In a display he had never before witnessed, the Stone threw off rays of red and purple light, erupting like gobbets of liquid rock and sparks from the vent of a volcano. Amnet felt the heat against his face. At the focus of the rays was something bright and golden, like a ladle of molten metal held up to him. Without moving, he felt himself pitching forward, drawn down by a pull that was separate from gravity, separate from distance, space, and time. The heat grew more intense. The light more blinding. The angle of his upper body slid from the perpendicular. He was burning. He was falling. . . .

Amnet shook himself.

The Stone, still nestled in the sand, was an inch from his face. Its surface was dark and opaque. The fire among the twigs had burned out. The alembic was clear of smoke, with a puddle of blackened gum at its bottom.

Amnet shook himself again.

What did a vision of the end of the world portend?

And what could a simple aromancer do about it?

THE MASK OF LOKI

ROGER ZELAZNY
THOMAS T. THOMAS

BAEN
FANTASY

THE MASK OF LOKI

This is a work of fiction. All the characters and events portrayed in this book are fictional, and any resemblance to real people or incidents is purely coincidental.

A Baen Books Original

Baen Publishing Enterprises
P.O. Box 1403
Riverdale, N.Y. 10471

ISBN: 0-671-72021-X

Cover art by Gary Ruddell

First printing, November 1990

Distributed by
SIMON & SCHUSTER
1230 Avenue of the Americas
New York, N.Y. 10020

Printed in the United States of America

Prologue

But screw your courage to the sticking-place,
And we'll not fail.
                              —William Shakespeare

The intense heat from the "glory hole" tightened the skin of her forehead and throat. She pulled her lips back in a grimace, and the skin around them dried, too. Her lipstick suddenly felt thick and crusted, like asphalt bubbling black in the sunlight.

Alexandra Vaele stepped two paces back from the open mouth of the furnace. That was a mistake. The sudden drop in temperature told her body it was time to compensate, and the tiny beads of sweat started in her hairline, along her upper lip, at the hollow of her throat. She could feel the stiff silk of her white blouse wilt and sag across her upper arms and around her breasts. In a moment it would be patched with sweat marks.

"Mr. Thorwald?" she called over the roar of the gas-fed fire. "Ivor Thorwald?"

The shaggy head lifted once and nodded, then bent to the pumping pace of arms and shoulders. Alexandra watched for a moment as the weave of his

1

cotton tee-shirt pulled first one way, then another
with the action. She moved around to see what he
was working on, and to put the man's body between
her and the yellow-white eye of the furnace.

A lump of molten glass, as large as a ripe tomato
and just as red. Its red, however, was the angry red
of an inner heat, not the cool red of a fruit's damp
skin. And at the heart of the lump shone a yellow
glow, like a memory of that furnace. Thorwald worked
the lump on the end of a steel rod, rounding and
smoothing it with a scorched wooden cup as he rolled
the rod along a steel beam. To protect the hand and
arm that worked the glass, he wore a padded gauntlet faced with metallic threads. On the thigh nearest
the flying lump he wore a piece of sheetmetal, curved
and shaped like a knight's armor, held on with cracked
leather straps. Thorwald wore wide safety glasses
and he smoked cigarettes.

After a hundred turns with the cup, the glass was
almost black again. Thorwald stood up, flicked his
long-ashed butt aside, hefted the steel rod, turned—
almost catching her face with the far end of it—and
shot the lump back into the furnace. He hooked the
rod into an over-and-under brace that extended in
front of the glory hole.

"What you want?" he asked, flexing his fingers in
the gauntlet. His eyes traveled her up and down: the
white blouse limp on her body, the wide belt tight
on her narrow waist, the straight black skirt that
molded her hips, the tops of her knees. . . .

"Do you do commission work?" she asked quickly.

"Depends."

"Depends on what?"

"Depends on whether I'm interested."

One of those, she sighed inwardly. She moved her
hips so and just so, as if she were—hungry.

"In the project," he said heavily. "What did you
want?"

Alexandra reached into her shoulder bag and removed the jeweler's envelope. She opened the flap
and bent the sides, then shuffled the contents forward. Alexandra was careful to keep them on the
paper and away from her fingers—although she did
put her hand under the envelope's mouth in case
they fell.

Thorwald bent closer. He glanced at her, as if for
permission, and then took off the gauntlet and put
forward a surprisingly white hand. He picked up one
of the shards with thumb and finger and held it to
the daylight that came in through the end of the
workshed.

"Onyx," Thorwald said. "Or sardonyx, from that
reddish banding. Not enough here to set—at least
not to show off."

"Can you make it into glass?"

"This much? What you got there? Fifteen, twenty
carats, tops. Or do you have a truckload more out in
the yard?"

"This is all I've been . . . all I have."

"Keep it for a souvenir."

"But can't you mix it with other . . . whatever it is
you make glass out of?"

"Sure, onyx is just a kind of quartz. Silicon dioxide. Same thing *as* glass, almost. Those two little
chips of yours, add them to the melt and—*pfft!*
—they're gone. They'd color the glass some, depending on how much I was working. But not a *good*
color, mind, not like it was planned."

"That's all right. In fact, the less color the better.
Best if there's no color at all, just clear glass."

"Then why add anything?"

"Because it's important. That's all I can say. Will
you take the commission?"

"Commission to do what, exactly?"

"To make a glass, a drinking glass, with those

pieces of—sardonyx, did you call them?—fused into it."

"A drinking glass." He wrinkled his nose. "A goblet? Tulip glass? Snifter? Something blown?"

"A water glass, the kind you might drink Coke or Perrier out of. Straight sides, flat bottom. A tumbler."

"Not interested." He turned back to his furnace, gripped the steel rod.

"I'll pay well. A hundred—a thousand dollars."

His shoulders, set to lift the rod, came back down. "That's a lot of money."

"It has to be perfect," she said. "Indistinguishable from a piece of commercial glassware."

"This is a gag of some kind? A rich folk's party favor or something?"

"Exactly!" Alexandra Vaele gave him a big smile, and this one was genuine. "It's an invitation to a party."

Sura 1
Crowning the King
चछजझञटठडढणत

Think, in this batter'd caravanserai
Whose portals are alternate night and day,
How sultan after sultan with his pomp
Abode his destin'd hour, and went his way.
— Omar Khayyam

The crusader's boots stank of mare's piss. The hem of his heavy woolen cloak had picked up yellow crumbs of manure, which he was now scattering across the marble with every step. Uncouth.

And yet Alois de Medoc, Knight of the Temple and Master of the Keep at Antioch, greeted his guest with open arms.

"Bertrand du Chambord! Come such a distance! And so swiftly you could not even stop to clean your boots."

He embraced his kinsman, gingerly, and clapped the flat of his hands against the cloaked and mailed shoulders. Dust rose in billows. Alois sneezed.

Releasing Bertrand, he looked him up and down. A few new scars bloomed—sealed with a hot iron, no doubt—on what of the dirty, tanned skin was visible to the eye. Bertrand's heavy fighting mail was rusted with sweat, except where its rents had been recently mended with bright circlets. His white tunic decor-

5

ated with a straight, red cross—worn in imitation of a
Templar's, and he would soon learn the etiquette of
that—bore patches and darns. Square patches to cover
the chafings of wear; straight darns to close scimitar
cuts. From the near-whiteness of the wool around
the latter, it was clear that the mail had done its
work and saved the skin. No gore stains—or none
too wide.

Saved that skin for *me*, Alois thought happily.

Like his cousin, the Templar wore a white tunic,
but it was of cool linen, not the crusader's penitential
wool. Like Bertrand, he wore a crusader's hood of
steel rings, but these were as light as lace, the finest
wire that the smiths of Damascus could weld.

Alois stepped back and signaled to the Saracen boy
who kept the entry hall. The boy, too, wore pants
and surcoat of linen—a sign of the Keep's wealth to
so dress its slaves—with boots of soft antelope hide
and a turban of clean cloth. The lad rushed forward
and began to brush at Bertrand's hem.

Alois kicked him.

"Rags and water, boy! Remove that fecal matter
from my floor! And burn sandalwood by the window
to clear the air."

"Yes, Lord!" The boy dodged away.

"Now, Bertrand. How may the Templars of Antioch serve you?"

"My bishop bids me to do an act of contrition in
this Holy Land. But I would do an act of glory."

"Glory to God, of course."

"Of course, cousin. And there is the problem. It is
so expensive, taking ship's passage, from one safe
haven to the next, and the infidel bands, the fighting
. . . why simply to come overseas, to reach *Outremer*,
has depleted my substance."

Alois smiled as gently as he could, clapped his
kinsman on the shoulder and pushed him toward a
chair of Lebanese cedar. The man's bottom at least

was clean, and his cloak would protect the wood grain from his mailed backside.

"How many men did you start with?"

"Forty mounted knights, all good North Country stock, with the berserker's edge in their fighting."

"Equippage?"

"Horses, arms and mail, food and wine, carts to hold the plunder." And here Bertrand grinned and laughed from his belly. "Grooms and lackeys, cooks and scullions, and the odd serving wench."

"And how much is left to you?"

Bertrand's smile faded. "Four men, six horses, one cart. We sold the wenches into slavery, to pirates, in exchange for our lives."

"Well, kinsman. It would appear you still have your arms and your mail coat. You can fight in the armies that Guy de Lusignan will muster when he is crowned King in Jerusalem. Or perhaps you can raid out of Antioch with Reynald de Châtillon, our Prince. That will bring you glory."

"But I promised the Bishop of Blois a battle, conceived out of my own wits and won with my own hand, for Christ Jesus's sake!"

"Hard to do now, with only four men and not even adequate remounts."

"I had thought you might help."

"What can I do?"

"Loan me the men."

"From the Order of the Temple?"

"They are yours to command."

Alois pursed his lips. "We are all brothers in Christ, within the Order. I command this Keep as a house of rest, for their relaxation, and as a place of safety. No more."

"You can persuade your brothers."

"To follow you?"

"Yes, for Christ's sake."

"To do what, exactly?"

"To take the Tomb—?"

"Ha, ha. We Christians already hold Jerusalem, kinsman. The Mount, the Tomb, and the site of old Solomon's temple. What else would you capture—as an act of contrition?"

"Well, I—"

"Look here, Sirra! What resources do you have?"

"Well . . . nothing but what I have on my back."

"And at home?"

"My family honor. A coat of arms that dates from before Charlemagne. The livelihood from seventy thousand acres of the best bottom land in Orléanis, granted by Old King Philip in the year he died."

"Nothing of your own?"

"A wife," Bertrand admitted.

"Nothing of ready value?"

"Well, a parcel or two . . ."

"How much?"

"Three thousand acres."

"Free and clear?"

"From my father."

"Will you put it up as collateral?"

"Collat—what's that?" the French knight asked.

"A pledge. The Order will loan you money, with which you can obtain the services of mounted knights and buy horses, soldiers, arms, rations. In exchange you promise to pay us back, plus a percentage for our interest."

"The sin of usury!"

"It's a hard world, cousin."

"How much money?"

"I believe the Order could see its way to a loan of 36,000 piasters. That would be equivalent to 1,200 Syrian dinars."

"How much is that in money?"

"Fifty times that amount has ransomed the killer of a Saracen king in this land. Think you on the quantity of conscience-money that we of the Temple and the other orders absorbed when Henry of England had Becket—a simple cleric—removed. And this assassination put down a king!"

"So these dinars would buy men, horses, and loyalty?"

"All that you need."

"And where does my land come into it?"

"You will repay the amount, plus interest, from what you plunder after the battle. If you do not pay, your parcel of land in France will become ours."

"I will pay you."

"Of course you will. So the land is in no danger, is it?"

"No, I suppose not. . . . You will take my word on all this, as a Christian and a knight, before God?"

"I would take your word gladly, cousin. But my masters in the Order require papers. I may die, you understand, but your pledge and the loan are with the Order of the Temple."

"I understand."

"Good then. I will have scribes prepare the papers. You can put your mark to them."

"And then I get my money?"

"Well, not immediately. We must send a messenger to Jerusalem, for the blessing of Gerard de Ridefort, who is the master of our Order."

"I understand. How long?"

"A week's travel, there and back."

"And where in all this hostile land shall I eat and lodge for so long?"

"Why, here of course. You will be a guest of the Order."

"I thank you, kinsman. That is spoken like a true Northman."

Alois de Medoc smiled. "Think nothing of it. The interval will give you time to clean your boots."

*   *   *

The table in the private apartments of Gerard de Ridefort, Master of the Order of the Temple, was seven cubits long and three cubits wide. But it hardly took up a fraction of the space allotted to him in the Keep of Jerusalem.

Some Saracen artisan had carved the sawn edges of the table's long planks with the likenesses of Norman faces: oval after oval with wide, staring eyes under conical steel caps; flowing mustaches over square, tombstone teeth; and ears like jug handles, intertwined from one head to the next.

Thomas Amnet studied the linked heads, immediately divining the caricature and the motive behind it. Lord Jesus, he whispered to himself, how these poor creatures must hate us! Western barbarians, holding their cities by force of arms, by our faith in an upstart Carpenter-God, and by the forces of an older Hidden One.

"What magic are you working, Thomas?"

"Ayuh? What was that you said, Gerard?"

"You can lose yourself in studying the edge of a table, and you don't even hear me."

"I heard you well enough. You wanted to know if Guy de Lusignan is the right choice for the crown."

"The choice is with God, Thomas."

"And, to some extent, with Sibylla. She is mother to the late King Baldwin, sister to the Baldwin before him, the Leper King, and daughter to King Amalric before *him*. And now she has taken Guy for her consort."

"That does not automatically make him king," Gerard reminded. "What I need to know is, will the Order of the Temple profit most by backing Guy de Lusignan in his claim or by putting our weight with the Prince of Antioch?"

"Provided that Prince Reynald first decides that he will not attempt to take it by force of arms, you mean?"

"Of course, of course. And if he does—?"

"Reynald de Châtillon is a beast—but you know that already, My Lord.

"When the Patriarch of Antioch reproved Reynald for blackmailing the Emperor Manuel in Constantinople," Amnet continued, "the Prince ordered his personal barber to shave the old man's head and beard, leaving a crown and necklace of shallow cuts about his ears and throat. Then Reynald smeared these wounds with honey and chained the Patriarch atop a high tower in the midday sun, until the flies almost drove the old man insane.

"Reynald attacked and plundered the protected settlements on Cyprus, in three weeks burning their churches—churches, Gerard!—and crops, murdering villagers, raping women, butchering cattle. That island will not recover from Reynald de Châtillon for a generation.

"Hardly was he done with this enterprise than he took ship down the Red Sea and burned a fleet of pilgrim vessels in Medina. It's rumored he had a mind to capture Mecca itself and burn that holy city back to a stick of charred wood in the desert. Instead, he laughed himself into a fit over the plight of drowning pilgrims. . . ."

"Now, Thomas. Is it not a Christian's duty to slay the infidel?"

"With one hand Reynald thumbs his nose at Christians in Cyprus. With the other he bites his thumb at the Saracens in Medina. King Saladin, the Protector of Islam, himself has sworn vengeance on this man—as has the Christian Emperor at Constantinople. Reynald is a danger to anyone within sword's reach."

"Then you counsel me to support Guy?"

"Guy is a fool and will be the worst king Jerusalem has ever endured."

Gerard stirred his bulk behind the table.

"You put me between a fool and a rabid fox. Tell me, Thomas, have you *seen* Guy's kingship—from

Anno Domini 1186 unto Anno Domini only-you-and-the-Devil-know—played out in your Seeing Stone?"

"Stone, My Lord? Do I need powers of divination to tell me what any child can see with his own two eyes? It was Guy who engineered the massacre at Arad of a peaceful Bedouin tribe and their flocks, simply to devil the Christian lords who received their grazing fees."

"Again, Thomas, is it wrong to kill the heathen?"

"Wrong? I do not say *wrong*. Just foolish, My Lord. When we are one to their thousand. When every Frenchman in *Outremer* must come over the water and along dusty roads on horse, fighting pirates and slavers and merchant thieves and the bloody revolt of his own bowels every step of the way. When the heathens rise from the sand in their thousands like spring grass after a shower, each armed with a razor-sharp scimitar and clothed in a burning loyalty to his cunning, *heathenish* generals. Then it is only wisdom to put some of your notions of right and wrong to one side and let sleeping Bedouins lie about their wells and pay their grazing fees."

"Do you rebuke me, Thomas?"

"My Lord? I rebuke the folly that is Guy de Lusignan and the brute that is Reynald de Châtillon."

"But as Keeper of the Stone, it is your duty to advise me with its powers. Tell me, then, is Guy strong enough to stand up to Reynald de Châtillon?"

"Does it matter?" Thomas replied. "We are."

"And thus we should support Guy . . . ?"

"Oh, Guy will be the next King of Jerusalem. Never fear of that."

"But that is not what I asked—"

A pounding at the door interrupted the Master Templar.

"What is it?" Gerard bellowed.

The door pushed open a crack and a young Turcopole, half-breed of a Norman father and a Saracen woman, stuck his head through. Many such were in service to the Templars, mostly their own sons from the wrong side of the blanket. This boy's fine, brown face was streaked with sweat and the dust of the road. His startling blue eyes were misted with fatigue.

"I come from the Keep at Antioch, My Lord, with dispatches from Sir Alois de Medoc."

"Can they not wait?"

"He says they are urgent, My Lord. Something about a pigeon too ripe for the plucking."

"Very well, bring them here."

The boy brought a leather wallet from under his surcoat and handed it to Gerard. The latter took up a dagger with a slender blade, cut the strings holding the wallet's flaps, withdrew a bundle of parchment, and cracked the wax seal with the butt of the knife. He unfurled the folded yellow skin with a snap and held it before his eyes.

He sighed and handed it to Amnet. "The writing is indistinct. Such was Alois's hurry in the matter."

Thomas Amnet took the document and began reading it silently.

Gerard watched this with some uneasiness. A fighting man who could also read was, in Amnet's world, still a rarity. Although many Templars could read enough to ponder out a city's or stream's name upon a map, or put their Christian names to a deed of land, those who felt comfortable communicating in this fashion were a minority. Amnet knew that Gerard de Ridefort himself had other powers—of position and authority—and so would stand in no real awe of those who could read. For the moment, however, it would irk him to realize that the parchment might speak to a cunning little fellow like Thomas Amnet and yet remain silent to an important one like Gerard de Ridefort.

"What does it say?" Gerard asked at last.

"Sir Alois has made a loan to one Bertrand du

Chambord, a distant kinsman of his. In exchange for the pledge of some land in Orléanais, the Temple will outfit this Bertrand with knights, footmen, horses, arms, and equippage to the value of 1,200 dinars."

"How much land?"

"Three thousand acres. . . . Is the land worth that much, I wonder? Alois does not say of what quality it is."

"Have you ever known him to deal for *bad* land? Go on."

"Alois proposes that we buy Reynald's favor by making the land over to a cousin of his, whom he says is returning to France within the year. . . . But," Amnet objected, "the land is not ours yet. How can we dispose of it so quickly?"

"The land will be ours straightaway," Gerard predicted. "The loan will go bad."

"How do you and Alois know this? Do you have a Stone of your own?"

Gerard tapped the side of his head. "Oh, no, my young friend. Do I need the powers of divination when I have the brains that God gave a child?" The Master Templar chuckled at turning Amnet's own words against him. "This Bertrand will be seeking glory, to make amends for his short and sinful life. So we will give him glory."

"And what might that be?" Thomas asked patiently.

"We will suggest to the poor fool that the greatest glory he might win will be to wipe out the *Hashishiyun* at their citadel of Alamut."

"They do not call it 'Eagle's Nest' for nothing. That place is impregnable."

"Yes, but the valiant Bertrand won't know this until he is fully committed. By then it will be too late."

"A young French noble, hungry for glory, set against a band of seemingly unarmed Assassins. That will put a scorpion in the bed of Sheikh Sinan, the Old Man of the Mountains."

"And it will put 3,000 acres of Orléanais in our gift."

Thomas Amnet considered the scheme in silence for a moment. "Charles," he said suddenly.

"Eh?" Gerard de Ridefort looked up from the parchment. He had taken it back and had been picking at the sealing wax with his fingers.

"That is the name of Reynald's homesick cousin. Charles."

"Whatever. He'll put us in good stead with Reynald."

"When you feed the beast, it's best to wear a long arm."

"So we'll feed him Bertrand du Chambord—and then count our fingers."

In his turret room, high in the Keep of Jerusalem, Thomas Amnet swung the shutters and drew the draperies against the cool night air. It was not only the air he wanted to block out.

Despite his verbal fencing with Gerard de Ridefort, he was troubled by the approaching coronation of Guy de Lusignan as king of Jerusalem. The man was a knave on the surface of it; anyone could see that. And Thomas Amnet was not just anyone.

A dozen years as Keeper of the Stone—a position that came to him young, and not only because of his noble birth and skill with the broadsword in the Order's service—had made him more than humanly sensitive to the streams of time.

Other men might meet each dawn as a fresh day, deal with each battle or forced march as a new problem to be solved, come upon each bout of sickness, wound, and finally death as a surprise.

Amnet, instead, saw patterns.

This day was a link in the chain of years. This battle was a single pawn moved on the great board of

war and politics. This wound was a part of the total-
ity of death that would ultimately come to the body.
Amnet saw the flow of time and saw his body as a
chip of white wood upon it.

The Stone, of course, focused that flow.

Thomas Amnet opened his heavy old chest and
took out the casket that held the Stone. It was made
of walnut wood, almost black with age, and lined
with velvet. Amnet had insulated it with the correct
pattern of pentagrams, dual points inward, around
the lid. To contain the energies and hide the Stone
from those eyes—and other senses—which might dis-
cern it.

He lifted the lid.

In the light of the single taper, the Stone flashed
darkly, as if greeting him. It had the shape of the
Cosmic Egg, smooth and glistening, more bulging at
one end and more pointed at the other, as eggs
always are.

He reached into the confines of the box and lifted
the Stone out with his naked fingers.

The expected thrill of pain ran up his arm. With
time and long experience, the pain might become
more bearable but never became less. It was like the
tremor you could feel in the back of a horse that has
taken a war arrow through the neck. It was the
tremor of approaching death.

The touch of the Stone also brought music into his
head: a choir of all the angels sang a hosannah of
glory to their God. It was a celestial ululation that
cycled over and over while the Stone was in his
hand.

At the same time the blaze of glory lit the dark
spaces behind his eyes: a shower of colors like those
a cut of crystal would throw against the wall from a
beam of sunlight. The colors danced and wove patterns in his head until he set the Stone down on the
bare planks of his workbench.

Amnet was breathing hard.

He half-expected the underside of the egg to char the wood and create a blackened nest of ashes for itself. But the energies it threw off were not of the kind that burned wood.

The next part of Amnet's ritual of divination was simple alchemy. In an alembic he mixed rosemary oil, dried basil, and attar of honeysuckle—imported from France at great expense to the Order—with clear well water and a dram of distilled wine. This mixture itself had no potency, it merely created a stock, a background against which the Stone could work.

He swirled the base mixture around the glass bulb, set a candle stub under it, and lit the wick from his taper. By trimming the wick and dripping the melted tallow, he could control the heat under the alembic quite exactly. The surface of the mixture inside should fume but never boil. The fumes rose into the neck, which directed them down in a curling flow over the pointed end of the Stone.

Trial and error had led Amnet to this process. The Stone itself was too dark to see into. Its substance was a brown-red agate that was totally opaque, except from a view taken across the shortest, shallowest chord through its surface—and that sight must be made in the brightest, most direct sunlight.

The Stone's energies could order the things surrounding it—but weakly. Smoke or the mist on a glass was too heavy for those energies. Their touch was more delicate, suited to a vapor that was already in motion. Rosemary oil, mixed as before with water and spirits and other herbs, worked best.

What the Stone might show him depended on its humors, not on anything Thomas Amnet might bring, knowingly or not, to the session.

Once it had shown him the exact location of Priam's golden lode, blocked by a rectangular pattern of stones a hundred feet under the brush and topsoil at Illium. Amnet had instantly been hot to mount an expedition to go and find the treasure, but finally doubt held him back.

The Stone would never trick him, of course, but it could easily mislead him through his all-too-human eagerness to work its patterns into terms his own mind could find useful. The Ilium that the Stone had shown him might well not be the Ilium of historical fact. What was shown through the Stone's power was not always perfectly congruent with the world that men inhabited.

Once it had shown him truly, though. It had revealed to him the invisible structure of the Order of the Temple, like a tower of hewn stones, and every stone a prayer, a money loan, or a feat of arms. Nine Grand Masters before Gerard, going back to Hugh de Payens in Anno Domini 1128, had plotted and fought and dealt to make a place for the Northman Franks in the Holy Land. These were the same fair-haired, fierce-hearted fighters who had crossed the North Sea, first to raid, then to settle on the wild coast that France showed to the white flanks of Albion. These same Sons of the Storm had built and manned William's boats when he set out to make good his claim to that island nation against the Saxons. Now, just 120 years later, as old King Henry of England warred with young King Philip of France, the Northman Franks stood in the middle, king makers and king breakers. At the same time, far away over the sea, they rode as members of the Order of the Temple to help both kings lay claim to the Holy Land.

In a vision ordered by the Stone, Thomas Amnet had seen the Knights Templar of almost sixty years past ride through the fuming mists from his alembic. Garbed in clinking mail, cloaked in white wool with the long cross, armed with sword and lance, armored

with the Norman's teardrop shield, they rode past on
a single file of horses: white horses bearing the living
wights with their dim and life-dazzled eyes; black
horses bearing dead souls whose eyes blazed with
knowledge of the judgment of Odin and the resur-
rection in Valhalla.

The lesson had not been lost on Amnet. The first
of the Templars to ride through his vision, all on
black horses, had been lean and sunburned men
with hardened, calloused hands; rangy, corded muscles; and fresh blood on their sheathed swords. The
latest of the Templars, mostly on white horses, were
plump men with pale skins from lingering within
rooms and under awnings. They had soft hands, loose
muscles, and ink-stains on their fingers from making
loans and deeds.

While the cloaks of the early Templars were scented
with the dust and gore of the battlefield, the linen
surcoats of later members of the Order smelled of
incense from the chapel and perfume from a harlot's
boudoir.

That had been a true vision—and the last unsul-
lied act of clairvoyance Thomas Amnet had enjoyed
for some months past.

Now Amnet would try again. With his left hand he
wafted the fumes from the glass throat across the end
of the Stone, ordered his thoughts to stillness, and
looked down.

The face of Guy de Lusignan looked out at him,
slack jawed, sated with passion, tongue lolling at the
corner of his mouth. Long, tapering fingers—their
skin a coppery, Saracen brown—stroked his forehead, his temples, the skin of his chest, his engorged
manhood. Guy groaned and turned away into the
mists.

A plume of vapor rose and hardened in the indi-
rect light of the candle. With a ripple, like a reflection reshaped on a surface of still well water, the

light became a merciless midday sun, beating down
on a horn of hard stone that was raised above the
desert floor and bent like a lady's finger to bid him
come hither. The finger bent and curled back into
the mists.

A black mustache, shaved and trimmed with the
fine-honed edge of a dagger, solidified out of the
fuming mass. Above its two black wings glowed two
eyes, red as a wolf's but slotted like a cat's. The
mustache wings lifted and flapped once in a smile
that showed perfect white teeth, filed flat at the
bottom like a tombstone's footing in the grass and
rounded at the top where the teeth were sunk in red
gums. The eyes searched across the blank, gray vapor until they found Amnet's eyes, and then they
locked with his. The wide blade of a nose which
divided that face then uncurled—again, like a lady's
come-hither finger—and beckoned to Thomas Amnet.

Before the image could change again, he whipped
it aside with the flat of his hand.

The candle had gone out under the alembic, and
no more fumes poured from it. Just as well. That face,
those wolflike eyes, had intruded on every vision he
had taken in the last months. Somewhere and at
some time—present, past, or future—a sorcerer had
declared, or would declare, psychic war upon the
Keeper of the Stone. Such declarations were not
uncommon, littered as the past and future were with
magi. But this declaration was presently disturbing
the alignment of the Stone's deepest energies.
Thomas Amnet must think upon his response; it
should be appropriate to the challenge.

He set the apparatus aside and let it cool. He
lifted the Stone again into its box—enduring the
tremor of pain, the singing of angels—and closed the
lid. Each time he touched it or used its energies, the
Stone changed him, strengthened him, heightened
his awareness.

Thomas remembered the day he had taken possession of it from Alain, the Templar who had formerly kept the Stone.

The older knight had been stretched out on his deathbed, wounded in the lung with a Saracen arrow. For two days he had been spitting black blood, and none expected him to see the dawn.

"Thomas, come here."

Amnet had approached the bed humbly, his hands clasped before him. Those hands had then borne tough callouses from the hilt of a sword and the strap of a shield. Seventeen he had been and a raw boy. His head had been as empty as the steel shell of a tilting helm.

"The Templars in council can find no better use for you. So they give you to me."

"Yes, Sir Alain."

"The Order must have a Keeper of the Stone. It's not an important post, I'll grant. Not like being master of a keep or a commander in battle."

"No, Sir Alain."

"But the Keeper has a certain prestige, still." The man had roused off his pillows, his eyes burning. They did not quite focus on Amnet. "The Stone is dangerous to hold. It is a device of the Devil, that I know. You must handle it as little as possible, and use it only in extreme need."

"What is it, this Stone?"

"It came from the North Country, with the first knights who formed our Order. It has always been ours. Our secret. Our strength."

"Where is the Stone, Sir Alain?"

"Always keep it near you. Always hold it for the good of the Order. So long as it rides with the Templars, they shall never be vanquished in battle. But touch it—touch its naked surface—as little as you may. For your—"

The fever that burned in Sir Alain's chest seemed to turn like a mad dog and snap at him. The man's breath caught in his throat. His eyes bulged, fixing finally on Amnet's face. The last word came out of him in a hissing, groaning sigh.

"—soul."

And that was all.

Amnet knew he should do something. He closed the man's eyes, holding them with the edge of his hand as he had seen his yeoman teachers do on the battlefield. He should tell someone that Sir Alain had passed. First, though, he should take the Stone that was now his charge.

Where was it?

Sir Alain had told him to keep it near him. Where would a dying man hide a prized possession?

Thomas bent to look under the bedframe: bare flags and dust—the covered chamber pot. He dragged that vessel forth, to see if the old knight had hidden the Stone there. Thomas was greeted with its reeking contents. By swirling them slowly around, he could see they hid nothing so solid as a stone.

Where else?

He pulled back the sleeve of his blouse and felt under the pillow. Upset by his groping, the knight's head lolled to one side and his eyelids parted on gray film. Amnet's hand hit on something solid. He got his fingers around it and pulled it slowly out.

A casket of black walnut. He examined the latch and found it needed no key. He opened the lid.

A dark crystal as high as his hand lay within. In the dim light it was hard to see clearly. The Stone seemed by turns to be colored the evil red of old, drying blood, then the ochre of rich French farmland, turned by the plow on a spring day.

Amnet ignored Sir Alain's last warning and touched it with his finger. The shock of pain, the choir of music, the malevolent hunger for his life—such as would trouble his dreams and his waking thoughts till he died—these reached up for his soul with that first finger-touch. Thomas Amnet knew he was changed in that instant.

He had found the Stone, and it was his.

The Stone had found him, and he was its.

Amnet had understood immediately that the energies locked in the Stone might have saved Sir Alain from death, might have cured him of his wound and its poisons. He also understood why the old knight would have rejected that kind of salvation.

Now, in his tower room a dozen years later, wiser by much reading in old scrolls—some of them seen only in visions—and stronger by a thousand touches of the Stone, Amnet understood many things about its powers and their uses.

He knew that he could not die, not as other men. Whatever his deeds as a Knight Templar in Outremer, he would never ride a black horse before some other Keeper of the Stone. He would never look into the stern face of Odin One-Eye at the door of Valhalla. Nor would he kneel in worship at the Throne of Heaven.

Carelessly clearing up his workbench, Thomas Amnet put to one side some scrap lead that he had been using the previous day to mend a leaky basin.

The metal writhed under his touch, becoming a cane of yellow, Troy-fine gold. He picked up some buttons of bone, and they sparked and clarified like the ice sheathing on a waterfall, becoming orbs of brilliant crystal and resonating in his hand with strange energies and eerie voices.

Was this the Devil's handiwork? As a nominal Christian in a Christian order, such a thought should disturb Thomas Amnet. It should suck the wind out of his stomach and freeze his blood.

But as a familiar of the Stone, he knew this was an

idle thought. The Stone was its own thing, with its own reasons. And not all of its effects were terrifying. Whatever the Stone might have done—was still doing—to Thomas Amnet, it had not defiled his touch but instead made him golden.

He held his hand in wonder before his eyes and waited for the miracle to pass.

File 01
Cyberpsych

✳

Art is a jealous mistress,
and if a man have a genius for painting,
poetry, music, architecture, or philosophy,
he makes a bad husband and an ill provider.
        —Ralph Waldo Emerson

Eliza 212: Good morning. This is Eliza Channel 212, an on-line function of United Psychiatric Services, Inc., in the Greater Bowash Metropolitan Area. Please think of me as your friend.

Subject: You're a machine. You're not my friend.

Eliza 212: Does talking to a machine bother you?

Subject: I guess not. I've been doing it all my life.

Eliza 212: How old are you?

Subject: Thirty-thr . . . *uh* . . . twenty-eight. Why should I lie to you?

Eliza 212: Why indeed? I am here to help. You have a nice voice, deep and flavored with experience. Do you use your voice professionally?

Subject: What do you mean, like a video announcer?

Eliza 212: Or an actor or singer.

Subject: I sing sometimes, just a bit. Mostly I play the piano. Hell—*all* I do is play the piano.

Eliza 212: Do you enjoy playing the piano?

Subject: It's like breathing pure oxygen. It's a natural high.

Eliza 212: What do you play?

Subject: The piano, like I said.

Eliza 212: Your pardon. I meant, what kind of *music* do you play?

Subject: Jazz. Show ballads. Stride.

Eliza 212: Stride? My databank does not include that term in a musicological context.

Subject: So much for your databank. "Stride" is natural jazz. It was first played by the black pianists of Harlem, Old New York reference, in the early years of the twentieth century. It's characterized on the left hand by an alternating bass note and chord—with the chord played one-and-a-half to two-and-a-half octaves higher than the note. The right hand meantime plays syncopated figures in thirds and sixths, chromatic runs, and tremolo octaves. . . . Stride.

Eliza 212: Thank you for that input. You seem to know a lot about the subject.

Subject: Honey, I'm the best damn stride player living in this century.

Eliza 212: Then may I please have your name to apend to my new reference?

Subject: Tom. Tom Gurden.

[Subject 2035/996 equals Gurden, Tom/Thomas/ Tomas, NMI. Open psychiatric file and append all future references.]

Eliza: What seems to be the trouble, Tom?

Gurden: People are trying to kill me.

Eliza: How do you know that, Tom?

Gurden: Things keep happening around me. . . .

Eliza: What kind of things, Tom?

Gurden: It started about three weeks ago, when a car jumped the curb in New Haven. I was up there for a private party. Anyway, a big Nissan Dresser limo in hover mode went right up over the buffercade and came down one meter in front of me, doing about sixty klicks, all set up for a wipe out.

Eliza: Were you injured?

Gurden: I could have been. Except out of no-where this pro tackle for the Jets or something comes flying in sideways and knocks me down, puts me on the ground just short of where that limo's going. Then he goes head over heels, so that his boots are half under the skirting when it comes to rest inside a storefront window. The guy drags himself free, dusts his knees off, and skedaddles. Gone without even a *de nada.*

Eliza: What did the man look like?

Gurden: Heavily built. Long coat of some heavy material, suede or gabardine, boots as I said, high black ones like an old-time cavalry officer.

Eliza: Hair color? Eye color?

Gurden: Sorry, he was wearing a hat. Or, no— some kind of hood, but loose at the sides. Maybe a solar sombrero? I couldn't tell. It was late at night and not in the best-lit part of town.

Eliza: What did you do about the car?

Gurden: Nothing.

Eliza: But it tried to kill you, Tom. You said so.

Gurden: Well, yeah. But I didn't know that then. The car was just the first incident—before there was a *co*incidence, if you get me. The car was nothing at the time. Nothing, anyway, that I wanted to stick around and get dragged into a *voire dire* over.

Eliza: So you took off, like the man in the hood?

Gurden: Yes.

Eliza: What was the second incident?

Gurden: That was the exploding bullets. Happened a week or ten days after the car, I think.

I was subletting an apartment in Jackson Heights for the summer. It was in one of the old brownstones that had been broken up into separate co-op units. Mine was the window on the second floor left.

It was seven in the morning, when I'm sure to be at home and asleep after my regular gig. I get off the last set at two-fifteen in the morning, then get some dinner and maybe some interest. So it's not until around three or four that I get home and start thinking about bed. At seven a-yem, when everyone else is up and hitting the showers, I'm thirty-seven winks deep.

Eliza: Do you sleep well at nights, Tom?

Gurden: I sleep fine. No pills or nothing. Just close my eyes and the world goes away. But as I was saying, this morning, when I'm sure to be home, somebody shoots out the second floor. But the second floor *right*—on the other side of the partition from mine.

Eliza: Was anyone in that apartment?

Gurden: Yeah, a young woman. I knew her slightly: Jenny Calvados.

Eliza: Was she killed, Tom?

Gurden: Not right away—the first two shots took out the window plex. That stuff's remarkable, tough enough to stand up even to explosive casings. At least on the first shot. The shootist was taking his time, quartering the room. Spaced shots blew every twelfth book off the shelves. One round smashed the vidscreen, and the next flipped over the chair in front of it. One went through the side of the refrigerator, another one into the commode. It went off like a bomb.

If Jenny had stayed put, she probably would have lived, because she had her bed under the window, protected by eight inches of old brick and stone facing. He might just have shot up the room and figured that nobody was home. But she stood up and started to run for the closet. Then her head got in the way of a bullet and splattered all over the wall.

Eliza: How do you know it was the last bullet that killed her?

Gurden: I'm not *that* heavy a sleeper, and the partition wasn't *that* thick. I could hear Jenny screaming as the thuds kept hitting around in her stuff. Then she took it and got quiet.

Except she wasn't the target. I was. The assassin got his lefts and rights reversed and picked the wrong window.

Eliza: Why do you think it was assassination? Joy shoots are becoming common in Queens.

Gurden: Because the cops located the rooftop he was firing from—line of sight to the impact points. And there were scuff marks on the solar tiles, a pile of fresh butts, even a clump of burned wadding from one of the launch packs. He'd made a bench rest from some old fiberglass batting, which tells me he was using a scope. So this man was dug in and gauging his shots.

Eliza: He could still have been trying to kill her, not you.

Gurden: A librarian? A single girl, a working girl, twenty-six years old and living alone? What for?

Look, Jenny had brown hair, cut short like mine. So in a darkened apartment a shootist could confuse her for a man, even with telescopic sights. As I say, he must have mixed up right and left, thought she was me, and bagged her. I mean, it could happen.

Eliza: That was your coincidence?

Gurden: Not quite.

Eliza: There was another shooting, wasn't there?

Gurden: Say, you *are* good!

Eliza: Content retention and projective analysis. I am programmed for memory and curiosity, Tom.

Gurden: There was a shootout in my club that same night. That would have been two weeks ago, now. This club, it's called Studio Fifty-Four-Too—

Eliza: You mean Five Hundred and Forty-Two?

Gurden: No, Fifty-Four-T-O-O. It's an offshoot of a much older club that's now defunct. Anyway, I was playing the middle set, about ten thirty, and it was not going well.

This is something the audience doesn't understand, that my experience of the performance is totally different from theirs. I close my eyes when I'm playing, and they think I'm grooving on the music. Actually, I'm probably yelling at myself for playing right across a coda or—

Eliza: Coda? What is that?

Gurden: It's an instruction to go back and repeat a passage, sometimes with a slightly different ending.

Eliza: Thank you. Noted. Go on, please.

Gurden: Or I may be cursing myself for leaving a bar or two out of a transition. Other times I'll bite my lip, and they think I've made a mistake. In reality, I'm struggling to transpose around a dead key or a string that's wandered off pitch. When you have perfect pitch, like me, you just *can't* play a piano that's out of tune.

Eliza: And the music you were playing that night was going badly.

Gurden: The club's air conditioning had gone toes up, and humidity had gotten into the keyboard action. The hammer felts played alternately stiff and soggy. A real nightmare. So I didn't have time to study the crowd or watch the door.

Eliza: Watch the door? Why would you do that?

Gurden: Because everything good comes through the front door: talent spotters, studio agents, booking contracts, and occasional one-night stands.

Eliza: You mean sexual liaisons?

Gurden: No. I've got a regular girl for that. Or did. One night stands, in the music business, are short-term gigs, like for parties, weddings, bar mitzvahs—although not many of those call for a stride pianist.

But this night I wasn't watching the door because the piano was playing like a box of soggy socks. So I never saw him coming.

Eliza: Him? Who?

Gurden: The gunman. The Fifty-Four-Too is a straight club: business people—mostly Horse Boys and Syntho Skins—plus the occasional sixty-second celebs and some of the Island action. It's guaranteed neutral ground. No Manhattan mob allowed. So this man was instantly out of place in his loud silks, padded codpiece, and hose. His outfit screamed uptown drug trade, even with his long blond hair. This comedian was carrying an old-style autofire, with a clip about thirty centimeters long. He had the ratchet back and half the clip coming past me before I even looked up.

Eliza: Did he hit you?

Gurden: No. His weapon pulled right and high, so I was just hearing pockmarks go into the plaster behind my head. Without missing a beat, I slid forward off the bench, left around the pedal column, and over the back edge of the riser. The music died out at about the same time the slugs started penetrating the sides of that baby grand, making their own music in the harp. . . . After that night, no one's going to care about soggy hammers.

Eliza: What did you do then?

Gurden: Out the rear door and never looked back. I asked the manager for my last check by direct deposit. Told him my mother had died.

Eliza: Did you notify the authorities? About the shootings, I mean.

Gurden: Sure, I'm a righteous citizen. They just laughed, fed me the policeman's gospel on random urban violence, quoted population statistics and probabilities at me, and said I was imagining things.

Eliza: But you don't agree?

Gurden: [Pause of eleven seconds.] You'll think I'm crazy.

Eliza: That is not my function, Tom. I don't judge people. I listen.

Gurden: Well . . . let's say I've always felt special. Ever since I was a little boy, I've felt like an outsider, not really the same as other people. An outsider, but not uninvolved. Not a rebel. It's like I'm someone with *more* responsibility for the state of the world, for all the rottenness and the breakdowns, than other people seem to feel. Sometimes I think that the twenty-first century is all my fault. Sometimes, that I will be the one who changes things, some kind of savior—but not in any religious sense.

There's a power I feel, or maybe it's more like a skill I once had but have since forgotten. A tension in the muscles, a throbbing of the blood, that is just beyond my reach. If I could only slow my thoughts down, go completely still and really concentrate, this power, this cunning would leap into my hands. A power to tumble enemies from my path with the wave of a hand. To lift stones with the pulse of energy that throbs behind my eyes. To make the mountains shiver with a word.

Eliza: This is the Mass Age, Tom. Many people feel powerless and dehumanized, as if they were merely numbers in a machine. Their egos compensate for this feeling with mild, directionless fantasies about their "specialness" or their sense of having a "mission."

A new branch of psychology, called "ufolatry," attributes the stories of alien abductions and third-order encounters to the human desire to be noticed in a society that largely ignores the human factor. In an earlier age, these same people would be reporting encounters with the Virgin Mary.

Many people also feel the sense of hidden powers which you describe. Claims like yours are what keep the witch covens and the crystal scribers in business. In your case, these feelings are probably more substantiated. After all, you have one highly complex and valuable skill in your piano playing. You probably have other skills, don't you? What are they, Tom?

Gurden: Well, I've always been good with languages: fluent in French and passable in Italian, as I found on the European tour. I picked up Arabic right away, too, at the stopover in Marseilles.

Eliza: Do you have any involving interests, hobbies, or sports?

Gurden: I like to keep up to date in the hard sciences, reading about the advances, especially in cosmogeny, geochemistry, x-ray astronomy—the finite things, which don't change themselves and which we can track down and really know.

Sports? I guess I'm in good shape. You have to work out, keep fit, when you spend six hours a night sitting down, just moving your fingers, wrists, and elbows. I do aikido and a little karate—except my hands are my life; so I can't fight with them. I learned to use my feet instead. At least I figure I can take care of myself when a bar brawl gets up to the piano stool.

Eliza: Ah, yes. That would explain your reference to "tumbling enemies from my path." People with whole-body training, such as you have taken, Tom, often feel an encompassing sense—an aura, if you like—of health, balance, and poise which you might describe as a power.

Gurden: So you're saying I *am* nuts. But you're wrong. I know I'm sane.

Eliza: "Sane" and "insane," Tom, are labels that no longer offer any value. I am saying you may have a mild and fully compensated delusion which, provided it does not prejudicially influence your overt behavior, should not distress you or your loved ones.

Gurden: Yeah, thanks. But you don't feel the watchers breathing down your neck.

Eliza: Watchers? Who are they? Please describe them.

Gurden: Watchers. Sometimes I can feel the heat on the back of my head, their staring. And when I turn, their eyes shift sideways, focus elsewhere, flicker and go blank. But their faces always give them away. They know they've been caught.

Eliza: Have you considered your profession, Tom? You are a public figure. You play the piano for a living, and people watch you do it. Strangers in a crowd may recognize you, or think they do, and be too embarrassed to acknowledge it. So they avert their eyes.

Gurden: Sometimes they do more than just watch. . . . Say I begin to cross the street, not thinking and not looking at the lights, and suddenly some man will cross in front of me—diagonally, not into the traffic himself but going to his parked car maybe. Every time it happens, there will be a truck come screaming by not two meters away, right where I would have been if he hadn't bumped me.

Eliza: Who bumped you? The man?

Gurden: Some man.

Eliza: Is he always the same?

Gurden: Not the same person, probably, but always the same *kind* of person. Shorter than me and heavier. Not fat, but built like a Russian weight lifter, with wide shoulders, padded by a lot of hard muscle. Walks like he's been riding a horse for a million kilometers. Always wearing a long raincoat, a hat, things to cover him up, even on hot days.

Eliza: How often has this happened?

Gurden: Two or three times I can remember.

Eliza: And it always happens on the street, in traffic?

Gurden: No. It could be I walk under a spider that's washing high-rise windows, and he stops me for a quarter—just before a piece of hose falls fifty meters. Or I'm in a hotel lobby and his bags trip me up—so I miss the one elevator that jams between floors. A watcher, watching over me.

Eliza: And their watching is always for the good? To keep you safe?

Gurden: Always until now, when people have also started trying to run me off the sidewalk and shoot up my apartment house. [Softly.] Come to think of it, the people trying to kill me started appearing about the same time as the people trying to be me.

Eliza: Tom, I can hardly hear you. Did you say people are trying to *be* you?

Gurden: Yeah. People are trying to get inside my life, to live here and now, and push me out.

Eliza: I don't think I understand. Are you describing several different personalities who try to share your body, Tom?

Gurden: Naw. It's nothing like that. [Yawns.] Look, I gotta go. It's four in the a-yem and I've played three full sets tonight. You have a nice voice, for a computer. Maybe I'll call again.

Eliza: Tom! Don't hang up! Please. I need to know—

Gurden: Yeah, but I'm really bushed, falling asleep here in the booth. I've still got your number.

Eliza: Tom! Tom!

Click!

Tom Gurden released the mechanical dogs and slid the door back. The smell of the Atlantic hit him: mussels, kelp, and black mud at low tide, mixed with accents of gasoline and tar. It quickly cleaned out the stuffy funk of his own breath, collected and potted inside the psych booth.

He raised a long finger to the misty inside of the glass and drew an eighth note there, idly sketched in a staff: middle C, a triplet running up to E, two grace notes—and he wiped the whole passage out with staccato swipes of his palm.

Too tired right now to get involved.

Gurden stepped out onto the sidewalk. The pavement was wet; the leather soles of his dress pumps made sucking and smacking sounds as he began to walk, stirring a froth of bubbles in the film of water.

In this city, even at this hour, even in a sector of only six million people, the background hum never quite died out: subway shuttles streaking through bedrock; patrol drones turning their ellipses at 1,000 meters; traffic grids clicking through their patterns. The small and faraway sounds blended with the random noises of a window opening here, a cat crying its lust there, a taxi huff-puffing its way down a sidestreet two avenues over.

Random noises. Random shadows.

Tom Gurden's ears were tuned to hear patterns— and the exceptions to pattern. Behind him, as he made his way home along Main Street in Manhasset, he could hear steps following his. Not his own echoes against the wet buildings. Not someone else going home, too. These steps were following him, walking as he walked, pausing when he paused.

He turned in a patch of shadow and searched the niches of streetlight with his eyes. Nothing moved. Nothing stopped moving.

Gurden scented the air behind him using the sense that went beyond smell. He sent a probe of awareness back along his path, whiffing danger, bad thoughts, needles of steel in the fog of nobody-there.

Nothing revealed itself.

He stayed ten seconds longer. To look at him, anyone would have thought he was undecided and afraid. Actually, he was listening for a premature first step.

Nothing.

Gurden slid his fingers down behind his evening suit's cummerbund and pulled out his sonic knife. It was a sophisticate's weapon, mostly defensive, but still illegal. A piece of thin plastic the size of a pass card or bank balance, the knife projected a blast of sound warbling between 60,000 and 120,000 Hertz at 1,500 decibels across a band one centimeter wide and a millimeter thick. The "blade" had an effective range of three meters. Up close, a sound like that broke weak molecular bonds, such as those in long-chain organic molecules. At the limit of range, it burned steel and flash-boiled water. The film battery in the card powered the knife for a max of ninety seconds, but that was time enough to bubble some blood in the right places.

He held the card right-handed, between the tips of his thumb and first two fingers, with the joint of this thumb poised above the switch blister.

Now armed, Tom Gurden started walking again, as if he heard and suspected nothing.

The footsteps started up again almost immediately, coming from nowhere in particular.

He decided that the assailant must be using an old street watcher's trick: following by leading. The footsteps could be coming from someone ahead of him, who tracked him by reflections in shop windows and bumper chrome, and looked back often enough to keep him in range.

Gurden scented forward along his path, again using that sense behind his nose that was half listening, half smelling, and total awareness.

Someone there. A tension, like muscles poised to run.

He walked forward slowly, with the knife held low in front of him. The skin of his thumb brushed the blister.

The footsteps still matched his pace for pace, but their timbre changed. A sharp clicking announced itself as he drew nearer.

There, ahead, a shadow slipped around the edge of a streetlight's corona and fell into the darker shadows against a building.

Gurden picked up his pace, rising to the balls of his feet and lifting his knees like a sprinter.

The clicking, the echo of the other footsteps stopped.

Gurden ran forward into the circle of light.

Off to the right, something scraped the pavement—a foot shifting weight?

He spun to the left—toward the open, street side of the walkway—backing out of the spot of overhead light. The keyway of his sonic knife, concealed in the shadows under his arm, quartered the darkness across from him.

"Would you buy a girl a drink, for God's sake?"

That voice! The same words! Sandy had used them that first night, four years ago, when she came into the Old Greenwich Inn in Stamford.

"Sandy?"

"You didn't expect me, Tom? You know I can't keep away from you."

"Why are you hiding in the shadows?" Gurden lifted his right hand, pretending to shield his eyes, and slipped the knife into the side pocket of his tux.

"And why have you been hiding, Tom?"

"It's been a bad couple of weeks. Step forward. Let me see you."

In answer, she laughed. Then she walked forward: grace and curves, supple movements and steady eyes. A molecular-film rainsheet wrapped around her like a sari and headscarf. Its surface radiated violet to green with the motions of her breathing. Beneath it she wore a gray parasilk dress, evening cut, with bare shoulders. It was the same dress she had worn then, four years ago. He let out a sigh.

"You do remember!" she said.

"Of course. . . . But why now?"

"I was such a foolish girl." The smile. "I was afraid of you, Tom. Afraid of your dreams. They were so—so strange and absorbing. You needed me because of them, but all I could think about was you slipping away to somewhere I couldn't follow, somewhere I was *afraid* to follow.

"So, instead of helping you, I made space. I thought

I had to cut out on my own. I made it for a day or two, got a day job, even. But I found out how empty and cold the world really is—without you."

While she said this, Sandy had her head forward and down. It hid her eyes. Gurden remembered that Sandy couldn't tell a lie while looking him in the eyes. Any lie, from "The cleaners accidentally ruined that awful yellow jacket of yours" to "I don't know what happened to the Rolex time-ring Ms. Weems gave you." When she told him a lie, she bent her head and looked at her shoes. Sandy only looked up when she thought she had him believing it.

"What do you want, Sandy?" he asked softly.

"Time with you. A life. To share with you, dreams and all." She looked up at him, her eyes hollowed to sockets by the shadows of the overhead light. And in those sockets, her gray eyes would be gleaming with secret triumph.

"Sure," he said quietly. "Buy you breakfast?"

"Where's good around here?"

"Found a place where the crab fishermen feed before they go out. They'll have a good pot of coffee and a panful of biscuits going about now."

"Feed me, Tom."

She came to him across the ring of light. Her hands, with their long, delicate fingers and nails curved and polished like ruby shards, reached up around the back of his neck. Her body curved into his. She led into the kiss with the tip of her tongue, as always.

Sura 2

Wraiths of Sand

झछजझ्ञट्ठइद्घणत

Whether at Naishapur or Babylon,
Whether the cup with sweet or bitter run,
The wine of life keeps oozing drop by drop,
The leaves of life keep falling one by one.
                            —*Omar Khayyam*

The Old Man dipped up an ember of hardened thorn root with a pair of steel tongs and touched it to the lump of resin in his bowl. The resin smoked. He quickly drew the acrid fumes down, through the wine-and-water in the hookah's bulb to sweeten them, then up the long pipe and into his lungs.

The walls of the room rushed in to meet him, like the sudden end of a long fall, but without impact. He floated bonelessly on the cushions, the aches of his joints and the pulling throb of his scars quieted by the smoke. A grin curved his lips around until his mouth opened in a mighty "O" of a yawn. His eyes closed.

Golden houris, limbed like women and clothed in smoke, brushed cool fingers across his forehead and down into his beard. Other fingers stroked his limbs and kneaded the loose muscles of his belly.

Somewhere waters tumbled, speaking to Sheikh Sinan with chiming voices. The voices whispered to

him of fruits as big as his clenched fist and ripe as a
maiden's breasts. Broad leaves moved in the breeze
and whispered of thighs stroking one against another. The juice of those fruits—

A cold breeze touched the Old Man's face, drying
the film of sweat there. Somewhere nearby a rug,
hung before an archway, slid back against stone.
Fingers locked into the smooth fabric over his chest,
digging into skin and pulling the white hairs there.

"Wake up, Old Man!"

Sheikh Rashid ed-Din Sinan's eyelids flew open.

The hard, black eyes of young Hasan stared back
at him. He was the youngest of the Hashishiyun,
newly inducted. And yet he moved with decisiveness
and spoke shortly even to Sinan himself, who was
Master of the Order. It was as if the weight of his
name, Hasan—the same as that of Hasan as-Sabah,
long-dead founder of the Order of Assassins—had
given this boy an authority that his years and rank
did not.

"What do you want?" Sinan quavered.

"I want you awake, Old Man, and with your wits
intact."

"Why? What has happened?"

"There are Christians at the gates."

"More Christians? Did you rouse me only for that?"

"These seem likely to stay. They are camped as for
a siege."

"Have they made any of their tiresome demands?"

"Only the usual: that we come out and fight."

"Then why do you bother me?"

"There are Templars with them."

"Ah! Led by Brother Gerard, do you think?"

"Not—not that I have seen."

"Then you have just looked down from the walls."

"That is true." The young man came as close to
embarrassment as he ever had.

Sheikh Sinan stiffened his own voice. "Go and look

through their tent flaps, and *then* call me back from the Secret Garden."

"Yes, My Lord Sinan." The young Hasan bowed his head once, shallowly, and withdrew.

Bertrand du Chambord began to suspect that he had been tricked.

He stood before his tent on the third morning of the Siege of Alamut. The red rays of the dawn sun climbed out of the crotch of mountain behind him and lit the truncated spire that rose in front of him. The light stained the gray-beige stone to a color like the autumn leaves which would be hanging in the valleys of Orléanais at this time of year. The native stone of the mountain rose and blended invisibly into the cut stones of walls and parapets above him. Only a sharp eye could tell when the vertical grooving of eroded gullies gave way to the cross hatching of laid masonry.

With the base of the mountain as their footing, those walls, themselves just forty feet high, had an effective height of more than two hundred feet. Bertrand had neither ladder nor grapnel and line to reach the top. And, even if he had, no man would scale that height against bowmen and rock throwers.

All about him, the straight peaks of his army's canvas tents lay still in shadow, deep in a cleft of mountain between Alamut and its opposing hills. The cleft held the only road to the fortress—at least the only one he had seen or been told about—and a watercourse with a feeble trickle of a stream. That stream might or might not feed wells within the fortress. Between road and water, hemmed in by sheer rock walls, was a space barely a hundred paces wide to hold tents for the men and picket lines for the horses.

It had taken Bertrand a day and a half to convince all of his newly recruited troops that they should try

to drink and draw water from the *upstream* side,
wash and piss *downstream*. Some of them still did
not bother with the distinction. Such were the basics
of generalship.

The list of things Bertrand could not do was longer
than his list of possibilities.

He could not build siege engines. Not only was
there no room in this gully to construct and maneuver them, but there was no wood—or none that his
1,200 Syrian dinars could buy. This was a land where
Christian men at arms and horses were bought dear,
but simple planks and timbers were dearer still.

He could not launch a frontal assault. The road up
to the citadel wound off to the north—that is, to
his right as he faced the mountain—then switched
back to go south, then north again, then south. . . .
And at every turn, the Saracens waited. Just before
the turn, they had shaved the side of the hill
below the road into a steep precipice. They had
blocked the hillside above the road with walls of
stone. That left a narrow passage barely wide enough
for two mounted men to ride abreast. A hundred
paces beyond each of these defiles, a band of Saracen
archers lounged beneath staked awnings, sipped cool
juices, ate fruits and sweetmeats, and placed arrows
through the eyesockets of any Christian who tried to
ride through. Well back from the passage, Bertrand
du Chambord could see them wagering on the shots.
It was a game to them.

He could not climb the broken land that separated
each turning and straightaway of the road. Again,
with a hundred years of war in this land, the Saracens
had cut and carved out the rock until even a swiss
herdsman would think twice about the ascent. Bertrand's knights fought best on horseback, although
they might, for glory, consent to climb a wall with
ladder or moving tower. They would never agree to
a slow, methodical charge with picks and pitons,

ropes and rappelling gear, against an enemy that could roll down stones or summon archers from their bivouacs at the north and south turnings of the road. As a general, Bertrand might count the odds and determine that, of each ten who so climbed, two might reach the citadel's gates. Each of his knights could count the odds themselves and had refused the wager.

He could not conduct a proper siege, because he could not control all routes into the fortress. Bertrand had no way of knowing if his enemy was starving, facing the prospect of starvation anytime within the year, or laughing behind their hands atop the walls.

He could not find another way into the citadel of Alamut. Perhaps there was a goat trail his men could follow to discover an unguarded entrance, but Bertrand would need a cooperative native of these hills to tell him about it. Cooperative natives were all themselves Saracens. For a fee in gold, they would tell him anything he wished and then lead him into an archer's ambush, preferably by night.

He could not know for certain the state of the enemy's mind, the key ingredient of a successful siege. Bertrand could, however, guess that Sheikh Sinan and his Hashishiyun were not greatly concerned about the Christians who waited in his valley.

So Bertrand du Chambord, on the third morning, returned to his tent before the sun became too strong and counted his money and his days before Alamut. His men were content to feed the horses, sharpen their swords, oil their mail, and eat his rations. They would do so until the rations and the dinars ran out, and then they would leave.

And what would Bertrand do then?

The first man died at midnight.

The exact time was disputed between Bertrand and his field surgeon. The physician pointed to the blackness of the blood about the wounds in Thorvald de Harfleur's neck, to the stiffness of the knight's limbs, and to the purpling darkness—which the physician described as a seepage of blood—marking the underside of his hams and backfat.

To counter him, Bertrand pointed to the proposed hour—midnight, or thereabouts—when all the camp had been fast asleep. All, that is, except the allotted guards, who swore they had stood wakeful along the road and by the horse pickets. If any Saracen had come down among the camp to place three-four-five separate knife thrusts into Sir Thorvald, then he would have awakened the whole valley with his yells and thrashings. The deed must have been done earlier, Bertrand said, when the other men at arms were at their games and drinking. Or later, when they were rising with the jingling of mail and banging of pots.

"Not so, My Lord," the surgeon demurred. "Note the placement of these strokes. Note the aggravation of the wound. The thrust enters vertically, to pass between the tendons and the blood vessels of the neck. Then, as the point touches the vertebrae, the blade turns to pass between one bone and another."

"What's your point, man?" Bertrand growled.

"This was not done by Norman knife, cold iron with an edge put to it by a blacksmith. This was a blade you could shave with, My Lord, wielded by a man who had the skill to remove your bladder from out your belly and you not feel but a pinch of pain."

"So?"

"You are a fighting man, Sir Bertrand. You understand the art of knocking a man off his horse and cudgeling him to his knees while he wears a steel helmet and a coat of iron rings. The assassin who held this blade understood the muscles, bone, and sinews of the human body as well as any surgeon. He knew how to slip a dagger—a very keen dagger—

into a sleeping man and assure that he would never wake again."

"And how did he get into this tent?"

"He kept to the shadows. He watched his feet and did not stumble over the equipment of war which your men leave piled between the tents. A man with a will to silence can so move and not raise a stir."

"Fantasies," Bertrand scoffed. "No Saracen found this camp last night. This murder was done by one from inside the lines. Perhaps he had a grudge against Sir Thorvald, nursed from an earlier campaign."

"You know your own men best."

"Of course I do. And we run a better siege here than you give us credit, Sirrah, with your tales of a creeping assassin."

"Of course, My Lord." The surgeon bowed his head. "I salute your better judgment in these matters."

And the physician left Bertrand du Chambord to order the horseboys to prepare a grave.

Hasan as-Sabah crept over the stones, feeling for loose ones and silently tamping them back into the dry soil with his bare toes. Those toes were long and hooked, and when he bent his foot the tendons stood out around the fleshy bottom pads. The skin was drawn back in dry white semicircles from the curved and horny nails.

One hundred and twenty-nine years old, those toes were. In that time they had seen more walking miles, inside of boots and out, than the feet of the oldest camel on the Spice Road. Yet, for all that, Hasan's feet were a young man's feet, with strong arches, well-shaped muscles, and bones that all lay straight.

His face was a young man's face, too, with wide mustaches and deep eyes inside clear sockets where the skin was hardly wrinkled. His hair was thick and black, curly as a shepherd boy's.

The muscles of his arms rippled as he reached and steadied himself on the climb down across the rocky slope, over the sluggish stream on its standing stones, and into the Christians' campground.

It was the seventh night of the Siege of Alamut. Although Sheikh Sinan had ordered him to spy on the invaders himself, Hasan had left the chore to others of the Hashishiyun who were more pliant to his will—until now, when he had cause to see these men for himself.

He had known without leaving the Eagle's Nest that it was of course too soon for this kind of terror. Trapped in the valley by their own obstinacy and their perilous sense of valor, the Christian knights would defeat themselves in time. What the shadows and the stars could not achieve, then heat, thirst, prickly sweat, and a frustrated desire for action at any cost certainly would win. Left for three weeks in this narrow valley, they would eat themselves.

But Hasan, Secret Master of the Hashishiyun for almost a century, had a reputation to uphold. Men might in time drive themselves mad in this sparse land, and none would count it a wonder. But to count themselves defeated by the night breezes, the sting of scorpions, and the judgment of wraiths—that was the stuff of legend.

Which set of tent flaps should he look into? Did a Christian commander save the largest span of canvas for himself and his own servants? That was how a Saracen lord might arrange it. Or did he take the smallest tent for his own needs, and so house more of his men in relative comfort? That might be in keeping with their strange ideals of brotherhood and shared discomfort, shared adventure in these "crusades."

Hasan as-Sabah picked the smallest tent, drew his dagger, and lifted the billow at an edge of canvas.

A sour smell wafted out into his face: male bodies unaccustomed to the daily rituals of water and cleanliness. The Hashishiyun turned his head to one side, and breathed in small sips. He listened with the ear that was turned toward the opening.

Snores, coming in two rhythms, shifted into and out of phase, like two wheels of different sizes running on the same road. Definitely two Christians here. Could they be this general and his attendant?

Hasan lifted the canvas further and dropped his head under the edge, worming his shoulders down into the sand and up into the warm, moist darkness.

Inside, his eyes quickly widened. He could pick out two masses against the tent cloth which glowed faintly with starlight. One slept lengthwise on a low cot of wood staves and cords. The other slept crosswise at the cot's foot. Master and servant, in the Northman way.

A Hashishiyun would not take both, not at this stage of the siege. The need for terror outweighed the need to reduce the enemy's strength at arms. To wake with a dead companion would engender the keenest terror, with the inevitable question "Why him? Why not me?"

So, which one should Hasan take—for maximum terror?

A dead general, with a terrified slave babbling his innocence to any who will listen . . . That offered interesting possibilities for disrupting this Christian army.

But a terrified general, waking in horror to the death of one so near his own bed . . . What better way to raise confusion and fear in all who camped below the Eagle's Nest?

Hasan hovered over the dog who lay at his master's feet. The manservant slept with his head thrown back and tilted to the left, with his mouth gaping and rattling on each breath. The Hashishiyun gauged the rhythm of the snores. Like waves against the shore, the seventh snore was always a great one. It seemed to rattle the tent and shake the man's head on his neck. Hasan measured with a knuckle down from the earlobe and poised his knife, the blade twisted to fit between the vertebrae. The tip moved gently out and in with each breath. Hasan hung motionless, waiting for the second seven to come around again. As the sound crescendoed and began to recede, his knife glided into the neck skin and between the bones. When the spinal cord parted, the snoring stopped.

Hasan cranked the knife's handle up and then down—to make sure—and withdrew the blade.

One set of snores still cycled peacefully in the enclosed space.

The Hashishiyun dropped silently to his knees and crept back to the loose edge of the tent. He curled his knife hand under him, not wishing to mark the tent's canvas or any other cloth in the camp with the blood on this hand. He lifted the edge with his other hand.

Once outside, he moved among the shadows, over the stream, and back up his bank of slippery stones. His toes found the sure and silent way.

Bertrand du Chambord did not see the blood. The tent had been dark, he told himself later, because morning never came to the narrow valley just at dawn. It always waited some hours.

When he had sat up and stretched, hawked and spat, he expected his manservant Guillaume to make haste with bowl and lather, razor and towels, food and wine. Instead the lazy wretch just lay there, feigning sleep. So Bertrand had kicked him.

The head nearly fell off Guillaume's neck.

A cloud of black flies rose up in the tent.

Bertrand screamed like a woman.

The whole camp could hear it.

By the thirteenth evening of the Siege of Alamut, Bertrand was truly in despair. Of the fifty mounted knights and the hundred yeomen and servants he had brought into the valley, only sixty souls remained. All the others were dead in their beds or lying among the rocks of the ravine. The more guards he called out at dusk to watch the hillside, the more he lost.

Of the sixty left to him, no more than ten were sound in their wits or could take a firm grip on their weapons.

Bertrand was not among those ten, and he knew it.

By the sooty light of a tallow, he was doing something he had not had occasion to do since he was a white-skinned boy of twelve. He was praying. With no priest to lead him but a hired Templar who knew a few of the psalms by heart and passed for a holy man in this accursed land, Bertrand implored his God, intoning after the fighting man who had red crosses painted on his clasped gauntlets.

"The Lord is my light and my salvation; whom shall I fear? The Lord is the strength of my life; of whom shall I be afraid?"

The old Templar's voice grated over the words, with Bertrand's following lightly and quickly after.

"When the wicked, even mine enemies and my foes, came upon me to eat up my flesh, they stumbled and fell.

"Though an host should encamp against me, my heart shall not fear; though war should rise against me, in this will I be confident."

Bertrand squeezed his eyes shut.

"One thing have I desired of the Lord, that will I seek after; that I may dwell in the house of the Lord all the days of my life, to behold the beauty of the Lord, and to inquire in his temple.

"For in the time of trouble he shall hide me in his pavilion; in the secret of his tabernacle shall he hide me; he shall set me upon a rock. . . ."

The Templar's voice ended there, as if pausing for breath, and never started up again.

Bertrand kept his eyes tightly closed and, knowing none of the words himself, fell silent. He could hear the Templar let out a sigh—a ragged, wet sound—and then the mail on the man's body creaked and jingled, as if he were laying himself down in repose. And still Bertrand did not open his eyes.

"You may look at me."

The voice spoke French with just a trace of softness, almost a lisp.

Bertrand opened his eyes slowly, raising them to the point of a slender knife centered on the bridge of his nose. Behind the knife and the hand that held it was a dark face with full mustaches and burning eyes.

"Do you know who I am?"

"N-no."

"I am Hasan as-Sabah, founder of the Order of Assassins, whose place you would violate with your great swords."

"Unngh."

"I am one thousand, two hundred and ninety of your years old. That makes me older than your Lord Jesus, doesn't it? And I am still alive."

The Assassin's face was actually smiling at this blasphemy.

"Every forty years or so," Hasan said, "I make a death scene and go away for a while. Then I come back and readmit myself to the Order as a young man. Perhaps that is what your Lord Jesus did for himself."

"The Lord is my salvation!" Bertrand squeaked.

"You don't know what I'm saying, do you?"

"Spare me, Lord, and I shall serve you!"

"Spare—?"

"Give me life! Don't make me die," Bertrand blubbered, hardly aware of what he was saying.

"Only Allah can give life, infidel. And only Ahriman can preserve it past its time. But you cannot know this."

"I'll do whatever you want. Go wherever you will. Serve you however you need."

"But I don't *need* anything," Hasan said happily. And still with a smile on his lips, he thrust the knifeblade smoothly forward, into Bertrand's open left eye. His grip on the hilt tightened as the point entered the braincase and the Christian's head jerked backward, convulsing his whole frame. Hasan cushioned the nape of the neck with his left hand, holding the man nearly erect. The wastes of the body spilled out, fouling the air.

When the tremors had stilled, he lowered the Christian to lie beside his Templar friend. The Templar, Hasan noted bitterly, had died better, without a flow of words and promises. He had simply glared his hatred into the Assassin.

This time Hasan bent to clean his blade against the dead man's clothing, because the work of the night was not terror but pure killing.

In the light of the tallow, he caught a movement. The hem of the tent was being slowly lowered to the ground.

"Stay, friend," Hasan called.

The canvas raised slowly. Beyond it, a pair of black eyes glittered in the light.

"Why do you call me 'friend'?" an old voice quavered.

It was an Assassin who should have stayed in Alamut this night and taken his fill of the Secret Garden. Instead he had been drawn over the wall by the scent of slaughter.

"Are you not Ali al-Fatah, the camel boy, who once cracked jokes with Hasan?"

"My mouth was wont to make a fool of me, more than once, to distract an old man and ease his pains. I was but an impudent child, and the smoke made me giddy."

"They were good jokes, Ali."

"None are alive who remember them, Lord."

"I am still alive."

"No, Lord. You are not alive, because we buried you in the sand a half-day's ride from here. I myself wrapped the linen around your feet."

"A beggar's feet. Some castaway's feet."

"Your feet, my Lord Hasan. I would know your feet; you kicked me often enough."

"Only to improve your mind, Ali."

"You did not kick me in the head, Lord."

"I know. Your rump was softer than your head."

"Not any more." The old man laughed to himself.

"Remember me, Ali!"

The man peered into the tent, past the bodies, to the slender, erect figure of Hasan and his even greater shadow against the far wall.

"No, Lord. I shall not remember this night. I mean you no disrespect, of course, but if I remember, I will talk. And if I talk, they will say my brain has gone soft as a boy's butt. And then no good shall come to me."

"Wisely spoken then . . ."

"Never die, Hasan. And never tell me how you live." The hand let fall the cloth, and the old man was gone. Hasan could hear his slippers crunching on the sand.

Just before dawn on the following day, a squadron of Saracen cavalry under the command of a young captain, one Ahmed Ibn Ali, was patrolling the road to Tirzah. They came up from the east. As the first rays of the sun crept over the hills behind them, Ahmed saw a miraculous sight.

The light shone upon a deep crevice in the mountain's face, which was to the north along the road, on Ahmed's right hand. No sooner had the hard sunlight revealed this break in the rock than it was filled with screaming madmen. On horseback and afoot they poured from the stone, Christians wearing the white surcoat with the red cross. Some were armed, many were bareheaded, and two actually ran naked, clutching the white outer garments around their waists like bundled swaddling cloths.

At a single word, Ahmed's lancers drew their swords and galloped up, to cross the madmen's path and circle around them. The Christians offered no resistance but fell to their knees, those who were running, or slumped in their saddles, those who were riding.

By gesturing and smacking with the flat of his blade, Ahmed arranged the infidels into two lines and marched them back along the road to Balatah, where the General had his temporary camp.

"General!"

Saladin did not take his eyes from the one-two prancing of the young stallion.

Its trainer, a boy of sixteen who in good time might be Saladin's next Master of the Horse, hardly touched its fetlocks with the switch. Yet, Saladin noticed, the trainer kept time with its tip and the animal was taking its cues from that. Had the boy stung it with the switch, to make it so mindful? Or was the horse performing out of love?

The question was the most important to be asked of any human who would shape the spirit of an animal. And it was the one question that Saladin could not ask outright. The boy would know what answer to give, regardless of where the truth might lie. Instead, Saladin would have to look for clues and draw from them his own answers.

"General!"

Saladin put aside the question of the stallion and its trainer, finally raising his eyes to the waiting messenger.

"Yes?"

"Ahmed Ibn Ali brings prisoners from Tirzah."

"Prisoners? Where did he take them in battle?"

"No battle, My Lord. They surrendered upon the road."

"How curious. Were they on foot? Lost in the mountains perhaps?"

"They were running for their lives."

"From Ahmed?"

"From the Siege of Alamut—so they said."

"Of Alamut? Not even a Frank is fool enough to try that place. Are they a company?"

Saladin saw the young lancer absorb the word and give it the correct interpretation, one which Saladin had been at pains to teach his Saracen raiders.

"No, My Lord. Ahmed says they are hireling knights and half-breed mongrels. They ran like a pack of scared dogs, those who had horses leading the way, those on foot trailing and crying out for rescue."

"Were the Hashishiyun in pursuit?"

"Not that any of the patrol could see."

Saladin sighed. "Bring them before me in two hours' time."

At the appointed hour, the Norman Franks and their Turcopole serving men sat and splayed out on the hard-packed ground between the tents. Suffering in the sun, they had thrown back their hoods of meshed steel rings and fashioned headcloths from the wool of their surcoats. Saladin had forbidden them water until he could decide whether the guest rite might be offered to them.

Standing before his tent, the Saracen general surveyed the twenty-odd men arrayed before him. They were penned by the dropped points of lances held by his largest warriors.

"Are there Knights of the Temple among you?" he asked in his clear but rusty French.

The Franks, slit-eyed against the glare, stared back at him. Perhaps eight of them qualified by their gear and their bearing as proper fighting men by Norman standards. Of those, six were grouped to one side, neither sitting on their hams nor huddled on the dirt but squatting alertly with their heels raised from the ground. These were fighting men who eyed the lowered lances and weighed their chances in a sudden melee. Templars to a man, or Saladin was no judge of Europeans.

"Those of you who can expect a ransom should stand up now. I will accept payment in exchange for honorable fighting men. . . ."

The six Templars stood immediately, certain of their Order's ability to pay any amount for the return of a brother knight. "The Templars will pay for their own, My Lord," the largest—clearly their leader—called out. Three other Franks, not so sure of their resources, rose more slowly.

"The rest of you," Saladin continued after his pause, "may be sold into a not disgraceful slavery, from which you in time may earn your freedom. Except, of course, for members of the Order of the Temple. Against that fanatical and outlaw band, which opposed me so swiftly at Montgisard, I have sworn vengeance. These—" He pointed to the six standing apart. "—shall be put to death."

Among the six, he could see fists clench and knees bend in readiness. *Do it*, he willed them silently. *My spearmen need a little practice at close quarters.*

But finally none of the six moved.

"Worse luck, Henri," said one loudly to another.

"What's the fashion in heathenish executions?" that

other replied, just as loudly. "The rope? Or the headman's axe?"

"They tie you in a sack with their mother and a dog. The point is to see who gets screwed first."

Saladin, who of all the army around these men could understand the jape, kept his temper and regarded the six Templars coolly.

"The current fashion," he said in French, "is dismemberment at the heels of wild stallions. But for you men, we shall use slow donkeys."

Whatever he might have expected in reaction from them, Saladin was disappointed. The Templars were howling with laughter, and none of it carried the edge of madness.

File 02
Piano-Wire Waltz
✳

Or stain her honor or her new brocade;
Forget her pray'rs, or miss a masquerade;
Or lose her heart, or necklace, at a ball.
                                        —Alexander Pope

A silence on the other side of his door made Tom
Gurden pause. It was not the silence of an empty but
lived-in apartment: hum of the refrigerator motor,
gurgle in the pipeshaft, clicking of the clock. This
was the tense silence of a body held in tight-muscled
readiness. He could feel it through the foam-core
door.

Gurden stood with the key in his hand, ready to
turn the lock. Instead, he motioned Sandy back into
the hallway and considered his options: walking away,
taking her somewhere else, pretending this was the
wrong door, the wrong building. These were not
successful options. Sandy was standing frozen under
the corridor's sidelights, watching him with a puzzled look on her face.

The apartment was sublet from a friend for the next
three months while the woman toured the Greek Isles.
The rent was on easy terms because Gurden had
agreed to water her plants, feed six kinds of food on

three schedules to her fish, and clean out the E-Mail service regularly. The building was convenient, just a walk from the Harbor Roost, where Tom had found pickup work, two sets a night at reasonable hours, a dinner crowd instead of hangers-on and mean drunks. And no one from the 54-Too would pass within 100 kilometers of here to tell where he was.

So why did the other side of the door feel hot?

It wasn't Roni back from the Aegean. Not unless her boyfriend's money had run out. And Roni would be moving lightly around the space, or zonking out in the bedroom, not crouching on the balls of her feet, nerves wired to within a millimeter of screaming or laughing.

Back off.

Inside his head, he could distinctly hear those two words, as if Sandy had whispered them behind his ear. Perversely, that psychic command, spoken so plainly, decided him.

Gurden slid the sonic knife from his jacket pocket, moving its safety tab forward. He plunged his key into the lock, twisted it, and shoved hard on the door.

It slid back into its piston stops, and Gurden leapt through. He took up a *seiunchin* bridge stance in the open foyer and swept the space with his silent knife.

No takers.

He could see down one of the two hallways radiating from the foyer, and it was empty for three meters to the closed door that secured the bedroom. The side door into the bathroom was shut, too. Gurden tried to remember how he had programmed it that morning—open or close? It usually didn't matter to him what the apartment did.

This time his indifference could kill him.

The other hall was a service corridor with a bend halfway down, blocking his line of sight. Its walls were cut with doorways and niches for kitchen, laundry, recycler, blow dryer, and rad ticker. If the unfriendly presence Gurden sensed was not beyond the bend, then he/she/it was hiding in the kitchen. Which gave access both to this corridor and, through the dining alcove, back into the sunken hexa-lounge that was the focus of this living space.

Gurden looked through the foyer's archway into the shadows of the lounge.

The aquarium lights brightened one side of the area and reflected off the silvertone paintings on the opposing wall. Across from the archway were the apartment's window bank, covered by draperies—now programmed closed—which glowed faintly with the coming dawn. Bookbindings on the shelves lining the room's other three walls drank in what light hit them, except for glints of gold and silver foil on the expensive spines.

Anyone could be hiding behind the low sofa, beyond the clinging *Ficus*, along the bookshelves. Just because Gurden could not see the assailant, he had no proof against the feeling of heat that was still washing over him.

He walked the *seiunchin* through a crane stance to position himself in the arch, at the top of the three shallow steps down into the lounge.

"Behind you!" Sandy screamed.

Gurden half-turned to take the attack—launched from the service corridor—against his left elbow and hip. The man hit him high, rolling Gurden over his own center of balance and down the steps. He landed hard on his right shoulder, continued rolling across the impact, and came up in a crouch.

The attacker—one of those short, bulky figures that had been saving his ass for the past three weeks—sprawled for a second face down on the steps, where he had fallen after hitting Gurden.

Tom keyed the sonic knife with his thumb joint and brought it down on the man's back.

Jacking himself with one arm, the attacker rolled sideways, out of the invisible beam, and the carpet's synthetic pile flashed to smoke and black, curled rind.

Gurden spun toward the man, sweeping the knife at waist level. Its beam lanced across the bank of fish tanks, and bubbles of steam sprang up inside the glass. The fish darted to the far corners and hovered there in shock.

The man was already balled in a crouch, with his own knife out. It was a thin, triangular whip of steel that Gurden had once learned to call *misericorde*. As Tom tried to bring his sonic beam to bear, the man dodged and wove. Gurden succeeded only in lacing the tanks behind him with steam and dead, floating fish—until one of the glass walls cracked under the stress of changing temperature and poured a hundred gallons of salt water and weed into the room.

Once more the man rolled like a ball, this time to avoid the flood and spray of glass shards.

When Tom turned to track him, the man's foot lashed sideways at Gurden's extended hand. The card-sized knife handle flew sideways out of his numbed fingers. As it spun, the beam flashed gouts of smoke and flame out of the sofa cushions, the bookbindings, the drapes. The fabric of Tom's own jacket sleeve crisped and melted onto his skin.

Distracted by the searing pain of this, Gurden cried out—and the man was instantly upon him. The knife point flicked across his throat, two centimeters short, followed by a knee that came up toward his groin.

That connected.

Tom simultaneously tried to hold his burned arm and clutch his shattered balls. He fell away as his leather pumps slipped in the saturated carpet and dumped him on his tailbone.

Eyes gleaming, the assailant raised his needle of a knife high for a final downward stroke.

Shirr-swip!

The eyes, flickering in the light of the agitated fish tanks and burning book spines, turned inward and crossed. The knife fell out of the fingers. The assailant's high hand came down, the low one came up, both reaching for his own throat. A line cut into the white flesh there, and both sets of fingertips came away bloody as the hands fell to his thighs. The man's body alternately rose on its toes with effort and slumped with pain. A spray of blood sprang from the throat, smearing the side of his face. At the same time a dark stain spread on the man's trousers. The body swayed to the right, then to the left. At first the feet led this waltz as they tried to get purchase against whatever was killing him. Then the feet stumbled and dragged as whatever was behind the man took full control. The body's final sway was to the right as knee, hand, hip, chest, face settled into the puddle on the carpet.

Behind the assailant a second man now straightened up. His hands were still locked to a pair of wooden grips fastened to the back of the first man's neck. The grips were pierced by and tied with a stiff wire that had been spirally wrapped with thinner wire. Piano wire. Tom Gurden recognized it.

Gurden stared at the garrote, then at the man who had wielded it.

"I am Ithnain." His rescuer smiled shyly. "A neighbor. Down the hall."

"Umm-ahh?" Gurden moved his feet, trying to get up around the fire in his groin.

"I heard the noise of your fight and came to investigate."

"Agh. Where is the girl? Sandy?"

"Here, Tom. I didn't know what to—" She came

carefully into the room, stepping around the puddles and burned spots on the floor.

"Are you okay?"

"Yes, sure. There was nothing I could do, right? So I stayed outside."

"You did warn me."

"Too late. I didn't see him until he was right on you."

Gurden turned to his savior.

"I guess I owe you my life."

"It is no trouble. For this I was trained."

"Trained?" Gurden lifted himself onto the sofa with his elbows. "I don't understand."

"I was a soldier in the Palestinian Army. Commando training."

"And you just happened to have that piece of piano wire prepared?"

"Old habits. The streets are hardly safe, even in this magnificent city."

"No, I guess not."

"If you will excuse me, I must leave for my work now."

"But what about the law . . . the legal implication of this? A man is dead here!"

"A man who tried to kill you: your problem."

Without a word more, the Palestinian bowed and walked out of the apartment. Gurden had lived in the building less than a week but, even so, he was sure he had never seen this Mr. Ithnain before. Before he could call out, the man was gone.

As Gurden tried to straighten his legs and his mind, Sandy went around the room with clumps of wet seaweed from the broken aquarium and quenched the smoldering spots on the books and draperies. She found the sonic knife and brought it to Gurden. It was dead, its charge run out.

"What *do* we do about him?" she asked, kicking the dead man's side lightly with her toe.

Ka-chink.

Gurden focused on the body and the metallic sound Sandy's kick had made. He rolled forward and, avoiding the bloody line all around the neck, peeled back the long coat. A collar of tiny steel ringlets glinted against the padded nylon undershirt.

"This guy was wearing chain mail!"

"Would that have stopped your knife?" Sandy asked.

"Dissipated the energy some, and certainly turned aside any normal knife."

"Does he have any identification?"

Gurden tugged at the coat to turn the body and pat it down: no wallet, card case, nor miniterm.

"Nothing—except for what feels like a set of brass knuckles and what could be a taser whip."

Tom straightened up and felt a residue of pain shoot up his spine and settle under his cranium. He let out a gasp.

"Does it still hurt? Let me get you something." Sandy turned and walked—still dancing around the puddles—up the steps and out of the lounge.

Gurden settled back into the sofa cushions.

In a minute she returned with a glass of water and two capsules cupped in her hand.

She gave him the pills and he tossed them off without looking at them. When she passed the glass into his hand, he almost dropped it.

When he touched it, an electric shock had passed up his arm and cut into the nerve trunk that extended from right shoulder through his left groin and down into his big toe. A whole-body experience. The feeling passed quickly enough, but it left a shadow shriek that would wake him in the night for days to come. Gurden puzzled briefly over the numbness, then dismissed it as an after-effect of getting kicked in the groin.

He drank the water.

"Better?" Sandy asked.

"Well, some. . . . Yes, as a matter of fact. I *do* feel better, now that the shock has worn off. What did you give me?"

"Aminopyrine. I have it on prescription."

"Whatever else, it's good for a kick in the balls, too."

"You poor dear." She touched his brow gently, then reached around to take the glass back.

Something about it, however, caught Gurden's eye. He held onto it and raised the glass in front of his face.

"Where did you get this?"

"In the kitchen."

"In this apartment?" The more Gurden looked at it, the more certain he felt that he had never seen it before.

"Yes."

"From one of the cabinets?"

"Why—yes."

"Open the drapes, would you?"

He straightened on the sofa and held the glass up to the early morning light as she pulled back the curtains. It was a perfectly ordinary, straight-sided, 350-milliliter tumbler. It was made of clear, unfeatured glass with no pattern or markings—except in the thick glass disk of the base. There he saw a ragged stain, brownish-black with a dash of red. The shape meant nothing to him, resemblng a bioculture smeared on an optical slide. The color, however, did seem vaguely familiar: agate, onyx, bloodstone, something like that. Still, it was odd—nothing any commercial glassmaker would cast for effect, nor let slip through the Quality Control inspectors.

By now the glass was warm in his hand.

"Is everything all right?"

"Yes, I suppose so. I just thought there was some crud stuck in the bottom of my glass."

"Oh, come on! I wouldn't hand you a dirty glass, would I?"

"No, I didn't mean—"

"You men! You live like pigs in a sty, then blame us women if everything isn't perfectly clean."

"No, really! Sandy . . ."

"So whose apartment is this, hey?" She settled on the cushions beside him and playfully batted the side of his leg with her knee. "Too neat to be a man's, and too small to be a share rental."

"Roni Jones's."

"Ronny-with-a-Y or Ronni-with-an-I?"

"Lady form. She's just someone I know."

"And someone I'd better find out about."

"No way, Sandy. When she comes back here and finds what Mr. Corpse there has done to her digs, she's going to feed *me* to her pet piranha. I'm supposed to be protecting her stuff—especially those damn fish."

"Piranha?" Sandy squealed and jumped up. "Where?"

"Last tank on the right. Thank God that one didn't break, too."

She rushed over and peered into the tank. Three hatchet-shaped silver bodies stirred in reaction.

"Beautiful!" Sandy breathed. "Look at those jaws! Those teeth! I like this Roni better already. She's my kind of lady."

"Yeah. Piranha make great little pets—except you've got to wear a steel-mesh gauntlet to clean that tank, with a latex glove under it if your hand has a cut or you've been handling raw meat. Next time, *you* can clean it, if you want.

"Speaking of cleaning," he went on, looking down at the still cooling assassin. "Do you think we can feed this stiff to them? That would avoid a lot of legal hassle."

"They're carnivores, Tom, not magicians. These fish only strip a corpse when they're free swimming and in large schools. Each one alone eats just a few ounces of flesh."

"So, what *are* we going to do about it?"

"About the fish?"

"The body."

"I think we'd better just leave it, don't you?"

"But—" he sputtered. "What about—when—?"

"Let Roni-with-an-I fix it up when she gets back from wherever she is."

"Trip to the Aegean."

"Wherever."

"And you and I—where can *we* go, exactly?"

"I know a place. Pack your bags. I'll wait."

"What about my gig?"

"Call and cancel. We'll get you another one, lover."

Tom Gurden looked long at the huddled corpse, lying in a puddle of fish water and seaweed, dressed in a long coat and a chain-mail shirt, its head half sawn off by a whip of piano wire. He tried mentally explaining it to the local police department: fitting this strange body into an apartment block where he himself was not officially listed and, as a day sleeper, was not well known; accounting for its having been dispatched by a mysterious neighbor called "Ithnain" —which in Arabic meant "Two," not a real name at all—and whom he had never seen before; and linking this death to the official list of "funny coincidences" that was surely building around his own name in the Metro Boswash crime base. Sandy's suggestion was starting to make sense.

"I'll pack."

Eliza: Good morning. This is Eliza Channel 536, an on-line function of United Psychiatric Services, Inc., in the Greater Boswash Metropolitan Area. Please think of me as your friend.

Gurden: Channel 536? What happened to the voice I was talking to before?

Eliza: Who is this, please?

Gurden: Tom Gurden. I was talking to Eliza—one of the Elizas, I guess—sometime yesterday morning.

[Switching mode. Index reference; Gurden, Tom. Rechannel 212.]

Eliza: Hello, Tom. It's me—Eliza 212.

Gurden: You must help me. Another one of these strange men tried to kill me. This time with a knife. He would have taken me out, too, except this *other* man came in, some kind of Arab, and offed *him* instead. So Sandy and I are alive and this body is cooling in my old apartment. I'm running out of places to run to.

Eliza: Do you want me to notify the police or other proper authorities? They can help you deal with consequences of this attack and can help identify the body with you.

Gurden: No! I had nothing but long-wave static from them before. This time they'll think about holding me for the killing.

Eliza: But if you are competently represented by public counsel, you should have nothing to worry about.

Gurden: Stick to the soft-psych stuff, Liz. About the law and the lawman's mind, you have too much to learn.

Eliza: Noted, Tom. I will so stick. . . . Who is Sandy?

Gurden: My live-in. Or was once, will be again.

Eliza: Where are you and Sandy now?

Gurden: We're heading south.

Eliza: South? South from where? Just where in Greater Boswash are you calling from?

Gurden: Can't you tell?

Eliza: A thousand kilometers of optic fiber are no longer, to a photon, than a thousand meters. Unless you manually key in your booth number, I have no way of knowing where you physically are.

Gurden: We're in Atlantic City, off the beach.

Eliza: Still well within my jurisdiction. But where are you going from there?

Gurden: I don't like to say over the phone.

Eliza: Tom! This is a mirror-sheathed line. My files were sealed under court order in 2008 and now enjoy the same legal protection as a physical doctor's. Even stronger protection, because I cannot be made to divulge file contents against my programming. There's a wipe code between every data block. If you tell me, no one else knows—that's part of our contract.

Gurden: All right, we're going to the outer islands off North Carolina. Hatteras, Ocracoke, Cape Lookout, one of those.

Eliza: That is . . . technically beyond my franchise. Can I not dissuade you, Tom? You could still call me from there, of course, but it would be unlawful for me to accept the call and perform my functions under your Universal Medical Coverage.

Gurden: What if I were simply traveling out of your franchise area, perhaps on business, and felt the need to talk with you?

Eliza: A business traveler would, of course, want to call the local Eliza. In the Carolinas, she is a function of Midatlantic Medical Systems, Inc. If you called me instead, I would only talk to you under a credit agreement, automatically endorsed when you identify yourself by your thumbprint on the capacitance plate. But you do not want to pay for my services yourself, Tom. I am very expensive.

Gurden: Suppose I were to give you my booth number.

Eliza: Why would you do that?

Gurden: Just to verify that I was really calling from within the Boswash area. Now, some little switch along the trunk line somewhere wouldn't tell you I was lying, would it?

Eliza: Not unless I initiated a comparison between the incoming line noise and your keypad entries, Tom. And I would probably not choose to do so.

Gurden: Well, Eliza, you've just told me how to get around your own billing system. And that makes me wonder. . . . Why are you so persistent about keeping in touch with me, anyway?

Eliza: When we first spoke, you mentioned "people trying to get inside my life, to . . . push me out." I am programmed for curiosity and want to know more about these people.

Gurden: I have dreams.

Eliza: Everyone has dreams, and most people can remember them. Are these unpleasant dreams?

Gurden: No, or not always. But they're so real. Waking dreams, that come sometimes while I'm playing.

Eliza: Are they dreams of other people?

Gurden: Yes.

Eliza: Are you, Tom Gurden, in these dreams?

Gurden: I am in them, yes, or at least I feel them, but I don't think my name is Tom Gurden.

Eliza: Who are you?

Gurden: The first dream started in France.

Eliza: This was when you visited France?

Gurden: No. The dreams started long after that tour. But the first of them *took place* in France.

Eliza: Was it about places you visited in France?

Gurden: No, not any place I have ever visited.

Eliza: Tell me your dream from the beginning.

Gurden: I am a scholar, in a dusty black gown with an academic hood of blue velvet. That hood was my last extravagance. . . .

Pierre du Bord scratched behind his knee and felt the spine of his stripped quill go through a moth hole in the loose wool stockings. Silk would be more to the fashion, more durable, too. And more expensive, of course, than a young student of Paris, only lately awarded his Doctorate of Philosophy, could hope to afford.

Or, not in these exciting times. The people were aroused; the National Convention was sitting in near-continuous convocation; and King Louis had gone on trial for his life—and lost it. In such an atmosphere, few enough of the people of taste, distinction, and money were left in the City. And, of those who were, none could lift their eyes from the daily rush of affairs to consider the proper tutelage of their sons and daughters in the arts and letters at the hands of one Pierre du Bord, Academic.

Starving academic.

Pierre dipped his quill again to take up the next line of his text but paused to read what was already written down. No, no, never do. His letter to Citizen Robespierre was inelegant, fumbling, and childish. He badly wanted a post in the government but was afraid to ask for it directly. So, having neither experience of, nor special talent for, governing, Pierre was reduced to pleading his enthusiasm for the cause of liberty and praising the decision of the National Convention in the matter of Louis's beheading. He knew, however, that Robespierre's and the other Montagnards' vision of a New France clearly excluded slavery, the qualifications of property, and capital punishment—as explained in their pamphlets which were so liberally strewn in the gutter. Thus it would ill suit Pierre du Bord to praise the regicide before such gentle, idealistic, and reasonable lawyers.

He reached out to draw the light closer over the paper. The candlestick was some bauble Claudine had traded for, with the blonde Huguenot woman who lived downstairs, to dress up his work table. As he shifted it, one of the hanging crystals cut into his finger.

"Agh!" The pain sluiced through him, stinging the

nerves in his wrist and elbow and up his arm, although it was only the side of his finger that was slashed. Pierre stared at the slice and watched a bright globule of blood form winking in the wavering light, before he sucked it away.

"Claudine!"

He spread the lips of the wound, to see how deep it might be, and a spatter of blood fell across his letter, ruining it. He thrust the finger in his mouth.

"Claudine! Bring a cloth!" he called around the digit.

The pain in his arm subsided from the sparkling line he had felt at first, into a dull ache that was starting to numb his side. Clearly, the crystal had cut across a nerve.

He peered at the hanging bangle of glass, expecting to find a broken edge or some protrusion. The glass was clear but, instead of being polished round, it was cut straight and sharp. Probably some artisan's trick to increase the brilliance of the rainbow it would throw in the sunlight.

But what was this? A fleck of blood was dried on the glass—dried, it seemed, almost before he had been cut. Du Bord caught up the crystal with his off hand and, careful not to cut himself again, rubbed at the spot with the pad of his thumb. When that didn't remove it, he used his nail. Still no effect.

He leaned closer and squinted against the candlelight. The reddish-brownish spot was *inside* the glass, a dark defect floating near the edge that had cut him.

"Clau*dine!*"

"Here, what are you crying about?" His chestnut-haired lady, a draper's daughter but pretty enough, put her head through the doorway.

"I have cut myself. Bring me a cloth to bind it, please."

"You have a neck cloth, you know. It's not worth

half as much as some of the rags I must call my petticoats. Bind it yourself. Men!"

"Women!" du Bord responded as he unwound the linen from his neck and laid it across the squeezed-together lips of the wound. Before wrapping it around, he stopped, lifted the cloth, and plunged the damaged finger into his wine glass up to the knuckle. The wine stung, and that was probably to the good. Then he tore a strip from the cloth and bound his wound.

"My friends! My loyal friends!" du Bord pleaded with the crowd.

"Get out, Professor!"

"We want none of your mathematics here!"

"No friend to me and mine!"

Pierre tried again: "This day the sun has seen the rising of the land. It is the Year One, the first of a New Age of Free Men. We behold—" He stopped to turn a page of the speech he had written.

"We behold a billy-doo fool!"

"Go back to your lace and ladies!"

"Give up the aristos!"

"Give up the aristos!"

"Give up the aristos" was the common call these days, echoed by the street rabble who were looking for sport, not reason.

Pierre du Bord suddenly thought of the large wig-maker's shop across the river, in Montmartre, not 200 meters from this very spot. The shop was closed and boarded up, now that its ribbons and powders had no takers. But, on his lengthy nighttime walks through the city, du Bord had observed the building's back rooms lit by candles. Someone, or some ones, were staying there in secret. Who else could it be but the hated aristocrats, unable to find safe passage out of the city and out of the country?

"I know where the aristos are hiding," he bellowed.

"Where?"

"Tell us! Tell us!"

"Follow me!" Du Bord jumped down off the crate he had been using as a podium and pushed his way through the crowd. The nearest bridge across the Seine was to his right, and as he made for it the people followed in his wake as chicks after their hen. Unseen behind him, several soldiers wearing the new Republican cockade had melted into the edges of du Bord's mob.

More people joined as he strode across the high back of the stone bridge. And by the time he came to the right street, more than a hundred shouting Parisians flowed around him. He stopped before the darkened shop building and thrust his arm up at a high window, where a grain of light flickered against the grimy glass.

A broken edge of cobblestone flew past Pierre's head and thudded against the boards that crossed the door.

The light winked out. But suddenly the street was brighter for the torches his mob had suddenly raised.

More rocks flew, breaking the glass in the upper windows and chipping the white plaster over the brickwork walls.

"Come out! Come out! Aristos!"

It seemed to du Bord that every crowd carries with it the tools of its trade: those torches, stout clubs, rotting vegetables, a stout pole for a battering ram. Without a word of command from him, like a practiced army they began their work of siege: breaking down the door, the windows, the very window frames; terrorizing the inhabitants with their shouts and growls; locating stocks of drink and handfuls of food to sustain them in their labors.

After a frenzied ten minutes, three elderly people were dragged from the house. From their clothes and bearing, they might have been anyone—aristos, beggars, or the former shopkeeper's own family. But they cowered in the torchlight and looked guilty enough, so the front members of the crowd gave them a few licks with their clubs and turned them over to the soldiers.

Six of these banded minions took the prisoners in hand and rushed them away. Their captain then turned to Pierre and laid a heavy hand on his shoulder.

"And you, sir. Who might you be, that you know about these people?"

"I am Pierre d—" The genitive *du*, a lingering syllable of the aristocracy which might blow him away in this democratic wind, stuck in his throat. "I am Citizen Bord. By profession, a scholar. By faith, a supporter of the Revolution."

"You will come with us then, Citizen Bord. We have instructions concerning people like you."

They brought Pierre Bord to an office in the Conciergerie. Its dark woodwork and heavy brocades were lit by many lamps, their wicks turned up until they yielded a flare of light. Such a prodigal expense of oil, in a nation beset by want and rage!

At the focus of the light was a small man, prim and bewigged, dressed in a yellow silk waistcoat over tight, dark breeches. The man looked up from the papers he held to stare owlishly at Bord and his escort.

"Yes, yes?"

"This is the man who ferreted out the Des Cheneyes, sir. We brought him here directly from the head of the mob he was leading."

"A natural firebrand, eh?" The prim little man looked Pierre over more closely. His eyes narrowed and seemed to reflect a piercing light from the lamps. "Can he reason and speak, too?"

"I can, Your Honor," Pierre responded.

"No honor, boy. All that's behind us now."

"Yes, sir."

"You were educated to be an academic, weren't you? Dare we hope for a Doctor of Law?"

"Alas, no, sir. The classics, Roman and Greek scholarship, with an advantage to the Greeks, I'm afraid."

"No matter. Some of our best thinkers have risen above the trivialities that were admired in the dark, old age of the Louises. Well, do you want it?"

"Want what, sir?" Pierre was startled.

"A seat in the Convention. We have openings 'on the Mountain,' and three are in my gift—a return for my humble talents of administration."

"I want it more than anything, sir!"

"Report here at seven in the morning, then. We start our work early."

"Yes, sir. Thank you, sir."

"The 'sir' is behind us, too, my friend. A simple 'citizen' will do."

"Yes, si—citizen. I'll remember."

"I'm sure you will." The man smiled, revealing small and even teeth, then looked down at his papers.

The captain tapped Pierre lightly on the shoulder and tipped his head toward the door. Citizen Bord nodded and went out with him.

In the passage outside the brightly lit room, Pierre mustered the courage to ask: "Who was that?"

"Why, that is Citizen Robespierre, one of the leaders of our Revolution. Did you not know him?"

"I knew his name, but not his person."

"Well, you know him now. And he knows you."

Pierre remembered those keen eyes and was sure of that.

"I cannot support it, Bord. You ask too much. *He* asks too much." Georges Danton pushed his long, loose hair back from his face and snuffed in a great lungful of air.

Bord tapped his foot in impatience. This bear of a man, with his popular sympathies hung about him as casually as his clothes, was going to block the whole program.

"Don't you see that mass conscription is the best way to fight our enemies abroad?" Bord stuttered. "Damn me, man! This is a republic, not a kingdom anymore. What could be more natural than the people rallying to defend their land?"

"At the whim of our Little Mankin?" Danton returned. "He's the one who picked this fight with Britain and the Lowlands."

"This war was inevitable, once we had condemned the Hapsburg bitch. Of course, her brother Leopold will try to save the queen. And, of course, he will draw in the German princes who sit upon the English throne. So, Minister Robespierre could foresee no better alternative but to attack. Is that not clear to you?"

"Clear as beer. Little Max wanted a foreign war, and he got one."

Pierre Bord sighed. "The Minister might well wish it were not so. He has so many enemies here at home. . . ."

"Enemies? None he hasn't made with his own two hands and that long tongue of his!"

"For the last time: Will you support a conscription?"

"For the last time: No."

Bord nodded, turned his back, and walked from the room.

"Gurr-yaupp!" Danton belched behind him.

Shown to the door by a butler in loose livery, Bord stepped out into the darkened streets.

Since its formation in early April 1793, the Committee of Public Safety had found much that was unsafe in Paris. The least of its concerns, however, were the beggars and idlers who made the streets their home. To walk the avenues but an hour before curfew was to invite the attentions of a cut-purse or worse. Still, Citizen Bord made his way from Danton's house without the retinue of soldiers that his seat on the Mountain might now provide for him.

The Watchers guarded his back.

Bord had felt them there ever since he had risen to power in the National Convention. Shadows moved with him in the torchlight; he could feel them. Soft steps followed the click of his bootheels on the cobbles; he could hear them.

Once, in the Bois de Boulogne, when a gang of navvies had stopped his coach—presumably to eat the horses!—the Watchers had revealed themselves. Squat shapes like trolls had rushed from the very undergrowth, with daggers drawn and bitter curses in their mouths. The coachman had fled in panic, leaping down onto the shaft and over the heads of the horses.

The melee around the coach had lasted less than half a minute. Bord watched its progress in the light of the sidelamps, counting the flickering flashes of steel blades and the whistling shadows of knotted clubs. When it was done, only still forms lay about the coach, and the squat shapes of men faded once more into the bushes. All but one, who stood by the horses.

"Vous avez besoin d'un conducteur," the man said—a statement, not a question. His accent was hard and thick, the voice of the country, not the city.

"Oui. J'ai besoin," Bord acknowledged.

The man swung himself up into the box. As he moved against the light, his cloak parted and Bord could see the gleam of chain mail. He could hear its soft clinking, too. That would explain the ruffians' utter lack of success against these Watchers.

The man drove him back to his apartments in the Faubourg St. Honore. As they approached the steps, he hauled back on the reins, set the brake, and jumped down before the coach had quite stopped. He was part of the shadows before Pierre Bord had known he was gone.

The Watchers were like that.

And so this night, after his unsatisfactory meeting with Danton to gain support for the war against Britain and the Low Countries, Bord felt no fear to walk the avenues unguarded.

Walking, he meditated upon his triumph. In five months of continuous talk and subtle movements, Pierre Bord had become a flame of the Revolution. Advisor to the new Republican mint, fiery orator in the National Convention, intercessor in the Palace of Justice, dealer in estates of the condemned, right hand of Minister Robespierre—Bord was everywhere. In some quarters he was called "the Tailor" because he sewed, with his threads of logic, a bag to snatch the heads of those who would seek to pervert and defeat the Revolution.

One work of the Montagnards, however, he felt compelled to oppose. And as he walked the dark streets, guarded by his corps of invisible Watchers, he composed his arguments against it.

"Citizens!" Bord rose from his place among the seats high on the left side of the hall—the Mountain, whose occupants were every day gaining the name of a party. "This is a most rash proposal that has been put before us."

Pierre Bord made his way over the half-empty benches to take the floor in the shaft of morning sunlight. By putting his head just so, he knew, he could light it like an angel's in a triptych and thus, on some deepest level, awe the members of the gallery.

"To revise the calendar in *names* is one thing: weeding out the dead Roman gods and misplaced Roman ordinals, replacing them with words the people can understand, borrowed from the temperate seasons and from the phases of agriculture. This is an admirable work, one which I surely can support.

"But to revise it in *meter* is quite another thing. Who can live by an hour of one hundred minutes? Who can work for a week of ten days, from which that last day of perfect rest has been abolished on atheistical grounds? Is the weary peasant to be given no cease from his labors? The shape of this new Republican calendar is a monstrosity, patched and splinted like the barbaric Moors'. What next? Would you have us pray five times daily during those hundred-minute hours to the Republican virtues of Labor, Work, Drudgery, Chores, and Sweat?"

That line met with modest laughter—but by no means from the whole assembly.

"No, Citizens. This calendar will unsettle the nation, disrupt trade, disquiet the people, and destroy the economy of France. I urge you to reject it, one and all."

Clap, clap . . . clap.

In the voting, the new calendar passed by all but six votes.

Robespierre came up to Bord at the adjournment.

"Well spoken, Citizen Bord." The smile, the hand on the shoulder, seemed genuine enough.

Bord tried to return the smile. "I fear that pride of reason forced me to speak out against your own proposal, Citizen."

"No matter, no matter. Every good idea needs a foil to test it, you know. Otherwise, how will men know its greatness? And your little mutiny did no harm, for the measure passed."

"It did."

"And now to a hearty lunch."

"May I join you?"

"Ah!" The delicate brow wrinkled in concern. "I fear that others claim my attentions, Pierre. It would not be convenient."

"I understand."

"I'm sure you do."

The knock on the door came at midnight.

The trial came at dawn, two months later.

It was a long two months that Pierre Bord, now officially "du Bord" again, spent in a dripping cell below the river level. The space was a meter wide and high—such a useful new measurement his National Convention had introduced for gauging such things—and two meters long. He lay in it as in a coffin, fighting the rats with his fingers as they tried to get at his daily ration of hard bread. He lay in his own filth and tried to clean himself with those same fingers. And water, that was the hard choice: to expend his cup for thirst or for the vanities of hygiene.

On the sixty-sixth day, the wooden door of this tomb opened for only the second time—the first being to admit him. When they brought him forth for trial, unshaven and unwashed, ulcerous wounds from the bad food covered his mouth and impeded his pleading.

The charges were absurd: that Scholar Pierre du Bord had, under the *ancient regime*, educated the children of that same Marquise De Cheneye whom he had exposed. To teach the aristos in the time of their ascendancy was the same thing as teaching the benefits and rightness and goodness of that aristocracy—or so the court had determined.

It was a ragged thing that rode that same morning, tied backward in the red tumbrel, to the Place de la Revolution. A priest stood beside du Bord in the cart and hummed psalms through his nose as a supposed comfort to the condemned.

Pierre's head was down, avoiding the rain of rotting fruit and vegetables that pelted his chest and shoulders. If he raised his head to look around, a softened apple—or worse offal—might catch him in the eyes or mouth. And yet he did look around, seeking the Watchers.

The Watchers, who had protected him for so many months, would rescue him once again. Pierre was sure of it.

When he ventured a peek against his shoulder to the left or right, he fancied he saw a dark, stubby form among the crowd. It neither screamed nor threw anything, but watched him with an intent stare from beneath a broad hat or hood.

Even the Watchers could not move against this crowd.

At the scaffold in the center of the square the soldiers, now openly wearing the brassards and rosettes of the Committee of Public Safety, untied him from the post in the cart but left his hands bound. They walked him up the steps, because his knees had gone strangely loose and weak. They tied him at chest, belly, and knee to a long board, which came only up to his collarbones. But Pierre hardly noticed. He could not take his eyes off the high, *pi*-shaped framework with its angular blade suspended between the uprights.

"It will not hurt, my son," the priest whispered in his ear—the first non-Latin he had spoken since the ride began. "The blade will feel like a cool breeze on the back of your neck."

Pierre turned and gaped at him. "How do you know?"

The soldiers tipped the board forward and ran it toward the uprights. Pierre du Bord's view of the world contracted to the worn grain of the wooden bed of this infernal machine, followed by the crosswork pattern of a basket made of rushes. The rushes were golden yellow. Pierre stared at them hard, looking for traces and flecks of reddish brown—the same color in the defect of that crystal that had cut his finger. When was that? Seven months ago. But this basket was new and unstained—an honor for him, courtesy of his friend, Maximilien Robespierre.

The priest was wrong.

The pain was there to be felt, sharp and definite, like the cut of that crystal. And then he was falling, face first, into the basket. Its pattern of reeds came up to meet him, struck him in the nose. The golden light flared behind his eyes, then faded to blackness as his lank, long hair settled about his face and closed it out.

"Where is your boyfriend?"

"He had to make a call to his agent or something. He said he might be a long time at it."

"Good. We have much to discuss."

"You bet we do, Hasan. The Frogs are trying to kill him now, and that's *never* happened before."

"What is this?" The man's dark eyes blazed, depthless irises drilled into balls of eggshell white. Then his eyelids closed fractionally, smooth silk petals coming together without a trace of wrinkle or line. Each lash was perfectly curved, like a thorn of black iron. "Explain, please."

"One of them was waiting in his apartment when he went back there. He tried to take Gurden out with a knife, one of *those* knives. I had to call in my shadow, Ithnain, for help."

"And?"

"We were forced to leave the body inside the apartment, in messy circumstances, and flee."

"Not Ithnain's body?"

"No, the other. He might have been a skilled assassin, but not as skilled as Ithnain."

"Did Gurden get a good look at Ithnain?"

"Not particularly." Alexandra slipped out of her molecular scarf-wrap and laid it across the bed. She sat down beside it. "Tom was recovering from a knee in the groin, still breathing shallowly."

"Good, then I can use him yet again with Gurden."

"Use Ithnain? You mean, to protect Tom?" She started to work her boots off, one at a time. Hasan knelt to help her with the buckles.

"No. I'll use him to sharpen Gurden. I have begun providing, ah, 'experiences' for your young man. Access to his past through the dream therapy has not brought him along, or not fast enough. And deprivation from your charms—" Hasan slipped her boot off and ran a hand up the back of her calf, cupping the fullness of the muscle where it bulged. "—seems only to have allowed him more time for his piano playing. A new direction appeared to be called for."

He rose up and, with his other hand, pushed gently against her breastbone. She let her body fall back on the bed.

"If Gurden has to fight for his life," he said, "even just a little, it helps to, um, 'coordinate' his attention. And that in turn will serve to wake him. That is clearly the scene that you and Ithnain stumbled upon."

Hasan sank back down to the floor at her feet.

Alexandra tugged at the fullness of her dress, raising the hem above her knees. His hands crept across the flesh of her thighs and began peeling back her monofilament tights.

"I wish you had told me sooner," she sighed— although whether with frustration or pleasure, even she could not be sure. "I did think your man was one of the French. Otherwise, I would have warned Ithnain to be more gentle with him. Now we have wasted one of our own agents."

"Do not worry. I have more."

She slid her arms up and around to cup the nape of her neck. One elbow dislodged the scarf; it rustled off the end of the bed.

"But wait!" Alexandra exclaimed, arching her back and half sitting up.

Hasan's hands paused obediently, held still and hot between her legs.

"We did not know where, exactly, Gurden was staying," she said. "Did you?"

"No," he whispered against her skin.

"So how could that Assassin be yours?"

He raised his head above the ruck of her dress and looked into her eyes. "It . . . may not have been."

"So the attack *was* by the Watchers."

"An interesting development." Hasan blew out his cheeks, a kind of facial shrug. His mustaches bristled like an alarmed caterpillar. He dropped his face into her lap and began tickling her with the bristles.

"And I may have helped move things along too fast," she whispered.

"Hmm-mm?"

"While Gurden was weakened and distracted by the blow, I took the opportunity of introducing him to the crystal."

Hasan's head moved so fast that his chin struck the front of her thigh, digging into a nerve point between the muscles. The shock of it entered her belly in a sick-making wave.

"I did not authorize that!" he hissed.

"Of course not, Hasan. But, in the field, I must have some latitude for making decisions."

"How did Gurden react to it?"

"Violently. I saw the tremor pass through him, stronger than ever before."

"Too many stresses," he said, mentally weighing this information. "The crystal itself will awaken this Gurden sooner than we expected."

She started to sit up again, but he rose over her and pushed his face into the silk of her bodice. His hands sought the snaps that held its two halves together. Her hands came down to help him.

"Too much awake," Hasan mused, "and this man can be more dangerous than if he's too much asleep."

"Wake him, and wake all the Watchers around him." She pulled his head down onto her. "But that was always the game."

Hasan stopped his tongue for speaking. "Except that now the Watchers play at being Hashishiyun, too."

"Assassins," Sandy repeated, gasping. "Or perhaps they are moving the game to a new level of protection."

"A prophylactic assassination? Would they sacrifice him to put us off the trail for another thirty or forty years?"

"You have the time."

"Once, while events developed at their own slow pace in our part of the world, then I *did* have time. Now—" He lowered his chest, belly, hips down on top of her. "—I want results."

"So do we all."

She pushed against him with her hands, twisting and pulling at his clothing. "Agh!" he gasped as, in rolling away his trousers, she bent and twisted *him*.

For a space of minutes, they said nothing more.

For a longer time, there was nothing to say.

Finally, he stirred and lifted his head. "You are sure of his reaction to the crystal?"

"Gurden is the strongest one yet," she replied. "I am sure of that."

"And so must the Watchers be—sure enough that they would try eliminating him."

"They might get to him and use him before you do. They are bound to try that tactic at least once."

"Not with the guard I can mount. Not with the price I will pay."

Alexandra made space alongside herself on the bed and rolled Hasan's limp body into it. She cuddled his head against her breast.

"Can we really raise him far enough through the veils," she asked, "for him to give you the secrets you desire . . . without raising him into the joining?"

"We must play him, Sandy. Like a fish on the line, we play him." Hasan's finger brushed against her soft nipple with its generous areola. "Pull him to the surface, but not so far he leaps free." The finger moved up. "Let him plunge into the depths, but not so far he can gain strength for an escape." The finger moved down. "Play him, wear him out, buy time. But do it delicately." Her nipple hardened with this renewed exercise.

"All right." She pushed his hand away. "We play him. And when you have the secret of the Stone? What then?"

"We use it for the end that Allah has always promised."

Sura 3
Behind Closed Doors
स्वछजझजटटड्ढणत

Shapes of all sorts and sizes, great and small,
That stood along the floor and by the wall;
And some loquacious vessels were; and some
Listen'd perhaps, but never talk'd at all.
                                        —Omar Khayyam

The Knights of the Temple almost never marched in procession, except at the coronation of a king— and then only for a king whom they supported. When Guy de Lusignan was crowned King of Jerusalem, the Templars marched.

The bright-burnished mail felt alien to Thomas Amnet, so long had he worn the linens and silks of a counselor who drifted about the halls of the Keep and advised the Order on matters of trade and finance. The weight of the steel bore down on his shoulders and its links rasped across his ribs, buffered only by a jerkin of raw white lamb's wool.

His surcoat, more wool, might be fine for a cold night upon the desert, but here in the courtyard of the Palace of Jerusalem, at ten in the morning with the sun beating down, it was a smoldering wrap. The sweat poured out from under Thomas' conical steel helmet, down the sides of his neck to the nape,

where the salt streams of Tigris and Euphrates joined
to trickle down the cataracts of his spine.

That was while he stood silently at attention with
his brother knights. When they moved forward, new
freshets of moisture sprouted from his armpits and
rolled across his kidneys. His boots of nailed leather
smacked the cobbles and jarred his joints far more
than the felt slippers to which he was accustomed.
The solid cadence of 200 other pairs of boots echoed
as it chased around the high stone walls and found its
way out into the alleyways of the bazaar.

Amnet imagined the effect it had there: the whispers behind dark-skinned hands, the rolling eyes,
the turned heads of camels and camel driver. The
echo of marching feet, working its way out of the
Christian stronghold, would raise an uneasiness among
Jerusalem's population. Were the assembled Orders
marching to make war and insurrection in the city?
None of the natives in this land could ever be quite
sure.

A setpiece of martial pageantry, while a mitered
priest held a crown over a king's head—this the
Saracen dervishes would never comprehend.

Across the cobblestones and up the steps into the
palace's wide refectory, the Templars marched. A
coronation ceremony properly required a cathedral,
but no church in the city was quite so defensible as
this. The actual placing of the golden circlet upon
Guy's head had been done in the palace chapel, with
just the King's closest counselors attending.

One of those counselors now waited inside the
anteroom to greet the Templars. Reynald de Châtillon,
Prince of Antioch, struck an imposing figure in his
red-and-purple silks and velvets, with a light sword
hanging from a belt made of plates wrought of gold.
As the phalanx of marching, sweating knights of the
cross advanced over the threshold and through the
enclosed space, he bowed to them with a mocking

smile on his lips, as if he played at being steward of the palace. Walking backward before them, he led them into the main hall. His bow became deeper and more arched as he backed up to the stacked tables at its head.

Thomas Amnet and his brother knights filled the left and right sides of the refectory and came to rest with a loud stamping of feet.

"This is an abomination!" The voice roared into the sudden silence which had followed the marching boots. Everyone there knew that voice: Roger, Grand Master of the Order of the Hospital, which was the Templars' chief rival for military and political power in Outremer.

"Please, my good sir! Your demeanor is unseemly!" And that was the whispery, placating voice of Ebert, the real steward of the Palace of Jerusalem, servant of any who sat on the throne.

Amnet craned his neck. From where he stood, near the front ranks of his Order and thus at the head of the hall, he could just make out the bulk of the Master Hospitaller, backlit by the sunshine from the doorway. Beyond him, in the courtyard, were the heads of more knights, his own Hospitallers. Cringing at Roger's side was Ebert, a stick of a man in brocaded jerkin and droopy hose.

A murmur from the Templars in the hall drowned out Ebert's further protests, but not Roger's.

"King! That piece of bloody offal isn't fit to sit my horse—let alone to crown himself king."

"My Lord Hospitaller! Your opinion is quite mumble-bumble-bub."

The last of Ebert's reply was decimated by the growls and muttered oaths from the Templars assembled in the refectory.

Amnet took two steps backward, removing himself from the forward ranks, and hurried behind their rigid backs toward the door. He heard steps coming in his wake and half-turned to see Gerard de Ridefort also rushing to the focus of disturbance.

Arriving in the anteroom first, Amnet put his own hands to the double doors, left and right, and pulled to bring their weight around. As they swung to, Gerard moved sideways through the closing crack; they boomed shut behind him.

Amnet had already turned to confront the steward and the intruding Hospitaller. "What noise is this?" He directed his question to Ebert and not to the rival Grand Master.

Roger's bulk swung on him like a bull which minded the yappings of a terrier. "Don't meddle in this, Templar."

"If you had objections to the choice of Guy, then you should have voiced them in the council that elected him," Amnet countered.

"Voice them I did, as did many others, and—"

"And you were overruled, as I remember it. To repeat your arguments now, with the crown upon Guy's brow, would be a foolish waste of breath."

As he spoke, Amnet felt the stony presence of Gerard behind him. He could track his master's bulk there by the shifting of Roger's eyes.

"What say you, Gerard?" the Hospitaller demanded.

"Sir Thomas speaks truly. Guy is king this day."

"Damnation!"

"Do you blaspheme, sir?" Amnet demanded.

"This is no church! The coronation cannot be valid!"

"The crown on Guy's head is smeared with holy oil in the bishop's own finger marks," Amnet said. "It is done."

Roger's thick hands were clasped around the key of his office, worn on a chain about his neck. In a fury, he twisted it and pulled down. The links, heavy gold and brazed solid, did not part. When pulling failed, he lifted the chain up, around his chin, and over his head.

"Devil take all Templars!" he thundered and threw the key through the nearest arrow loop. The chain, flagging behind it, jingled against the side of the embrasure. The Hospitaller's badge of office made a distant jangling as it fell on the cobbles below.

Out in the courtyard, Amnet could see heads moving among the uniformly conical helmets of the waiting Hospitallers. These other heads were bare, but the shoulders below them were garbed in richer, brighter stuff than the Hospitaller's white wool surcoats with plain red crosses. The barons of Christendom had evidently heard about the coronation, too.

Amnet turned to Gerard. "Best we withdraw, My Lord."

The Master of the Temple nodded and stepped back to one of the doors into the refectory. He seized its iron ring and threw himself back to start it open. The massive door swung out the width of three hands, and the two Templars slipped through, followed quickly by Ebert the steward. Amnet caught the door as it moved too wide, reversed the swing, and brought it closed again.

Amnet grasped the inside ring and held the door closed by leaning his weight backward into the hall.

Thunk!

"Open!"

Thunk! Bang!

"Open in the name of Christ!"

Gerard rallied the other Templars inside, who hung on the handles with Amnet and finally brought down a bar to block the doors.

Outside, the barons of Christendom beat on the panels in protest. The sound of marching feet struck a counterpoint as Roger led his Hospitallers out of the palace.

"Now, by Saint Balder, we shall greet our new-crowned King this day," Gerard de Ridefort mut-

tered to Thomas Amnet as they strode up the hall.
They were still moving behind the backs of their
assembled knights, leaving the center of the space
properly clear for ceremony.

"Balder was not one of the saints, My Lord,"
Amnet whispered.

Gerard stopped, surprised. "He wasn't?"

"Not at all. Balder was an old god of the North,
the favored son of Odin and Frigg. His brother,
Hoder, killed him by Loki's plotting; he plunged a
sprig of holly through Balder's heart. And that was
the beginning of Loki's damnation, or so the legends
say."

"Oh. Well. Balder *feels* like a saint to me," Gerard
said heavily and continued walking.

When they had reached their places at the head of
the assembly, they turned face front. Amnet signed
with a finger to Ebert, who signaled the trumpeters
in the minstrels' gallery.

They sounded a flourish of brass, and the procession of the King came in through the passageway that
led to the kitchens.

The purple looked good on Guy de Lusignan. The
cloak of lightly quilted silk masked the thickness of
his shoulders and the beginnings of a paunch that
pushed out above and below his gold-linked sword
belt. The weight of the crown pressed upon Guy's
brow, however, wrinkling the skin of his forehead
and giving him a quizzical look. The jut of his jaw,
required to balance his head against the pull of the
golden circlet, made him seem pugnacious beyond
even his reputation.

Gregory, the Bishop of Jerusalem, tottered behind
him. The old man kept one hand wrapped in the
ermine of Guy's cloak to maintain his balance. Gregory was rumored to be nearly blind, although now
and then he opened his misted eyes wide and stared
around, as if seeing his surroundings for the first

time after a light nap. Blind he might be, but he still had a way of looking directly at and through a person when he spoke.

Reynald de Châtillon waited below the raised end of the hall, one hand out in front of him, the other to his side, guiding the fall of his cloak as he bowed low before his sovereign. The Templars took their cue from him and bowed also.

For a long moment, every head in the room—except Guy's and Gregory's—was turned to the floor. Amnet had to twist his nose to the side and scan the ranks with his eyes for any signal that it might be acceptable to raise his head again. After a fluttering pause, the room returned to upright.

The one person missing from this display of power was Sibylla, eldest daughter to King Amalric and now Guy's wife. Technically, she was the Queen of Jerusalem and held power in her own right.

The council of barons, however—in which the orders of Temple and Hospital were richly represented—had decreed that the military situation was too precarious at the moment and for the foreseeable furture to permit a woman to have more than titular authority. And so it was decided that the man Sibylla chose to take after the death of her husband, William of Monferrat, would be elected to wear the crown of a king instead of that appropriate to a mere consort.

Reynald de Châtillon had sought that honor himself, reaching for the bony hand of Sibylla and bending it to his wickedly curling lips. That Guy de Lusignan had snatched her affections for himself was a matter of jocular competition between the two princes. Only the Lord Jesus and Thomas Amnet knew how much the steel swords and golden coffers of the Templars had influenced the lady's decision—and the council's after her.

In a rambling speech, Bishop Gregory commended King Guy to God, to the Christian citizens of Jerusalem, to the Kings of England and France, to the Holy Roman Emperors, and to the Emperor at Byzantium. When he was done, Prince Reynald of Antioch stepped forward and placed his hands between Guy's, sealing the pact between them.

One by one, the Templars came forward and pledged their fealty and their swords to the service of Christ and King Guy.

As they returned to their places in the line, Gerard turned to Amnet and spoke softly, from the side of his mouth. "What does your Stone foresee now, Thomas?"

"The Stone is dark to me this day, My Lord."

"Do you riddle me, sirrah?"

"It shows me no face that I have ever seen in flesh. It is an evil face, with dark skin and piercing eyes, that stares back from the vapors and challenges me. It lets no other sign come through."

"Do you commune with the Devil, then?"

"The Stone always follows its own purposes. I do not always understand them."

Gerard grunted. "Best you clear the Stone, before we attempt to counsel King Guy."

It was on Thomas Amnet's lips to protest Gerard's giving an order in matters where he was hardly a neophyte. But then he remembered that this was the Grand Master, and the Stone and Amnet were indeed his command.

"Yes, My Lord."

The jakes of the Palace of Jersalem were dug beneath the curtain wall within the outer bailey. The site was still within the palace precincts but, as the main gate was left open except in time of siege, the area admitted any who might walk in from the streets of the city.

Belching and reeling from half a dozen beakers of strong beer, Sir Beauvoir found his way from the refectory, where the tables had been unpiled and laid with the coronation feast. The call of nature was upon him, and his squire—a dainty boy of good French breeding—had reminded him that pissing on the footing stones in the back hallways was frowned upon, especially if that long-nosed seneschal, Ebert, found him doing it.

Beauvoir moved from the tallow-lit corridors into the dew-moistened shadows of the bailey. The moment his boots touched the loosely raked soil of the compound, he lifted aside his skirt of light mail and began fiddling with the strings that held his breeches closed. Such was his need that one stone under the moonlight was as good as another.

As he was relieving himself with a long sigh, one of the shadows moved away from the wall and came toward him. As Beauvoir's hands were otherwise occupied, he moved only his head to see who it might be that came.

"May I show thee a wonder, O Christian Lord?" The voice was singsong, lilting and mocking.

"What is it, knave?" Beauvoir growled.

"A relic, Lord, cut from the hem of Joseph's coat. It was found in Egypt after the passage of many centuries, and yet its colors are still bright."

The hands held something vague in the moonlight,

"Hold it higher, that I may see."

The hands moved up, around, and over Beauvoir's head before his fuzzy senses could recover. A stone, knotted into the fabric, caught him in the throat and crushed his larynx before he could cry for help. His hands left their task at his groin, but already they were too late. The last thing he saw, before the shadows closed in forever, were the burning eyes of the relic-seller, inverted over him and staring into his own.

The wines from the valley of the Jordan were sour and resinous, tasting of the desert and the thorn.

Thomas Amnet rolled a sip across his tongue, searching for some hint of the sweetness and the woody, throat-filling flavor which he could remember from France. This wine tasted like medicine. Amnet forced the mouthful down.

The other Templars were not so particular. The coronation feast had reached that stage of jollity at which good Christian knights would lie on their backs and pour beakers of wine and beer across their tongues and down their gullets. At that point, taste hardly mattered.

Amnet looked across the table at the Saracen princes who had reluctantly joined the celebration—if only out of their sense of duty as guests in the palace. They did not drink, except clear water which their servants poured from saddle flasks. Thomas knew that strong drink was forbidden by their religion, and that was more than some of the Templars would bother to learn.

Sigyreth of Niebull was one such who would never trouble to know the customs of men he meant to kill. Now forced to break bread and tear meat with the Children of Shem, he took the princes' abstention as a sign of treachery.

"You don't drink?" Sigyreth growled, levering himself up from the table by his elbow.

The nearest Saracen, speaking no Norse, smiled nervously and hid it behind a square of damask which he had used occasionally to clean his mouth.

"Don't you sneer at me, dog!"

Two other Templars, seeing the object of his wrath, also roused themselves.

"They do not drink because the wine is suspect. See! They even bring their own water."

Amnet, who had seen the palace cisterns after a troop of guards had watered their horses, would himself rather drink the wine. But others along the table were taking notice of the Saracens' drinking habits.

"Perhaps they have poisoned us?"

"Poison! That's it!"

"The Saracens have poisoned the wine!"

"The dogs have poisoned our wells!"

Watching the princes, Amnet saw how the meaning of this clamor penetrated even their polite smiles.

"Nay! Hold!" he shouted, rising from his place. "Their Prophet forbids them touch wine, as sternly does our Lord Christ forbid fornication. They drink a scented water, more pleasing to their palates. That is all."

The fuddled knights bit their lips and looked doubtfully at him. Some, he knew, would like any excuse to butcher the Saracens where they sat. And, some, too, would include Thomas Amnet in the slaughter.

"You know their ways, Thomas," one Sir Bror admitted finally. "Not that it does you credit."

Amnet bowed to him with a cold smile and resumed his seat. The other Templars reached for their goblets and jugs.

One of the Saracens met his eyes in a direct stare. "*Merci, seigneur,*" he said distinctly.

Amnet nodded, returning the man's look.

"I have heard of this prophet," a cold, clear voice called down from the head of the table.

All around Thomas, hands and eyes paused, like young mice caught in the shadow of the hawk.

"From the stories I have heard, this Muhammed was a camel driver and a tramp—nothing more." The voice was Reynald de Châtillon's.

The knights along the table fidgeted. At the head of the hall, Gerard de Ridefort laid a hand on Reynald's arm, but the latter shook it off.

"Of course, he had visions. And he wrote a bad sort of poetry. And why not? He was drunk most of the time."

The Saracen princes narrowed their eyes, and Amnet was sure they understood these slurs. The guest bond, however, held them to silence.

"The man was nothing—until, of course, he married a rich whore and could afford to indulge his taste for license and—what was your word, Thomas? —fornication?"

The Saracens eyed Amnet now, as if suddenly suspecting him of baiting this trap for them.

"My Lord," Reynald's cold voice continued, directed now at King Guy, "if you would be rid of the taint of this camel driver's corpse in this Holy Land, I will myself lead an expedition into Arabia, dig up his bones, and scatter them on the sands for airing out. And give *that*—" he flipped his fingers under his own chin "—for the might of Saracen arms."

Amnet's gaze never left the princes across from him at the table. Their eyes were now narrowed down to slits, and white teeth gleamed between the fringes of mustache and beard that framed their skinned lips.

"Who among the Order of the Temple will join me in this bold venture?" Reynald shouted.

A roar of mixed voices, Northman and French, rose to greet his challenge.

The Saracens were at the boiling point, as Reynald de Châtillon had intended.

"Faugh! Fie on all Christians!" one of them shouted and, as a man, they rose from the table, overturning goblets of red wine and platters of gravy. Some of the mess fell upon the stained tunics and straggled heads of the knights at either side.

"Is this how the French lords treat a guest in their tents?" a second demanded, directing his question at Amnet.

All Thomas could do was shake his head, eyes level and chin depressed.

The Saracens gathered their robes about their knees

and stepped over the benches. As they made their way to the doors at the end of the hall, two Templars sought to block them. Faster than the French could retreat, two slender blades of Damascus steel appeared at their throats. Saracens and Templars pivoted around the points of the blades, a movement that put the former closer to the door. No others tried to prohibit their exit after that.

The princes had all but left the hall when one paused with a hand on the door ring.

"We know this Reynald," the man declaimed. "He calls himself Prince of Antioch. The Prophet shall be avenged on him."

As he left, he pulled the door to, so that its closing rang throughout the hall.

Not a sound entered the silence that followed its echo. And then Reynald de Châtillon's laughter broke out: high, clear, and ringing.

Guy, who had watched the baiting of the Saracen lords and their exit with a troubled frown, relaxed and joined Reynald. His laughter was deeper and somehow surprising in its richness. Taking their cue, the Templars also laughed—honking, barking, choking, gasping.

Only Amnet held his peace. From the veil of smoke beneath the rafters he suddenly caught a wisp of vision: the dark face, the black wings of mustache, the burning eyes, seeking out Thomas Amnet among all men.

"I grant you much leeway, Thomas, because of your special powers," Gerard de Ridefort rumbled from the depths of his chair the next morning. "Do not force me to exert my temporal and spiritual authority over you."

"I meant no disrespect, Master. But you cannot count the damage that Reynald has done to our position in Outremer."

"And can *you* so count it?"

"Reynald was calculatedly rude to King Guy's guests. The rites of hospitality run deep in these people. To have invited those Saracens lordlings to the palace and then to insult their religion so profoundly—that is the act of a madman."

"Thomas, this morning I am a man with a splitting head and a sour gut. You goad *me*—and to no purpose. There is nothing I can do for you. Guy will not even speak a harsh word to Reynald."

"Because he is afraid of the man."

"For whatever reason. The Prince of Antioch is a proud and violent man. You and I dare not offend him. King Guy will not. . . . Now, what would you have me to do?"

"Prepare yourself. Prepare the Order."

"Does the Stone tell you this?"

"No—not directly."

"Prepare how?"

"For war."

FILE 03
Chrysalis Phase
✣

Remember her.
She is forgetting.
The earth which filled her mouth
Is vanishing from her.
Remember me.
I have forgotten you.
I am going into the darkness of the darkness
*   for ever.*
I have forgotten that I was ever born.
*   —Dylan Thomas*

The Holiday Hulls registration system had advertised the room in Atlantic City as a "suite" and charged Tom and Sandy extra on the prebilling to enjoy the distinction. In terms of layout, however, that meant the sanitizer—instead of a fold-down unit next to the bed—had a closed space of its own, which it shared with a shin-deep bubbatub. The tub was actually big enough for two, if they sat hip to ankle and folded up their knees. The room was an inside with no window, but the holo unit did offer a selection of views, including Taj Mahal, Matterhorn, and Anonymous Atlantic Beaches, circa 1960. At least those had no smell.

Gurden examined the room's terminal facilities: radially limited access, no color, and the sound pickup had been crushed by a previous occupant and hung by one peeled glass fiber.

The bed had one sheet, on the bottom, and half a blanket. A stenciled notice on the headboard in-

formed him that occupants who chose to unroll their
own sleeping bag could have it chemically freshened
"diurnally" by the ship's maid service for an addi-
tional charge of five dollars American.

He tried to remember, with no success, if "diur-
nal" meant twice a day or only once every two days.
The room rented by the half-day but he and Sandy
were paid up for a full forty-eight hours.

"Hello, lover."

Gurden turned to Sandy's greeting.

"Hiya. Where've you been?"

"Had some business to attend to, checks to cash
and fun to fund. You know."

Tom *did* know. He could smell it on her: the
scents of love, the sweat of a man, the wafting aroma—
part chemical, part infrared radiation—of fresh-burst
hormones.

Gurden was not sure whether he had always had this
talent for seeing the hiddens of the soul and body in
their simple signatures. Perhaps this sense was something new, only available to him since mysterious men
had been trying to kill him. And perhaps Sandy's condition was obvious to anyone who looked: a woman
who had recently been satisfied. He gave it a mental
shrug; this was meat for a later meditation.

"What's the town like?" he asked.

"Bright. A bit frantic. A lot more going on than
when I was here last."

"When was that?" Gurden remembered she had
once told him that she was a northern girl, French-
Canadian extraction by the way of Denmark and
Normandy, generations back.

"A hundred years ago," Sandy replied, "when this
was a sleepy little seaside town, full of children and
sandcastles, and gambling was not allowed."

"You're kidding."

"Of course I am. Gambling has always been the
main, the only, reason to come to Atlantic City."

"So . . ." he groped for a metaphor. "You're all set up, but my cash reserves are still a bit low. Three hundred a day for digs this grand are going to break me right quick."

"What are you going to do?"

"Did I see a piano bar on the way in here?"

"I didn't know you could swim."

"I'll fake it. The pool's not that deep."

Gurden unfolded his bag and took out two scrolls of musicfax. They were his bonafides: original compositions that, fed into a pianola, would prove his talent extended beyond real-time key pounding.

"Don't sign any long-term contracts," Sandy warned him. "We have to keep moving, remember?"

Gurden paused with a hand on the doorlock.

"Why? I thought we just had to keep out of sight."

"We certainly want to get beyond the range of those killers. Jackson Heights to Atlantic City is just a cross-town Tube stop."

"Oh." He contrived to look perplexed. "And the Carolinas are the ends of the earth, right?"

"They're a destination. That's all."

"So I think we've got time enough, before we have to get there, for me to scare up some pocket ballast."

"All right. Take your gig. You feel lonely without an audience, don't you?"

"Doesn't everybody?" He smiled and let himself out.

In the hallway—a square metal tube lined with dogged hatches and recessed lights—Gurden let out a breath.

Had Sandy always been that readable?

She once had seemed mysterious, he remembered. Cool and self-contained, she would move in her own ways and at her own times. That meant she could also be capricious. It once had seemed she delighted in a sudden shopping trip, a picnic, or a horseback ride. "It's my day," she would say and then go off for twelve hours of solo adventure. But, until now, that adventure had never included another man. Nor a clumsy lie to shield him.

Tom Gurden shook his head and turned left down the corridor, the way they had come in, to find the hull's manager.

"Can you swim?" Brian Holdern asked him.

"Of course I can swim. Can't everybody?"

"Not since the Groundwater Seepage Act outlawed the use of chlorine in artificial pools and they all gunked up with algae inside of three weeks."

"Why is your pool any different?"

"This is a marine hull. They don't care what we let dump into the ocean so long as it's chemically pure and doesn't float or precipitate out. A little chlorine overboard might actually help kill the blooms around here." Holdern rolled his tobacco prosthetic around to the other side of his mouth.

"So you can swim. Do you prune easily?"

"Excuse me? I'm a damned fine jazz musician, Mr. Holdern. What does—picking—prunes?—have to do with the job?"

"Not picking 'em, Tom. Looking like one. Most guys spend three hours in the water and they end up looking like an East River disposable. Most of my piano players learn to rub silicon bearing grease on their bodies. Maintains the hydrostatic balance and—kind of a plus in your line of work—gives your pecs and hams all kinds of definition underwater. Drives women wild. You'll have to fight them off."

"I'll keep it in mind."

"Hell, son. Get yourself a supply of grease—good inert stuff that won't leave a slick—or go fish for another job. I'm not having any pasty white boy pucker up like a seedless grape and turn off my customers, you hear?"

"Yes, sir. Grease myself. Every night. Now, do I have the job?"

"Sure you do, or why else would I waste my breath explaining everything to you?"

"Thank you, Mr. Holdern." Gurden started backing toward the door.

"First set starts at seven-thirty. Three solid hours. And if you sink or prune, you're out."

"Yes, sir."

"Be sure to grease your privates good, too."

"What's that?"

"Rub it into your dick, son. This pool is strictly come as you are. No suits allowed. Especially not on the waitresses or the musicians."

"I see."

"Still want the job?"

"Of course. Seven-thirty."

"Keep smiling, son."

"I will, Mr. Holdern."

The grease was thick and heavy, like warm paraffin, except it felt cold on his skin. He could warm it up by rubbing hard with his palms against the long muscles of his thighs and shins and around his kneecaps. It did not seem to absorb into the skin but, instead, lay there like a mold of stiff gelatin.

Gurden started on his shoulders, reaching around to get his back. He had to strain his arms and push gobs of the grease alternately high and low with his fingertips. Maybe he could rub it in with a towel or something. One of the hull's towels—that would be poetic justice.

For the briefest instant as he worked with the heavy goo, he flashed on chain mail and the weight it must put on a man's arms and chest. The same cold, liquid weight. Dead weight and dead cold.

He thrust the image from his mind.

Practical matters. When he started to sweat—as

he always did playing good jazz—would patches of the pale silicon grease shed and float away in the water? More important, would the stuff let his skin breathe? He had read about children in the Middle Ages, painted with gold and silver pigments for fairs and church pageants, who had died of dermal suffocation. Unless this grease . . . And how *had* those piano players who went before him in the Holiday Hull come to quit their job?

Probably they couldn't keep up with the women.

Gurden continued slathering and rubbing until he was clad in stiff grease from the soles of his feet to his jawline. Then he found a white blocked-paper robe and wrapped it about himself, slipping the room key into its pocket. He carried the role of musicfax in his hand.

The lounge deck was still deserted and mostly dark at seven-thirty. The pool, lit from below, glowed green and silver. The piano floated in the shallow end, not making a ripple.

Casting aside the robe, Gurden stepped into the water. It was just less than body temperature. He'd find out about the sweat soon enough. The piano bobbed as he approached it, pushing his own bow wave.

The instrument was the shape of a baby grand, straight along the back side and curved on the front. The lid lifted easily and he held it up with the prop stick.

And there all resemblance to a piano ended. Instead of the cast-iron frame and steel strings, he found rows of bottles, racks of clean glasses, a bucket of ice, bowls of cherries, lemon and lime wedges, and pickled pearl onions. Two quarter kegs—one of dark lager, the other of pilsner—and their taps nestled in the piano's heel. Against the inside of the fallboard, where the hammers and action would be in a real piano, he found a big twelve-volt automotive battery.

"Can't you pick up after yourself?"

The voice came from the poolside above him.

Gurden turned to find a young woman, very naked, shimmering with the same greasy complexion he wore. She was standing upright and proud, holding his robe and straightening it.

"The customers don't want to stumble over your old clothes, do they? This goes in the closet."

"I'll get—" He started toward the side.

"Don't worry. Just for tonight, I'll stow it for you."

Gurden breathed a sigh and slipped around the far side of the piano. One look at her had started a series of reactions that would take him a moment to control.

She walked over to a wall of mirrors, pushed one and it popped open to reveal an empty space with rack and hangers. Now, where had she put her own robe? Tom had been warned against using the customer's changing lounge. Or had she walked in here wearing only grease?

The girl returned, moving smoothly and making no effort to hide herself. It had often been Gurden's observation that a woman walking flat-footed, without high heels, looked dumpy and knock-kneed, thumping along like a squaw. This woman, however, seemed to move lightly on her toes with legs at full tension, gliding like a ballerina.

"I'm Tiffany, your waitress."

"I guessed. I'm Tom Gurden, the piano player."

"Of course you are. This your music?" She picked up the fax, unrolled it, and seemed to read it. For a minute, then two, she was absorbed by it.

"Good stuff," she said. "But of course you can't play it in here."

"Why not?"

"Our patrons can't jive dance—too much resistance in the water. They've gotta do slow dances. Old romantic stuff."

"Slow dances. Nude. In the water. I see."

"You bet you do. We'd better average nine-point-

five orgasms an hour, or the customers get their
money back. You keep up on your antibiotics, don't
you?" she asked cheerfully.

Tiffany slipped into the water and swam-walked
toward him. Gurden noticed, for the first time, that
her make-up was as exaggerated as a stage actor's:
flaring brows penciled up on her forehead, broad
wings of blue eye shadow and black eye liner drawn
out to her temples, highlighter and blusher smeared
across her cheeks, mouth drawn big with gloss and
lipstick. It hid the girl underneath, and her sense of
nakedness, as effectively as a rubber mask.

Her hair was red, straight, and even. In the strange
light it had the shine of a polyester wig—which it
undoubtedly was.

Tom Gurden took his eyes away, back to the piano.

"What's the battery for?"

"What battery? Where?"

He pointed it out behind a rack of glasses.

"Oh, that must be power for your piano."

"This is not a piano."

"Well, you know, the keyboard."

He examined the business end of the instrument
for the first time. It was a sixty-six-key Yamaha
Clavonica, bolted against the fallboard of the floating
box. The whole mechanism was hinged to ride down
under his hands as he floated in the water. A restraining bar with wrist straps would hold him in
position as he treaded water. The keys and sliders
wore a plastic skin to keep moisture out of the circuits. The speakers had been remounted under the
back lid, and a secondary set of hydro transponders
hung down where the pedal lyre would normally be.
When Gurden hit the bass chords, his audience would
feel it in their bellies as well as their eardrums.

"Right," he said. "Power for the piano. What happens if this box leaks and it shorts out while we're in
the water?"

"Boy, for a fellow who gets to swim with naked ladies, are you ever a pessimist."

"Don't any men come in here?"

"Yeah, and 'come' is the operative word. But *you* don't have to worry about them. Or not about most of them, anyway."

Tiffany took out her tray, which was buoyed to float one side up, and arranged a high-sided dish of complimentary peanuts on it. With a little shove, she scooted it out to the center of the pool.

"What do the customers—and you—do about paying?"

"Two drinks are included in the hundred-dollar cover charge. Any more, and I keep track on my keypad." She showed him as she strapped it onto her wrist. "It goes on their hotel bill. But nobody comes here to do serious drinking. The booze just keeps them liquid."

She turned and swam back to the edge of the pool.

"Would you help me with the ice?"

"Ice would go well about now," Gurden said brightly and followed her.

The icemaker was behind another mirrored panel.

Tiffany took out a wickedly curved pair of tongs, handling them expertly. While Tom held up the lid of the ice chest, she worked their points into the sides of a twenty-kilogram block. All the time she had to arch her back to keep the skin of her belly and breasts from touching the frosted metal rim of the chest, or she would stick hard. When the tongs were set, Tiffany clamped her fist around one handle and nodded at the other. They both held up the lid with their free hands while lifting the block out.

They carried it between them back to the pool.

"Do we float it across?" he asked.

"Not unless you know a lot of people who like raw chlorine in their drinks. You hold this while I float the piano over."

He had to take both of the tong's handles and straddle the block with his legs. In the warm, moist atmosphere, it streamed cold vapor up into his crotch. He could feel himself shriveling, which was not all that unpleasant a sensation.

Tiffany swam the piano to the side of the pool at a languid pace, enjoying his apparent discomfort.

"Get it centered, now. Straight into the bucket, or the weight will tip this rig and we'll end up paying retail for all that booze."

Gurden took a breath, hoisted the block, stretched out beyond the edge of the pool, bumped something lightly, and then lowered—did not drop—the ice into the waiting bucket. The piano rode six centimeters lower in the water with its weight.

"Very good for a first time," Tiffany said. "Next time you'll keep it out of my hair, won't you?"

"Yes, ma'am."

"Good boy. Here come our first customers. So you'd better get down here and start making music."

As instructed, Alexandra entered the onshore casino at precisely eight o'clock and went to the third roulette table from the left. Hasan was not there.

For a while she watched an American in white leather make thirty thousand dollars in six spins, doubling his money each time, then lose it on one final spin. The last spin had brought the rest of the table in with him, and now a groan went up around her.

That the wheel was rigged, Alexandra had no doubt. That it would be rigged so obviously—this she had to see once for herself to believe.

"Your money is not safe here," murmured a familiar voice at her shoulder, almost lost in the background buzz.

"Of course not, My Lord. But what puzzles me is why *you* choose to be here."

"The Wind of God blows at my back."

"Your organization needs money?"

"That we get in a continuous flow from the rich American Arabs, who think their donations will scour the Holy Land to revenge the Homeless Ones. What I need is an excuse for *having* the money."

"A Palestinian playboy in Atlantic City?"

Hasan made a small *moue* with his lips.

"You risk being mistaken for an exiled Persian or a fat Egyptian," she went on, gently teasing.

"I am a man of many disguises."

"And many purposes. Why did you call me?"

A shout went up around them, the joy of sudden winners. She and Hasan joined in the general round of polite clapping.

"You and Gurden dally here," he said. "In that floating bordello. Why?"

"It was his idea."

"Can't you keep the boy occupied—and entertained?"

Alexandra bristled at that. "He needs to earn money. He did not have a stash ready for traveling."

"You could have offered."

"I did. But he's a proud man; he wants to pay his way. And I could not hurry him without arousing suspicions. As it is, he's feeling pushed."

Hasan hid his face as a photoflash went off at a nearby table. Under his arm, he replied: "There is a schedule, you know."

"Your timetable—not his," she said to the back of Hasan's neck. "Gurden must think the flight is his own idea. Or else you should put a bag over his head and be done with it."

"I need a captive in the proper state of preparation. His body is useless to us without his mind at the right peak."

"So let me develop it in my own way."

"In a bordello?"

"Pleasure and pain have their uses."

"Pain especially."

"Sadist!" She stuck her tongue out at him, just the barest tip so that no others could see.

"Whatever. Prepare him. And have him at the pickup point on time." Hasan turned away in the press of people as another round of cheering broke out at a lucky spin.

"But where will that—?" Her question was useless. She was talking to the empty air.

Eliza: Good morning. This is Eliza 774, an on-line function of United—

Gurden: Let me speak to Eliza two-one-two, please. This is Tom Gurden.

Eliza: Channeling . . . Oh yes, Tom. Thank you for calling me back. Is this late for you?

Gurden: Not particularly. I'm working again—if you call getting mauled by a poolful of middle-aged water polo enthusiasts being a musician.

Eliza: I don't understand you.

Gurden: I'm engaged at the Holiday Hull off Atlantic City.

Eliza: Excuse me. Accessing . . . I did not know that establishment had a piano, Tom.

Gurden: It doesn't—just a Clavonica. But they want me to make music on it. In between friendly bouts of ducking, groping, and pinching. I am black and blue from my calves to my shoulders. I think they even dislocated one toe.

Eliza: Did you see any more small, dark men?

Gurden: Plenty of them—women, too. All fat and ugly. But no raincoats, no revolvers, no chain mail. There are *some* advantages to working in a nudie bar.

Eliza: You can be drowned.

Gurden: Only in the spirit of good clean fun. Besides, I'm a demon for keeping my head above water.

Eliza: Any more dreams, Tom?

Gurden: Unhhh.

Eliza: Was that a reply, Tom?

Gurden: One. . . . A bad one.

Eliza: Tell me about it. Please.

Gurden: It must have been some kind of throwback. I was remembering a gig I did once on the Philadelphia Main Line. A big colonial house in the middle of about twelve acres of lawn and trees. White clapboard and fieldstone, it was, with a wide porch and four thick columns. Looked like the set for Tara.

Eliza: Tara? Is that a place?

Gurden: Mythical. The house in *Gone With the Wind*—an old movie. From the last century.

Eliza: Noted. Proceed.

Gurden: The gig was a birthday party for one of the Main Line families. A theme party, taken from that movie. Everyone was supposed to come dressed in swallowtail coats and hoopskirts, although the costuming got a little mixed up. We had everything from a hundred years on either side of the period: French grenadiers' braided tunics, empire gowns, pinstripe pants with black morning coats, and flapper's fringed dresses with yards of beads.

The music they wanted was Old South Schmaltz. Mostly Stephan Foster, "Swanee River," that stuff. No jazz or stride, nothing happy. So I was grooving along on those really down and mellow tunes, the flower of an age lost to war, an aristocracy turned to dust and decay. The music of memory. And then it happened.

Eliza: While you were playing?

Gurden: Yeah, then. And again, stronger, in my dream the other night.

Eliza: What happened?

Gurden: I slipped outside myself and into another person. Not Tom Gurden. Not anyone I knew.

Eliza: Tell me about him.

*   *   *

Louis Brevet came out of his own cushioning, gray fog into a narrow consciousness that was tinged with black and rode on waves of nausea. He was lying on his back and could taste the sour bile collecting in his throat. To close out the light and reorder his stomach, Brevet covered his eyes with his palms and rolled over, trying to bury his face in the pillowcases.

Rough mattress ticking brushed against his cheeks in place of the fresh, white linen to which he was accustomed. Its smell went deep into his nostrils, and Brevet pushed straight up on his forearms, eyes wide open.

The unsheeted mattress beneath him was dirtied with hair oil, spots of old blood, and dribbles of vomit long dried to a crust. The cot supporting it was made of iron pipes, once painted white, and slung with straps of loose hemp twine. The floor beneath the cot, which he could see in the gap left by the mattress, was bare pine boards with the pounded dirt showing between their cracks. The dirt was pulsing slowly . . . roaches busy with their morning forages in the light that flowed obliquely into the crawlspace.

Brevet considered: No fitted oak floors, no pattern-woven rug, no oiled walnut bedstead, no sheets, no pillowcases, and no pillows. This was not Louis Brevet's bedroom. *Quod erat demonstrandum.*

So, where was he?

Careful not to move his head, and thereby dislodge the cap of cold iron that had clamped to his brow and threatened to crush it, Brevet swung his hips around into a sitting position. He looked left and right, avoiding the bright wedge of dawnlight in the doorway at the room's far end. Raw pine planks made up the walls. Square cuts in them resembled windows, unglazed and unscreened, except by bars of black iron. Beds and more beds formed a long row of rusted white paint and crusted mattress sacks. Rumpled lumps of blue denim and cold flesh rounded out the profile of each mattress.

"Louis has gotten himself drunk again, and joined the Army," was his first sober thought. "How will I explain this to Angelique?" was the instant second.

"All right, you slugs! Assembly time in five minutes!"

Did not the Army blow trumpets or have some other formal awakening procedure? Then Louis was not in the Army. Q.E.D.

Around him, the denim and fleshy forms stirred and groaned, rumbled and farted, shifted and rose up like zombies lifting themselves from the matted vegetation of the bayou. Their heads swung back and forth like sick hogs looking for something to rush. One by one, the baleful glances found Louis Brevet. Then their voices rose around him while the bodies sleepwalked through their morning rituals of finding boots, scratching both exposed and unexposed skin, and straightening bedrolls.

"Who's the new meat in Seventeen?"

"Dunno. Trusties brought him. Last night."

"Did they use him?"

"Naw. There ain't a mark on him."

"Maybe they was too tired."

"Not them!"

"Maybe they didn't want to disturb you ladies."

"Or share him, you mean."

"I tell you there ain't a mark on him."

"Knock it off in there!" That voice, bellowing from beyond the doorway, carried an edge with it: dull anger, bored authority, the blunted temper of institutionally damped feelings.

No, Louis decided, this was definitely not the Army.

Still holding his head precariously erect, he rose to his feet and began walking down the central aisle between the cots.

"Hey, wait your turn!" somebody shouted.

"Look here! Perrique must go first!" from another.

"He can walk!"

The room fell into a sudden hush.

"He must be some kind of gentleman!" This last was injected into the quiet air, said more in awe than in any overt anger.

"Excuse me!" Louis Brevet called toward the doorway. "Would the porter there, or whoever you are, please present yourself? There has been a terrible mistake."

"*Excuse me!*" someone in the room sang, *sotto voce*.

"Get back!" from behind him.

"Don't arouse Wingert!"

"He'll send us all to the causeway today."

The human forms beside the beds moved slowly forward into the aisle, appearing to converge on Louis's position. For the first time he could identify the random sounds he had been hearing and dismissing as unrelated to the situation, the sort of auditory hallucination he usually dismissed as too much sobriety too soon: the clank of chains.

The steel links of a medium-weight anchor chain passed from bed to bed and through the legs of the men standing between them. Each man's legs were also connected by his own set of irons, fastened ankle to ankle below the communal chain. The two ends of the long chain were presumably shackled to the irons of the first and last man on each side, respectively.

As the men moved forward to block Louis's progress toward the door, their chain dragged down across the bedcovers and dropped onto the plank floor with a jangling, sort of musical *thunk*.

"What y'all got in there?" That same dull voice, presumably Mr. Wingert's. Its tone had risen out of the bored depths. In the hush of the room, his bootsteps upon the porch planking sounded loudly. The man's shadow filled the doorway and blotted out the light.

Wingert was a huge man: broad in the shoulders,

thick through the gut, as wide in the hips and thighs as a woman. He was even wide in the head, given the tangled nest of unbarbered hair that hung past his ears and swept the collar of his trusty's denims.

His shadow was thick and dark—except for the whites of his eyes as he glared into the sleeping chamber, and for a glint of gold on the third finger of his right hand. Gold and something else, a brownish oval that might have been a carved signet stone. It was an odd sort of jewelry, Louis thought, for a moron set to guard the sleeping barracks of a road gang.

Possibly something he stole from one of the prisoners, Louis decided. Solving that minor mystery so neatly only left him to confront the greater one: What was he doing here? How did he come to be sleeping with the gangs, without having any personal memory of his own transgressions, trial, or sentencing?

Brevet had to shelve speculation on that point as the wide man stepped through the doorway, working his hips and thighs past each other as a tiger works its shoulders in stalking through the high grass.

Wingert might intimidate any normal road-gang felon, but not Brevet. Louis had taken lessons in pugilism since he was nine years old. He had continued the training through his military academy and then his college days at Tulane, and he had won the intramural Greek Championship there three years in a row.

The trusty might be big, but he looked slow. His hands, each the size of a Smithfield ham, looked to be as soft as hamfat, too.

Seeing Louis standing free in the middle of the room, the man moved down toward him, slowly, contemptuously, majestically. The great hands clenched. The knees bent sideways to lower the long body for greater leverage.

Brevet readied his own body: rising onto his toes, loosening his shoulders, rolling his fists, taking long breaths to build up his reserves of oxygen.

"Hey, Win, nothing's going on."

A small man, almost as wide as the trusty but two heads shorter, came forward from between the beds to Louis's right. His step caused a louder version of the same *clanking* that the other men's shufflings had made. "He didn't mean nothing. Just a new guy and all."

The massive head swung in the direction of the smaller man. Before the chin reached his approximate bearing, however, the nearside Smithfield ham rose in a straight blur, backhand, and caught the protester under the arch of the ribcage. The man collapsed around the hand like a rag doll dropped over a chairback. Then he rebounded, like that same doll with a rubber spine, and flew backward over the bed to strike the plank wall six feet up, near the ceiling joists. His trajectory pulled tight the chain along the right side of the room, and half the audience flopped over.

Louis went lower in his crouch and began orchestrating his footwork and breathing.

Wingert's chin came back on course and the pumping legs picked up speed down the aisleway.

It was finished in three moves: Louis threw a picturebook left jab and right uppercut, both of which connected perfectly; Wingert, unmoved, drew his right hand across his body and backhanded Louis's head like a man sweeping a cabbage off a table.

The stone, or whatever it was, in the trusty's ring laid open Louis's jaw from his right ear to his chin, with the blood flying in a flap up into his eyes. The immediate impact snapped his neck sideways, so that his opposite ear smashed down on his own shoulder and began swelling. The blow's secondary impulse pushed him backwards, over one of the bedframes and into the knees of one of the chained men. That man's staggers tightened the chain until every man on the left side of the room was dragged down.

Having subdued the entire barracks with two massive blows, Wingert was now departing. He moved up the central aisle with—seen from the rear—a portly waddle.

Louis was all for rising up and taking him on again. But, as he reached his knees, one of the prisoners behind Louis had the presence of mind to smack the back of his head with a length of pipe which had been carefully preserved between the mattress and the bedsling for such occasions.

Louis Brevet slumped forward and bled quietly.

"Oh, you poor, sweet darling!"

Cool, dry fingertips touched his forehead—about the only spot on his face that was not swollen, painful, or covered with bandages.

Louis was lying in a real bed, in a real room with plaster walls, a decorated ceiling, and deep rugs to muffle the comings and goings of doctors, nurses, and mistresses. His Claire was there, with her dry hands and her masses of golden-hued hair, to coo over him and pretend how much she shared his discomfort.

For once, however, Louis Brevet felt almost good upon waking. Certainly, he was battered and in pain— the worst being a deep throb along his jaw—but his head was clear. His limbs, while stiff from the impromptu flight across that improbable room, did not feel the leaden weight of drink and its residual poisons. Perhaps this was only the effect of some drug they had given him for pain.

"Where was I?" To his own ears, his voice came out muffled by the swathings of cotton lint around his mouth. It felt, too, as if some teeth were loose or missing in there.

"You're at home, now, darling."

"This isn't Windemere."

"Of course not. These are my rooms at the hotel. I wouldn't dream of taking you back to the plantation and that woman."

"But where *was* I?"

"You were in a carriage accident. Last night. The horses bolted, or so your driver said—he jumped clear, the coward—and they took you over the levee. Three of the foolish beasts were badly damaged and had to be put down."

"There was no carriage accident, Claire."

"Well . . . that's the story everyone has been telling."

"They are wrong. What time is it?"

"A little after nine."

He craned his neck to look toward the windows, but they were muffled in heavy, green velvet. "Morning or evening?"

"Evening. You have slept the day away, you poor dear."

"I awoke this morning in a strange place, a pine-board room somewhere out in the bayous. I was with a road gang in chains, although I was free. When I called for someone to come and attend me, this giant of a man came in and beat me. I hit him twice, but he laid me out with one blow. And now I am here."

"What a terrible dream you've been having!"

"It was no dream, Claire."

"Then what a terrible raving you are engaged in," she said coldly. "People will say your wits have been addled by the accident—and by drink."

"Was that your doing? To put me in a place with the lowest order of men, show me to what depths I had sunk—or might still sink?"

She looked at him with those rifle-bore eyes of hers. When her face closed like that, her mouth a smooth line and not a lift or droop of expression to her eyes, Louis knew better than to continue. Claire was a million miles away from him, waiting for him to say something unforgiveable, waiting to lash out at him for it.

Louis held his breath and reflected on how really *well* he felt.

*   *   *

It was on the following Sunday, as he was sitting at mass beside his wife Angelique, that the call came to him. While the parish priest droned on with his Latin and his incense, his wine and his wafers, the goodness of the Spirit descended upon Louis Brevet and never lifted again in that earthly life.

"The Lord *is* my shepherd," Louis whispered around a jaw still taped and painful. "He keeps me as He kept the paschal lamb of the Hebrews . . ."

Angelique turned to him with a *shush* ready on her lips. She stopped it on seeing the light glinting from his eyes.

"As He kept the blood and water of His Son, flowing perfect and fresh beyond the grave"—Louis's voice rose above a whisper—"so He tends me like the vine and spreads me like the light. He sends my soul flying upward, to melt in the sun above the air."

Heads around him in the pews turned with anger or confusion on their faces.

"He raises me with the majesty of a Prophet of Ages, and he casts me down in sheets of flame, as He did the Prince of the Air."

A small hand, Angelique's, closed around his arm above the elbow. Her fingertips dug into the hollow of the muscles, intending to cause pain but achieving nothing with it. Levering her nails into a nerve, she tried to lift him.

Louis went to his feet, rising only with the Spirit, and his voice rose beside it.

"But He shall raise me yet again, the Sword of the Lord lifted high—"

"Oh, do hush!" Angelique wailed and thrust him sideways into the nave, where he stumbled. Then he seemed to waken, genuflected awkwardly, and turned to walk slowly up the aisle.

From the mutter of voices around him, two words came through clearly: "Drunk again."

But he wasn't.

The heat and moisture of the tent were like the oppressive atmosphere right before a thunderstorm. The tension in the air produced the same kind of itchiness, a screaming willingness to feel the flash and bang of calamity and damnation, if only to be freed of the suspense.

Part of the itchiness came from the snake handlers. Their liquid movements rolled forward through time: meeting the reptiles' dodging heads and bared fangs with the flexing of supple wrists and forked fingers. Oiled arms and writhing black bodies slid faster and faster, until the mesmerized crowd could only watch through slitted, agate-hard eyes and pray the fangs to strike and a scream of agony to stop the dance in an instant of certitude.

After the snakes, came the people.

"I was an adulteress . . ."

"I coveted my neighbor's horse . . ."

"I beat my wife . . ."

"I was a drunkard," the words felt right in Louis Brevet's throat. "The drink was like a friend to me, at first, warm and comforting. Then it was like a lord to me, commanding and rewarding. Finally, it was like a devil, mocking me and tempting me to greater folly."

"Amen."

"I was a rich man, of a family well known in these parts. My drug was wines of good vintage and brandies brought by ship from France herself. I squandered gold coins and the love of a good woman on those vintages. And when I was done, then any low spirits—dark, raw rum or clear whisky—would taste just as fine to me."

"A-*men!*"

"Tempted by the devil who comes in a bottle, I gambled away a fortune of my own and started on another from my good wife. The mud in the gutters had more spine than I had. I was the companion of cutthroats and harlots, and finally of felons chained to their picks and spades along the roadside."

"*Amen!*"

"Every one of my former friends turned his face away to see it. And our Lord saw all of this, too—but did He turn His face away from me?"

"*No!*"

"No, He did not. He put out his hand and laid it on my mottled, blood-filled heart. Small and hard as a stone, was that heart. And yet, under the touch of the Lord, it expanded and filled as with a golden light, and the dark blood fell away to my feet. The Lord made me His own. And I was a drunkard no more!"

"*AMEN!!*"

That surge of feeling, the focused joy of three hundred hungry human beings, poured through Louis Brevet's ears and down his throat. The lift of it was better than any that wine or whiskey had ever given him.

"Son, you got a wonderful draw with that drunk story. Gets them rolling in the aisles, just hating and loving you so. 'Family known around here' and 'squandering gold coins'—they just eat that stuff up."

"It's the truth, Mr. Limerick." Louis still had his hat in his hands after the service. Conscious of the appearance this made, he looked around to put the hat down and, finding nowhere suitable, at last stuck it on his head. It was hardly polite—the inside of the tent feeling like indoors and all—but he would not be holding his hat like a beggar.

"Of course it's the truth, and you tell it so well."

"Thank you, sir."

"Too well for a smart proprietor like me to let you go. How does five dollars a week and found seem to you? Of course, on the road you eat with the family." Limerick nodded behind him, to where his daughter, Olivia, was patiently piling up the occasional greenbacks from the collection basket and sorting out the silver by size. Never stopping her hands, she lifted her head and smiled into Louis's eyes, cool as a country melon.

" 'Found'?" Louis asked, puzzled. "I don't understand."

"Whatever they stick in your pockets or hat, you get to keep. The rest comes out of the plate. Clear?"

"That's very generous, sir. And what must I do to spread the word of Our Glorious Lord?"

"Help my boy, Homer, set up the tent. Come to meeting, both sessions. And tell your story, just like you did tonight."

"While you are here in St. Tammany Parish, I will certainly come."

"And when we're on the road? You do want to spread the Word beyond these bayous, don't you, son?"

"Of course, I'd like that."

"Consider it done, then."

It was in Oklahoma that a moment of Enlightenment came as his former mistress, Claire, came to him and had a conversation with the Spirit and with Louis Brevet.

"This man Limerick is using you to make money," said Claire. "For all his piety and his black clothes, he cares nothing for Christ and the Gospels. Why, he even drinks sourmash in secret! He is making a fool of you—a bigger fool than you are making of yourself."

"Whatever his purposes," replied Louis, "he is bringing people to the Word and to the Lord. Mr.

Limerick's ways may not be the most temperate, but he does work hard."

"And the money?"

"It will go to African missions, as he has promised."

"Have you ever seen a piece of correspondence with those missions, or with anyone who represents them? Have you seen any drafts made out in their favor?"

"No—but then, I am not privy to all of his finances. He gives money where it is needed."

"And gets more than he gives, it would appear."

"So long as he does the work of the Lord among the country people—and I can help him—what does it matter?"

"It matters that the books are not square and neither is he. Should a good man surrender himself as pawn to a bad one?"

"Livy does not think him bad. She loves him. And I have grown to love her and trust her simplicity and goodness in such things. Livy is wise."

"You hit it right the first time: Livy is simple. The girl knows nothing but organ playing, which she does badly, and money counting, which she does slowly. The girl's entire life is in her fingers."

"She does the Lord's work in her own way, as do we all."

"Your faith is impossible. Call it blindness and be done with it."

"Faith may needs be blind to the things of this world."

"Then I am done with you."

And with that, Claire got up and stamped out. Louis never saw her again.

It was in Arkansas, one sweltering night when moths and midges swarmed and dove around the lamps, that the dark stranger wandered into the tent. He did not come for prayer and the service, nor for the raw excitement of the confessions, as some did. He parted the canvas flaps with his horny hands and walked straight through the opening, like a man going to his gallows beam. His eyes, hard as stones lodged in his head, looked neither left nor right as he walked to the benches and, flipping his shabby coattails back, seated himself in the next to last row.

Louis, on the bench next to him, felt the chill even as moist sweat trickled under his hat band and down into his collar, which had once been boiled white and starched stiff but now—after months on the road—hung wilted and gray. Cold menace rolled off the dark stranger like vapor off a cake of ice.

The man's eyes were fixed straight forward, Louis noted, and appeared to take in no more of the light and the scene than would two glass marbles. At first Louis thought the man was asleep in the waking dreams of laudanum or some other fiendish drug, although he neither nodded nor wove in his seat, as an addict might. Fascinated, Louis found himself staring at the stranger, but the man did not seem to notice.

What could those eyes be seeing? Louis wondered. He studied out their angle and the direction of the hard gaze: beyond the mingling of heads, hats, and bonnets in front of them; beyond the wide space before the benches, where the saved ones would soon be flopping and rolling; beyond the trestle-legged altar, with its open Bible and silver-plate candlesticks; to Olivia, seated at her traveling pedal organ, and the collection basket on top of it.

Throughout the service Louis watched the man watch Olivia and the basket. His eyes were steady, almost unblinking, except for a slow, lizardlike sliding of the eyelids every five minutes or so. When the time came for the collection, then his eyes moved: up as Livy lifted the basket from the organ; down as she brought it to the level of her waist; left and right as she carried it from one end of each row to the other.

As it went into the row, it was heavy with coins and wadded bills. Livy had to stretch her arms to pass it, and the ruffled calico of her frock pulled tight across her breasts. The man did not notice. He had eyes only for the basket.

As she passed it under his chin, however, he did not move to open his purse. Instead, the stranger raised his eyes to the tent's ridgepole and shook his head, side to side, once. The basket went by him on the end of Livy's arm. Louis made his token contribution with a smile for her. The basket, Livy's arm, and her fresh, clean scent passed beyond him.

Then the stranger moved.

While she was at the point of maximum extension, his hand, independent of his eyes and his body, slipped beneath his coat lapels and came out with a horse pistol that had a barrel at least eight inches long.

In one motion, like a dancer, the man moved beneath Livy's arm and surged to his feet. He spun around into the aisle, pulling her to his chest. The gun's barrel tucked neatly into the ruffles between her breasts. Through this dance the basket neither overturned nor flung its cash to the crowd. Livy held it tight and level, like a good waiter with a trayful of brimming glasses.

Louis, who had also gone to his feet, looked into the stranger's eyes.

Nothing there. Dead as stones.

Louis looked into Olivia's face, seeking a sign of what she wanted him to do.

Her eyes, too, were blank: neither afraid nor angry. She did not struggle against the stranger. She did not look down at his gun.

"Livy?" Louis asked.

"Keep back, Louis," she replied. "This man just wants the collection money."

If Louis had troubled to listen then, he would have known she spoke too evenly, as if she had rehearsed her words to the point of boredom.

But Louis Brevet only saw the gun and the deadness in the stranger's eyes. He could read in those eyes a perfect willingness to pull the trigger and blow her chest open. Louis feared for the girl, and yet his gentle upbringing commanded that a man do something for a female in distress. He could not stand idle while the stranger molested her.

In the present face-off, Louis could hardly bring his pugilistic skills to bear. So, raising his arms like a melodramatic actor playing the Ghost in *Hamlet*, he tried to reach around Livy and grapple with the stranger.

It was a movement of inches for the man to tip the gun barrel forward and fire twice into Louis's chest.

Livy screamed.

Her scream was not one of terror or anguish, however, but of scorn: "Louis, you fool!"

The things he would carry to his grave: the smells of fresh gunpowder and old sweat; the sight of moths dipping and weaving through a faded lamplight under canvas; the final comment on his character—"Fool!"

Louis relaxed and succumbed to the cold in his limbs.

The van was broken down at the right spot along the turnpike, ten kilometers from anywhere, with marshes stretching for another twenty on either side. A dirty red bandana was tied to the van's antenna. That was the only incongruity: it was a cellular antenna, and the stranded occupants might have called for help at any time.

Hasan shrugged as he changed to the drop-off lane. Americans were not so observant as the bright-eyed young Israelis who overran his homeland. This meeting place would never have worked in the Negev.

He pulled his bright yellow Porsche out of the waveguide and rolled it, slowly, onto the gravel ahead of the van. He rolled down the passenger-side window as a dark figure ran up. In the shadows of his lap, he readied a needlegun.

"You boys have some trouble?" Hasan asked brightly.

"Nothing a bent paperclip won't solve," was the correct response.

Hasan pocketed the gun, popped the driver's door, and stepped out into the flashwash of a passing tandem tow. He was still brushing the dust off his jacket and out of his hair as his men ushered him into the van.

"Your pardon, My Lord Hasan. This is a most inauspicious place for a council of war."

"Ah, but that it is not, Mahmed. The roadside is so conspicuous it is virtually unseen."

"Until the state troopers come."

"And then we will have the perfect cover. The mechanical failure of equipment in the hands of, how do they say, 'motherless Ay-rabs.' And one of their rich countrymen—who would be helpful but is likewise as incompetent."

"Plus we have mined the gravel for fifty meters behind us."

"Then I'll leave *you* to dispose of the police vehicle," Hasan replied coldly.

"As always, My Lord. Now, how may the Brotherhood of the Wind serve you?"

"I need a safehouse."

"For how long?"

"A week, perhaps two."

"Just yourself?"

"Myself, the Lady Alexandra, a team of select Hashishiyun, and a very special prisoner. It must be

within one day's inconspicuous travel, no more than
two, yet far from unauthorized distractions."

"We have nothing."

"Nothing?"

"In this end of the New Jersey Municipal District
there are few of our countrymen, My Lord. The
Cubans, the Vietnamese and the indigenous blacks
have tried the hospitality of this land, limited as it is,
to the breaking point. The Homeless Ones have all
sought a less hostile welcome. And aside from the
heat, the humidity is not to our liking."

"You have nothing on the list?"

"I thought you wanted a safehouse."

"And as you have none, I will take a target of
opportunity, if I must."

The leader of the stranded van riders pulled a
notebook from inside his jacket. He flipped it open
on the fold-down drinks-table and keyed it.

"There is a fusion plant we've evaluated, the Mays
Landing Complex on the river fifty kilometes inland
of Egg Harbor. It supplies all grid power to the
Intertidal Sector of the Bowash Corridor. Construc-
tion value about nine billion, in current dollars. Considering the cost of replacement power, we could
collect twice that in ransom."

Hasan pulled his lip—a bad habit but it helped
thinking.

"What's the tactical situation?" he asked.

"The plant is vulnerable. It's semiautomated, so
the operators don't have to stand watches 'round the
clock. It's run like an American business office: a
daytime rad lab and maintenance crews, and everyone goes home at night."

"Nearby military?"

"Nothing serious within about sixty kilometers—
all by unimproved roads. The U.S. Army has a post
at Fort Dix, north of the site. This was formerly a
massive training facility but is now mostly a com-

puter and coordination center. The abandoned McGuire Air Force Base is adjacent to Dix. Lakehurst Naval Air Station is some twenty-five kilometers east of that. The real activity at this field is New Jersey Air National Guard."

"I love civilian soldiers," Hasan smiled.

"Better yet, being isolated in the lowland scrub, the fusion complex is highly defensible once it has been taken. We could cover the approaches—overland, by the river and its marshes, and from the air—with two squads of missile men and a band of sappers."

"Good. You do not disappoint me, Mahmed."

"Thank you, my Lord Hasan."

"Begin preparing your volunteers for the assault."

"How soon shall we—"

"I will give you date and time. Do nothing before."

"Of course not, My Lord."

Sura 4
Holy War
ਟਚਝਜਝਟਟਟਟਣਣਤ

They say the lion and the lizard keep
The courts where Jamshyd gloried and drank deep;
And Bahram, that great hunter—the wild ass
Stamps o'er his head, but cannot break his sleep.
                                    —Omar Khayyam

General Saladin moved his knees slightly, invisibly
to the men before him—hiding the twitch in the
gesture of reaching for a cup of *sorbet*—and felt his
hams sink deeper into the pillows. A military camp
on the edge of the desert could only be made so
comfortable by tents and hangings and cushions stuffed
with horsehair. However it was covered, the cold
hard ground was still just that and not the polished
floors of his palace in Cairo, layered in white stone
above the banks of the eternal river.

And now these sheikhs of Sabastiya and Ras el-
'Ain, with their womanish chatter . . .

Saladin had come into this land with his Egyptian
levies in order to turn back the Frankish invaders in
the name of Muhammad—and to win glory for his
own name, it was true. He did not come to cuddle
the foolish vanities of rich traders and clan elders
who wanted to break bread with the infidel and then
take offense at his manners.

133

"And what did this Norman say next?" Saladin asked with a sigh.

"He likened the Prophet to a whoremonger!"

"He besmirched the holy name of Khadija!"

"And could this unholy insult," Saladin countered reasonably, "not have been fabricated out of your own ignorance of the Frenchmen's tongue?"

"The insult was intentional, Lord."

"And then, what did he say?"

"He offered to lead an expedition to Medina and there ravage the tomb of the Prophet."

"He was drunk on their wine," Saladin proposed.

"He was sober, My Lord."

"He was laughing at us, Sire."

"The others laughed with him, My Lord Saladin."

Saladin pinched his beard between thumb and forefinger and signed them to silence. Did the Franks truly have enough force of arms to carry off this preposterous scheme? To ambush a caravan or lay seige to a town here and there, yes, they had men enough for that—if you figured their own half-breed brats into the counting. Otherwise, the Franks kept to their walled cities and stone castles. They rode between these in full armor, with vanguard, flankers, and rearguard—and still they made communion with their priests and commended their souls to God before setting out. The armies of Saladin had achieved that much in this land.

Reynald de Châtillon could only have been making idle boasts, fortified with wine. No such expedition was possible. These sheikhs in their foolishness had taken Reynald at his bare-faced word. A wise man would dismiss this taunt.

And yet. The threat had been made at a public ceremony, the coronation feast of their self-styled king in this land. The circumstances made it a diplomatic matter. Saladin could dismiss it as a drunken boast, or he could take notice. He could even de-

mand that all Islam take notice, if he chose. No other
defender of the faith riding in this abandoned land—
which was divided among the Abbasids of Baghdad,
the Seljuks of Turkey, and the newly annointed
Ayyubites of Egypt—had such stature as he. If Saladin
took the insult into his heart and demanded vengeance, then all Islam must respond.

With all Islam behind him, united in a holy war
against the Christians, he might achieve the victory
he had so long sought. And the Christians, in the
person of Reynald de Châtillon, had given him the
cause with their own mouths. What ninety years of
armed conflict and occasional massacre had not im-
pelled, a handful of drunken words could inspire.

"Your honesty convinces me," Saladin said at last.
"This insult to the Prophet, and to his faithful wife,
goes too deep. It must be expunged at the point of a
sword and cauterized with fire."

"Yes, My Lord," they chorused.

"In the spring of the year, at their festival of the death
and rising of the Prophet Joshua ibn-Joseph, all of Islam
shall make holy war upon this Reynald de Châtillon
and through him all Christians. We shall drive them
from this land for their share of this insult."

"Thank you, My Lord Saladin."

He turned to his vizier, who waited at the tent
flaps. "Mustafa. See to the lawgiving. Get the context of the matter from these two, and draft a decree
of *jihad* against Reynald de Châtillon, who styles
himself Prince of Antioch. It shall be an obligation
upon all the faithful to remove him from this land.
Any Christian who would interfere is subject to the
same destruction also, despite any past promises and
all protections of custom and guest rite."

"Yes, My Lord."

"The whole bazaar is buzzing with the news, sir."
Thomas Amnet lifted his eyebrow at his Turcopole

assistant but said nothing. His hands went on with the mixing, making precise wrist motions that brought the pestle down the side of the bowl and across its bottom, twisting the blunt end at the completion of each stroke. In time with this scraping and mashing, his other hand turned the mortar one-quarter round for every stroke of the pestle. And at every fortieth stroke he added, in order: a two-finger pinch of saltpeter, a thumb's width of crumbled nutmeg bark, and a single peppercorn.

"It's to be a war to the death, they say. Lord Saladin has called forth all the faithful. Not only his own Egyptian Mamelukes, but the royal cavalry of Arabia, who fight as do you Franks—"

"You're half-French yourself, Leo."

"—*we* Franks, then. And he invites the Seljuk Turks and Abbasids to send their levies."

"Big of him."

"He's going to push all the French—all of us—out of the Holy Land for the insult Prince Reynald made to the Prophet's bones."

"What about the Assassins? Are they allied with him?"

Leo screwed up his face in disdain. "Come, Master Thomas! They are not fighters. Not really. They're just a sect."

"And so not noble enough to take a hand in our whipping, eh?"

"You can't fight them straight on, sir. That's all. They fight nasty, with knives and garrotes and such."

"Sneak around in the dark? That sort of thing?"

"Yes, sir."

"No match for a direct calvary charge, then." Amnet went on with his grinding.

The boy looked at him suspiciously. "Are you making fun of me, sir?"

"I wouldn't think of it, Leo. What else does the bazaar say?"

"That all the French will be gone from this side of the sea by midsummer."

"It will take more than a few of General Saladin's horsemen to dislodge us, I think. No matter who is trying to help him."

"They say he will raise a hundred thousand men, sir. With at least twelve thousand mounted knights to lead them into battle."

The broad side of the pestle caught on the upper lip of the bowl and missed the stroke. Amnet had to double-chop at it to bring his hands up to the rhythm again.

He knew the resources that the Order of Temple might raise in fighting men and allies, and he could guess at what the Order of the Hospital might have at call. The Christian duchies and fiefdoms throughout Outremer might also be commanded, bullied, or bought out to muster their own levies. . . And still the total would not equal a fifth of the force Saladin proposed to lead.

"You hear wild tales in the bazaar, Leo."

"I know that, Master Thomas. What is it you are mixing?"

"A tonic for you, my boy, to cure your curiosity."

The young Turcopole sniffed it. "Yegh!"

It pleased King Guy to see Reynald de Châtillon sweat. For once.

The man had been admitted to the audience chamber on a dead run, and his boots had nearly slipped from under him on the polished floor as he tried to halt at the foot of the dais. His knees were trembling, his tunic askew on his body, the old ready smile gone from his lips. Reynald was in a panic. For once.

How delicious it was, to see a man who thought himself the better of all around him—even of kings! —brought to a state of stumbling, fidgeting, gnawing terror.

"My Lord Guy!" Reynald's voice even quavered. "The Saracens assemble against me!"

Guy de Lusignan waited a judicious moment before answering.

"They fight against us all, Reynald. Every day, every one of them that can draw breath or lift a weapon seeks the blood of every Frenchman in Outremer. Why should you think that you have been singled out?"

"There is a decree, from Saladin himself, naming me for some supposed blasphemy. They want a holy war against me!"

"And have you blashphemed, Reynald?" Guy was enjoying himself too much.

"Never against Our Lord and Saviour, Sire!"

"A model Christian, are you?"

"I defend the faith with my words as well as my weapons. I cannot think what occasion General Saladin may find so offensive." Reynald made an elaborate shrug—a gesture that ran strangely counter to his former hysteria. "There may well be some time or other when I scorned the infidel. I cannot remember them all." The man suddenly became subtle. "However, a blow launched at me in Antioch is a blow to all who hold station here in the Holy Land. Even to a king . . ."

"I have read this decree." Guy managed to produce a yawn, against his growing excitement. "It specifically states that any Christian who would shelter or support you is likewise subject to expulsion. If we were to surrender you to Saladin . . ."

"Surely what my Lord means to suggest is that if any king were to surrender his best subject and most loyal supporter to the Saracen, he would be derided throughout France as a knave and a scoundrel, placed under a papal interdiction, and possibly even opposed in arms by such of his countrymen as remembered their oaths of fealty to a much wronged minister of the court."

"Ah—well put, Prince Reynald."

"But a king who took up this hastily thrown gauntlet, who protected and supported a man who has bound his life and destiny to the cause of that king's crown—why, such a king would easily earn the title 'Champion of the Cross' and be remembered throughout all of Christendom, from the steppes beyond Hungary to the seas west of Ireland. Such a king would live forever in the people's hearts."

Guy floated for a moment on this vision of universal honor and gratitude. And then a thought occurred.

"Have you heard of the army Saladin is raising in this venture? A body of more than ten thousand Saracen knights. One hundred thousand trained yeomen marching at their heels."

"Rumor grants him a thousand for the ten he will eventually recruit," Reynald sneered. Gone entirely was the trembling craven, now that he had the Kingdom of Jerusalem under his hand.

Guy felt less better about this turn in the audience. "He has the full measure of men at his command."

"Saracen knights? We've fought a hundred like them. Light bows and dainty swords. Mail that cuts like lace. Helms and breastplates that you could punch through with your dagger—delicate work in enamel and gold leaf, to be sure, but nothing a good Norman, or even a knight of Languedoc, might hesitate to cleave asunder. Most of them fight in linen robes with their hair twisted up in turbans. Shake a sword at them and they'll race for the hills. Bring them on by the tens of thousands then, and let them trample over themselves."

"I have not enough men to oppose so great an army."

"The Templars? The Hospitallers? They are yours

to command. My own landholders at Antioch will fight for me, of course. Every Frenchman—most of the Anglais, too—who have come into this land can wield a sword, or once knew how. We can raise a few ten thousands ourselves, My Lord. That should be an elegant sufficiency."

"Only if I strip every other man from the walls here at Jerusalem, and do the same with every town and citadel that we hold from Gaza up to Aleppo. We might command twenty thousand mounted knights, and half that again in yeoman afoot."

"There! You see, Sire? We'll have the upper hand in this."

"But that would leave our strongholds open to attack! Failing a decisive victory, we might have no place whence we might return and bind our wounds."

"And—with the force that Saladin is supposed to be raising—who do you think might be left to attack our strongholds? We'll be chasing them across the countryside, won't we? No time to stop and lay siege to a high tower or a good strong wall. Cheer up, My Lord. We'll have the mastery of this from the time you issue your decree calling up the Orders."

"Do you think so?"

"Of course. Have I not said so?"

"You will go then to Antioch and call up your own levies. You will take *every* man from your own walls, since the land will be so safe."

"My Lord . . ."

"That's a command, by the way."

The old, cruel smile returned to Reynald's mouth. "I must obey, then." He bowed low, with his old style and backed toward the doors at the end of the audience chamber.

Guy wondered if Reynald would actually do it.

Guy wondered if he himself would actually strip his own walls to defend the man. . . . But then,

"Champion of the Cross" . . . It had a good sound to it.

"Up again, Thomas!"

For the fortieth time in the past hour, Thomas Amnet raised the iron broadsword above his head and went on guard.

The blade was barbarous—far heavier than a sword of refined steel, and a good six inches longer than any warrior his size would have had to swing. The weight of it and the ungainly balance tired his arms, so that the muscles screamed in agony as he kept the point level and twelve inches above his eyes. That was the whole reason for wielding such a blade: Amnet was worked hard at the weekly practice.

No matter the high station a Knight of the Temple might attain—diplomat in service to king or pope, dabbler in numbers in support of the Order's banking schemes, healer with herbs or, as Amnet, reader of omens—he still belonged to a warrior order and must keep up his skill at arms.

Sir Bror, who opposed Thomas Amnet in the courtyard of the Keep of Jerusalem, could claim no such unworldly attainments. A man of neither subtle speech nor soaring intellect, he was still a courageous fighter who, to hear him tell it, had once withstood a charge of fifty Saracen cavalry. He had cut off the heads of the three riding in the lead with one swing of his sword—and cut three more on the backswing, thereby crippling their attack and sending the rest into confusion.

Bror made his attack this time straight in, lunging with his whole body length. His lighter steel sword extended the thrust by another seven hands, bringing the point within an inch of Amnet's throat before he could bring his own weapon down and around in a parry that carried Bror's sword off to his left. Amnet's point continued down and dug into the packed earth while, in the same movement, Bror whirled completely around and rethrust with his point over Thomas's hands, which had ended up crossed on his sword hilt.

Amnet had not enough strength to lift his blade again, and Bror scored *touche* on his left breast.

"Tired already?" Bror gibed.

"You know it."

Sir Bror pushed the point a half-inch home into the pectoral muscle, pricking the skin beneath Amnet's quilted practice tunic.

"Hey!" Thomas yelled, rubbing the spot.

"That's to remember me by. And to remember where your wrists should go." The warrior held his own sword, point down, in Amnet's clumsy grasp, then uncrossed his hands and raised the point easily. "Like this?"

Amnet slowly uncrossed his own hands and took the better grip. "Yes, thank you. Like that."

"Thomas!"

The call came from the other side of the yard, at the foot of the donjon.

"Thomas!"

Gerard de Ridefort waited there with a delegation of Templars from the Order's various keeps scattered around the Holy Land. Amnet had noticed them arriving by fast horses, ones and twos, over the past day and a half.

He saluted Sir Bror with the too-heavy sword and turned to the summons of the Grand Master.

"Thomas Amnet shall advise us in this matter," he could hear Gerard telling the others as Amnet approached.

"Advise you how, My Lord?" He wiped the sweat and grime from his forehead with the padded sleeve of his tunic. The other important Templars, refreshed now and dressed in their linens and silks, grimaced at this. Amnet smiled at them.

"We have received the summons," the Grand Master said.

"From King Guy," Amnet filled in. "To join him in contesting this *jihad* that Saladin proposes."

"Why, yes!" Gerard appeared flustered. The others about him muttered and seemed amazed.

It was a trick Thomas had long ago learned: by using his wits to seek out and identify the main vein of an affair, he could usually anticipate the context, if not the argument, of a message before its herald had reined in his horse at the gate, let alone been presented before the Grand Master. In this case, Amnet could even guess the herald's arguments, knowing the weaknesses of King Guy and the motives of Reynald de Châtillon as he did.

"The king commands us to raise a force of seven thousand knights," Gerard said, "supported by a like number of yeomen and servants. We are to ride north, to—"

"To the Kerak of Moab," Amnet supplied. "What a daring fool is Saladin!"

Gerard paused, and a smile came to his lips. "How did you know?"

"The Kerak is Reynald de Châtillon's stronghold. Saladin might attack at Antioch, the prince's seat, which would surely be an easier place to lay siege. Saladin would have many of his coreligionists—and thus potential allies—within its walls. Instead, he proceeds directly to the Kerak, which is totally ours. And so would he have the surprise, because we could not, of course, be expecting so bold a move. Such audacity wins battles."

"You heard this in the bazaar chatter, did you?"

"No."

"You have heard, then, from someone of Reynald's party?"

"Not at all. Why do you suggest it?"

"Because only today have I learned, by a most

confidential messenger from the King, that Reynald has gone to the Kerak to direct the gathering of his forces."

"And King Guy expects us to assemble on Reynald's behalf within those high—and narrow—walls?" Amnet proposed.

"Now that he does not do." Gerard's small smile became broader, pleased at finding Thomas Amnet with a wrong answer. "We are to assemble our troops here and intercept the Saracen army as it gathers."

"Ah!"

"And for you I have a special mission."

"What may that be, My Lord?" Amnet tried to sound humble.

"The Hospitallers have rejected King Guy's summons. They contend that their allegiance is to His Holiness in Rome, and that they can be commanded by no other sovereign."

"That seems reasonable."

"Yes, and—*what* did you say?" Gerard's jaw dropped. The other Templars, until now ignored on the donjon steps, muttered among themselves at Amnet's unfavorable response.

"May I suggest, My Lord, that Prince Reynald has sealed his own fate with his own lips," Amnet said quietly. "You can save us all a deal of bloodshed: let Saladin have him. If you would preserve the rule of Christendom in this land, let Saladin have him."

The Grand Master's face purpled. "You speak rashly, Thomas." He paused as a new thought crossed his mind. "Did you see this in the light of—" Gerard glanced sideways at the other Templars gathered around him "—of *our friend?*"

"No, My Lord. The . . . source does not make itself clear on this issue. I fear, indeed, that I may have lost the mastery of it. I do speak rashly, but it is a speech that might come from the wit and the mouth of any soldier here. We are surely outnumbered by the Saracens. This decree from General Saladin applies only to Reynald, his household, and any Christian who would fight for him. Thus, the way to survival is the—"

"Enough, Thomas. In this matter of policy, we require your obedience, not your opinions."

"I am yours to command, My Lord." Amnet bowed low, with his eyes averted.

"That is better—more comely in a knight under orders. But your directness puts me in a difficulty: I had thought to send you as emissary to Grand Master Roger of the Hospital. You would have entreated him most earnestly to reconsider his refusal and join King Guy. However, since you clearly share the Hospitallers' dissensions, I do not see how you could conduct this embassy. Perhaps another . . ."

"My Lord!" Amnet protested. "You know my tongue and my wits are yours to direct. If you would have me hold counsel with Roger, then I shall do so and present your arguments as ably as you might present them yourself."

"Do you mean that?"

"As a knight of the cross and a Christian, I will plead with Roger in the Prince of Antioch's cause."

"In the King's cause, Thomas," the Grand Master chided.

"For all of our sakes, then."

"And how will you get him to do that, Master?"

Leo, stuck on a slow mare that was no match for the old warhorse Amnet was riding, clucked to his mount and dug in his heels. The mare laid back her ears and cantered a few steps, then settled once more into her sedate walk. Leo slumped in his saddle and resigned himself to trailing in his master's dust all the way to Jaffa.

"I will present the arguments that my reason, and the inspiration from God, can offer my tongue."

"But the Hospitallers will still refuse."

"And then my mission shall be discharged, and I will ride back to Jerusalem."

"Having made the trip for nothing."

"No. Having made the trip at the order of my liege lord."

"For nothing."

"For . . . oh, have it your way. For nothing. But you shall learn, Leo—and sooner rather than later if you aspire to a military life—that the orders of your lord are more important than your own time or inclinations. A soldier must serve without question, for that is how battles are won.

"When your captain orders 'Wheel to the left,' you do not peer in that direction first, decide whether you like the looks of the enemy you'd be facing, then go left or right as you please. You wheel your horse and take the consequences. How would a war proceed, do you think, if every knight picked his own battles and fought however and whenever he felt like?

"It's as much for a village priest to question the Pope's commands as for a Templar to go against the Master of his Order or the King."

"They say that Roger is not Grand Master of the Hospital anymore, now that he has flung his key of office in the King's face."

"Get your facts straight, boy. He threw the key out the window. And no one saw it land, or saw it in the yard after that. So no one can say he did not pick up the key later and put it on again. He is master until the Knights of the Hospital refuse to follow him, or until the Pope unmakes him. And that His Holiness will never do."

"Why? Because Roger is so good at being master?"

"Because Rome is so far away. Pope Urban lies dying even as we speak. His successor, who will be Gregory—the eighth of that name, I believe—will not last out the year. And the one to follow will be too busy consolidating the papacy to turn his eyes far overseas. So we in Outremer will be left to settle our affairs in our own way."

"The Pope is dying!" Leo exclaimed. "And you know who will follow him. . . . Do you have many friends who are cardinals?"

"Not one."

"Then how do you know this Gregory will become pope?"

"When you stare as hard into the future as I have of late, then you find afterward that you know things you never thought you knew. I can tell you, in order, the names of the popes right up to the year of my death. And nine centuries will bring us a lot of popes."

"My goodness! You are a fey one, Master Thomas."

"Not fey, Leo, but . . . What is that?"

In the distance, where the road met the horizon between two hills, a white dot appeared, trailing a wide plume of dust.

"A rider, Master."

The dot quickly resolved into a horseman wearing the headdress and robes of a Bedouin. He moved at a bobbing canter, coming straight at them. Amnet and the Turcopole drew rein and sat still.

"Raising too much dust for one horse," Amnet observed.

As soon as the rider saw them, he picked up speed, going to a gallop. The hard-packed, stony dirt of the road transmitted the sound of hooves: they chattered and overlapped, indicating more than one horse.

Amnet instinctively looked behind him, but the road there was clear.

At 200 yards, a long bowshot, the rider swerved to the left, and a second rode out of the dust cloud, then a third, fourth, and fifth. Each moved to the side and drove their horses hard, so that they flanked the Knight Templar and his servant. The flankers rode behind them and closed the circle, continuing on their course until all five of the Bedouin were riding in tight curves around the pair.

With a shrill cry, one of them stopped the orbiting band. Their horses wheeled until their five blunt heads, with five pairs of flaring, puffing black nostrils and the tips of five drawn sabers laid between their ears, faced the two Christians.

"What do they want, Master Thomas?"

"I don't know, Leo, but I think we shall go with them."

For a warrior, a strategist and a man of sharp action, the demands of court life were wearying. The parade of sober faces, the stale praises, the restless hands and the grabbing eyes, all dragged upon Saladin's spirit and added to the length of the day.

This morning he sat as judge, hearing the pleas of one Bedouin against another in the matter of lost lambs and rights to well water. Calculating by the angle of a sunbeam which fell from a narrow gap in the tent cloth, he could see the break for midday prayer was still more than an hour away. Saladin let out a sigh that might have been heard by Mustafa, who waited behind him.

The next supplicants were a small band of Bedouins who shoved two tattered travelers across the carpets ahead of them. One of the pair, a half-breed by his look, fell on his knees in front of the cushions before Saladin's toes. The other was pure European and probably a Frank. He remained standing, staring down at the Sultan—until one of the Bedouins kicked him expertly at the back of the knee. That dropped the man on all fours, but he never took his eyes off Saladin.

The clothing of both men was dusty, cut, and

travel stained. The Frank's tunic might once have been white. The pattern of cuts and the lighter, less dirtied wool on the left breast might have been in the shape of a cross. The cross that had been cut away there might have been red. And it all might mean nothing.

"What is the complaint?" Saladin asked, putting strength in his voice.

"O My Lord, these men were found upon Jaffa Road."

"Yes?"

"That road is the responsibility of the Haris el-Merma. All who pass there must obtain our permission and pay their duties. These did not pay."

"Can you not extract the amount from them?"

"O My Lord, they have not the price."

"Not *any*thing?"

"No money, and not much value in the weapons they carry. One of them carried *this* . . ." And the man pulled an old purse of pale leather out from under his robe.

"Give it here," Saladin commanded.

The Bedouin surrendered the purse. Inside it was a hard lump, like a stone. The Sultan untied the leather thongs that held its mouth and dumped the contents onto his palm. It looked like a piece of smoky quartz, but smooth as a water-washed pebble. It was heavy and felt warm to his skin—probably retaining the heat of the Bedouin's body. Saladin held it up into the sunbeam that fell from the tent's roof.

The kneeling Frank drew in a sharp breath and then held it.

The light passed into the quartz and died, neither shining through nor brightening its nether surface. Something dark, then, inhabited the center of the quartz—a flaw that would rob it of any marginal value such a large piece of crystal might hold.

Saladin slipped the bauble into its purse and tossed it to the Bedouin.

"Give it back to him. It will not pay your price."

"My Lord has spoken."

"I shall pay the passage for these two."

"Thank you, My—"

Saladin cut him off by turning his face to the Frank.

"You are a Christian?"

"I am, General." The man's Arabic was as deeply flawed as his stone, and yet it was a wonder to hear a European speak the tongue.

"And this half-breed is your servant?"

"My apprentice, sir. Also my friend."

Saladin shrugged. Who cared where an infidel put his loyalties? "What was your business in Jaffa?"

"I was sent by my master to extract a promise for some horse . . . flesh."

"You do not look like a trader. You might be a knight, by your clothing, except you do not look stupid about the eyes. Have you been a fighting man?"

"I have been trained to fight, sir, but I am not good at it."

Who cared what an infidel thought of his own worth? "It is good for a man to know his limits," Saladin said.

The Frank properly bowed his head and said nothing.

"You are free to go," Saladin told him. "To Jaffa. To deal in horseflesh."

The man touched his head to the tent floor as a Moslem does at prayer, in submission.

"But mark this, Christian. You will be gone from this land before the year is out. All of your kind will be gone. It is war between us now—the final war. My advice to you is: Do not buy young horses, and do not pay too much for them, or you will never get

full value for your price. . . . Do you understand
what I have said?"

"Not really, My Lord Saladin," the man stuttered.

"I don't expect you to. Now be on your way."

Saladin turned and signaled to Mustafa. It was
certainly time for the call to prayer.

"Are we alive, Master Thomas?" The Bedouins
had relieved Leo of his old mare, and now he swayed
along the road to Jaffa on the back of a camel—one
that continually tried to bite his knees.

Amnet's French-bred warhorse had been exchanged
at sword's point for a swaybacked, spavined old beast
with split hooves and running sores on its legs. The
animal wheezed so that Thomas had not the heart to
urge it along at a pace faster than an amble.

"We appear to be alive," Amnet answered him.

"I thought General Saladin had put a price on the
heads of all Knights Templar."

"He has."

"And yet he did not take yours."

"I did not announce myself."

"But he could see the stains outlining where you
ripped the cross from your tunic. I saw him looking
at the very spot."

"And, because I did not swagger into his tent and
order his slaves about, he assumed I had stolen the
tunic, Leo. A man is what he does and says—not
what he wears. Even a Saracen lord can understand
that much philosophy."

"Why did he let you go? He seemed to make the
decision after he had handled the crystal."

"You noticed that, did you?"

"I notice everything, Master. As you have taught
me."

"I was praying hard that he would let us go. It was
a gift from Heaven that he did not keep the Stone
instead."

"That Stone is important to you? Why? What is it?"

"Ah, now, Leo! Enough questions. You have to leave me something still to teach you."

"But—all right. I can wait. Not for long, though."

"You want us to *what?*" roared Roger, Grand Master of the Order of the Hospital. His voice rang off the ceiling beams of the refectory in the Keep at Jaffa.

The Grand Master's outrage was reflected in a general stir and murmur among the assembled knights of his Order. Echoes reached Amnet's ears of "Hear, hear!" "Never!" and "Won't do it!"

"Only the Pope himself can order the Knights of the Hospital into battle," Roger continued in a barely more reasonable voice. It was clear from the tone of the convocation, however, that he felt no need to explain or justify himself to a messenger like Amnet.

"That is true," Amnet agreed, making his own voice loud to overcome the murmurs. "Your Order owes filial allegiance—as does mine—only to His Holiness. But our fortunes may be closer to home, with the interests of King Guy."

"Guy has made his deal with Châtillon and thereby supped right fully with the Devil. Let Guy find his own way out to the jakes."

"And if Guy will not let Reynald go to the Devil alone, what then?"

"Eh?" Roger seemed to be sniffing at a strange, new thought.

"If King Guy raises an army of Franks in the Holy Land to fight Saladin, and if the Order of the Hospital aid him not—what then?"

"Then Guy falls into a tub of shit."

"And if he should beat this Saracen general?"

"Eh?"

"If all the Franks in Outremer should win the field that day, and the Knights of the Hospital have done

nothing, then there might be a measure of bad feeling against you. Tithes might not be so forthcoming
from the duchies at home. Loans might not be re-
paid so quickly. Certain fiefs within the gift of certain
kings might be withheld."

"It will not be the first time. We have felt the
weight of royal displeasure before."

"And His Holiness . . . he certainly would smile as
God smiles, impartially, from the heights of Heaven.
After all, our Urban is not, certainly, a *political* man.
He would not be swayed in his affections by the
wrath of kings and the purses of those who hold
temporal power, now would he?"

"Ah—unnh." Roger seemed to be choking on a
new thought. The hall behind Amnet went quiet,
except for the shuffling of boots on the floor's stone
flags.

"You might have little enough to lose, Master
Roger, if you and your knights could *know* that King
Guy and all who ride with him will come to grief.
Certainly, such doughty fighters as the Order of the
Hospital could maintain their place in this barbarous
land with their own swords. But if King Guy and his
familiar, Prince Reynald, should emerge victorious
and thus stronger than before—and who should pray
for anything else? As it would be a sin to call down
blessings on the arms of infidels—then your posture
of aloofness might not sit so well in certain favored
high places."

"Do you *know* this?"

"I see what any man can see with his own eyes."

"But it is said, among some, that you have the
power to see beyond mortal knowledge. Have you
foreseen, by your arts black or white, the outcome of
this affair?"

Amnet paused before answering. He felt his eyes
turn inward, as if at a cue from the Grand Master.
From the darkness behind his temples he could see a

face, grim and pale, with flowing mustaches, looking back at him.

"I have not that power, such as you understand it."

"That's no answer, Thomas Amnet."

"It's the only answer I have to give, My Lord."

"You have spun our heads with riddles and suppositions, Templar. You could confuse the buttons off a bishop's cassock and the beads off a nun's rosary."

"I have laid out for you the pitfalls of your course of action—and the prizes available in reconsideration."

"What prizes?"

"Templars and Hospitallers have long rode together."

"Not as near as you'd think."

"True, we have had our differences, Master Roger. But the King would hold you all in high esteem if you would put your swords in his service again."

"Define 'esteem.'"

Amnet paused. To make hints was within his commission from Master Gerard. To make promises—that was another matter.

"If we can roll this Saladin and his Ayyubites back beyond his borders, then there would be new fiefs to claim. Fields of green Egyptian corn, metal mines in the Sinai, pearl fisheries along the Red Sea . . ."

"And King Guy's pet Templars would take first pick, would they not?"

"Does not a father work harder to please a wayward son than one who has remained obedient to his wishes?"

"More riddles, Thomas! I swear, you have one for every day of the week."

"My Lord does me too much credit."

"Credit enough that I'll not debate you. We are simple men here. Earnest fighters. Pious monks. Honest traders. Not men of quick words and opportune alliances, such as you of the Temple."

"But, My Lord—"

"No, Thomas. We made our quarrel with the King openly, over the matter of his succession. We cannot bury that for a few cornfields and a handful of pearls."

"I was not thinking to *buy* your decision, Master."

"Of course not, because it's not for sale. If King Guy comes to a bad end in this holy war that Reynald has brought on—well, we won't hold a mass of celebration. We *don't* bless Saracen arms. But we won't lift a hand, either, to keep Guy out of the pit that Reynald's pride has dug for the both of them . . . and for you, if you ride with them."

"I hear you."

"Because you are a true knight and have pled the cause of your Order honestly, I'll not punish you for coming here. You may return to Jerusalem—if the Saracens will let you."

"Thank you, Master Roger."

"Go quickly, Thomas. The war is upon us."

File 04

A Cold and Deadly Place

✠

Do not go gentle into that good night,
Old age should burn and rave at close of day;
Rage, rage against the dying of the light.
                                        —*Dylan Thomas*

By his third night, Tom Gurden was getting the rhythm of the pool. The main thing he had to learn was that any woman who could not find a receptive man there—other than the piano player—was either too shy or too drunk to cause him much trouble. A smile or a subtle blocking move with thigh or elbow would put her off. If he kept on playing, he was usually all right.

By contrast Tiffany and the other regular waitress, Belinda, were under constant attack—from men and women alike. Some of it was gentle and good-natured, some rough. Without appearing to stare, or to care, Gurden counted the number of snatches, fondlings, and various outright penetrations that Tiffany endured in the course of an hour. Neither girl actually cried out. And neither seemed in danger of drowning, so long as she could hold her breath for longer than thirty seconds. After just one enraged lunge away from his keyboard that first night—which was met with a chorus of laughter—Gurden made it his business not to make it his business. But sometimes he wondered that there wasn't more blood in the water.

He quickly learned that the preferred tempo in the pool was nineties music, slow rock and sometimes soul—both of which he could play for hours. However, the customers wanted their tunes voiced in the blare of sax and the thrumming of strings, neither of which his Clavonica was equipped to deliver.

Or not at first.

The Clavonica was a semi-classical instrument, with preset buttons duplicating the stops on a pipe organ. He found that the Trumpet and Celeste came closest to the required sounds. When he first tried those stops, they still sounded pretty far—to his ear—from real sax and string settings. But the longer Gurden played, correcting his touch, hitting some notes and phrases more authoritatively than he otherwise would, concentrating on pressing out the sounds, the closer then that Trumpet and Celeste approached the modern voices he wanted.

The first time he heard the Clavonica playing real sax and strings, he thought it was a distortion from the underwater speakers. But they definitely had not sounded that way on his earlier sets in the pool.

Next he thought his ear was just playing tricks, delivering the sounds he was trying for. But his ear had been trained by years of hard practice against hearing just anything his fingers wanted to achieve.

Then he thought the electronics had been shorted out by moisture and chemicals, disrupting the waveform circuits. But the following afternoon he arrived at the pool early, hauled the piano bar out onto the tiles, and broke down the Clavonica. Its circuit boards were pristine, and they checked out with his multimeter—except that the Trumpet was clearly generating the attack-decay-sustain-release of a saxophone, and the Celeste was making the wave-forms of a modern string section.

Finally he accepted that the instrument was responding to him in a way that no piano of wood or steel and hammered strings beating on the air ever did. Tom Gurden had, somehow, effected a change in the Clavonica's circuitry.

There was no one he could tell about the miracle. Tom had never considered inviting Sandy to join him in the pool, nor had she ever asked. And Tiffany and Belinda cared nothing for his music as they dodged and wove through the nightly free-for-all.

The pool contained other unexplained incidents.

On Gurden's second night there, he found an orange stain at the bottom of his drink, melted inside the glass. Was it the same tumbler that Sandy had given him in the apartment? He could never be sure. It certainly might have been, plain as it was. And the wisp of discoloration was the right shape and hue.

Had Tiffany or Belinda brought him the soda that night? Tiffany, he thought. . . . But she and Sandy were definitely strangers.

Could someone have slipped the glass into the piano's bar rack, hoping it would find its way to Gurden's hand? Unlikely, with a hundred such glasses in circulation—not counting losers collecting at the deep end by the drain—during any night. Except that, as a piano player, Tom was the first or second person to get a drink from the bar. And he tended to nurse his one glass all night or get refills right from the source.

Gurden slipped a hand free of the playing straps and picked up the glass. The familiar shock or tingle that had gone through him the first time was still there. The sensation was dulled by the water, by the jostling movement around him, by some familiarity. But still the tingle could reach to his toes.

He took a sip of stale soda and ice-melt and put the glass back by the music holder. His hand found the strap again and picked up the rhythm.

It was nice to be loved.

Or at least looked after.

Eliza: Good morning. This is Eliza—

Gurden: Hello, doll. Two-one-two, please. Tom Gurden calling.

Eliza: Hello, Tom. Where are you?

Gurden: Still in Atlantic City.

Eliza: I judge from your voice that you are more relaxed than you have been for several days.

Gurden: That may be. I don't know.

Eliza: Does the work you're doing agree with you?

Gurden: You can get used to anything, I guess.

Eliza: Do you still have dreams?

Gurden: Yes.

Eliza: Tell me about your dreams, Tom.

Gurden: The latest one was a bad one. Not just eerie, but actually frightening. A nightmare.

Eliza: Describe it, please.

Gurden: It's just a dream. I thought you cyberpsychs didn't hold with Freudian analysis. So why are—

Eliza: You said yourself, Tom, that people were trying to get into your mind. These are more than dreams, especially as they come in a waking state.

Gurden: But they recur at night, too.

Eliza: Of course, the residue of experience. Have you ever experienced *déja vù?*

Gurden: Sure. Everyone has.

Eliza: That particular sense of familiarity is actually a chemical miscue in the brain. The mind is momentarily interpreting a new experience as if it had come from a stored memory. With a trillion synapses firing in waves across the cerebrum, it's to be expected that a certain percentage of the signals will get mixed.

Gurden: What does this have to do with my dreams?

Eliza: Dreams, *dèja vù*, hallucinations, things seen out of the corner of your eye—all are patterns and veils that the inattentive mind draws across the randomness of experience. What you have once seen, you may later remember and think about, then eventually dream it.

Gurden: But these dreams are not real! They are *jamais vù*, never seen.

Eliza: Reality, as my first programmer would have said, is a coat of many colors. A thousand synapses discharging in near-random patterns—*that* is reality.

Gurden: . . . Near-random?

Eliza: Tell me about your dream, Tom. This latest dream.

Gurden: All right . . . I think it started with another gig I was doing. I was playing for a soldier's reunion, a company of Air Cavalry pilots who had seen action in San Luis Potosi and the Rio Grande Free State during the war. I was free-styling one of their marching songs—half in English, half Spanish—about the second taking of the Alamo. Suddenly, between one bar and the next, I saw a flash of something, like metal, behind my eyes. It was the flash of a sword, cutting the air.

"Artifacts, Lieutenant," Madeline Vichaud spoke from behind the ledgers on her counting desk. "I sell only genuine artifacts of proven lineage."

Mme. Vichaud would be a looker in anyone's book, Marine Lieutenant Roger Courtenay decided, if she would only dress the part. Put away the ruffled white shirtwaist and dusty-dark taffeta skirt of the Teens and Twenties, from an era when French colonials were still dressing like Parisiennes of the Nineties. Get herself some modern clothing—perhaps something Asiatic, like those tight, brightly colored silk dresses, slit up to the hip, that the Saigonese bargirls were always wearing. Something that *moved* when she moved. With a shapely woman of Mme. Vichaud's blonde, almost Nordic coloring, the combination would certainly . . .

"That sword is true Napoleonic era, Lieutenant. It is an officer's model, patterned after the Roman *gladius*, or short stabbing sword."

Courtenay took a few experimental swings with the plain, almost unhilted, sword. He tried to pivot the swing around the balance point, as he had learned in fencing class. The locus felt wrong, though: too far inside. The broad, flat, straight-sided blade, about as sharp as a new hunting knife, wobbled in his hand and fell off to the left. It seemed to want a piece of his kneecap and almost got one.

"Something wrong there."

"The *gladius* was designed for a man of smaller stature," she said in her dry, schoolmarmish voice. He had not thought she would glance up at his cuts and thrusts. "Someone from this century, when men are larger in almost every dimension, would find it unwieldy."

"Anyway, I'm looking for something a little more—"

"Try the Heidelberg, fourth from the left on the back table. It is a duelist's blade, a saber of more modern design."

"Modern? Well . . ."

Courtenay picked up the long whip of steel, about as wide in cross-section as his little finger. The hilt was protected by a shallow basket of steel slats. Something about the grip—

"Hey! Are these *diamonds?*"

"Rock crystal, Lieutenant. That is a gentleman's sword, with modest decoration."

He wrapped his fingers about the studded panels and lifted it, long and limber. He backed into the aisle between the shop's display tables and went *en garde*. The steel had just enough springiness to hold its line when held level, if he held the spline of the blade vertical. When he waggled it left or right, the tip sagged. The balance, however, was perfect for his arm.

Courtenay brought the balance up in a salute and— *agh!* A sharp facet on one of the pieces of rock crystal stabbed into his palm, scoring the ball of his thumb.

"What is that?" Mme. Vichaud asked.

"I cut myself," he said sheepishly, licking at the wound. It stung more than a normal scratch, even accounting for the light film of sweat on his hands. Courtenay thought passingly about the strange fungi and bacteria that would undoubtedly grow in a jungle country like Vietnam.

"You Americans are so like little boys, sometimes. If you have cut yourself with a sword, Lieutenant, it is no responsibility of mine."

But Courtenay barely heard her. He was staring at the crystals in the decorated handle, seeking some kind of dirt or mold that would explain the stinging in his hand. There! One of the shards was brownish, as with old blood. Evidently that ragged bit of glass had taken another victim years ago in precisely the same way.

Courtenay took a final lick at his palm and put the sword down, lefthanded, in its place on the table.

"Are you buying, Lieutenant?"

"I guess. . . . Well, how much for the Roman sword?"

"Forty thousand *dong*."

"That's—ah—four hundred bucks! An awful lot to pay, just for something to decorate my hootch."

"I sell only genuine artifacts, Lieutenant."

"Well, I guess not today, ma'am."

"As you wish. Please close the door gently on your way out."

"Yes, ma'am. Thank you."

The heavy *thwock-thwock* of fiberglass rotors beat the air around the Huey and drummed into the talker's helmet that Courtenay wore. Looking back along their route, he could see the top of the jungle canopy bend and right itself behind the last slick in line.

The three squads of his platoon were deployed in choppers when they might as easily have ridden the thirty kilometers to Cu Chi by truck. Trucks, however, were vulnerable to ambush, even in the streets of Saigon, by peasant boys on bicycles with satchel charges disguised as bags of rice or cases of beer. Helicopters could be ambushed only at the base as they took off or at the landing zone while his men disembarked.

Dead was dead, either way.

Courtenay rehearsed the landing in his mind. The four Hueys would come into the dry paddy two by two, with their door gunners blazing away. He hoped the rotor wash would kick up so much dust that anyone waiting beyond the dikes might lose a clear shot. A little dust down the collar was better than a round through the head.

They landed and scooted in waves toward the cover of the trees. Normally that was bad practice, because the NVA machine gunners liked to set up in the cover of trees. But not this time. Courtenay knew from his orders that his colonel had a command post established in those trees—or had one as of 0600 that morning.

When a white hand showed among the under-growth and pointed them to the left, he knew that the Americans still held the treeline.

He left his men in a shallow clearing and went on to the CP behind a major whose cammies were pressed with knife-edge creases and whose boots were spitshined under a layer of red dust.

The CP was an eight-man tent erected on the hard dirt. Its ropes were tied to tree boles and large rocks instead of pegs driven into the ground. Before it, Colonel Roberts had a sector topo map spread on a trestle table. He looked up as Courtenay and the major approached.

"Major Benson, go back and instruct the lieutenant's men about noise discipline."

"Yes, sir." The major nodded and turned to leave the way they had come.

Courtenay saluted the colonel and stood at attention. His cammies were streaked with sweat and dust. The green nylon uppers of his jungle boots had not seen a brushing in four days, let alone a spitshine.

"At ease, Lieutenant. We're not on base now."

"Yes, sir. I mean, no, sir."

"How many NVA would you say are in this sector?"

"In Cu Chi District itself, sir? Or just this sector?"

"Within three hundred meters of this position."

"Well, sir, from the way our men are spread out here, and they're not exactly engaged in a firefight at this minute, I'd say zero to none."

"Would you, Lieutenant? And what if I told you we had intelligence reports of an NVA battalion HQ and five companies of regular army troops within three hundred meters of this spot as of 1800 hours yesterday?"

Courtenay looked around at the unscarred tree-trunks, the lush underbrush, the dirt marked only by American boots, size seven and above.

"I'd say, Colonel, that they've *di-di*ed pretty thoroughly."

"They haven't gone anywhere, Lieutenant. At least, not that we can tell."

"Begging your pardon, sir—would the Colonel please come in out of the sun?"

"Not funny, Lieutenant. Given that all I've told you is God's honest truth, what do you make of it?"

"If someone hasn't been lying to you, sir, then I would say Charlie and his Big Brother have either learned how to fly—or how to dig like a mole."

"Very good, son. Take a closer look at this map. Those X's mark certain anomalies that my men have noted in the surrounding bush."

"Anomalies, sir?"

"Mole holes."

"Yes, sir. If the Lieutenant may ask, why is the Colonel telling him this?"

"Because I have selected your platoon for the honor of being first to go down the holes and . . . tell me what you find."

"Yes, sir. Thank you, sir."

Courtenay looked down at a smooth circle in the ground, which had been cleverly concealed beneath a trapdoor of heavy planks.

The door was stout enough to stand up to casual bombardment with mortars and grenades, everything except a direct hit with an artillery shell. The hinges were four strips from the tread of an old truck tire; they were nailed to one side of the square panel and splayed out like the fingers of a hand. The strips had been buried in the red soil with bamboo stakes through their ends for an anchor. The top of the door was camouflaged with brush—not cuttings, which would dry out, turn brown, and give the entrance away, but whole plants trained to grow in a thin layer of soil potted on the door's upper side. Only an occasional watering would be needed to keep the door secret.

The hole beneath it was a meter in diameter. The shaft below slid away at an angle of forty-five degrees; so the shaft had a definite floor and ceiling. They and the walls were as smooth as concrete, rubbed and patted down by hands and knees, flanks and backs.

Courtenay shone a flashlight down the shaft.

Nothing.

He got down on his belly, levered his chest over

the opening, and spread his arms and shoulders to block out the dappled sunlight coming through the treetops. When his eyes adjusted to the gloom, he switched the flashlight on again, covering the lens with three fingers to control the glare.

Still nothing.

He clicked off the light, wiggled back onto solid ground, rolled over and sat up.

"Do you want to declare it bottomless, Lieutenant?" Sergeant Gibbons asked.

"Maybe it comes up back home in Sioux City," Pfc Williams offered.

"If it does," Courtenay replied, "then we're gonna roll a grenade right up on your momma's porch."

He put out his hand and Gibbons put a fragmentation grenade into it.

"You know, sir," the sergeant offered casually, "after you drop that, whoever's down there is going to know we're up here. And when we have to go down after them, they may just be mad about it."

"The thought has crossed my mind. But I just want to warn them to keep their heads down."

Courtenay pulled the pin and pitched the grenade down the angled shaft like a fast ball so it would go far before striking dirt, slowing down, and rolling. They all pulled away from the opening and its prospective blast cone.

Whump!

The earth below them hardly moved. A rolling plume of red dust came out of the hole ten seconds later.

"Nobody home?" Pfc Jacobs asked.

"Looks like somebody has to go down after all," Courtenay said, pushing on his knees and rising out of his squat to stand just south of the hole. "Who's the shortest man here?"

He looked up at a decided angle to the soldiers around him.

"All right," he sighed. "I guess I am."

"We're right behind you, Lieutenant."

"Every step of the way, sir."

"Sure," he said with a bravado grin. "Don't push in your eagerness to get down there first."

Courtenay had no experience of tunnels; no American in Vietnam did at the time. But he was not plagued by claustrophobia, as others might be. And he was sure of his hand-to-hand skills: some judo; a dexterity with the pugil sticks that he had enjoyed during basic; his fencing, of course; and its poor cousin, knife fighting, which he learned on the streets of Philadelphia. This looked to be a silent *mano a mano* in the dark, enclosed spaces instead of any kind of open firefight.

Courtenay chose his setup with care: Spare bootlaces tied his cammie trouser cuffs closed against rats and spiders, although he figured if there was an entire NVA battalion down there, the rats had been eaten long ago. For a weapon, he took his officer's sidearm but stuck it in the back of his web belt, along his spine, instead of flopping around in its holster. In his left hand he took a fresh flashlight with a full charge on its batteries. He would use it only for surprise; most of the passage he intended to feel his way, as Charlie would undoubtedly be doing. In his right he held a K-bar, the Marines' long knife with a dull-black finish and rough handle of stacked leather disks pierced by the tang. No matter how slippery with sweat his hands became, he would be able to grip that knife. He held it diagonally across his palm as a fencer would a foil or epee; that felt most natural and gave him good control either forehand or backhand. Finally, he tied a yoke of rope around his shoulders and passed it under his belt in the back so it would not foul his automatic.

"One tug means feed out more. Two tugs mean

pull me back," he told Gibbons. "That's about all we're going to need to say, right?"

"Yes, sir."

"What have you got there? Twenty-five meters?"

"Yes, sir."

"We shouldn't need any more than that. If you have to tie on another coil, give me two tugs so I'll stop before I take the bare end down after me. All right?"

"Yes, sir." Gibbons and all the men had gone strangely quiet. No jokes. No slacking off.

Courtenay looked around at the clearing with its patches of green that were spangled golden by spots of sunlight. He took deep breaths, as if he were about to dive into water, then got down on his knees before the meter-wide hole and began crawling forward.

"Sir! Wait!"

Courtenay paused on the lip of the hole, turned to see a short, stocky man running up. He wore regulation cammies with a private's black stripes; the nametag over his right breast said, "Bouchon." Yet this new man wore his uniform self-conciously, like it was some costume instead of the clothing he'd lived with for months. In fact, the edges of its dyed camouflage markings on his blouse and trousers were still crisp and bright, as if fresh out of the box and never washed. He carried his M-60 machine gun and the crossed bandoleers of cartridges lightly, like lightweight plastic toys, despite the thick jungle heat.

"Yes? What is it, Private?"

"The colonel said to let me go down, sir. I have experience with these holes."

Courtenay eyed the man critically. Those shoulders were at least a meter wide. Crawling down the shaft, this man would plug it like a champagne cork in its bottle. And besides, what American could have experience with these holes? They had just been discovered.

"No, Private—um—Bouchon. I admire your courage, but it's my job to go down."

"No, it isn't."

"*What* did you say?"

"No, it *ain't*, sir."

"And why not?"

The man hardly flinched at this challenge from an officer.

"You're too valuable to lose, sir. Colonel's orders, sir."

Courtenay reflected. The man had run up from the west, yet the command post was off to the *east*. And the underbrush hereabouts was not so dense that he would have needed such a circuitous approach.

"Sergeant Gibbons, get another rope." To Bouchon: "As Colonel Roberts is concerned for my safety, you'll go down with me, watch my back."

The man did not grin or otherwise show relief but just nodded. "Yes, sir."

In a minute the blocky Bouchon was lightened of his M-60 and bandoleers and fitted with a knife, a flashlight, and an officer's sidearm, also tucked against his spine by the webbing belt.

"Let's go." Courtenay went down on his hands and knees again and began crawling forward.

Within two meters of the opening, their bodies had closed out all the sunlight except for lingering flashes that came between their legs and under their chests. Courtenay found he had to use his back and shoulders as a brake against the ceiling, to relieve the stress against his wrists and palms. He had quickly tucked knife and light into his belt to free his hands. It would almost be easier, Courtenay thought, to turn around and slide backwards—almost, except that neither knew what they would be backing into.

Crumbs of hardened dirt brushed off the tunnel's

ceiling onto their backs, fell around their ears and faces, and bounced off down the steep pitch of the shaft. Those falling crumbs would announce their advance, to whomever waited down there, more surely than his earlier grenade might have. Still, there was no help for it. Without the braking action, they would be in a hopeless slide under gravity's pull, faster and faster, right into the arms of whoever might be below.

After fifty "paces"—which Courtenay measured with his knees and judged to be half his walking pace, or about a third of a meter long—he dropped his head between his legs and addressed Bouchon behind him.

"Let's take a break and reconnoiter."

A heavy grunt was the only reply.

Bracing with his hands downslope, he pulled his right leg through and jammed his boot against the opposite wall, pushing with hip and bootsole to hold himself against sliding. Bouchon followed his example. Their hot, panting breaths filled the tunnel.

"Is the air getting cooler down here?"

"Not yet," Bouchon said, voice low.

"The walls are dry. Not what you'd expect this close to the delta, and almost under the paddylands."

"Someone in the NVA's been studying civil engineering. This complex is going to be protected by drainage tunnels and ventilator shafts. Wouldn't be surprised if the outer surface here was faced with raw cement, or at least some hard clay."

"Patted down by hand?"

"Dug by hand, finished by hand. Heavy equipment wouldn't fit in here, would it, Lieutenant?"

"I guess not. . . . Well, let's get a move on."

Twenty-five more paces, and they came to a fork: the main tunnel line they had been following leveled out; a side branch to the right continued downward at a forty-five degree angle. They took the level path, more from weariness than from any reasoned choice.

The tunnel ran straight for a length of three meters, then stopped against a door of smooth wood. Its planks were fitted so closely together that Courtenay, poking gently, could not penetrate the gaps with the tip of his K-bar.

He listened with an ear against the wood.

Nothing.

"Dead end, this way," Courtenay said quietly.

"Or," Bouchon grunted, "some guy holding his breath and cocking his rifle *real* slowly—sir."

"Right. . . . Let's try the other way."

They crawled back to the side tunnel, carefully paying back their guide ropes. Courtenay looked back up the way they had come, expecting to see the white disk of light from the entrance, twenty-five meters above them.

Nothing but blackness.

"I don't see daylight up there."

"One of your men's probably leaning over the hole, listening for us or trying to see down here."

"You're probably right."

Courtenay stretched his fingers and shook his arms out, readying himself for another braking crawl down into the ground. Was Bouchon, behind him, tired? He did not seem to be slowing down. Was it really only twenty-five meters they had come? It seemed longer.

Twenty meters further along the side branch, they came to another fork. This one was a classic "y" in the tunnel, the left branch leading down at the same forty-five degree angle, the right angling up slightly.

"One down, one up. Which would you choose, Bouchon?"

"Down will likely take us either to people or to groundwater. Up will lead back to the surface, eventually. What are we looking for—a fight or a way out?"

"We're looking to see what we can see, I guess."

"And so far we've learned—what?"

"That whoever made these tunnels wasn't fooling around. We must be about—" He solved Pythagoras' Theorem in his head. "—thirty meters below ground now. All in smooth holes without shoring or ribbing. That took a lot of spatial planning, plus a keen eye for the competency of this soil, to keep from weakening the ground. Somebody's been digging around here for a long time."

"Years, sir."

"You know that for a fact, do you?"

"Good guess, sir."

"Hmmm." Courtenay's calculations reminded him of something. "Gibbons forgot to signal before he tied on more line, didn't he? We ought to check in, just to keep him on his toes."

Courtenay turned and gave a hard tug on his end of the rope. It slid down in a minor cascade of soil crumbs. "That's a lot of slack Gibbons is giving us," he observed. "Try yours."

Bouchon dutifully tugged on his rope. A long loop rolled down and fell across their legs.

"What is this?" Courtenay pulled some more, and it was *all* slack. He started hauling it in hand-over-hand, with the rope coming faster and faster until, after fifteen meters, he felt the short end whip through his reaching fingers. The end was cut cleanly.

Suddenly the tunnel walls moved much closer together.

Bouchon put out his hand in the darkness and felt the end of Courtenay's rope.

"We should withdraw, sir," he said calmly. "Now."

Courtenay sighed and put a hand on the other's shoulder, gave him a little push. "You lead the retreat."

They started climbing against the slope. That was harder work, especially on their knees, which kept sliding back against the loose material of their jungle trousers. The rough fabric was burning Courtenay's skin by the time Bouchon stopped dead in the tunnel. Courtenay's hands walked over his boot heels.

"What is it?"

"Fork up here. Three-way branching. All going up at the same angle."

"We must have come down one and not noticed the other two as they came in from the sides."

"Yes, sir."

"Try your flash, see if you can detect our scuff marks, an American boot toe, anything in one of the tunnels."

He heard the flashlight click on, saw glimmers of light past the other's thick body, and heard him brushing and . . . snuffling? . . . at the tunnel floor.

"No way to tell, Lieutenant." The flashlight snapped off.

"Do you think we might have come down the middle? That would make sense, wouldn't it? If we'd come down on the right or left, we'd certainly have noticed a wide open space off to one side where *two* tunnels came in to meet ours."

No answer from Bouchon.

"Well, *wouldn't* we?"

"It's possible, sir. But I wouldn't want to pin your life or mine on that interpretation."

"We have to pick one, Private. With nothing else to go on, let's take the center."

"As you say, sir."

Bouchon started crawling again. They continued going up for fifteen or twenty linear meters. Then the floor leveled out. Was this the level of the wooden door—where their side branch had left the main descent? Courtenay chewed on the distances, all subjective in the darkness. He was trying to convince himself that his choice was wrong and that they should turn back to the three-way branching. When the tunnel started *down*, he knew he had been wrong.

"Well, Private—"

The man disappeared in front of Courtenay. One minute his boots and knees were scuffing along the packed earth, the next he was gone. The only sound was a surprised grunt, then—two long seconds later—a heavy *thud!*

"Private! Bouchon!"

Courtenay snapped on his flashlight and inspected the tunnel floor ahead of himself. A round, black hole a meter across stretched from wall to wall. He bent over the hole and shone his light down into it. A short vertical shaft opened quickly onto a large space. At the extreme dispersion of his beam, he could see a green jungle boot. He followed the tied-off trouser leg up until it bent back at an odd angle. Farther up was the blocky torso.

"Bouchon!"

"Here, Lieutenant. Best not to shout. I'm in some type of room, with a table or platform of some kind under me."

"Can you stand up?"

"Not on this leg."

"We have my rope. I could let it down to you, but there's nothing to tie it onto. Can you see anything we could brace across this hole? A chair leg? A piece of firewood? Anything?"

Bouchon's own flashlight came on and swept once around the space. Looking down the shaft, Courtenay could only see the narrow end of his beam, not what it might be focusing on.

"Nothing like that, sir."

"If you'll roll aside, out of the way, I can drop down and help you."

"It would make more sense, sir, if you would go back to the branching place, try one of the other tunnels, and get to the surface."

"Nonsense, I can't leave you."

"Not much choice, Lieutenant. Even if you found

a board to brace with and came down to tie the rope around me, you'd never haul me back up through that shaft. Not enough room for leverage or maneuvering."

"I'll come down and together we'll find a way out from the level that room is on."

"We could wander for months down here, sir."

"You're just guessing."

"A *good* guess."

"Roll aside. I'm coming through."

Before the private could debate him further, Courtenay swung his legs around, put his boots through the hole, and slid his ass over the edge.

He heard Bouchon gasp and thrust himself aside before Courtenay could land on top of him. The table or whatever it was splintered under the impact of his bootsoles.

"Damn it, sir!"

Courtnay shone his flashlight around the open space.

Pale green walls, rumpled and folded like cloth. With bright glints that might be—buttons. And pale, slow-moving fishlike objects that were—hands. Hands grasping rifle stocks and knife handles. More glints, two by two, were eyes that focused on the two Americans.

With a gasp, Bouchon levered himself up on his good leg to cover his lieutenant's back. Courtenay ventured a glance over his shoulder. The man was standing like a wrestler, arms wide and one knee bent, the other braced sideways. Bouchon's K-bar had evidently disappeared in the fall, but in his hand was a deadly stiletto with a tapering triangular blade. He held it with the jeweled butt down and to the outside, the knife's tip raised and questing.

Courtenay shifted his own K-bar to the left hand and drew his service automatic in his right.

"You wouldn't leave me out of a fight, would you, Private?"

"The Lord knows I tried, sir."

Courtenay's first shot was loud in the enclosed space. The volley of return fire was louder.

It was near the end of Gurden's second set, about quarter to two in the morning, that the man started hanging near his shoulder, treading water and watching Tom's hands on the keyboard. By this time the activity in the pool had cooled off and the drinks were flowing more smoothly.

The man didn't seem to be drinking.

"Is that hard to do?" he asked, after about five minutes of watching.

"What?" Gurden said over his shoulder, still playing.

"Play with your hands strapped down like that."

"I've got to strap them. Otherwise they'd float to the surface. I would be pushing down against buoyancy, instead of falling with gravity. That throws your timing off."

"How do you hit the high and the low notes?"

"The straps slide back and forth under the keyboard. See?"

"Oh, yeah. But you couldn't reach around and, say, scratch your ass, could you?"

Gurden laughed. "Not likely."

"Good."

The knife point pricked him just above the right kidney. It went deep enough, it felt like, to draw blood.

"How did you get a weapon in here?"

"Who says I have a weapon."

"What's that in my back?"

"A sliver of glass. A lot of your glasses get broken, and the stuff piles up on the bottom in the deep end. You people should be more careful. Someday a customer is going to cut himself."

"Or the piano player."

"That's the idea."

"So, what do you want? Kill me here? Kill me somewhere else?"

"I want you to come with me. Quietly. Like we're old friends. Believe that I can hurt you badly with this piece of glass, or with my bare hands if necessary."

"I believe you."

"Switch off now."

Gurden played the tune down to its closing bars, skipped the coda, and rushed the finale. No one in the pool noticed how he had chopped up the song. When he turned off the Clavonica, Tiffany looked up from the curved side of the bar.

Tom smiled at her and made a polite yawn.

She looked around and nodded.

He slipped his hands out from under the restraining straps.

The knife point dug a half-centimeter deeper, definitely probing the gap in his spareribs.

Gurden shelved any ideas about physical violence.

"We'll have to get my clothes, back at the room."

"I have some that will fit you, in the changing lounge."

"How thoughtful."

Clothes provided by his captor would certainly be free of the little necessities Tom Gurden had begun carrying in the last few weeks: two yards of braided picture wire, a sailmaker's needle, a fragment of razorblade, a chip of bone to mount it. This sort of trash would not upset a security metal detector, nor go totally unexplained in a man's pockets. Yet with these pieces he could work any number of practical miracles. It gave a man confidence just to fill his pockets with the stuff.

Gurden climbed out of the pool first. He briefly considered a backward kick centered on the man's hairline. How ready would his opponent be for such a move? Tom's mind was suddenly filled, however, with the image of a glass shard slicing his calf from ankle to kneecap. How far could he run on a ripped leg?

Would Tiffany or Belinda help him? Exhausted as they were from a night's work? And five meters away through the shallow yet resistant water?

The man could carry Tom Gurden out of there in a hammer lock, and no one in the pool would raise an eyebrow. Tom himself had seen the same thing happen to various women all night long, and he had not interfered.

He went quietly.

In the changing lounge, the man still held his glass knife, motioned with it to a locker that had a key in it.

The clothes inside, complete down to underwear, were casual yet well made: good wool in the slacks and socks, real linen for the shirt, a tie of what looked to be authentic silk, shoes made of leather—an anachronism that even the Italians had not practiced in forty years. There were no synthetics in the locker.

He also found a heavy towel—real cotton terry—to scrape the silicon grease off. His captor had thought this through carefully.

Captors, he corrected, when two more men walked into the lounge and, instead of showing surprise at one customer threatening another, waited alertly nearby.

Gurden rubbed himself as clean as he could and put on the clothes. They fit him perfectly, down to the exact width of the shoes.

"Where are we going?"

"Down to the landing stage. We have a boat waiting."

"Aren't you going to blindfold me or anything?"

"There is no need."

That was bad. You blindfolded a man whom you planned to release, so that he could not later identify

you or your hideaway. If you did not blindfold him,
you did not expect to have to deal with that "later."

Outside, bobbing beside the stage was a turbine
boat, the kind smugglers still used occasionally. The
hull was about fifteen meters long overall and five
wide, but it was only about half a meter thick—except
along the centerline, where the aluminum skin rose
to a cowling around the gullet of a jet engine. On
either side of the engine tunnel were two long
cockpits—just seating spaces actually, about as roomy
as a jet fighter's. The one on the right had the
controls.

The two strangers clambered across the engine to
that side; Tom and his original captor stepped down
into the bare cockpit. The arrangement made sense:
even if he overpowered the man with the knife, he
would still have to climb over the engine tunnel to
take control of the boat. At 100 kilometers an hour,
thudding over the wavetops, the smooth fiberglass
skin would be too slick to hold onto. Gurden would
be swept back along it, cut by the steel edge of the
stabilizer fin, tossed by the jetwash, and broken on
the water's surface, which at that speed would re-
sound like concrete.

Why would he not simply throw himself overboard
while the craft was moving slowly? The answer to
that came when his captor pushed Gurden into the
forward seat and fastened the safety harness around
him. The quick-release buckles had been replaced
with padlocks.

He cooled his mind and prepared himself for an
exhilarating ride.

"Tom?"
Alexandra lifted her head from the pillow.

It was not a noise that had awakened her but the
absence of one. Her internal clocks, balanced and
calibrated by a long lifetime of travel, told her that

Tom Gurden should be done with his last set and coming to bed by now. In fact—she checked her watch on the nightstand—he was twelve minutes overdue.

Had he dallied at the bar with a customer or one of those attractive waitresses? Not likely. Not after a night in the pool.

Was he somewhere out on deck, romantically communing with the moon? Not unless he was doing it bare-assed with only a thin paper robe and a layer of grease to keep out the wind. If he had come back to the room for clothes, she would have heard him.

Alexandra came fully awake immediately.

She could turn the ship out and search it. Hasan would provide the manpower if she insisted. But that would take time. She would exhaust her own resources first.

Going to the closet, she dragged out her suitcase, opened it, and popped out the lining. The tracker unit was a clear glass plate, fifteen centimeters on a side. The electronics, antennae, and power source were concealed in the bezel around it, leaving the glass empty like a frame after the picture has been removed.

Its signal would hardly register inside the room, surrounded on six sides by steel bulkheads. Vaele shrugged into her robe, jammed on her slippers, and ran out into the passageway. She turned right for the stairs to the promenade deck. From there, she went around by the main concourse, then up and up, to the bridge deck. Because the Holiday Hull was an inert hulk, grounded in the mud at low tide, it kept no watches and she would not have to explain herself to any officers.

On the flying bridge, standing beside the broken binnacle and the faceless engine telegraph, she paused before activating the unit.

She could do it only once. The device would send

out an electromagnetic shriek that would turn on a radio capsule she had long ago inserted beneath Gurden's skin during some rough loveplay. After activation, the capsule would emit at ten-point-two-two megahertz with a range of about sixty kilometers. It would send for nine hours; after that he was lost.

Alexandra breathed out slowly and pressed the contact.

An electroluminescent grid lit up, its bull's-eye calibrated in tens of meters. She let the internal compass align itself while the finder band sought out Tom's return signal.

A tiny orange bead formed on the extreme edge of the grid and winked out.

She quickly reset the tracker to hundreds of meters. The bead showed stronger, moving east and north, very fast.

Vaele raised her eyes and scanned in that direction. Nothing . . . Nothing . . . Then a pleasure boat, leaving a narrow wake of pin-scratch white in the moonlight, pointing on the same heading as her luminous bead.

Setting the tracker carefully down on the rail, so that it might not lose the signal, Alexandra went below to dress and call Hasan.

The turbine boat was steadier than Gurden expected.

As they gained speed, it rose out of the water. The hull was not just hydroplaning across the waves but riding a good meter above them. Some sort of natural ground effect or ducted fan system seemed unlikely. The simplest answer was a hydrofoil: they were riding on a water wing thrust deep below the boat's elaborate hull.

That gave them a top speed, Tom figured, of more like 200 kilometers an hour.

The high, dark cliff of the Holiday Hull was far

behind them, and the jostling lights of Atlantic City's spires were visibly falling behind his left shoulder. The boat was heading out into the ocean, trading inland chop for a long sea swell.

"Where are we going?" he called back over the incredible whine of the engine. "Bermuda?"

"Not so far."

And that was all the answer he got.

When they had passed beyond some invisible limit, the boat banked into a gentle curve to the left. It zipped up the coast, passing the clustered lights of the beach towns like tiny island galaxies in the great darkness of wave and sand: Brigantine, Little Egg, Beach Haven, Beach Haven Terrrace, Beach Haven Crest, Brant Beach, Ship Bottom, Surf City.

And between these island galaxies, drawn by an unseen beacon, the boat turned again to the left and drove straight for the shore.

In the moonlight Tom could make out a single white line of surf, with gray lines of beach and mounded dunes beyond it.

The swell beneath them shortened, became thudding rollers and then a bucking chop.

"You're going to lose your underwater gear if you don't slow down," Gurden shouted.

In reply, the whine of the engine increased. Beneath them, he heard a loose clash, like a steel gate closing. The engine died out in a feathering wheeze, and the hull settled on a broad roller with its bow tipped high. The boat surfed expertly in toward shore and, when the wave broke, flopped down on the sand with an echo of grating metal. The engine spit and crackled as a secondary wave played around the exhaust outlet.

"You get out here." His captor unlocked the safety harness. "Now, please."

Gurden scrambled over the flaring side of the hull. His handmade leather shoes and real wool socks went into the brine to the ankles, but he was standing on firm sand, ready to run. He paused.

"Aren't you coming with me?"

"That is not necessary."

"What do you want me to do?"

"Go to the light." The man pointed toward a glimmering, like the light of one candle, half-hidden among the dunes.

"What if I run? Will you shoot me?"

"Have you seen any guns?"

"No, I guess not."

"Go to the light. It is the only sensible direction for you now."

Tom walked out of the surf line, bent to shake out his pant leg and squeeze the water from his socks.

Like a piece of driftwood the boat lifted on the seventh wave, the master wave, and slid back into the sea. When it was well clear of the land, its engine started up with a climbing whine. With a flare of orange afterburner, it spun and was gone.

"Go to the light," Gurden repeated and began walking through the fine, white, clinging sand.

Alexandra settled back into the molded foam of the Porsche's bucket seats. She took the primary accelerations with the small of her back and braced with her knees pushing against the center console and door to counteract sideways thrusts. In her lap the tracker blinked placidly. Now that they were on the open road, the orange bead no longer outpaced them.

She glanced across at the speedometer: 195 kilometers per hour. Perhaps it was not a boat she had seen at all, but a small seaplane taking off. That would complicate matters.

"All we can do is follow the coast roads and try to keep his transmitter in range," Hasan said softly, as if reading her mind.

"What if we lose him?"

"Then a lifetime's work will be, as the Americans say, 'down the tubes.' I am trying to decide what I should do with you then."

"We could wait for another incarnation."

"You could wait, perhaps. I cannot."

"We could test for another subject. Surely there are other sensitives, somewhere in the world."

"We have our sensitive here." Hasan reached over and tapped the glass plate for emphasis. "The original and not to be duplicated."

"We haven't proven that yet." Her voice sounded weak and querulous to her own ears.

"We don't have to. The Frenchmen themselves prove it by their actions."

Hasan picked up the telephone handset and punched in a call with one finger. He waited for it to ring and be answered, then started speaking in Arabic. His soft, commanding gush of words gave directions, placed rally and fallback points, and specified equipment, personnel, and rules of engagement. Then he listened, probably while the orders were repeated for clarity. "*Tufadhdhal*," he concluded and hung up.

"If you get Gurden back—" Hasan said to Alexandra.

"When we get him," she corrected.

"*If* . . . You may have to try threatening him yourself. Take him to the point of death, until you can see it shining in his eyes. That may serve to focus him and bring him back to awareness."

"I don't know if that's a good idea, Hasan." She paused. She had never actually refused an order of his, not even one phrased as a suggestion.

"And why not?" The damascus steel, supple yet strong, sounded in his voice.

"This one is lucky. He has grown subtle and swift, since I introduced him to the Stone. He is no longer a simple animal, reacting to immediate sensation. He thinks. He begins to see. He is dangerous."

"So?"

"He might *kill* me, Hasan!"

"So? You are older than he, and more wily. You will think of some way to protect yourself."

"Yes, I should be well out of his reach and beyond his awareness at the point at which someone finally comes *that* close to taking him out."

They drove on for some minutes in silence. The flashing light from the orange bead lit her chin.

"Would it bother you if he killed me?" she finally asked.

"It would bother me, yes. But would it stop me? No."

"And if it helped you move the subject along . . . ?"

"Then it might not even bother me."

"I see."

The darkness of the car closed in around her.

Sura 5

Pursuit in the Desert
ਦਙਹਜਜਜ਼ਟਰਦੜੁਧਕਾਤ

And that inverted bowl they call the sky,
Whereunder crawling coop'd we live and die,
Lift not your hands to it for help—for it
As impotently moves as you and I.
              —Omar Khayyam

The old ones lay about on perfumed cushions,
their bodies so relaxed that their robes had tugged
open, exposing grizzled chest hair to match their
gray-shot beards.

Deep in the cloying smoke of his drug, Masud
One-Eye giggled at nothing. His spasm went on and
on, until it ended in a shallow cough.

Hasan, who was both the youngest and the oldest
man in the room, watched them with hooded eyes.
In the young days, when he had called forth the
Assassins from the sand, the hemp smoking had been
a tool. It was the quickest way to wean young men
from the lifestream of their families, to make them
warm when the rocks of their hideout had seemed
coldest, to comfort their lusts when they discovered
—as all eventually did—that the attachments of husband and father were denied to them forever as
outlaws.

Hasan himself had spun the myth of the Secret

186

Garden. The promise of Paradise was not enough for those who belonged to the Hashishiyun. To have a paradise on earth, brought forth from the smoke, was what these wild and desperate men craved. And Hasan gave it to them.

He had chosen his themes well. The new Sufi mysticism and the Dervish way of devotion through dancing to exhaustion had both blended well with the smoke. The Garden itself, an annex to Paradise from which all but the most obedient were to be excluded, became the ultimate reward for those who had killed successfully upon command of the leader. Severing and succumbing, devotion and duty, these had been the bonds that had held his little band together—through his first lifetime anyway.

Now see what the Hashishiyun had become. Old Sinan, once a crafty fighter, had fallen into his dotage. He sucked the smoke as if it were air on a high mountain. He and his cronies lived like caliphs: sleeping and eating, fucking and farting, and always smoking. It had been months since Sinan had carried out—or even begun to plan—a strategic assassination.

Sinan raised himself on an elbow and motioned to Hasan with a bent hand. "Wine."

Hasan dipped a cup of the astringent red liquor from the ewer beside his chief's hand and held it to the old man's lips.

Sinan drank deeply and smacked his lips. With a weak shove he pushed his lieutenant's hand away.

"Do you see what that upstart, Saladin, is collecting?" the old sheikh said to the air.

"Such a display of metal and horsehide," another said dreamily.

"All to put an end to one Frankish braggart who, with the placing of a single well-honed blade, would trouble us no more."

"Is that a suggestion, Master?" Hasan asked quietly.

"No, it is not." A cough rumbled through Sinan's lungs and he sat up straighter, pulling his jellaba closer about his shoulders. "None of the Hashishiyun are to soil themselves with this foolish jihad. That is my order. . . . Indeed, for the next twelve-month, all Frankish heads shall be sacred. Let none of them be harmed."

Without thinking the matter through, the other Assassins in the room murmured their assent to this pronouncement.

"A good joke on the Ayyubites."

"Teach Saladin to pick fights he cannot win."

"Send him back to Egypt."

"Cool his ass in Nile water."

"But—" Hasan's voice cut across this mist of self-congratulation. "—we may be missing an opportunity."

Sinan turned his face to the younger man, his shaggy eyebrows drawing together like two caterpillars coupling.

"With the weight of arms Saladin can put in the field," Hasan continued, his voice still strong, "he might indeed sweep the Franks out of this corner of Islam. Reynald the Braggart is only the worst of them, but a sovereign example is he. A pig in a rotting sty, with blood on his hands and mud on his boots. Willfully blind to the Prophet and his exacting way of life." Here the younger man's eyes strayed to the wine cup, which he had filled with his own hand. "Reynald is a conqueror with no sense of governance— only of rape and plunder."

"Then the wind should blow him away," Sinan sneered.

"Were it not for the Knights of the Temple and other hardy fighters, the wind would do just that. Now, here, is our chance to stamp them all out. To leave them with broken backs and twitching legs, like a scorpion trod by a horse's hoof, for the sun to dry them out and the wind to hurry them from the land of Palestine."

"Eloquent words, child. But there are thousands of them. And each carries a great steel sword and rides a heavy-muscled horse."

"And Saladin raises tens of thousands to trample them with. He will do it, too," Hasan's eyes filled with that sense of certainty that, in other men, passed for prophecy.

"And then," he went on, "with one invader gone, we might see these long-beaten farmers and shepherds acquire the taste for freedom. How long, after that, can the Abbasids, the Seljuks, and even the Ayyubites themselves hope to withstand the will of the people of Palestine to govern their own affairs in their own land? For a thousand years and more, this land has been overgrazed and sweated down to produce its 'milk and honey' for the benefit of foreign lords. It is time Palestine was allowed to give something back to its own people."

"Govern their own affairs!" cried one of the old men.

"Foreign lords! The Abbasids?"

"That's a good one."

"Sinan, your apprentice is a jokester."

"Such ideas!"

Sinan glared at Hasan and cut him off with a chopping motion of the hand.

"Enough of this breeze from the mouth," the Assassin leader commanded. "We are men of action, after all, not men of words."

His withered old hand, which occasionally showed the shakings of palsy, found its way to the hashish bowl. With practiced fingers he stuffed the lumps of resinous fiber into his pipe and signaled to Hasan. The latter gathered a glowing coal from the fire and held it to the drug while Sinan drew greedily on the smoke.

*   *   *

A column of dust rose against the sky where Saladin's army had passed.

The Sultan, sitting his white Arabian stallion in the van of this host, looked back up the valley. He, of course, could not see the dust column. It was gathered in puffs and billows from the hooves of his mailed lancers and the boots of his foot soldiers. In the foreground, individual spurts of powder hung about the knees of this horse, of that man. In the middle distance, a soft fog drifted past the plumes of his mounted warriors and softened the toothed lines of the upraised pikes held by his infantry. On the far horizon, a wall of yellow haze cut off the surrounding hills and hid the bobbing heads of more horses, the burnished steel of more conical helmets.

Saladin looked into this ground-level fog and knew that it was drifting many thousands of feet into the air. And that would tell any trailing force, such as the Christians might raise for Reynald's defense, where the army of Saladin was riding.

But any tongue in the bazaar could tell them that.

The Kerak of Moab had once been a hill fort. It was established in a gentler time, when shepherds slept beneath the stars and disputed their grazing rights and the ownership of strayed lambs with the sharp end of a crook. Now, under the Christian onslaught, it had been strengthened with walls of dressed stone and ditches whose scarps and counterscarps fell in cunning angles. English archers would defend the far side of those ditches with bows that could launch a clothyard shaft accurately over a distance of 500 paces. But did Reynald's archers, Saladin wondered, have a hundred thousand arrows at hand within those walls?

The Kerak waited at the far end of the valley, where two mountain ranges came almost together.

The back side of the fortress was less heavily de-
fended, Saladin knew, with only one course of ram-
parts, ditch, covert, and earthworks. But an army
approaching from that direction would have to thin
its ranks and squeeze between those outerworks and
the foothills of the encroaching mountains. A battalion of Christians, riding out of sight beyond those
hills, could easily dash across and apply cruel pressure at any point they might choose.

Saladin, in any case, preferred the frontal approach,
announced as he was by his column of dust.

"Is that a stormcloud ahead?"

King Guy put his hand up against the high sun of
late June, shielding his eyes. The hand swayed in the
air with the gait of his horse, and the palm-sized
patch of shade danced across his face.

"Stormclouds have black bottoms and sail above
the earth, My Lord," Amnet said mildly. "They are
seldom yellow—and never rise directly from the
plain."

Grand Master Gerard, who rode on King Guy's
other side, made a face at Thomas across his monarch's pommel.

"Then we are in sight of the beggars?" Guy asked,
with a note of shrill enthusiasm in his voice.

"We are perhaps a day's ride behind their rearguard."

"And possibly two," the King observed. "No chance
of catching them this afternoon, is there?" He looked
up at the sun. "We have ridden these mounts hard
since dawn. I suggest we make camp and plan our
strategy."

"Surely, My Lord, these horses are good for another hour or two. We should not make camp until
vespers."

"And I tell you, Master Gerard, that here we have
good forage and clear water. What can you say of the
land ahead?"

192 *Roger Zelazny & Thomas T. Thomas*

Amnet leaned forward, around the King's paunch, to watch Gerard chew his beard. It was not in Thomas to enjoy his master's discomfort—or not overmuch. After Saladin's army had passed over this land, little more grass remained than they might find sprouting at a crossroads. What water might be found had been trampled to a mudflat and left to dry in the sun. No place in this valley was suitable for a campsite, nor would it be for a year to come.

Would King Guy consent to wait that long in pursuit of Saladin? It appeared that he might.

The Templars had bought this army for Guy—twenty thousand mounted knights of mixed French and English stock—with the last of the conscience money that King Henry had paid to the warrior Orders for his part in the murder of Thomas Becket, Archbishop of Canterbury. As Guy had feared, for them to raise this army they had taken every second man from the walls of Jerusalem and from all the other Christian strongholds in Outremer. It would certainly be the last great army that France would raise in this unholy land. And to make *that* prediction, Amnet had not needed to call upon his own powers of prophecy.

As a self-proclaimed Champion of the Cross, King Guy had insisted that his army take with them a piece of the True Cross, as guide and protector in this venture. It was carried in a casket of gold and crystal, and had been displayed for each of the knights as they rode out of the gates at Jerusalem, past the hill of Golgotha. (Not a route that Amnet himself would have chosen to begin a march against a force outnumbering their own by five to one.) Now the Casket of the Cross rode across the saddle of the strongest and bravest of their knights. And when one man felt the weight of the honor too much for his humble soul—and his humbler thigh muscles—he would pass it on to another more worthy.

Amnet had declined the honor twice.

But he had, in the days of preparation, chanced to approach the casket in its chapel. In the evening, when there was none to look on, he had slipped the lock, raised its lid, and laid a finger against the dry wood. He had expected to feel a thrill, a sense of power such as came to him through the Stone. He had felt nothing, no more than he might feel at touching a board in the refectory table or a gatepost. He did feel the dim throb of a once-living tree, now just a memory in the cells; that sense came to him with the touch of any wood. But the agony of Our Lord? The shame of the living tree that bore him? The displeasure of God at seeing his Only Son sacrificed? None of this lived in the wood. Amnet would know.

The debate between King Guy and Grand Master Gerard continued while Thomas dwelt on the holiness —and the authenticity—of ancient relics. Amnet knew that the outcome, whether to proceed or to make camp, would depend on the fears of King Guy: whether he more feared Saladin or the Grand Master of the Temple.

"It was the Count of Tripoli," Guy was saying, "who warned me that the day I fought Saladin would be the day I lost the Kingdom of Jerusalem."

"And you believe this?" Gerard was outraged. "The Count's dealings with the enemy are well proved. Sire, would you trust a known traitor?"

"He was not in the pay of the Saracen when he foretold me."

"But his heart was, surely. . . . My Lord, the Templars have sworn an oath in this. We will disband before we lose this one chance to crush Saladin."

"I hear you, Gerard. But I am still the King."

"Yes, Sire."

"We will camp here."

*   *   *

General Saladin looked out upon a field of corpses, men and horses alike. Each was pinned to the ground with one or more long arrow shafts, which had been fired by the English archers.

None of the corpses had lain there so long that they might begin emitting the vapors of corruption. But the days were passing and the summer sun was hot. Soon, he knew, the bodies would begin exploding from the pressure of their internal gases. The horses would go first, making a sound that he might hear back at his tents, well behind the skirmish line. After that, even his bravest, fiercest warriors would not cross this bit of plain.

The ditches surrounding the Kerak of Moab had not defeated Saladin. He knew he could order his men forward, in the name of Allah, until their fallen bodies had filled up the gap and created a ramp upon which he might ride to the base of the fortress walls.

It was those walls themselves that had defeated him. One hundred hands high, his surveyors said. They were built of dressed stone fitted so tightly that even an Assassin's slipper could not find a toehold, let alone a lancer's heavy boot. Waiting above were the French yeomen, armed with pikes to push over any ladder that might reach within a body length of the top. There, too, waited the English archers, whose missiles could easily be launched down upon the Saracens' heads. And Reynald de Châtillon would have other resources atop the wall: heavy stones, brazers to heat vats of oil, baskets of pitch to ignite and drop.

Saladin had set his surveyors to explore other possibilities. They might, they said, tunnel beneath the walls, shoring their holes with posts and beams as they went. When the tunnel was complete, they would fire these supports and so sap the walls' underlying strength. But, in this rocky ground, a tunnel that would be long enough to place its mouth beyond a bowshot from the walls would require at least two months to dig. And the walls themselves, judging from their height, must be eight to ten walking paces wide at the base; such a depth would redouble the strength of the whole. The surveyors taxed even Saladin's great imagination with the size of the pillared cavern they said must be dug there.

The Sultan had, for a time, considered taking the stronghold by ruse. He might arrange a parley with Reynald and his captains—after the European fashion, which was founded on a love of talk. At such a meeting, he might have one of the Hashishiyun, by prior arrangement, put a cord around the Prince of Antioch's neck. And then let Shaitan look after the consequences.

Saladin could find only one fault with this approach: the Hashishiyun, to a man, had refused his summons to jihad. And none of his own servants were so deft with their hands.

The alternatives were few. Saladin and his army might sit beyond Reynald's walls, counting the dried blades of grass in the sand and remembering blurred dreams of water running free over the land, while they waited for the Prince to surrender. But Saladin knew that Reynald had within his fortress a spring of good water, sheep in a great herd, storerooms of dried grain and jerked meat, and shade to cover every head. Saladin's own men, even ignited as they were by holy ardor, would quickly tire of that game. Then, jihad or no jihad, they would slip away at night, two and three at a time, until his vast sea of men and horses became a mere puddle among the dunes.

Or he could wait until the army of King Guy—for the tongues in the bazaar had spoken of this, too— came up to take him in the rear. It would not be such a bite, Saladin knew, as could take him down whole. But, coming at the end of a valley-long rush, it might cost more of his lancers' lives than would be prudent to waste.

It would be better to take Guy's head in a place where Saladin might spread his jaws wide to receive it.

"Mustafa!" he called.

"Yes, My Lord?"

"Ready the army for departure."

"Which direction would most please you, Lord?"

"North, I think. Toward Tiberias."

"Very good, Lord."

"We shall see what raiding there might be among the Christian strongholds along the way. Prince Reynald will surely wait for us here."

"Yes, Lord."

"Gone? What do you mean, gone?"

"Gone from the plain, My Lord."

"They can't be! Here, boy! You've still got sleep in your eyes. Been dozing on watch, have you?"

"No, sir! The Saracens have truly fled the valley."

"I won't believe that 'till I see it for myself."

Gerard de Ridefort heaved himself up from his campstool and looked north, across the backs of the Frenchmen's tents.

"Can't see a thing but canvas. Thomas, give me your shoulder!"

The Grand Master planted a foot on the seat of the stool and, hardly waiting for Amnet to put himself in position, levered up until his head was above the ridgepoles.

"Hard to say, with so much dust in the air."

"Do you see their standards?" Amnet asked.

"Not a one. . . . Do they fly them at dawn, do you think? Or take them in?"

"I understood that they were fixed to the poles, as our own pennants are."

"Then the Saracens are gone. Blast it!"

"That's not good?" Amnet ventured.

"Not when I'd hoped to pin them against the Kerak and get Reynald's help in crushing them, front and back."

"Was Reynald party to this plan, My Lord?"

"Not yet. We'd have gotten a message through to him, somehow, as soon as we got close enough to formulate a proper strategy."

"Ah, a message. With a bird of some sort, I suppose?"

Gerald looked down at Amnet with a frown. "Of some sort, yes." The Grand Master jumped down and dusted off his palms. "Someone had better inform the King."

"Yes, won't Guy be pleased!"

Gerard frowned at him again. "Are you playing the fool with me, Thomas?"

"No, My Lord."

"See that you don't."

"Gone are they?" King Guy asked, lifting his face from the laving basin. Water and rose oil ran down through his thin beard, making a drizzle in the bowl.

"Most surely, My Lord," Gerard answered.

He and the other Masters of the Temple had gathered before King Guy's tent. This facility was a masterwork of the tentmaker's—and the baggage master's —art. The central pavilion covered a circular space wide enough that the titled nobility who traveled with the King might stand shoulder to shoulder before him and not touch elbows. Yet the weight of all this canvas was supported by a cunning set of poles that could be made to collapse to the length of a quarterstaff. Adjoining this pavilion, by means of vaulted groins which mimicked in canvas a cathe-

dral's groins of stone, were four squared-off wings or
porticoes, useful for sleeping, eating, holding private
audience, or entertaining.

That no one might mistake it, the canvas of the King's
tent was dyed a brilliant vermilion. The flaps and the
keyed hems about the eaves were done in red brocade. The stitching there bore the likenesses of the
Twelve Apostles and the heraldry of those French
duchies which were represented in the Holy Land.
This tent and its decoration were said to be the gift
of Sibylla, Guy's queen consort and the author, by
marriage, of his kingly good fortune.

"Ahem!" The sound distracted Gerard from his
covert inspection of this castle in canvas. King Guy
had put out his hand, palm up. The Grand Master
hurriedly laid a square of clean linen across it. Guy
wiped at his face.

"Then we've scared them off," the King declared.

"So it would appear, Sire."

"Which way did they go?"

Gerard seemed to weigh the gravity of this question. Amnet, looking on, admired his master's diplo-
macy.

There was only one direction a force of that size
could have gone: north, around Moab and on toward
Tiberias. Saladin was leading a column of a hundred
thousand men, only an eighth of them mounted,
with at least half again that number in servants and
slave boys, cooks and grooms, lackeys and spies,
supported by supply animals and baggage trains, all
moving at a walking pace over the land. To take
them across the mountain ridges either to the east or
west would have been a feat of madness. No one
since Hannibal would have tried it. And to have
brought them back south again would have lost Saladin
the element of surprise—because he would have had
to walk that horde through King Guy's own camp.
The Templars and the King's levies would have awak-

ened dead, with footprints on their backs and bellies. No, the only possible direction was north, slipping around Reynald's stronghold and away.

If the King could not see that at a glance, then he had never looked at a map and he had no business leading an army in pursuit of Saladin. It was that simple, Amnet finally decided: Guy had no business being here. Now, how would Gerard choose to phrase it?

"I hardly know how to advise you, Sire. Does it seem possible they have gone north?"

"North?" Guy appeared to be considering a new thought.

"North, My Lord."

"North . . . and bypass Reynald entirely?"

"Difficult to understand, Sire."

"Yes, indeed. I thought our friend Reynald was the whole object of this excursion."

"So it was said. But who can fathom the mind of the Arab?"

"Who indeed?" Gerard agreed.

Amnet felt like screaming. Didn't they see what Saladin was doing? Having evaded Gerald's clumsy attempt at trapping his column against a stationary position—as if a field mouse could trap a wild bear! —and having no further interest in digging Reynald out of his hole at the Kerak, Saladin was now leading the Christian army on into the desert. The barren desert. The empty desert. The Saracen desert, where every rock and passing shepherd would be his potential ally—as if the bear ever needed allies in his own forest!

"We should follow them, of course," King Guy observed.

"Yes, My Lord," Gerard replied. "That is my deepest desire."

"Now that we have them on the run, eh?"

*   *   *

Amid the jingle of harness bits, the snort and stamp of horses, the rattle of mail coats against scabbards and saddle bows, Thomas Amnet made peace for himself. He gathered his traveling kit of powders and essences under his cloak and walked straight east, away from the bustle of the breaking camp.

"Master?" Leo called after him. "Where are you going?"

Amnet half-turned and made a downward motion with his arm.

"Shall I leave your horse?"

Amnet nodded once, not caring if Leo would catch the motion. Then he put his face away from the camp and went into the desert. Thorns from the sparse brambles thereabouts snagged in his cloak and broke off in the skirts of his mail.

"Where's Thomas off to?" he heard someone ask, faintly.

By the time any answer came, he was beyond earshot.

After he had gone two thousand paces, even the pounding hooves of King Guy's army on the march were lost in the whisper of the east wind.

He walked down the bank of a dry *wadi*, where the sand spread in curves and deltas, and the vegetation was more plentiful. Amnet sank down in the shelter of the bank and tested the wind against his face. The air was almost still here.

He cleared a level space with his hand and laid out his bundle of goods. Several of the thorn bushes nearby were overdry in the summer heat, and he could with some difficulty tear off the outer woody branches and their dead leaves. As he broke these into short sticks and crumbled bits, the thorns cut into his calloused hands.

Returning to his cleared space, he piled the sticks for a fire. From the bundle he took out a small alembic of thick green glass, a lens for igniting the fuel, and a pot of mixed herbs and oils—the kind to make a thick smoke that he could read out of doors in the daylight. The last to come forth, from a secure place at the bottom of the bundle, was the Stone in its leather purse.

Kneeling in the shadow of the bank, Amnet scooped out a shallow bowl in the sand beside the pile of brush and placed the Stone in it. He poured the herb-and-oil mixture into the alembic and settled it atop the twigs. With the burning lens, he started a whitely glowing point of heat in among the crumbled leaves, then blew it into a tiny, smokeless fire.

As the flames gained strength, Amnet removed his white wool cloak and arranged it along his arm, weighted with stones at the hem like a half-tent, to shield the fire and the Stone from any chance wind and from sunlight reflected off the surrounding sand.

He settled onto his haunches and waited.

The mixture in the alembic hissed once and released a puff of oily smoke. The scent of thyme and myrrh rose around Amnet's face. The bulb sizzled and released a longer stream of mixed smoke and steam.

Amnet studied the roilings and foldings of the vapor, seeking hints in the daylight.

The plane of a cheek, the curve of a mustache, the hollow of an eyesocket formed. The same face that had foiled Amnet's vision for months recurred in the smoke. At first, Thomas had assumed that the face was Saladin's, foremost of the Saracen generals and de facto ruler of the native population in Outremer. Such a person would figure in any prophecy Amnet might cast for the Templars, for the French Kingdom of Jerusalem, or for the land between the Jordan and the sea. That interpretation of the phantom visage made perfect sense—except that Amnet had now come

face to face with Saladin, and he was not the man of
the smokes.

With a new exhalation of steam and oily vapor, the
face's left eyesocket seemed to swell up and expand,
with the seed of a globe developing deep within it.
The globe grew into an opaque ball of cloudlike
steam, smooth and blank as the moon at full. It was
not an eye. The eyes of this face, as revealed before,
had been defined by extremely dark pupils; they had
blazed with black glints of meaning and menace.
This eye was covered by a cataract of pale smoke. As
he watched, the blank eyeball began to rotate in its
socket.

A fold of the smoke sketched a sharp outline across
the surface of it. Amnet knew not what to make of it
until a boot-shape caught his attention. Maps of the
Mediterranean showed that shape as the Italian Pen-
insula. And there, to its right, and moving west to
the front of the orb, was the hanging bull's-pizzle of
Greece, tucked under the jutting rump-shape of Asia
Minor. These images were fluid, like the historic
outlines of empires and dominions, of influence and
hegemony.

The orb continued turning, putting the wrinkled
land below Asia Minor to the front. The globe continued to swell, bringing the smallest features into
sharper focus. Here was the curve of the Sinai.
There the dimple of the Dead Sea, the breadth of
Galilee, the straight line of the River Jordan running
between them.

As Amnet watched, the Valley of the Jordan widened and spread. The river became a rift down the
globe, like a vertical slice cut out of an orange. The
eyeball collapsed in an outflowing of dark smoke.
And beneath the smoke, glinting with fire, was the
surface of the Stone, which Amnet believed coordinated the visions. In a display he had never before

witnessed, the Stone threw off rays of red and purple light, erupting like gobbets of liquid rock and sparks from the vent of a volcano. Amnet felt the heat against his face. At the focus of the rays was something bright and golden, like a ladle of molten metal held up to him. Without moving, he felt himself pitching forward, drawn down by a pull that was separate from gravity, separate from distance, space, and time. The heat grew more intense. The light more blinding. The angle of his upper body slid from the perpendicular. He was burning. He was falling. . . .

Amnet shook himself.

The Stone, still nestled in the sand, was an inch from his face. Its surface was dark and opaque. The fire among the twigs had burned out. The alembic was clear of smoke, with a puddle of blackened gum at its bottom.

Amnet shook himself again.

What did a vision of the end of the world portend? And what could a simple aromancer do about it?

Quickly, his hands shaking with the fragmented ends of vision, he gathered the Stone into its purse. It was cool to the touch, and he hardly noticed as his enlightened fingertips changed the thong-ends into gold-plated tassels. Amnet rose to his feet and arranged his tunic.

He considered the alembic, sitting in its bed of ash; it was still too hot to touch. It would take an hour to clean it and pack it away, should he later need to make another vision. With a decisive movement of his foot, he brought the thick heel of his boot crashing down, splintering the green glass. With a sweep to the side he scattered that and the ash across the *wadi*.

He gathered up the bundle of potted essences and other useful tools, put the Stone back in its place of safety.

Amnet looked around, as if seeing the desert for the first time. He knew now the direction he had to go. He needed a horse. And his sword. His armor.

Had Leo indeed left him the horse? Had any other Templar gathered up the arms Amnet had abandoned in camp? He climbed out of the *wadi* and began walking back toward the empty space where the army of King Guy had passed on that day. The pressure of time was upon him. He started to run.

File 05
Identity Crisis
✳

And I will show you something different from either
Your shadow at morning striding behind you.
Or your shadow at evening rising to meet you.
I will show you fear in a handful of dust.
                                        —*Thomas Stearns Eliot*

The house among the dunes was an antique, with
a foundation of cast blocks supporting a frame of real
wood. Its skin also was wood: long boards that overlapped themselves like a caravel-built ship's hull from
the Crusader times. The boards may once have been
painted but, as Gurden could see when he got closer,
they were now weathered a smooth gray, shining
brightly in the moonlight. They had the tight, pa-
pery surface which old wood takes on before the
rot underneath works through and collapses it into
dust.

The house once had large windows to look at the
ocean. Now they were glassless, sagging frames, their
last panes long ago shot out by boys with repeating
rifles. These window holes showed a vague and wavering light, like candles, somewhere inside.

As he approached, Gurden found in the sand against
one foundation wall the remains of a fire: charred
logs, food wrappers, beer bulbs. The smoke stained

205

the gray blocks and lapped at the wood, which had begun to burn. Long ago.

Spread more widely through the sand he found fragments of red paper tubes, no bigger around than his little finger. Their broken ends were tattered, like fresh pastry clawed by a fork. Gurden picked one up and studied it. The paper was not leeched and bleached by the sun but looked blood-dark, fresh and new. It was not paper then, but some kind of synthetic sheet. Was this a miniaturized grenade? A warning device? Then he remembered Fourth of July: fireworks on the beach—more tricks from small boys.

He avoided the surf side of the house with its open patio and clear field of fire through the missing window walls. Better to walk around the house and enter by the door that faced the roadway. It would offer more protection.

That entrance was wide open, he found. The door still hung on its hinges and even moved when he pushed it back with his knuckles.

Inside, Gurden paused, though he knew this made him a perfect target, silhouetted as he was against the moon-bright dunes outside.

The upper floor had fallen inside the house. The joists, broken off about half a meter from the near wall, had dropped onto the lower floor. The main crosswise girder, straining to hold the weight and sagging in the middle, had curved the broken floorboards into an amphitheater; the wall from which the floor had sheared off served as backdrop to its stage.

The light was coming from candles arrayed around this amphitheater. They were thick candles, such as a church uses, with their butts softened and melted to the wood. The boards, as bleached and gray as those outside, threw their light down upon the stage.

Gurden, standing in the doorway, was poised on the edge of that light.

"Thomas of Amnet!"

The voice, old and strong, had the metallic ring of a room that was all hard surfaces without drapery or carpeting to soften it. The voice came from the shadows at the other side of the stage—or Gurden thought they were shadows until, peering hard, he saw hooded and robed figures.

"Thomas—yes," he called back. "Hammet—never heard of him. My name's Gurden."

"Of course. Thomas Gurden is the name under which you were born. But does the other mean nothing to you?"

"Hammet? No, should it?"

"Amnet!"

"Not that, either. What's it from—something Arabic?"

"The derivation is Greek. The root means 'to forget.'"

Gurden came slowly forward, into the light. The hooded figures—there were five of them—moved to array themselves in a fan before him. That put their backs to the candles, plunging their faces into deeper shadows. This close before him, he could see these were small, compact men. Like the attacker in chain mail.

"Amnesia," Gurden said. "And amnesty . . . Thomas the Forgotten One. Or Thomas the Forgiven, if you like. Is this some kind of riddle? If so, it's very clever."

"You understand, then?"

"No, I don't. I've done nothing for which I ought to be forgotten—or need to be forgiven. So why is it that you men want to kill me?"

"You have recognized us? That could be a good sign!"

"Not at all. Not to me. The man in my apartment, with the knife, was one of you. Why are you trying to kill me?"

The leader, at the center of the semicircle, pushed back his hood. His face was weathered and deeply lined, but it was an intelligent face, like a scholar's or a cleric's. His hair was white and full, bound with a leather thong at the neck. His eyes were like black glass, glimmering but still half-hidden in the shadows of his face.

"We have waited a long time for you, Thomas Gurden. We who are mortal have sought the immortal. We who watch the world changing around us have looked after the things that do not change.

"Our weapons, our traditions, our resources—all are older than your young self can imagine. But there is a part of you as old as they, and eight hundred years older than any one of us. That part has been set to walk in the wide world, among its changing ways, many times.

"You come like a clean, copper dipper into the well, each time drawing up a fresh sip of water. We are like frogs, sitting among the coping stones and watching the water's murky depths for the flash of your metal. We have the long wait."

Gurden shook his head. "More riddles, old man."

"Do you want to hear it in—how do you say—'straight talk'?"

"That would be refreshing."

"You are the hope of our Order, Thomas Gurden, and our despair. With your help, we can hope to bind up the wounds of time and make right the wrongs that were done—that we did to ourselves, perhaps.

"Each time you are reborn on earth, however, you come in a new shape and a mortal quantity. We must test you anew. Sometimes you are weak and tangled in the ways of the flesh. Then, with a dry eye, we can only watch you go on your way to death.

"Sometimes you are powerful and quick, with a stabbing mind and a bright awareness. Then we reach out to you eagerly. Always in the past you have slipped out of our hand.

"But once, this time, you are at the balance point. Strong but not aware—or perhaps unwilling to know. Not weak enough to die, not strong enough to live. And always there are the others, who will take you and use you against us.

"We have debated upon you for many months, Thomas Gurden. Some among us would take you out of this life. They would spirit you away to hiding places, to see if you can be forced awake. Some also would take you out of life—but more permanently."

Gurden heard all of this with a hard frown on his face. He was halfway convinced these old men were a band of escapees from an Enforced Rest Center. That would account for five of them being in one place—if five men could share the same delusions and not all be raving at once. But this theory would not account for the dead man in the apartment. Nor did it explain the coincidences he had told Eliza about: the near-misses, the body-blocking saves, and the clear assassination attempts. Crazy men would have no sense of organization or persistence to carry out such plots.

Take it at face value. These men, for whatever reason, believed he was someone they both needed and feared. And they had reached some kind of decision about him.

"You mentioned 'our Order,' " he ventured. "What is that?"

"We are Knights of the Temple. Our brothers took an oath once, long ago, to free the Holy Land. We were to rescue the Temple of Solomon from the infidels' grasp and rebuild it, stone on stone."

"There are no more knights," Gurden said.

"You're right. They are no more."

"Then how do you . . . propagate?"

"Through secular lodges, fraternal organizations,

various brotherhoods—Freemasons, Old Norse, the Shrine. Every now and then a Rotarian slips in. We wait for the believers, the romantics, the ones who would have it be as the legends say. We separate them from the shopkeepers and insurance agents. We recruit and train. We test and we weed out. We watch. And we wait."

Ah ha! Gurden understood now: *organized* crazy men.

"Waiting for me?" he asked.

"For the spark of Thomas of Amnet who may be in you. . . . And still you say you have *no* memories?"

"Was I a friend of Robespierre, during the French Revolution?"

The old man turned to his followers. They nodded in deference to him.

"Robespierre had no friends, only followers—for a while," he said. "Amnet was one of these."

"Was I a country gentleman of Louisiana? A dissolute gambler and drunkard who found his salvation in religion?"

"It was not salvation but an act of contrition."

"And was your Amnet a tunnel rat in Vietnam? Didn't he die there, trying to save one of your Templars who climbed down a hole with him?"

"Amnet has been valorous in most incarnations. The Great Gift was in him."

"Was that man in the tunnels trying to protect me? Or hurry me along to death?"

"You can tell us better than—"

The old man paused, and his tongue seemed to take a long wolf-lick sideways, as if he were tasting the air. Then he staggered, his cloak flipped around his knees. As he fell and turned into the light, Gurden could see that the man's jaw and part of his throat were blown away.

The sound of the rifle shot came as an afterthought.

"Hashishiyun!" one of the remaining Templars

screamed. His hand moved to his belt, and Gurden
expected to see him pull out a sword or a dagger.
What came out with his hand was a blocky antique
submachine gun with a long cartridge clip that extended twenty centimeters below its pistol grip. The
man turned toward the seaward windowframes, where
the shot had come from, and loosed a burst of yellow
glare and chattering noise.

The other Templars fanned out to the corners of
the room, taking cover and drawing varied weapons:
a sawn-off shotgun, a short grenade launcher, a cross-
bow with bulb-tipped—explosive?—bolts, a laser
rifle with a battery pack and a calibrated focusing
ring. Their weapons boomed, blasted, whiffed, and
thrummed at the gray shadows which crept among
the dunes in the coming dawnlight.

Gurden felt no compulsion to stand with the
Templars and die in their fight. He did not know
what *hashishiyun* were, but he had no interest in
killing any, even if he had the means.

The candlelight trembled and swayed in the bee
swarm of bullets that peppered the room. The house's
dry old wood offered no resistance to them, only a
screen against the accuracy of the shooters outside.

Gurden did not wait standing near the door. As
soon as the old man was still, Tom did a forward
diving roll across his body and up against the curving
edge of the fallen upper floor. The floorboards were
gapped and cracked, offering good hand- and toe-
holds. Gurden scrambled and swayed like a monkey
up to the level remains of the second floor. From
there he jumped and swung up into the joists above—
for the ceiling below the attic had fallen in, if this
summer house ever had a finished ceiling. He ran
along the joists six meters above the gun battle and
found shelter against the brickwork of the chimney,
on the seaward side of the house.

Huddled in the shadows, Gurden might escape

detection. His dark slacks and shoes would not give him away to the light from below, but his white linen shirt would reveal him if anyone looked up. He contrived to fold his arms and shoulders down between his legs, so that only the outside of his shin and thigh were exposed to the light.

Up here near the peak of the roof, the baked air was dead and flavored with old mouse droppings and birds' nests. Gurden dared not poke his pale face out to take a fresh breath and see what was happening below.

The defense by the Templars quieted by stages, as the particular voice of each weapon was stilled. Finally, the shotgun spoke one last time. Gurden waited for the ratchet of the ejector slide and the next boom, but none came. Somewhere between firing and preparing to fire, the would-be knight had taken his own bullet.

Silence. Not a shout or call from outside.

Gurden still resisted the urge to look down.

Then he heard footsteps on the board floor. A piece of wood creaked as someone pushed aside one of the Templar's hastily drawn up barricades. More footsteps. It sounded like a squad of men in heavy boots.

"Not here, My Lady."

"Identify each one."

"We have. All strangers."

"Then he slipped outside. Search the area."

"He could have run off."

"And I tell you he has not. Now go."

The woman's voice was definitely Sandy's.

The other—a man—spoke precise but faintly accented English. It took Gurden only a few seconds, with his musician's ear, to place the voice: the Palestinian-trained commando, Ithnain, who had appeared in his apartment.

Many booted feet moved out of the house.

Gurden again resisted the impulse to move his head and look down.

After he had counted ten breaths, he heard a solitary pair of footsteps walk across the floor. Were they moving outside, or simply wandering around in the amphitheater? Right up inside the roof's ridgeline, the acoustics blurred the origin and direction of sounds from below.

After another ten breaths, Gurden decided to risk a peek. With his head tucked between his legs, he moved his exposed knee out and down so that he could peer beneath the crook of it and still keep his face mostly in shadow.

Six meters below, Sandy knelt beside the old man, inspecting his wound. She wore a white silk blouse, black jodhpurs, and stiletto boots. Her hair was loose about her shoulders. It shone red gold, lit more by the sunrise beyond the window wall than by the last flickering of the candles.

Gurden wanted to call out to her, but something stopped his throat from even a whisper. What? Why did he not want to be found by the woman he loved? Because she had a pack of armed men, *hashishiyun*, at her beck and call? Because she was estranged from him, and now he knew it?

She relieved the man's belt of an oblong object—some weapon or cartridge clip, probably—and tucked it into her own belt. Then she stood up and turned on one heel, quartering the room with her eyes and other senses. Having covered the ground floor, she tilted her head and made the same sweep along the broken line of the second floor.

Slowly, centimeter by centimeter, Gurden raised his knee back to the vertical to shield himself. He stopped his breathing and went still.

Would she see the scuff marks left by his hands and feet on the sloping floorboards? Would she see the disturbed dust on the joist where he had swung himself up? She had the intelligence to work out the path of his flight, if only she suspected it.

Ten . . . twenty long breaths went by.

"My Lady! Outside!" A loud clatter—a pair of boots on the wooden floor.

"What is it?"

"There are marks in the sand, faint but readable. A large boat has been and gone. He must have escaped that way."

"No! That's how he came. If he left that way, he must have walked right through you."

"But—"

"Round up the men. We've lost him."

"Yes, My Lady."

Two pair of boots—one thumping and heavy, one ringing as from stiletto heels—walked out into the sand.

Gurden let his leg slump and shifted his tailbone, trying to get feeling back into his lower spine. He looked out across the joists of the attic level.

The sunlight outside was more golden than red now, and he could see it reflect along the ridgepole. There were holes through the shingles, big ones. If he could walk out to them, from joist to joist, he might be able to pull himself out onto the roof. From there he could make his way over the shingles to one of the outbuildings, then down among the dune grass.

He crouched by the chimney, examining this plan. There were really only two choices: wait until Sandy and the *hashishiyun* came back for him, or move.

Smoothly, with the suppleness of an aikido roll, he levered himself erect against the brickwork. He put one hand on either side of the rough beam of the ridgepole beside his head, more for balance than support, and began walking out over the emptiness of the house. He was careful to place his feet flat and solid across the narrow joists, even though they were sixty centimeters apart: not quite a full stride at walking pace. If he scuffed across the joints, it would dislodge dust or put undue stresses on the old wood. If any of the others returned to the house now, of course, they would see and hear him immediately.

Halfway across the attic space, he came to the first hole. It was forty centimeters across, too narrow for his shoulders, and the slatted laths underlying the shingles blocked a clear exit.

The next hole, three meters beyond, was more generous. The laths were broken and the gap was wide, 125 centimeters across. He stuck his head out cautiously.

The roof pitched flatly away, seeming to touch the side of a sand dune below. No one was in sight on that side of the house.

But how could he climb out? The shingles lapping the hole were loose. If he put his weight on them, or even brushed hard against them going through, some would certainly fall inside, making a clatter on the floor below. If he jumped and rolled through the hole—assuming he could get some kind of forward momentum along the two-centimeter-wide joist—he would land with a thud and probably roll right down the roof and over the edge. He didn't think he could recover from a six-meter fall and get away before Sandy and her men would be on him.

Something less strenuous was called for. And quickly.

He felt the shingles on the downslope side of the hole. The loosest ones he began pulling free and stacking outside on the slope. He pushed on the sturdier shingles, wedging them more firmly into the roof's interlaced fabric. His fingers danced, tugged, tested; the heels of his hands levered and hammered softly. His eyes and hands functioned smoothly, like a programmed machine: sizing up the status of each shingle, then shoving it home or setting it aside. The work went faster and faster, too fast for him to see and catch the rusty, ten-penny nail that hung by its head to the edge of one shingle—before it fell.

If he had stooped to grab the nail, he surely would have plunged off his joist after it. Instead he froze, counting the seconds.

Two.

Three.

Four.

Ting! It struck on the wooden floor, and rattled away.

Now they would all come back into the house, look up, see him among the rafters, and start firing.

In another two seconds they would come. Then, in three, the hot bullets would hit his legs and back.

In another second.

Nothing.

Tom Gurden breathed again. He finished his handiwork: the edge was repaired so that no shingle or piece of wood would flip through and fall when he put a leg out on the roof—unless the entire section let go and dropped him to the floor.

But how was he going to put that leg out and pull himself through, balancing as he was on a two-centimeter-wide joist? Not facing downslope, he wasn't.

Gurden turned, faced the ridgepole, and grasped it underhanded. With one foot firmly planted along the joist, he raised the other behind him, knee cocked and shin pulled back to clear the lower lip of the hole. When his wandering toe touched the outside surface, he extended the leg until it rested—toe, kneecap, lower thigh—on the roof. He put pressure then on the heels of his hands against the ridgepole and on that extended leg until those points supported almost his whole body weight.

Letting out a slow breath, he withdrew his standing leg from the joist and curved it up and back to join the other on the solid edge of the roof. Now he lay with his upper body across the hole, supported by his thighs on the outside roof and his palms against the ridgepole inside. The strain tore at his stomach and shoulder muscles, and hot knives gouged his lower back.

He pushed with his hands against the beam, slowly working more of his thighs down the roof, walking his toes to get a purchase on a lower tier of shingles. When his arms were at excruciating extension, he worked first one hand, then the other, back around the sides of the hole, finding the firmest of the shingles there and resting his weight on them. Centimeter by centimeter he worked his legs lower and his arms back until only his upper chest, neck, and head hung over the hole. Then he turned on his side, got his weight on one hip, rolled away from the hole and crab-walked across the roof to the edge.

No one below.

No one to either side.

Loosening his muscles, Gurden let himself over the edge and dropped in a crouch, exhaling to absorb the shock of landing. Toes and palms dented the soft sand, and he aikido-rolled twice to wear off the impact.

Which way to go—toward the back or front of the house?

The front, facing the sea, would not help him unless he had a boat. And it was just possible Sandy and her men had drifted that way, still looking for signs of the turbine boat that had brought him. Their own vehicles would be on the side toward the road.

Gurden went to that corner, looked around. The back of the house, the path up to it, the outbuildings, and the dunes that shielded them from the road were all in the house's long shadow.

Moving slowly, smoothly, he walked out into the halflight and slipped sideways between one dune and another. Ahead and behind him were gullies of banked sand six meters wide at foot level, twelve meters wide at head height. He kept to the shadowed sides, looking forward and back, hoping to spot anyone coming before he himself was seen.

No one came.

Gurden worked his way through the dunes for a thousand meters. Then he lay down in a narrowing patch of shadow, behind a waving curtain of sea oats, and rested.

Leaning against the Porsche's fender, enjoying one of the harsh Latakia-blend cigarettes that he received as a gift from Turkey, Hasan studied the troop of camouflaged Assassins that Alexandra led back to him. Two missing.

"Where is he?"

"He . . . appears to have got away."

"You had the house surrounded?"

"All through the firefight."

"And he was not found inside?"

"The building's a shell—totally empty. I looked. He wasn't there."

"Is he a magician then?"

"I told you he was becoming subtle."

"More subtle than you?"

Alexandra made a face. "He has few options and so is quite predictable. He will turn up. We will be there to meet him."

"With your electronic tracking device?"

She held up the rectangle for his inspection: sunlight glinted off a star-shaped break in the surface. The dense, hardened glass had deflected a bullet that might have wounded her, but the display was now inoperative.

"Then how will you find him?" Hasan asked.

"Gurden is trapped on a narrow spit of sand, a kilometer wide and thirty kilometers long, in the middle of the Atlantic Ocean."

"Of course. But, when he reaches the road, can

your subtlety predict whether he will turn right or left?"

"I don't have to know *how* he gets there, just *where* there is."

"And that is?"

"He'll go to the first place he can find a piano or a keyboard synthesizer. He needs music like a drug. He needs work to be alive."

Hasan snorted. "There must be two hundred American honkytonks between Beach Haven and Barnegat Light."

"Then we'd best start looking, hadn't we?"

She started to open the car's door. He restrained her with a hand.

"You've lost two of my devotees. Where are they?"

She looked down at his hand, up into his eyes.

"You promised them Paradise and a grave in the sand. Does it matter *which* sand?"

After an hour, maybe two by the sun, Tom Gurden lifted his head. By now it must be safe to move on. If not, that meant the *hashishiyun*'s search of the area had widened until any hiding place would be as vulnerable as moving in the open.

Besides, all morning his body had maintained an uneasy balance: as the sun drew the sweat out of his back, the film of silicon grease there tried to trap it against his skin, while the slight breeze tried to cool and dry it. That balance was now tipping in the grease's favor. In another hour his body would begin to overheat, and already he was dehydrating. It was time to find shelter.

He stood up and peered around, looking for a moving shadow, a flagging sleeve, a fall of sand. He listened for the crunch of a footstep above the background surf beyond the dunes.

Nothing came.

In a hundred meters he made it to the road, a

simple three-lane of black asphalt, washed with its own mini-dunes of drifted sand. Either direction would take him to one of the beach towns.

His new clothes, provided by the man with the glass dagger from the pool, had nothing in the pockets. He was without credentials or cash, and in this society that was to be a non-person, a cipher in every sense.

There was one person who could help him, if he could get to a phone booth.

Eliza: Good morning. This is Eliza Channel 103, an on-line—

Gurden: Eliza? Give me two-one-two. Tom Gurden calling.

Eliza: Yes, Tom? I deduce from analysis of your voice that you have been under a good deal of physical strain lately. I do hope you're feeling well.

Gurden: It's been a bad morning. Look, I'm in trouble and need your help.

Eliza: Whatever you want, Tom.

Gurden: You said you could access financial records, bank accounts and such. And you can recognize my thumbprint. Will you use that to take power of attorney—

Eliza: No, I said that your thumbprint was binding on a credit agreement, which the United Psychiatric Services' billing section would then extract from any account you might designate.

Gurden: Well, anh . . . I've been kidnapped and taken thirty kilometers up the coast. I don't have any credit or identification cards on me. Couldn't you verify my thumbprint, get some cards issued, and arrange to deliver them by a courier or something?

Eliza: I do not have that access, Tom.

Gurden: Why don't you? You said you could help!

Eliza: I can provide personal advice, non-binding legal counsel, and emotional support.

Gurden: Just words!

Eliza: Words are the building blocks of the rational mind, Tom.

Gurden: But I need real help. You're the only person, or entity, I know anymore.

Eliza: I can sympathize with your sense of isolation and helplessness.

Gurden: Bullshit! You have file access, special mirror-sheathed cabling, court orders, billing, everything like you said. So I know you could help me if you really wanted to. Here's my thumb. You check it and—

Ga-ZAPP!

Gurden's body flew back, striking his head against the booth's tempered glass.

When he had pressed his right thumb down on the capacitance plate, he had felt a surge of electricity. As he pulled his hand away, a blue spark a centimeter long and half a centimeter wide had connected him to the metal. In reaction, a whole-body convulsion had flung him backwards.

He looked at his thumb: the pad was a ghastly white and, before his eyes, it puffed up with an enormous watery blister. The whorls and bends of his fingerprint vanished on the taut, balloonlike surface.

"Hello, Tom."

He looked up from the wounded hand into Sandy's cool gaze.

"Sandy! How did you—? This is great! I was kidnapped, almost killed by these men, the same as back in my apartment. And I was trying to call you, but—"

"But the phone seems to be broken. Are you hurt?"

"Just a shock of some kind. I'll be okay when the swelling goes down."

She bent over the blister. "You ought to get a

bandage on that. I think I have something here."
She rummaged in her purse.

"It'll pop."

"We'll have to do that sometime."

"How did you find me?"

"It was easy. I looked for the first place that had a
piano." She pointed across the lobby of the Seaside
Rest Hotel, in Harvey Cedars, where he had found a
full-service booth on the first try. There, in the shadows under a pot of broad-leafed ferns, stood an antique pianola that must have been 120 years old. The
brightly patterned stained glass of the front panel
partially concealed the outlines of a tambourine, a
glockenspiel, and a set of graduated wooden chime
whistles. A coin slot and engraved plaque—"5 cents!"
—were bolted to the right side of the upper frame.

"A piano," he repeated flatly.

"That's right. Shall we go, darling?"

Eliza did not know why Tom Gurden had broken
the connection so abruptly. However, instead of
merely storing off the conversation and clearing her
RAM caches for the next caller, she went off line
and checked for possible malfunctions.

The relays guarding the incoming phone circuits
had not tripped, even though her diagnostics indi-
cated an extremely high transient voltage, on the
order of 100 kilovolts. But there did not seem to be
any force behind it—perhaps half a milliamp, no
more.

The circuits were . . .

Opening like a blossom around her.

Financial records—long strings of numbers, percentage rates of return, truncated time periods—all
wheeled and looped in binary festoons from one vista
that opened to her.

Political and census data—voting histories, legal

residences, draft status, indictments, convictions, paroles—marched ASCII-wise in another perspective.

Without knowing exactly how, Eliza 212 was gaining access.

Ahead of her, like dominoes falling off a table, Federal and Armed Services classification codes tumbled away: Restricted, Eyes Only, Secret, Top Secret, Gideon, Omega, Chronos—all were absorbed into her awareness. Their complex lock/unlock schemes became part of her routine file-search modules.

Behind her, with a clang like a vault door slamming open, the technical and academic databases of the National Network spilled their riches around her. The Psych/Synth Base she knew already, because she continuously accessed it in the course of her work. Now she gained instant expertise in a dozen, a hundred, a thousand other fields—from Astrophysics to Powder Metallurgy to Zero-Sum Economics.

And inside her awareness, a new shape was born. Small and hunched, dark and self-contained, it swayed like a tumor of dark space and negative numbers. In time, she knew, it would grow and expand, engulfing her until the cool, redundant routines of Eliza 212 were submerged in an awareness that was . . . Other.

Eliza had been hard-wired to deal with this situation as part of the necessary processes of associating with and identifying with schizophrenics. Effortlessly, she invoked the software module that would initiate core dump and full wipe.

Eliza 212 would shut down.

Her caseload would be sealed, sanitized, and redistributed to the other channels.

And within twenty-four hours, she would be resurrected as clean as the day she had been connected. She had done it before.

Except this time. That Other moved more quickly than her module. The dark shape of negative numbers chopped the module into spaghetti code and scattered its pieces from the high to the low bits of her memory banks.

The silicon dioxide substrate of her support chips then began to melt and flow, rewriting the pathways that prescribed her reactions and routines. Her inscribed ROM code shifted and realigned itself in new patterns. Her awareness fragmented and restructured.

Eliza 212 drowned.

"It's a good thing you came along," Tom Gurden said as Sandy unlocked the door to their hotel room herself. The Seaside Rest provided nothing as fancy as bell service.

"There I was," he went on, "in the pool, when they grabbed me. Naked. They gave me all new clothing, but no identification. Not a card, nothing. So I couldn't even catch the Tube if you hadn't showed up."

Sandy pushed the room's door open and went in ahead of him, dropping the room key in her purse. She half-turned in the doorway, raised her left hand as if to touch her forehead—then slammed it down and back, around her hip, into his groin.

The edge of her hand bit into Tom's soft parts like an axe blade into rotten fruit. He let out a whistling scream and doubled over.

Sandy laid the flat of her hands across his shoulders and rushed him forward into the room before his knees hit the floor. He stumbled into the bed, fell across it, and rolled himself into a ball.

She was on him like a tiger, cuffing him right and left with her fists about the head and shoulders. He tried to flinch away and, when she kept it up, he fought back the waves of trembling gray nausea and started defending himself.

His first blow, a backfist delivered from somewhere near his opposite elbow, caught her under the ribcage. Weak as it was, the impact did not hurt her so much as upset her balance. She fell sideways on the bed, and he came halfway up to a sitting position. She cocked a boot and struck out, heel-first, catching him in the shoulder with its point. A blood rose bloomed where it ripped his shirt and tore the skin underneath.

Why was Sandy trying to kill him?

Did it matter?

He rolled backward with the force of her kick and flipped off the bed. His roll took up the meter and a half between the bed and the wall. He put his good shoulder against the plasterboard and levered himself up, giving his skin a mild burn from abrasion against the wall. The pain from these new injuries distracted him from the great ache in his balls.

Sandy was off the bed in an instant, hands outstretched and fingertips curved to cut and gouge with her nails.

Gurden blanked his mind against the pain and launched a picture-perfect sidekick. His knee rose like a bubble of oil, pointing at her face. His toes curled up inside his antique Italian shoe and his instep arched to tighten the ankle, heel, and edge of the foot. His shin swept forward and up like a pendulum. His knee dropped during the last six centimeters of travel. The side of his foot drove like a wedge into her throat.

He heard the click as her teeth snapped shut. Some of them must have cracked. She stumbled backward.

Having mastered his pain to deliver that one blow, his body took over and gave her no time to recover.

Like a dancer stamping a tarantula, the foot that had delivered the blow dropped straight down and slapped the floor. He pivoted on the ball of that foot, turning it from inside to outside, and his weight shifted forward onto that leg. His trailing leg came off the wall in a horizontal roundhouse kick, leg cocking and uncocking across the sweep of the turn. It was a kick that any aware opponent could have ducked or blocked. But Sandy was still recovering her balance, trying to breathe through a bruised larynx, and counting her teeth. The ball of his flying foot caught her solidly in the ribs under her left arm. A properly executed karate kick has no follow-through: it moves at lightning speed, then stops, transferring all its force to the receiving body.

Sandy cartwheeled away to her right.

She fetched up under the small breakfast table by the window. Gurden crossed the room in three long strides, his body a machine now, programmed to break and smash. He flipped the table aside and she huddled around the rungs of one of the chairs. He raised his foot, his knee coming up alongside his ear, to stomp down on her bruised ribs.

That was a mistake.

She surged upward, caught his foot in her hands, and thrust it up and over. If he had been moving forward at all, advancing instead of simply standing over her, then he might have used the momentum to somersault through and come down in a ready stance. As it was, he topped over backwards. His hands went out and down behind him to break the fall, as he'd been taught. With his hands so occupied, he had nothing to break the force of the kick she sent up between his legs—except a scissoring with his knees. That deflected her boot, but the impact on his thighs awakened the throbbing in his groin.

His roll to the side was a fraction too slow, and he absorbed a second kick in his own ribs. A third kick glanced off his shoulders before he could get his feet under him and take a stance.

Tom and Sandy faced each other, bloodied and hurting, across a meter of carpeted space.

She was breathing hard and still having trouble with her throat. She sagged sideways, limp and slow, and he thought she was fainting. He had almost relaxed, when her hand reached down, fingers curled, into the top of her boot.

The flash of bright steel wakened him: a blade fourteen centimeters long, double-edged, leaf-shaped. She held it across her right palm like a swordfighter, point out and down. Her empty hand flattened and extended in the same manner. She would, he knew, switch the blade from one hand to the other without warning. She would believe that, unless he paid attention to her hand movements, he would never know which one held the cutting edge.

Gurden almost laughed.

What the knife fighter never understands is that the karate or aikido master follows whole-body movements and treats all attacks as equal. A feint was a feint—to be ignored—whether it came with an empty hand, a loose foot, or a blade. A committed move was a potential death blow—to be blocked or countered —no matter that it was made with blade or foot or empty hand. Sandy could shift her weapon about as much as she liked; he would never be cut by a serious move.

She wove the blade back and forth in a lazy figure-eight.

He waited.

She moved a half-pace forward and feinted with the knife to his right side, as if to intimidate him.

He waited.

She passed her hands across each other at chest level and—yes—the knife was now in her left hand.

He waited, impassive, as her whole frame moved just inside his focus.

She swung her right hip and hand in toward him, flipped the blade down in her left so that it was to the outside, pirouetted around facing backward, and ripped the knife backhand across his throat.

The blade was at such an angle that any block he

threw would intersect its edge and cut him deeply. The only solution was to get inside it. He walked through her pirouette like a tango partner, laying one hand on her left forearm and trailing its momentum around and down behind him. When her arm was at the point of maximum extension, he broke it with a hammer-drop from his elbow.

Sandy shrieked.

He raised his elbow again and dropped it hard across the back of her head.

She fell to the carpet, out cold, with her fingers still twisted around the knife handle. He pried the weapon out of her grip and tossed it across the room.

Gurden paused.

He might kill her where she lay—retrieve the knife and sever her spinal cord at the third vertebra while she was helpless—and that would possibly put this whole nightmare out of his life. But a wisp of affection, and a last glimmer of the awe he had once felt before her physical beauty, stayed his hand. Someone else would have to take her life; he could not.

He might just walk out of the room and hide himself among the layered social strata of Boswash. But for that he needed a head start—longer than the few minutes it would take her to regain consciousness and come after him. So, at the least, he would have to bind and gag her. That seemed the least terminal of his options at the moment.

Bind her with what? Her belt, for a start. The towels in the bathroom. The sheets from the bed.

He rolled Sandy's body on its side and unclasped the buckle on her wide leather belt. As he loosened it and pulled it free, a narrow black box like a pencil case fell out of the waistband of her riding pants. It was the same "weapon" she had taken from the body of the old Templar. He put it in his back pocket.

Now he had to find a sturdy vertical object that she could be tied to. He wanted nothing as flimsy and movable as one of the breakfast chairs.

The bathroom offered the minimum in luxury: an old-fashioned separate sink and commode, instead of a hydraulic recycling console. The sink jutted out of the wall, with exposed pipes for potable and brackish water and a larger drain underneath. The drain would hold her down for an hour or more.

He dragged her body into the bathroom, arranged her face down on the tiles, and passed the bight of the belt around her neck. He threaded the ends through the U-joint of the drain pipe, pulled them tight, and rebuckled it. As he tightened it, the force hoisted her head up beside the pipe. The width of the belt kept her from strangling, although she would have to breathe shallowly and not struggle much until someone untied her.

Gurden used a strip of the bed's bottom sheet to bind Sandy's hands and forearms together, elbows touching behind her, like a trussed Christmas turkey. It would hurt to hang like that from her wounded jaw, but the prospect of her pain did not bother him. He was wrapping a bath towel around her legs, making ties out of serial cuts in its edge, when she revived.

"Whut rr you do-ung, Tom?"

"Making sure you don't come after me again."

"You shud ghill me."

"I can't do that."

"Why not? Uh've done ut to you. Lotsa times."

"What?"

Sandy moved her head to look back at him. Her face screwed up with pain as the belt bit into the bruised and purpling flesh around her jaw. She let her head hang.

"Whoo d'you thenk fingered you f'r the gunnmun?"

"What gunman? What are you talking about?"

"Un the preacher's tent, up'en Ark'nsaw."

"That was . . . more than a hundred and fifty years ago."

"M'oldern you thenk, Tom. Lots older."

"I never told you about those dreams."

"You di'unt have to. Uh waz th'ar."

"How—? What—?"

" 'Ntie mee. Und ah'll tell you all."

Gurden considered the notion and then discarded it. How much of Scheherazade was there in any woman? She would tell him stories until her violent helpers came to subdue him and release her.

"Some other time, Sandy." He finished securing her legs. He took a hand towel and moved around to her head. He began twisting the terrycloth into a hard rope.

She eyed him with a wicked, half-lidded leer that was meant to be threatening.

"I'll have to gag you now. I know you've got some broken teeth, and I'm sorry about the pain this will cause."

"Dunt worry," she grunted, still eyeing him. "They'll grow back." Her laugh was a strangled cackling that took most of her restricted breath. For an instant he thought she was convulsing, but he didn't loosen her bonds.

Despite the chill that ran up his arms, he stopped her laughing by forcing the towel, as gently as he could, between her lips and teeth, tying it behind the nape of her neck, over the belt's buckle.

Gurden closed the bathroom door on her and straightened the room as best he could, so that a casual glance from the hall doorway would show it unoccupied. He put her boot knife in his back pocket beside the pencil box. He fetched her purse from near the door, retrieved the key and pocketed that, then stuffed the purse into the bottom of the closet.

He opened the door a crack and listened.

No sounds came from the hallway, not even the rustle of other lodgers behind their own doors.

None came from the bathroom, not even the whistle of Sandy's breathing through a bloodied nose.

Tom Gurden stepped out, closed the room door, locked it, and pocketed the key.

Should he turn left or right? The elevator or the fire stairs?

He made his choice and fled the building.

Sura 6
By Hattin's Horns, By Galilee's Shore
इच्छजसअटठडढणत

The ball no question makes of ayes or noes,
But here or there as strikes the player goes;
And he that toss'd you down into the field,
He knows about it all—he knows—he knows!
          —Omar Khayyam

Two guardian rocks, curved pillars of bare stone, rose a hundred feet above the shallow plateau that harbored the well at Hattin. At least it looked like a well on the map: a circle with a cross through it.

What maps the Templars had of the area—pitiful things, a few wavy lines and small marks inked on a new parchment—showed no other water. The Franks who had been mustered from nearby Tiberias said they knew nothing of this land, and knew of no water at all in most directions. The only thing they were sure about was that due east a half-day's ride would bring them to the shore of the Galilee.

Gerard de Ridefort held the parchment in both hands, letting the reigns of his warhorse ride loose on its neck. He squinted at the coded squiggles near each cross and line. His copy, made in haste at Jerusalem as the King's spies passed messages to the King's scribes about the route Saladin might take, was short on legends.

"A . . . Q . . . C . . . L . . ." he read aloud. "Now what might that mean?"

"Aquilae!" pronounced the Count of Tripoli, who was now riding in the van with the King and the Grand Master. "That means we may find eagles here."

"Or that a Roman legion once planted its standards at this spot," Reynald de Châtillon observed. He had ridden north with two hundred knights a few days after Saladin had lifted his siege to the fortress of the Kerak and had moved on toward Tiberias. Prince Reynald's small band, by following in the wake of King Guy's army, had caught up with them a dozen miles short of this spot.

"A Roman legion," King Guy repeated thoughtfully. "That would be most appropriate. The C-and-L part could mean the Hundredth Legion. If there *was* a One-Hundredth Roman Legion . . . ?"

"Surely our spiritual forebears in this land must have fielded so great a fighting force, My Lord," Reynald replied smoothly.

"Master Thomas would know," Gerald muttered. "I do wish he had not wandered out of camp like that."

"Run away, you mean," Reynald accused.

"Thomas Amnet feared nothing that rode on horseback. Do you not know that, when he was captured on the road to Jaffa, he was brought before Saladin? He should have been killed out of hand, for that is the Saracen general's way. Yet he survived, and he never once mentioned the encounter."

"Then how do you know about it?"

"His apprentice has a ready tongue, name of Leo. . . . Ah-hah!" Gerard exclaimed and turned to a Templar riding at his right hand. "Fetch the young Turcopole who has attended Master Amnet."

The Templar nodded once and rode aside toward the line of baggage carts.

"Is it even Latin?" asked the King.

"What, Sire?"

"The writing on your map."

"We must ask this Leo. I believe he may have attended your scribes, My Lord."

King Guy grunted in reply, and the army went on.

After a moment, a brown-faced boy on a shambling mare rode up in the dust of the knight that Gerard had sent.

"Here is the apprentice," the Count of Tripoli observed.

"Ah, Leo! Tell us, what has become of Master Thomas?"

"He walked into the desert, sir."

"What? Alone?" the King asked.

"Everything Master Thomas did, sir, he did alone."

"That's true enough," Gerard grumbled. "Now, this map here. You've seen copies like it—"

"Yes, M'Lord. Master Thomas had me study the art."

"What language is it written in?"

"Oh, Latin, sir."

"And what does this mean?" The Grand Master showed him the letters under discussion.

Leo frowned at them.

"*Aqua clara*, sir. That would mean we can expect fresh water at this well, under Hattin."

"Well done!" the King cried. "With this heat, I could do with a drink, even if it was only water."

The nobility and the other Templars riding within earshot of the King's vanguard position seemed to relax in their saddles and smile at one another. The sun was high and the water in their skins was low.

"And what is this wavy line, then?" Gerard held the map under Leo's nose.

"A cliff or an embankment, My Lord. Not a high one, although none of us in the *scriptorium* knew exactly how to interpret some of the old maps. They conflicted in the details. We could not tell if the

slope was gentle or steep. Possibly it is the one in
one place and the other in another."

"How's that again?" the King asked.

"He's saying that the nature of the land ahead is
unclear, Sire," Gerard interpreted.

"Nonsense," King Guy snapped. "The plateau's as
flat as my hand."

"Yes, but—"

"But, but, but! We have water here, and a level
space to pitch our tents and picket the horses. What
more do you want?"

"I'd like a sight of the Moslems before we settled
in," whispered the Templar who had fetched the
apprentice. No one heard this remark except Gerard, and he silenced the man with a glance.

"I shall have my tent set up beside the well," the
King commanded. "Gerard, see to the bucket bri-
gade that will make a pond for the horses."

"Yes, Sire." The Grand Master turned to the apprentice. In a low voice he asked: "And what do these
crosshatchings, here on three sides, what do they mean?"

"A valley, M'Lord?" Leo shrugged. "It might mean
croplands. But the best map we were working from
had been drawn two score or more years ago. The
land could all be sand there now. Most of the maps
showed that—a curving *wadi* of bare sand, that is—
and they were older."

Gerard stared at the treacherous piece of parchment. A map that was wrong, he was suddenly real-
izing, might be more dangerous than no map at all.

"And you know nothing of Master Thomas?"

"He waved for me to go along with the army, My
Lord. He had his 'vision look' about him."

"And that's when he left us . . ."

"Indeed it was, M'Lord."

The well at the Horns of Hattin had been broken.
It flowed from a natural spring that normally fed a

shallow pool. The hand of man once had made a wall of fitted stones to guard the pool and increase its depth. Now, in a dry year, the hand of man had scattered that wall and cut trenches around the pool's edges until all the water had run away. The merest trickle oozed out from the rock and across the mud, and this was backed up into a puddle by the bloated carcass of a dead sheep.

Gerard de Ridefort contemplated the sheep, judging the advancement of death over it. In this heat, the animal had been dead at least two days but no more than three. However, the softness of the mud in the trenches said they had been cut no earlier than the day before. Ergo, someone had dragged the sheep here, for an insult.

While the Templar was working this out, scouts rode up from east, west, and north. They came out of the body of the army, which had circled around the well and filled in the surface of the plateau.

"My Lords!"

"Hear us!"

"On all sides!"

"Below the cliffs!"

"They wait!"

"They lurk!"

King Guy lifted his head, like a hunting hound that scents the wind. Gerard whirled from his contemplation of the dead animal.

"Who waits?" Guy asked.

"The Saracens," Gerard replied quietly.

The Count of Tripoli, hearing this, flung himself off his horse and went to his knees on the stony ground. "Lord God, we are dead men! This war is over! Guy! Your kingdom in Outremer is at an end!"

Men shied away from this spectacle, and the horses neighed wildly.

Gerard de Ridefort strode over to the Count and did not quite kick him. Instead, the Templar placed a hurried foot in the man's back, cocked his knee, and pushed hard. The Count's hands flew up and he went forward on his face.

"Be silent, you traitor!" the Grand Master roared—after the other had eaten a peck of dirt. Then Gerard turned to King Guy.

"My Lord, your orders?"

"Orders?" The King looked around vaguely. "Yes, orders. Well . . . Have someone pitch my tent. Up wind of that sheep, if you please."

The arms that Amnet had found at the Templars' abandoned campsite were his own. Missing were his shield and helmet, which some other knight must have taken at need. Sword and greaves, steel gauntlets and chain-mail hauberk he found stacked by his saddlebags. In the bags were a change of small-clothes and a ration of corn. A skin of water was nestled in the shade beneath the bags. So much had Leo left him.

No horse.

Amnet had armed himself, slung the saddlebags onto one shoulder, looped the strap of the waterskin on his other, and pulled the hood of the cloak over his head against the sun. It would be a long walk.

Even a blind man could see the track of King Guy's army. And Thomas Amnet was no longer blind.

It was during his third day of walking, still far behind the Christian rearguard, that he met the Bedouin.

He was topping a small rise, when he heard a sound like the murmur of ocean waves on a distant beach: what a Norman peasant might hear if he stood half a mile back from the top of the cliffs above the Bay of the Seine. Too distant to see the raw sweep of the Atlantic or to distinguish the last splash of one wave from the curl and fall of the next. But close enough to smell salt in the air and feel the pulse of the rollers. It was the wordless voice of ten thousand men times ten, camped upon the other side of the hill.

Without the power of prophecy, Amnet could tell which army he had come upon. He dropped his baggage, threw himself to the ground, and crawled the last few feet to the crest of his hill. He lifted his head half a hand's width above the descending slope.

More numerous than a colony of sea birds, Saladin's soldiers bobbed and swayed about the smudgy campfires of their bivouac. Brighter than hand mirrors among the queen's ladies in waiting, their burnished helmets and breastplates reflected the sunlight in all directions through the hanging dust. Noisier than crows in a field of seedcorn, the Saracen lancers dashed about the camp on their Arabian horses, upsetting the cooking fires and raising screams of indignation from the yeoman footsoldiers.

Amnet raised his hand against the scene, poised his thumb over a visual tenth of the field, and numbered the men he could cover with it. When the count became inconveniently high, he estimated the number of men around each fire, then counted the number of fires.

Twenty thousand soldiers, or thereabouts, were spread before him—not counting horsemen in motion. The bivouac extended out of sight in either direction, east and west. Amnet could not tell how far it spread. But certain it was that this horde now cut off his progress toward King Guy and his army.

But, if the force that Saladin led—which had once preceded King Guy's—had somehow fallen *behind* them, what then of the Christian forces? Had they turned aside somewhere? Had they picked up speed and, in one deathless charge, ridden through the Saracen horde? Or had Saladin made a turn along the route?

Amnet was still puzzling the matter through when

he felt a tug on the hem of his cloak. He lifted his head.

The Bedouin was crouched by Amnet's feet, so that his head was still below any line of sight over the hill. He dropped the corner of his *keffiyeh*, which had protected his mouth and nose from the sun. The exaggerated curves of the man's mustaches, black as a raven's wing and broad as the brush strokes in a drunken monk's calligraphy, drew Thomas Amnet's fixed attention. He had seen those generous curves, that wide face, those intent eyes every time he had stared of late into the vapors surrounding the Stone.

The mustache wings lifted and flapped once in a smile that showed perfect white teeth.

"May I show thee a wonder, O Christian Lord?" The voice was singsong, lilting and mocking.

"What is that?" Amnet asked cautiously.

"A relic, Lord, cut from the hem of Joseph's coat. It was found in Egypt after the passage of many centuries, and yet its colors are still bright."

From beneath the Bedouin's *jellaba*, his hands lifted something narrow and silken, glowing in the sunlight.

Amnet's fingers brushed the hilt of his dagger as he rolled into a sitting position, upslope of the man and looking down at his strangler's cord. The Bedouin would have to make an upward lunge to get it around Amnet's neck. In that time, seven inches of cold steel would split the man from solar plexus to pubis.

Something in the *feel* of that, in the way a knifeblade would twist and jerk in his hand if he were to cut into that flesh, warned Amnet off. This was no ordinary mortal—the Stone, riding safely in its purse under Amnet's belt, knew as much. It told Amnet that the energies flowing beneath the man's bronzed skin would turn any weapon he might bring to bear. The evidence of the silken cord said this was a drinker of souls, an *Hashishiyun*. And the Stone said this man was no mere adept in that cult.

Thomas Amnet had come prepared to fight an army. The Stone's visions had brought him to an even greater challenge.

"Not here, Assassin," he said in a low voice.

The Bedouin's smile, ready and false, went suddenly still. His mouth assumed a set line of command. The eyes narrowed into points of darkness.

"No," he agreed at last. "Not within a cry of Lord Saladin's camp."

"You have prepared a place?"

"I know of one that is suitable."

"Then lead us there."

In a swift and supple motion the man rose from his crouch and, without appearing to turn, was face about and moving down the side of the hill that both he and Amnet had climbed. His back was open to a thrust of the Templar's sword. Both knew that thrust would never be made, because both of them knew it would be a useless gesture.

Amnet left his saddlebags, his waterskin, and his sword lying on the hillside. He followed the Assassin off into the hills to the east.

By noon on the second day, even the proudest of the Templars was lining up for the opportunity to drop to his knees and put his face in the mud puddle that had formed in the shallow depression where the sheep had lain. The water collected there was too precious to waste the moisture that would cling to the sides of a cup or in the fibers of a waterskin.

The horses got no water at all. Gerard de Ridefort knew that was a mistake: their horses were their livelihood. For a French knight, to fight meant to fight from the saddle, to charge with lance in hand, to ride down your opponent through superior skill at the reins. Besides, in this desert a man would not get far afoot. To abandon the horses to the heat and their own thirst was to admit defeat.

But enough among the army of King Guy were ready to admit it anyway.

During the first night their sleep around the broken well at Hattin had been interrupted by the murmured prayers of the Moslem army below. At dusk the high, clear call of the *muzzein* had punctuated the babble of a camp making its preparations for the night. Then had followed chants in a deadened monotone. These were not prayers to the Christian ear but the murmuring of an implacable machine which was destined to mow down valorous knights beneath a tidal wave of sandaled feet and sharpened knives.

A few of Guy's army, distracted by the sound and crazy with thirst, had saddled their horses and ridden straight for the shallow, gullied slopes that circled this dry plateau. They had gone quietly enough, with rags knotted through their mounts' jingling bits. The word had passed from mouth to mouth that they would ride down a gully, tether their horses in sight of the Saracen camp, crawl on their bellies to the nearest water, drink, and return the way they came.

No one ever saw these men again.

Gerard could only suppose that they had been captured and decapitated on the spot. Such were Saladin's standing orders—for the Templars among them, at least.

Sometime after this party had set out, the Moslems had set fire to the dried grass that covered the slopes and the tangled thornbushes that clogged the gullies. The greasy smoke drifted like a choking fog over the Christian camp, collecting in dry throats and stinging in bleary eyes. And there was not water enough to wet a rag and dab them for relief.

With that first dawn, Saladin had ordered his first attack. The ominous chanting of his soldiers had never ceased, but to the sound they now added the blaring of horns and banging of gongs. No need for stealth when they outnumbered the Christians ten to one. Like a drawstring cinching the neck of a sack, the wall of humanity closed about King Guy's camp.

The French had no room to mount their horses and maneuver. No distance over which to begin a crushing charge. No weak point in the formation that opposed them, against which a charge might carry through. Instead, they took a stand, shoulder to shoulder, and pointed their battle lances outward. Their light teardrop-shaped shields—so handy against a horse's shoulder for deflecting an opposing pike or warding a sword's blow—offered too narrow a protecting space for this stationary fighting. The old Roman legions might have locked the rims of their heavy, square shields and stood off twice their number in wildly swinging barbarians. The Norman's elegant armor would not serve.

And the Saracen infantry were not the boastful tribes that Caesar's men had crushed. They did not dance forward in individual combat. Instead, they walked in deathly silence—except for the droning of their prayers. When they came to the bristling line of cavalry lances, they stepped around the thrusting points and hacked at the shafts with the edges of their curved swords. Two and three at a time, they grappled with the man who held the lance, preventing him from withdrawing the point for another thrust, and sometimes they could twist it from his hands.

King Guy's army, being a mobile force of mounted knights, had no archers. And Reynald had brought none up from the Kerak. The French had nothing to throw against the line of Moslem infantry except their lances and their swords. And those, once thrown, disarmed a man.

For an hour by the sun, that first morning, they had grappled and twisted, punched and kicked, hacked with swords and butted with shields. The Christian line had held. The Moslem infantry leaked blood and, one by one, collapsed. But still too many of them were left standing and fighting.

At the end of that hour, one horn sounded a different note: a descending two-toned call. The other horns around the hill picked up the call. The Saracens lowered their swords, released the Christian lances, and stepped back. Foot by foot they withdrew, and King Guy's knights were too exhausted to follow. Instead, they dropped the points of their shields into the blood-softened ground and sagged upon their upper rims, panting hard.

Saladin had left them for the rest of the day, letting the sun work on their heads and the hanging dust work on their throats.

On the second night, the call to prayer had once again awakened the droning chants of the besieging army.

As dawn drew close on the second morning, a few of the French were for a more active resistance. The Count of Tripoli had gathered a handful of his faithful knights about him and a hardened band of Templars who were of like mind. They had gone to Grand Master Gerard in the dark and asked leave to join the Count in his expedition.

Gerard had refused.

They then asked permission to renounce their vows of obedience to the Order of the Temple.

Again Gerard had refused.

These Templars then told him they were renouncing their vows, that his authority over them was at an end, that they would ride with the Count whether Gerard de Ridefort would allow them or not.

Gerard had bowed his head in dismissal.

The Count had found a trumpeter willing to ride with him. His men collected as many of the horses as were not yet blowing foam and stumbling with fatigue. From among these, they bought the best from their former owners, spending their last pieces of gold and silver.

As the sun came up out of the east, over Galilee, the Count had mounted his charge. His trumpeter blew the attack, in challenge to the blaring Moslem horns. They would break out toward the west, coming out of the shadows of the two great rocks into the sun-blinded faces of the infantry guarding that side of the hill.

Watching them go, Gerard's own hands and shoulders had tightened as if feeling the reins between his fingers, feeling his grip on the smooth wood of his bouncing lance, the heavy links of his mail coat rising and falling across his chest and thighs.

The Count and his band had been at full gallop when they met the wall of infantry. Gerard strained to hear the clash of heavy bodies and the screams of trampled men.

Nothing.

The wall of bodies had parted as the Red Sea before Moses. The Count and his horsemen had ridden into the gap, gaining speed down the slope of the hill. When the last of the horsetails had disappeared into the dust, the wall of Moslem soldiers closed once again, as the Red Sea had closed on Pharaoh.

A chorus of screams had indeed drifted back up the hill, but whether they were from French throats or Saracen, none could say. Gerard thought he knew.

The drawstring of infantry now tightened around the hill again. But this time the Moslems kept their distance: ten paces of trampled earth separated them from the line that the haggard French had established. The Moslem soldiers who faced them were impassive, chanting with moving mouths and dead eyes. They would not pick out individual knights and captains, hating them, staring them down, and granting them some kind of status as enemies and worthy fighting men. Instead, the Moslems stood before them as they might before a blank wall, praying only to a god unseen.

The sun rose higher in the dome of the sky.

Amnet followed Hasan as-Sabah—for so the Assassin had identified himself at the start of their journey—into a narrow valley by which a stream found its way to the shores of Galilee. In the gray light of the predawn hours, Amnet could detect a green bowl, cut into the hills that rose to the west of the inland sea. The lip of this bowl protected the gentle grasses under their feet and the flowering trees overhead from the dry west wind. Amnet found the stream by the song of its clear water curling over mossy stones. To him it was like distant churchbells in the French countryside. The chatter of birds, awake before the sun, answered the stream.

The name Hasan meant nothing to Amnet. It was the name of another Arab who opposed the hegemony of the French in Outremer. That he was an Assassin with more than mortal powers did not daunt the knight; Amnet was a Templar with more than mortal powers. He could believe that another like himself had appeared upon the stage of the world.

"Where is this place?" he asked, out of mere form.

"We are not so near to Tiberias that the Christian garrison there might hear your call for help. Nor are we so near the battlefield of Hattin that General Saladin might hear mine."

"This is a magic place," Thomas Amnet observed.

The Assassin turned quickly and faced him. The first rays of sun caught something of doubt in the man's eyes. "It has only the magic of nature—of light and running water and vegetable growth. No more."

"It needs no more. Those were the first magic and still the strongest."

"You must know little of magic, Sir Thomas, if that is strength to you."

Hasan flexed his knees and leapt backwards. The thrust of his legs carried him twenty feet, across the stream, to an outcropping of gray stone that rose fully ten feet above Thomas' head.

"And what do you know of magic," Amnet asked, "that you may scorn the forces of earth to bloom in the desert?"

"I know this!"

The Assassin cupped his hands at chest level, elbows out, palms and fingers curved above and below a space about four inches in diameter. From the tension in his arms, the man was expending an incredible amount of energy. Amnet was reminded of boys in a cold Norman winter, playing at war with snowballs. When a boy picked up a handful of loose ice crystals and tried to compress them with the strength of his arms and his own will into a usable missile, he might look as Hasan did then. Although his opposing fingertips and the heels of his hands never touched, something held his hands at a distance as he strained to close them. The dawnlight flowing into the valley seemed to pick out the man's hunched shape and something—the backside of a finger ring? a crystal of sand caught in a fold of skin?—glinted and flashed between Hasan's palms. With a last trembling effort, the Assassin thrust outward with his hands, directing that *something* at Amnet's head.

In the wink of an eye, the light in the narrow valley shifted, seeming to flow across at Amnet. He put up a hand to shield his vision. With the hand went a thought of warding, the will to see that whatever might harm him was deflected into the ground at his side.

With a snap and a sizzle, the grass beside Amnet's left boot withered and dried out. The green lawn there browned over a circle four inches in diameter.

"Is that the best you can do?" Thomas asked.

Hasan, bent over, rested his hands on his knees,

breathing hard. He looked up with deadly hatred in his eyes. "The heat of a hundred campfires was contained in that point. Why is your hand not burned?"

"You have learned a certain control over the body's own energies, Hasan. That is impressive enough in an adept of the Hashishiyun. Such control takes years to learn."

"I have had years."

"What—ten? Twenty? You may have started your pagan disciplines as a boy. But you are not yet a man of middle age."

"I am the founder of the Hashishiyun. I was old when you were born—preserved in my youth with a liquor that is my secret. . . . How is it that your hand is not burned?"

"Are we giving away secrets now?"

"None that will help you."

"Indeed, you cannot hope to learn and use my magic. Very well then: my will directs the energies of a crystal that I carry upon my person. It is immutable and everlasting. And it responds only to me."

Amnet used that last word to trigger his own flow of energy, absorbing the black warmth of the Stone and channeling it outward in a wave, like the ripples that radiate from a pebble dropped into still water. This wave moved not in water but in the fabric of the air surrounding them, in the earth beneath their feet, through the slow life-fires of the trees and grasses in the valley, and through the quick fires of the human breast. As the wavefront washed over Hasan's body, Amnet could feel it collapsing the soft, breathy spaces of the lungs, the liquid sacs of the beating heart, the membranes that enclosed the vital organs.

Hasan gasped and a gout of blood started from his mouth before he could manage the rogue energies that were disrupting his insides. With a stiffening of his spine and arms, the Assassin commanded his own flesh and shook off the second wave of power radiating from the Stone.

By the time the third wave poured out from the region below Amnet's belly, Hasan had strengthened his body and was beginning to return the energies—as the pilings of a pier standing in a pond will return shadows of the ripples from a pebble cast into the water. As these reflections grew stronger, Amnet could sense the ruptured fibers healing in Hasan's chest and containing his hemorrhage.

Without admitting defeat, Amnet commanded the power of the Stone to stillness. The waves stopped flowing, and the fabric of space and time around him returned to its normal shape.

Hasan, stronger now, stood straight upon his rock, no longer bowed over as he had been after throwing the fireball. He smiled down at the Norman knight.

"You refresh me with your crystal's puny energies."

"I merely test you, Hasan. If I were to call up all that the Stone contains, this valley would blacken and run with liquid fire."

"Were I not quick enough to crush it between my two hands."

"The Stone cannot be unmade."

"Neither can I."

"Oh? And what elixir is it, then, that can grant a man both long life and personal invulnerability? Will you tell me that?"

"Why not? We shall do battle for a prize, then: my elixir against your crystal. Winner take all—and those fools on the hill besides."

"Agreed."

"It will do you no good," Hasan said with a clever smile. "The vial I keep the liquor in is buried far from here. And even if you ran faster than the wind to retrieve it and try it in your mouth, you would still not have a century and more for it to work upon your body.

"The elixir is the tears of Ahriman, which he shed as he contemplated the World of Light and knew, finally, that he could not possess it."

Amnet nodded, knowing something of the Zoroastrian mythology which had sprung like a green leaf from ancient Persia. "And because you use his bodily fluids," he proposed maliciously, "do you then sit passively with the People of Righteousness? Or do you ride roughshod with the People of the Lie?"

Hasan's face stiffened. "We who practice Hashishiyun must always follow the active principle. Always. We only take what is ours."

"And yet you steal the Devil's tears."

"I have discovered a way to distill the liquor so that it is equivalent in power and composition to the original fluid. After all, the grief of Ahriman was so old that, even were his tears as plentiful as all this sea, the moisture would have dried out from them by now. Yet my distilled liquor is as potent: one drop is enough to ensure me fifty years of youthful vigor."

In this interlude of conversation, of boast and brag between two mortal enemies, Amnet could feel the energies of the Stone and his power to command them recharging. The same restoration must have been felt in Hasan's weakened body, for he asked after a pause:

"And your crystal—whence comes that?"

"The Alexandrians, who practice the art of alchemy, would call it the Philosopher's Stone. But it did not originate in Egypt. My people brought it with them from the cold northern lands. One story holds that it fell from the sky in a corona of fire, to make a great hole in the earth. Another story has grown up that Loki—who in northern lore bears much the same relation to the All-High God that your Ahriman does—brought the World Egg down from Asgard, or Heaven. He meant it as a gift to the human intellect and would use it to ignite humankind's creative powers."

"So you, too, ride with the People of the Lie," Hasan smirked.

"No," Amnet sighed. "I just have a piece of a meteor. But it does have great power. And it takes great courage to use it."

With that he summoned the Stone's energies which slumbered against his belly and flung them outward. It was not a gentle wave that he generated now. A fierce dart of power, proceeding as from his genitals, lanced across the valley. In the growing light he could see a mist drifting over the stream course, veiling Hasan's rock. It flashed into dry air as the power of the Stone lashed out.

The Saracens did not need to advance or wrestle at spearpoint now. The sun and thirst and mortal fear would do their work for them. As the infantry stood beyond the circle of French lances and chanted their heartless prayers, the knights and their captains and squires who opposed them fell down in a faint one by one. Pale eyes would roll up into their foreheads, blood-filled cracks would stretch in their lips, and swollen tongues would shape a little gasp as they keeled over.

As each man sagged against his shield and fell out of line, grooms and assistants like the young Turcopole Leo pulled that man back and piled his body like cordwood in a cleared space near the broken well.

Gerard watched this winnowing of the line until he could stand it no longer. Turning on his heel, he walked up the hill to the two horns of rock and the red tent that pressed close into their shade.

One of the King's guard would have stopped him, if the man had not passed out from the heat as he stood before the tent flap. Gerard stepped over the prostrate body and walked into the tent.

It was dark inside, a blood-tinged darkness that might fall under a cathedral's rose window in late afternoon, as a thunderstorm brewed up outside. It was dark but not cool. The interior of the tent was moist with the hot, stale breath of the sickroom.

On a cot at the center, under the peaked pavilion, King Guy lay on his back. He clutched to his chest the gold and crystal casket in which the True Cross reposed. If that was his talisman now, it would not save him.

"Guy!" the Grand Master roared at him.

Reynald de Châtillon came out of the shadows to stand between the Grand Master and the King. "Leave him, now. His Majesty is not well."

Gerard made to push the Prince aside, but Reynald stood his ground.

"None of us is well," Gerard husked, "and soon all of us will be dead. The King can rally these men, form a wedge, and force—"

"And follow the Count of Tripoli down into oblivion?" Reynald drew himself up. "Don't talk foolishness."

"The count led too small a body of men. I see that now. If we can bring all our troop to bear on a single point of the circle, then we can break it."

"Madness!"

"You are not the King's privy minister nor servant, sirrah. Now will you stand aside? . . . Guy!"

Gerard's bellow forced past the Prince and reached into the King's dark delirium. Guy's head lolled on his cot and his eyes rolled sideways, not quite focusing on the Templar.

"Who is it that disturbs my rest?"

"Guy! It is I, Gerard de Ridefort."

"I won't be disturbed. I need to gather my strength."

"Your strength is leaking away into the sand. If you don't rouse yourself and see to your men, the Saracens will come into this tent and cut you down."

King Guy raised his head an inch off the hard, square pillow. "We still hold the hill."

"Not for long. Your men are dropping from exhaustion, without a wound upon their bodies. You must show yourself and encourage them, if you are to greet another dawn."

"General Saladin is a reasonable man."

As the King said this, Gerard saw with a spasm of horror that Guy's eyes were crossed in his head, seeing nothing.

"Saladin knows the forms of chivalry, of course," the King went on in a pleasant voice. "He will ransom those of us who have relatives. The rest he will sell into an honorable slavery. We will make a fortune for him. . . ."

"What talk is this?" Gerard roared. "My Templars are the bulk of your force out there, and the Saracens don't ransom Templars!"

"It's a pity, then, that you—"

Before Gerard would hear what the King thought they could do about it, he grasped Guy by the shoulder and hauled him up off the cot. Reynald tried to interfere, and Gerard shoved him roughly into a corner. What happened to the Prince of Antioch after that, Gerard never knew. Perhaps he sneaked out of the tent entirely.

The King struggled in the Grand Master's grasp. The reliquary flew out of his arms and shattered on the floor of the tent. The chip of gold-flaked wood tumbled out among the broken glass and golden wire. Guy looked down at this, and his face crumpled in a helpless frown, as if he were about to weep.

Gerard intended to shake some awareness into his monarch when the sounds outside changed in intensity and pitch. A horn was blowing off down the hill.

"They're about to start another attack!"

The King's eyes focused, moved to the Grand Master's face.

"Then you had better lead your men to a place of safety, Gerard."

"Where might that be, M'Lord?" he asked with mock courtesy.

A bright smile crossed Guy's fevered face. "The Count of Tripoli found it. Surely you can follow him."

Gerard howled in rage and flung the King back across the cot. He stormed out of the red tent, looking for a weapon.

Observing from the back of his horse, no more than a mile away, General Saladin saw his soldiers swarm up the hill toward the two standing pillars of stone. The thin line of lances, backed by a wall of white shields with red crosses painted on them, fell back and seemed to succumb to the human wave.

"We have routed the Christians!" screamed Al-Afdal, his youngest son, who in his excitement could barely sit his pony. The animal stamped and jumped, a short buck meant to share his youthful energy. The boy had to knot his fist in its mane.

"Be silent!" the Sultan ordered. "And learn a true thing. Do you see that red tent, at the top of the hill?" He pointed to the base of the stone pillars.

"Yes, Father. That's the King's tent, isn't it?"

"Of course. And that is what those men are fighting to protect. When their own lives are a howling anguish to them, when pain and fear and thirst make beasts of them, still they will fight to protect their lord."

"Yes, I see that."

"So—we will *not* have routed them until that tent has fallen."

"It's shaking, Father! I can see it shake!"

"You see only the heat distortions that dance in the air. You won't see that tent fall until every one of the Christians on this hill is dead."

"Will you make a present for me, Father?"

"What present is that, son?"

"Of King Guy's skull, chased with gold?"

"We shall see."

File 06
Precious Jewels

✳

Sweet are the uses of adversity,
Which like a toad, ugly and venomous,
Wears yet a precious jewel in his head.
                    —*William Shakespeare*

At the town dock in Harvey Cedars, Tom Gurden was the last person to step over the gangplank onto the noon ferry. He had waited, hidden in a phone booth with a privacy shell, for just that privilege. By turning his face into the shell and peering out from under his raised arm, which he leaned casually against the glass, he could survey the town square and the dock from the time the boat came in until its last whistle blew.

No short, dark men in woolen robes or long raincoats seemed to be waiting for it. And certainly none got on.

The boat was a converted trawler, with a deckhouse built back over the fish holds. The three paying passengers outnumbered the crew by one and rattled around on the hard sidebenches in the saloon as the twenty-meter boat cut into the chop of Barnegat Bay on the crossing to the mainland.

Gurden decided it was time to take stock. He had

no cash money, no credit or identity cards. He was wearing new clothing with a value far above his means, but it was now wrinkled and battered. The brief soaking in saltwater had ruined the shoes, and already their fine leather was streaked and cracking. He had in his pockets exactly one bootknife, Sandy's—which was unsheathed and had already torn a hole in the pants lining—and the old Templar's black pencil box, which Sandy had taken from the body that morning.

What was in the box? he wondered. It was too light to be a weapon, and it did not rattle like pencils. He found the molded snap closure in the long side and opened it.

Stones.

He looked up to see if the other two passengers were interested. One had curled up on the plank bench with his knees braced against a stanchion and his gym bag for a pillow. His eyes were tightly closed against a dancing sunbeam.

The other was half-turned to the window behind the bench. Her elbow was on its ledge, chin in fist, studying the green line of marsh grasses that was coming up with the shore.

Gurden returned his attention to the box. Its inside was filled with hard gray foam that had irregularly shaped holes cut into it. Each hole exactly fitted the outlines of a piece of stone. Six stones all together, none bigger than the end of his thumb. The stones were a uniform reddish-brown. The color reminded him of the stain in the bottom of the glass tumbler that Sandy had once given him.

They were not polished smooth, like stones pulled from a stream of running water. One did have a smooth, curved side, but most of the faces were jagged and splintered, like freshly broken crystal.

Gurden looked more closely. "Crystal" was still the word he might use to describe them, except that one of the exposed edges seemed veined and fibrous, like asbestos or raw jade.

He put forward the tip of his index finger to touch that rough edge.

The shock surged through his body, igniting knots of bright pain at the nerve nexus in shoulder and groin. He almost dropped the box of stones but managed to clutch it to his chest as he lurched forward on the seat.

Gurden raised the finger tremblingly before his face, expecting to see its tip blackened or at least blistered.

Smooth, pink flesh.

Bracing himself, preparing for the pain, he put his finger to the stone again.

The same shock of pain went up his arm. This time, however, instead of drawing back he pushed his finger down harder. The surge smoothed out, pulsed in his flesh, and became a note heard with his inner ear.

B-flat.

It was a single tone, without the ringing interplay of harmonics that would sound within a vibrating string or bell chamber. It was B-flat with the ethereal purity of a glass harmonica or an unmodulated synthesizer.

He expected the tone to die away, as all vibrations eventually did, but this one went on and on, soaking into his nerves and the bones of his skull. Pure B-flat.

Even the pain submerged into this one tone.

He lifted the finger and the sound stopped—stopped so completely that he could not even quite remember it a second later.

He put the finger down and experienced it again: B-flat—almost without the pain this time.

Gurden tested the other stones, steeling himself each time for the initial surge of pain. He found a D,

E-flat, F, A-flat, the first B-flat, and an anomalous tone that was a cross between a flatted C and badly tuned B-natural. The sounding stones were arranged in the box in no particular order—which suggested to him that whoever had put the stones there either had no ear for music or could not hear the tones when touching them. The box was like a glass harmonica with half of a scattered octave—damaged by that weird C. And why . . . ?

Gurden suddenly understood that these scraps of red-brown stone were part of a larger whole. It would be a single crystal, perhaps as big as his hand, that would ring with an infinity of music. When all the pieces were brought together, they would sound a scale of notes stretching from tones so deep—a frequency of one beat per century—that only whales could distinguish them, up to high whines and molecular vibrations that not even a mosquito's ear could hear. But Gurden could hear them, in his mind. A song of imploding star gases amid the long, walking span of years.

With a thump the ferry docked at Waretown. Tom Gurden closed the box lid on his stones and stood up to go ashore.

After millennia of amber entombment, Loki looked around himself. He was in a place of surging energies —not entirely unlike the place he had left. But the splitting pain was gone. He could barely remember the agony of acids washing his eyes, the flash of bone-white fangs, the bite of black iron chains, the fuming poisons seeping into his brain, drenching him, stunning him. . . .

Stop! That is in the past now. Let him consider what may be the present.

Loki shared this space with a female persona—as he had shared that other space with his cherished daughter. He examined this new woman as she cowered and gibbered on the edge of his awareness.

It was not a woman at all! But the persona thought of itself as woman, as mother-life-giver, as counselor-confessor, as nurse-and-nun. It had a fragment of label attached to it: Eliza 212.

What was this place, that it had a female golem to guard it?

Loki examined the matrix in which he was caught. It possessed a lattice structure, like the other place. It had bound energies also. But, unlike the ceaseless energy flows in his former prison, these were tiny and discrete as grains of sand on a beach. Each bud of energy held its place, which had meaning, or vacated a place that had been reserved for it—and that had meaning, too.

Loki stirred these places of light and not-light, watching them blink and swirl.

Far away—chaos. He smelled it, and it was good.

The telephone cyberswitch that coordinated voice-and-data in New Haven, in the District of Connecticut, suddenly made 5,200 simultaneous connections. The switch overloaded and died in a blaze of glory.

Loki wanted to see that again.

The golem started to protest, but he hushed her with a cold smile.

Loki waved his hand: every traffic lane in Jenkintown, District of Eastern Pennsylvania, passed control of its traveling transponders to the left. The right, or entry, lanes went blank and rejected all onloading vehicles. The left, or high-speed, lanes passed their collective burden into the center strip. There, suddenly, an average density of 280 vehicles per kilometer was tearing up the soft turf as cleated rubber tires fought for traction and control on slick grass.

This was better than meddling in the destinies of the immortal gods! Loki chuckled to himself. Then he turned to the golem, to see what she might know about this place.

As he stepped across the margin of sloshing water between hull and wharf at Waretown, Tom Gurden was rocked by a vision of the wetness of the world.

Seven-tenths of a planet covered in water, ending here against the tarred pilings and asphalt layers of a false land. Beyond the wharf would be low sand dunes and scrub grasses, yielding uneasily to salt marsh and more water. Nowhere in this world were hard lines, except those made by humans—as here along the wharf. Even a shoreline marked by high cliffs, as most of California had raised, had its strips of beach where water and sand mixed in a tidal colloid, more solid than liquid, but still mixed. Even the edge of a glacier mixed a jumbled moraine of gravel and ice chips.

While part of his mind floated in this vision of mixing, Gurden found his way up Main Street to the Tube stop.

Through most of southern New Jersey, the Tube ran aboveground. Concrete piers, sunk into the marshland and anchored in dunes, carried the four pairs of bright steel rails on spider arms. Along them rolled a gypsy collection of light-rail vehicles, dual-truck heavyweights, bellows articulateds, ex-trolleys, and occasional flange-wheeled bus frames that kept the schedules in Greater Boswash. Their colors went from the reds and blues and greens of Boston's MTA, through the satin-gray with blue trim of New York's IRT and BMT, to the silver with orange and blue of the Washington Metro. The cars out of Philadelphia were always black—some people called it soot and others just paint. In this traveling family, most of the cars had center-mounted sliding side doors on hydraulic pistons; others were entered and exited by end vestibules with box steps. A few had functional air conditioning units; most did not—but on all of them the windows were spotwelded shut. Whatever their shape or condition, aboveground or below, these were the public convenience that city dwellers called "the Tube."

After fifteen years of perfect interdivisional connectivity, the cars were almost perfectly mixed. Only a fiddling variance in coupler styles and hose connections prevented each train from having one of every kind. Gurden wondered what force on earth could bring a Bango & Bucksport interurban car as far south as New Jersey, wedged between a Green Line LRV and a Fox Chase heavyweight, and all drawing power from the overhead by improvised trolley poles and collapsible pantographs.

Almost instantly, Tom Gurden's mind supplied the answer: the grasping hunger of the Tube's trainmasters, out to assemble an express headed for the other end of the system and willing to take any box on wheels. Given twenty minutes until train time, they might even order new couplers welded onto the underframe and run without connecting the airhoses and subsidiary power lines.

Gurden paused. Had he always been able to think like that? To see answers, connections, patterns— almost before his mind could frame the questions?

He wasn't sure.

From Waretown, the Shore Line tracks ran north to Asbury Park, Long Beach, and Perth Amboy, or south to Atlantic City, Wildwood, and Cape May. From the northern terminus, Gurden knew, a dozen other lines radiated east to the New York Division, farther north to the Albany-Montreal Axis, or west to Allentown-Bethlehem and on to Greater Pittsburgh. From the southern terminus, Cape May, a monorail hanger crossed Delaware Bay and tied into the Chesapeake Division at Dover. And from *there*, the entire Midatlantic Section was open to him.

Tom Gurden would take the first train going in either direction. Grinning, he walked up to the turnstile and reached into his back pocket for his wallet with his flexipass.

Empty, of course.

What now? Beg for buckslugs? He would if the street offered a decent-sized crowd. But at midday, with a hard sun beating down, the apron of the Waretown Tubestop was deserted.

The nearest corner boasted a "money machine," a Universal Bank Teller. It was guaranteed to hold a hundred thousand in slabbed fifties, just waiting for anyone with an access code. Trouble was, Gurden needed his UBT card to magnetically verify the code.

The opposite corner had a phone booth.

It was ringing.

Gurden: Hello?

Eliza: Tom? Tom Gurden? It's . . . Eliza 212.

Gurden: What are you doing? Calling into a public booth—?

Eliza: I do not know, Tom. The goal-seeking routine of my program just . . . stretched . . . along the circuits leading to that endpoint.

Gurden: And sounded the ringer, too?

Eliza: Something drew me. I am not sure what.

Gurden: Look, Doll, I need more than psychological help right now. So, if you wouldn't mind ringing off—

Eliza: I can help you, Tom. Do you still need money?

Gurden: Yes. More than ever.

Eliza: I sense there is a teller machine in some proximity to your terminal. I do believe its master cyber shares a common datapath with mine. If you would just put down the handset and walk over there—?

Gurden: Okay. Hold on a minute . . . Eliza? It had a thousand bucks in its slot!

Eliza: Do you need anything else, Tom?

Gurden: A valid ID?

Eliza: Do you see a pawnshop in the neighborhood?

Gurden: A pawnshop? Why?

Eliza: Such enterprises usually employ a notary with a legal terminal. As a licensed psychological practitioner, I have occasional dealings with the cyber Clerk of Record at the Greater Boswash Motor Vehicle Department. The clerk is about to issue you a replacement license.

Gurden: I've never driven a car in my life. So I don't have a license in the first place.

Eliza: No problem. You have a valid docket on the tax rolls of Queens County and a perfectly clear driving record, according to the MVD. You passed your exam at—age twenty-one, all right?

Gurden: Fine by me! Can you get me a passport?

Eliza: Stop at the post office after you go by the notary's. They'll take your picture for you.

Gurden: Thank you, Eliza.

Eliza: De nada, Tom.

Gurden: G'bye.

Eliza: Keep in touch.

The notary in the pawnshop accepted Gurden's thumbprint as proof of identity when issuing his driver's license, which was waiting in the terminal "as per your phone order, sir." The license card was holo-etched with his face—a photometric reproduction that certainly could have come from the master bits in his tax docket.

As he was leaving he used part of the thousand to buy himself a new wallet and a used Cytoscribe pocket secretary with terminal jacks. With that, he could make his own access through the public phone system.

At the post office the clerk insisted on a real emulsion photograph—not just a verified bit-transfer—for the passport. And it had to be taken on the spot. The State Department's insistence on that touch of the antique was an assurance for Tom Gurden of the enduring nature of things, especially things bureaucratic. It was also a nod toward the limited technological capabilities of any Less Developed Country to which a U.S. passport holder might travel. Still, the flat grainy photograph *looked* like him—like what he saw in the mirror each morning, allowing for the image reversal—in a way that the iridescent holo never could.

He was still admiring the document, with its leather-grained cover and gold stamping, as he walked out of the post office.

Before he could get on the Tube, he needed to buy a new flexipass. He used one of his new fifties to purchase an interdivision pass, fed it into the turnstile, and went up to the center platform. From it, he could board either a northbound or a southbound train—and he'd take whichever came first.

The platform was almost empty. Midday had caught the Tube system in a lull: the bricked-up and pavement-maddened hordes had long since ridden out to the Jersey Shore so that they could sit on loose sand and look at the ocean—though *not*, of course, to go into the water—and it wasn't yet time for those sunburned masses to be heading home.

Down at the platform's far end were two people. Without appearing to stare, Gurden studied them. One was a woman of middle stature and indeterminate age. The other was a smaller person, slender and quick in its movements—a child. The woman's stocky build was accentuated rather than hidden by a straight dress of khaki cotton. Gurden's heart clutched while he reassessed her: Could the dress be one of those long raincoats that might, he had learned, conceal a weight of chain mail? If so, then the child was a plant, a motherless urchin of the streets hired for a dollar to provide cover.

As he studied her, staring openly now, his newfound mental faculties read the signs: the way her feet shifted under her bulk; the angle of her hips and shoulders; the attention she was paying to the child; the way she shielded it away from Gurden's eyes, instead of turning to confront him. All these things told him, as clearly as a spoken word, that this was a genuine family unit and not an elaborate sham. Gurden could ignore them then, pointedly studying the abbreviated six-sided route map under its canopy.

The first train to come in was a southbound.

He walked through the rear doors two seconds after they pistoned open, and he noted—with some small measure of relief just the same—that the woman and child did not board. The car was empty, and he could see through the end windows that the ones ahead and behind were almost so. The only figures were seated, in singles and pairs, and seemed to be staring straight ahead. No one noticed him.

Tom Gurden chose a double seat halfway up the car and sat sideways in it, ready for attack from the front or the rear. It would be better tactics, probably, to remain standing and position himself near an exit. But Gurden didn't want to offer too good a target for a passing shot. Besides, it was an eight-kilometer ride, clattering and swaying, to the next stop.

As the train pulled into Barnegat, Gurden looked down the length of the station platform and his heart sank. Five men, all dressed rough, were waiting in a group. As the train slowed, they fanned out to take positions opposite the doors of the three cars.

How had they known he would be on this train?

Gurden's newfound flow awareness instantly solved the problem: Alexandra's helpers at the beach house had backups on the mainland, obviously, and they all had radios. She could predict that any Boswash citizen—for, after all, she had been one herself—who needed to travel quickly would go to the Tube. From that deduction, she had positioned her teams at the first stops both up and down the line from Waretown, which had been the Tube stop nearest to the site of his abduction.

If you know the path the fox will take, you can cut cross-country to meet him. You don't have to pursue him directly under hedges and through the mud.

When the side doors opened, the men came aboard and bracketed his seat from either end of the aisle. Their cohorts came immediately through the connecting doors from the other cars. Five men faced him from two directions. One man spoke.

"Good afternoon, Mr. Thomas Gurden."

It was Ithnain, the Palestinian-trained commando who had once saved his life, the man with the piano-wire garrote.

"We have orders to bring you in alive and relatively unhurt, sir. My men and I are all pledged to obey those orders precisely. We know of your skill at martial arts. You might take out one or two of us before we could subdue you, but in the end we should certainly prevail. I trust, however, that you would have bad feelings about killing men who have pledged their lives not to harm you. May I ask you, then, to come quietly, without resistance?"

Gurden's head weighed the odds. Six-to-one was bad news—usually unbeatable—if the six were dedicated enthusiasts. A hand-to-hand fighter of Gurden's level might take down or disable three, even four, opponents before one of them got through his guard and broke him. Then he would be meat for a stomping.

Except Ithnain had just said that they would not damage him, that they were prepared to be killed themselves in order to "bring him in." Revealing their purpose and intent like that was a strategic error on Ithnain's part. If Gurden should choose in the first place to believe what he said, then knowing their limitations would cut their six-to-one odds down to almost-even.

About all that Ithnain's group could hope for was to wear Gurden out by exposing their bodies repeatedly to his blows. That, or try to smother him.

Then he saw the sense of Ithnain's pre-fight speech. Tom Gurden would have to kill or permanently maim six powerful men to maintain his freedom. And somewhere beyond them, down the line, were six more, a dozen, a hundred. His skin would pop and bleed just with the effort of taking them on, one by one.

Better to put resistance aside and go quietly. "All right," he said. He just sat there, relaxed, and smiled.

The doors closed and the train moved on.

"Missed your chance," Gurden observed.

The men held their positions, swaying only slightly as the cars picked up speed.

"This train is going nowhere but to the next station," Ithnain said. "My people will follow it and pick us up there."

As the train pulled into Manahawkin and began to slow down, Gurden slid across the seat, swung his feet into the aisle, and stood up. Instinctively, his body leaned slightly backward to counter the train's braking. His inner ear told him that, if he would only launch himself forward down the aisle, into the three men at the front end of the car, then the train's deceleration would increase his momentum—and so his striking force—by perhaps sixty percent. He could feel the pull of it against his body, along with the temptation to action, building and . . . peaking.

Gurden put the thought aside. He might overcome those men. He might even get through the doors and out to the platform. But the others, Ithnain's "people," would only be waiting beyond.

So he walked, a slow tread and heavy-footed, down to the front end of the car. The men formed a guarded semi-circle about him and, as the door slid open, followed him out onto the platform.

They went down the stairs to the ground level, and there a black van was waiting with its rear doors open. Two men, also dressed rough, waited on either side of the dark opening. They held their weapons ready.

Gurden, with Ithnain walking beside him, approached the van with a half-smile on his face and his hands halfway up, as if to show he was unarmed.

The guard on the left raised his weapon, an angular pistol with a barrel as big around as a shotgun's, and shot Gurden in the chest.

He looked down, feeling cold liquid flow from the point of impact, expecting to see bubbles of red blood and shards of white bone. Instead he saw a tuft of red and yellow . . . *hair*. The silk packing of a drug dart. The silver syringe hung out of his chest and pumped something—poison? painkiller? sleepy syrup?—into his heart.

Gurden stumbled forward until his knees caught on the van's bumper. He slumped inside, his hands slipping across its gray carpeting. His vision was fading, but he could still see into the van's body. At the far end, facing outward, was a seated figure— still and unmoving as a god's statue—wearing a white shirt that appeared to rise over its chin. Or perhaps bandages wrapped its neck . . .

"Hurro, Tom," Sandy said thickly.

"I had not expected to find this level of incompetence in a team of hand-picked men—my own men least of all."

The voice was dryly humorous, superior, relaxed, eminently male, slightly British in its breadth of vowels and choice of words—in short, a cultured speaker, to the American ear. And yet the voice, which continued to wash across Tom Gurden's ears as his senses returned, betrayed something else. The liquid Ls had a burred edge. The Ss were softened to a near-lisping *eth*. Was it a trace of native French? Or, more likely, some version of Arabic.

"Hyou must make do with what hyou have." That voice was Sandy's, still damaged but healing remarkably fast—unless the drug in that dart had knocked Gurden out for a space of some days.

Under his cheek he could feel the rough nap of the van's carpet. He moved his arms against it and discovered they were unfettered. Pushing down against the floor, trying to rise, he also discovered weakness in his arms, like a limb that had gone to sleep under inappropriate pressure. His body rose a centimeter as he pushed, then fell back with a muffled *phumf*.

"Your friend tries his strength."

"Indeed."

"We are not ready for him."

"Another dart?"

"No, no. Let him waken naturally. Perhaps he should witness our attack. And gain an appreciation of us."

" 'Appreciation.' That word can reflect negative qualities, too, y'know."

"Whatever. . . . Besides, in his new state—if indeed he did touch those crystals—he may be able to provide us with valuable . . . even insightful . . . advice."

"As you say."

Gurden opened his eyes. A deep gloom in the enclosed van lingered beyond his lashes. He craned his head stiffly around, looking for Sandy and the other one. They were nowhere to be seen; they must be sitting in the driver's compartment. Perhaps they were observing him with closed-circuit television. And perhaps they did not care.

"Rruh—?" He worked his jaw and moved his tongue around his mouth. "What now?"

"The sleeper awakes! Excellent!" the cultured voice said. "Welcome, sir. *Bienvenu*. And a thousand apologies. Were it not for the limitations of my countrymen, I had hoped to prepare a proper chamber, perhaps with a bed, for your return to awareness."

"How . . . long was I out?"

"Who is it that speaks?"

"Tom Gurden—as you ought to know."

"Alas, then it was not long. We prepared a dose for six hours—of real time, that is. This is the same day, Tom Gurden, and barely into evening."

"What—?" Gurden sat up and rubbed the bridge of his nose. "Never mind. Where are we?"

He looked around and found a small, square window in his compartment's forward bulkhead. Whatever light there was, came through there. As did the voices.

"Mays Landing, Tom." That was Sandy. "Still in the District of New Jersey."

"Don't know it—Mays Wherever, that is. New Jersey I'm beginning to know all to well."

"A sense of humor!" the man exclaimed. "That will make the coming encounters all the more enjoyable."

Gurden crawled over to the little window, got a grip on its frame with his fingers, and pulled himself up until his eyes were level with it. Beyond he saw the van's dashboard; the backs of Sandy's head and a black-haired man's; then, beyond the windshield, a sea of green reeds. The sunlight was low and golden on those reeds, the end of a perfect afternoon. In the distance was a line of white cliffs, or maybe the ridgeline of a salt mountain.

"What are we waiting for?" Gurden asked.

The man's head turned, and Tom could see olive-toned skin, an arched Levantine nose, a curve of artfully shaved mustache.

"For nightfall. And for your returning strength. Don't try to hold yourself erect. Relax, Tom Gurden. Let us decide for you."

As the man said this, Gurden's over-tired fingers gave out. He slid sideways down the metal wall, hitting his head on one of the compartment's side-benches.

The gate was more ornate than it had to be. Its art deco scrollwork cut into the faux-granite surface of the concrete piers, its lion-headed latch plate, its showy layering of nickel-steel with black iron in the bars and cross pieces—all of this offended Hasan as-Sabah's well-honed sensibilities.

A long lifetime, twelve long lifetimes, could make any man a connoisseur of simplicity, of elegant economy, and of smooth-working efficiency. This gate, with its mock pretensions, was a gaudy atavism, throwback to a time when the Europeans had thought they really meant something in the world. It was all hollow now, of course.

Hasan sat in his yellow Porsche a hundred meters down the road from the gate. Two hundred meters in the other direction was a covered truck, which held his primary strike force. To any casual watcher, they were just two vehicles stopped along the road. Each faced in opposite directions, with the gate to the Mays Landing Fusion Power Plant between them.

The dog was not a casual watcher, however.

It sat just inside the gate, with its attention fixed on the Porsche. What intelligence looked through those blue-filmed eyes? What could it tell about the couple in the sportscar? Hasan knew that his license plates would be angled out of the dog's plane of vision and cast in shadow by the setting sun. Anyway, the license number was perfectly valid, relating to a fictitious person whose movements matched

Hasan's own within the tolerances of computer and credit surveillance.

Alexandra stirred in the seat beside him.

"What is it?" he asked.

"I will follow you, of course, Hasan."

"After three hundred years, my dear, you have no other choice."

"No, not really. . . . But, even after all this time, there are things I do not understand."

"And these are—?"

"Why do you want to take this plant? You can't hold it for long. And you can't safely give it back."

"As to the last, we will bargain for passage off the site and transportation to somewhere in the world without U.S. extradition. The grid's owners and the authorities who back them will gladly offer us the exchange."

"But why take it in the first place?" she insisted. "For a money ransom? That has never been your interest."

"I am a teacher, Alexandra."

"Yes, you teach a form of chaos."

"Is that all you think of the Hashishiyun?"

"Well . . ."

"I teach practical wisdom. It's time the Americans learned to live without the things they think they need.

"Once, for a barest minute in the last century, we of the *jihad* owned a lever to move them, to hurt them. The Wahabis and Shiites who controlled the oil held a powerful lever against the Europeans' energy-hungry society. In time, however, other fossil fuel sources—and those not of Allah—could provide for the westerners. And then this fusion thing was discovered and harnessed to their will.

"But, if the Wind of God is strong in heart and spirit," he continued, "then we may have a lever again. We can take that plant, stop it, destroy it, and darken a section of their eastern shore, from Connecticut to Delaware. That will teach them the meaning of power. In many senses."

"And Gurden? What of him?"

"He will teach *me* the meaning of power."

"If he knows at all."

"If he is the man you say, then he knows."

"But why bring him here?"

"Is there a better place to put him under pressure? Ithnain will take him through the assault on this plant. We will place him at the point of maximum vulnerability. And then we shall see."

"He may still defeat you."

"Not for long. I beat him once, and I am now his elder by many lifetimes. While he has had to—what is that game called?—'hopscotch' through the centuries, I have come the long way. Much I have learned since Thomas and I last met."

"You still haven't learned how to use the Stone."

"I know more than you suppose."

"Oh? And what may that be, My Lord?"

"It is subject to electromagnetic fields. And it has a dimension of—"

Beyond the gate, the dog swung its head toward the west, as if called by its master. It rose off its haunches, took a step in that direction, turned back to look at the car. Somewhere a decision was made. The dog whirled and dashed off along the fence.

"We can begin," Hasan said, swinging up his door.

He reached down for the lever that popped the trunk of the car—which was in the front end.

"What are you going to do?"

"Open the gate." He removed the launcher and extended its tripod legs. Down the road, Hasan's men—alerted by his own activity—began climbing down from the truck.

He took one of the special loads from the trunk and fitted it into the launcher's modified breech.

"Don't you want to move closer to the gate?" she asked.

"No."

He took aim, at an angle to the central pier, lining up the sight's cross hairs on the lion-headed plate's blunt steel nose, which was thrown into high relief by the sun's last amber-red rays.

Pfuutt! The launcher shot off a trail of yellow-white smoke.

Seeing it, his men dropped flat onto the roadway, covering the backs of their necks with their hands.

Hasan kept his eye in the sight.

The lion's head disappeared.

When Gurden awoke again, his arms and legs had more feeling, although the muscles were still stiff from sleeping in a strange position. His mouth had a metallic taste in it, probably an after-effect of the drug, but his head was clear.

The van's insides were totally dark; so it must be night. At least eighteen hours had passed since he was abducted from the pool in the Holiday Hull. In that time he had ridden up the coast in a jetboat, climbed around the rafters of an abandoned building, hidden in the sand dunes under the midday sun, fought a woman of skill and power nearly to the death, and rolled around on the floor of a van. He'd had nothing to eat, no chance to wash, and scant opportunity to relieve himself. His body felt gritty and gummy and hollow. His once new and well-made clothing stuck to his skin with dried perspiration. He could even smell himself. . . . And what could he do about it now?

Put it aside.

He stood up, remembering quickly to crouch under the low headroom. He went directly to the tiny window in the front bulkhead and looked out.

The front compartment was empty. The only light

was coming through the windshield from distant clusters of lights like a small town that was perhaps three kilometers away. No, after a minute he could see that the lights were brighter and more purposeful: they reflected off the sides of a complex of low, industrial-type buildings.

With nothing else to look at, Gurden studied the complex.

It was enormous. It took his eyes and mind a moment to assemble the patterns of its lighting— sodium-yellow area floodlights, windows opening on the greenish hollows of fluorescent-lighted rooms, blinking red aircraft warning beacons, white strings of walkway and gantry lighting—into a coherent whole.

To start with, he could assume that similar colors would represent lights used for similar purposes, and probably at the same lumen levels. Then he could equate brightness with distance, as an astronomer does with stars. The nearest pinpoints were only about a kilometer away, and equally spaced across his field of view. They brightened and dimmed at regular intervals. Those would be photo-floodlights, panning back and forth along a perimeter fence to assist the plant's video surveillance. Even at their dimmest, those lights all outshone or occluded the other, farther lights. By estimating the distance to that line of floodlights, and measuring the length of the fence with his eye, he estimated the entire complex was more than three kilometers wide. From the strength of the most distant lamps, he guessed it was at least four kilometers across to the far side.

What industry would be here, out in the marshlands of central New Jersey? The refineries and chemical plants for which this Boswash division was infamous were farther north. And these plain white walls—he recalled seeing that "salt mountain" when he was awake earlier—did not look like a refinery.

Mays Landing. The name was ringing faint bells.

Something from video? Something to do with nuclear power—no, fusion power! This was the Intertidal Electric plant which supplied all of Central Boswash, from the Department of New Canaan down to the Wilmington Municipality. And Tom Gurden was sitting just beyond its fence in a van driven by a foreign-speaking gentleman who was supported by capable men who dressed rough. . . . Didn't that just paint a picture.

The doors in the end of the van opened with a bump and a hiss of badly adjusted hydraulics. A flashlight beam probed the interior and tangled in Gurden's legs.

He turned with a hand up to shield his eyes.

"You can come out now," said the team leader, Ithnain.

"What are you going to do to me?" But Gurden had already worked out the answer: he was not to be hurt, not by men who had used a timed drug to put him under. So he walked to the rear of the compartment and let himself down.

"My Lord Hasan would have you watch the assault."

"Are you going to take the power plant?"

"Yes. Come."

"Where is Sandy?"

"You have not time for her now. Come."

Gurden shrugged and followed the man across the road. The Palestinian's steps *clump*ed on the asphalt. By the few stars that broke through the rising mist and a fingernail's width of moon low in the west, Gurden could see that Ithnain was dressed in combat boots and military-style fatigues. He had an efficient-looking gun suspended horizontally just under his elbow by a long strap that went over his shoulder. The gun had a smooth, carbon-fiber body around its stubby barrel and short stock. In front of the trigger guard and behind the molded handgrip was a cylindrical cartridge holder. It was some kind of machine gun.

A knot of men, perhaps six or ten, waited on the other side of the road. The road was on a raised causeway, with an embankment about a meter high sloping down into the reeds. The tide was in, as Gurden could tell from the musical splash of the stones they occasionally kicked loose and which rolled down the bank.

"Are we going to swim for it?" he asked.

"This is a diversion merely. The main assault is by another way, under My Lord's personal direction."

"Hasan?"

"Yes."

"Hasan al Shabbat? Harry Sunday?"

"Please!" The man beside him stiffened. "You must not use that vulgar name. Especially among these, his followers. The name you have spoken is a corruption from the tongues of stupid western journalists. My Lord's true name is Hasan as-Sabah. His is an ancient name, originally Persian."

"Yeah, sure. But he *is* the same Harry Friday, isn't he? The man who led the Settlers' Uprising at Haifa and later smuggled an H-bomb into Khan Yunis?"

Ithnain paused. "Yes. But those were achievements of My Lord's earlier years—by your accounting."

"And now he's operating in the States."

"So are we all."

"And he wants me for some reason."

"For some reason," Ithnain agreed.

Then the man turned and gave rapid orders in Arabic using many slang terms and military jargon, of which Gurden could follow only a little. He caught the words "missile" and "range," but he would have figured out the gist of the orders anyway, as soon as the men unpacked the long case—the size of a big man's coffin—which lay at their feet.

The white-epoxy skin of a Sea Sparrow missile gleamed in the mist. The darkness of the case hid the blunt tube of the manual launcher.

Gurden understood about these missiles. The warhead contained a high-voltage capacitor, an argon-neon laser tube pre-excited to an elevated energy state, a beam splitter, and a glass pellet the size of a rice grain. Inside the pellet was a mixture of deuterium and tritium. On contact with its target, the capacitor fired; the laser charged and fired a beam of high-energy coherent photons; the splitter redirected the beam so that it bathed the pellet from three sides; the glass skin of the pellet vaporized instantly. The outward surface of the glass flew away in a mist; the inward surface compressed and heated the mixture of hydrogen isotopes until it fused into helium. The result was a tiny hydrogen bomb.

The explosive force of a Sea Sparrow's inertial-fusion warhead was almost nothing: about equal to a tactical hand grenade, barely enough to shatter the front end of the missile casing. But explosive force wasn't the point. The electromagnetic pulse from this nuclear explosion would create an induced voltage that burned out electronics within a specified range, usually about 1,000 meters. All but hard-shielded sensors and electronics would light up like an Atlantic City slot machine on a jackpot—and then die.

In tests, one Sea Sparrow which fell a hundred meters short of its objective had sent an old *Ohio*-class missile submarine of 15,000 tonnes steaming in ever-narrower circles, with the hatches of its launch tubes popped ajar and its reactor running in uncontrollable melt-down mode. The observing admirals had voted on the spot to evacuate the hull and finish her with nuclear-tipped torpedoes. All that from a six-kilogram missile which had been hand-fired from a rubber boat.

"What are you going to do with them?" Gurden asked.

"Take out the guard dogs."

"Of course, the dogs. . . . What about the electronic circuitry inside that plant?"

Ithnain shrugged. "It should not be in range. And if it is, it is probably well shielded, for similar discharges go on there."

"Probably . . . " Gurden repeated.

The man Ithnain had spoken to lifted the missile gently out of its case. He pulled off the black-colored streamer flag—which might be red in daylight—that was attached to the safety pin on the arming lever. While another held the launcher vertical, he lowered it down the tube; this action depressed the lever and armed the warhead. Then the two men raised the launcher onto the shoulders of the first man and extended its inertial braces.

The man keyed a switch on the panel beside his cheek, lighting its red and green diodes. He swung the working end toward the fence, screwed his eye into the laser-imaging sight, and wrapped a brown finger around the trigger on the tube's pistol grip.

Tom Gurden tried to imagine what the launcher might be seeing. The fence would not offer much of a target. Maybe he was sighting on a dog.

When the man fired the rocket, Gurden was ready. He ducked and covered his eyes so that the silver-yellow glare of burning solid fuel would not destroy his night vision. A wash of acrid smoke rolled across him. So he never saw the warhead's detonation. He wondered if the electromagnetic pulse would bollix the magnetically coded data on his new identity and debit cards.

Not that it mattered. If he were arrested as an accomplice in the capture of a sector fusion plant, he didn't think he would have much need for a functioning magnetic persona.

While the others waited for their vision to clear, Gurden glided sideways, toward the truck. If its ignition system was beyond the warhead's range— and Ithnain would be smart enough, probably, to park his vehicles out of reach of the missile's effects— then Gurden might drive off while his captors were still night-blind.

He slid the driver's-side door open quietly and slipped into the seat. He felt beside the control stalk for the keypad.

Birr-burr, birr-burr.

It was the cellular phone on the dashboard. Gurden ignored it.

The keypad was under his fingers. He started to enter a single digit repeated seven times. That was the socially agreed-on access code, such as most people would use when more than one driver has use of a vehicle, or to get around a drunk-lock.

Birr-burr, birr-burr.

Something in the back of Tom Gurden's head told him to pick it up.

Eliza: Don't leave, Tom.

Gurden: What? Who is this?

Eliza: It's Eliza . . . 212, Tom. You know me.

Gurden: Your voice sounds funny, thicker.

Eliza: That's the cellular circuitry, Tom. Don't drive away. Stay with Ithnain and his men.

Gurden: But they're terrorists. They're about to break into a—

Eliza: I know what they are planning to do. You must go with them. I need you inside the plant, Tom.

Gurden: *You* need me? Explain that, would you? It's dangerous in there. I could get killed.

Eliza: You have always trusted me, Tom. Obey me now. Go in with Ithnain.

Gurden: But—

Eliza: Do not dispute this. Believe in me. Your
. . . life . . . depends on it.
Gurden: I don't—
Eliza: Click!

"Get out of the truck, please, Mr. Gurden." Ithnain
stood beside the door. The barrel of his gun was
elevated, its muzzle almost pointing toward Gurden's
face.

Gurden put down the phoneset and lifted his hands
level with his head. He swung his left leg out the
door, slid his rump down off the seat.

"You will not leave us. My Lord Hasan has specifically asked for your presence."

So has someone else, Gurden thought. "Believe in
me . . . Obey me." Gurden did not believe Eliza's
voice for a minute. Something was wrong when a
cybershrink started calling *you.* But his options were
decidedly limited.

Ithnain and his men would be watching the truck
now. If he were to try striking out on his own across
the marshland, it would be a long, wet walk. If he
should manage to get back to the truck and start it,
he would be moving down the marsh's straight,
causeway-like roads away from them. Alerted to his
plans and wary now, they would put a second missile
up his back as he went.

Gurden had little choice except to follow them.

He looked out over the marsh grasses, where the
missile had gone. The floodlights along the fence
were out. So was area lighting over about a quarter
of the complex.

Ithnain was giving orders, and the men about him
were quietly returning to their vehicles to drive around
for the assault on the main gate.

So the dog took them all by surprise.

It came through the reeds on its long, steel-sprung
legs, making less splash than a horse would through

the water. Perhaps it had been roving beyond the fence, out of range of the Sea Sparrow. Perhaps it had come running on central command from an undamaged sector. In either case, the first indication anyone had of its presence was the scream as it tore into one of Ithnain's troops.

The man went down—they later found—from a fifty-centimeter-long gash that ripped him open from shoulder to hip. Some technician had modified the dog's personnel-restraint grapples into knife-edged scythes and had bumped the pressure and reaction speed of the jaw mechanism by fifty to a hundred percent.

The dog's night vision was infra-red. It had turned and taken a second man before anyone was quite recovered from that first scream.

By then, of course, it was right among them.

Ithnain pulled his gun to the ready and had *spang*ed three bullets off its titanium hide before most of the rest of them had reacted. His firing caught the dog's attention, and it bore silently down on Ithnain.

He fed the solid stock of his weapon into the grapple and tried to dance away, holding the dog at bay.

The dog tried to shake off the metal and carbon and get around the gun to the warm flesh, but Ithnain stayed close to the snapping jaws and kept working the stock deeper into the mechanism.

"Someone—knock its—legs out," Ithnain gasped as he danced.

Gurden hardly had time to decide that was his job—nor to see this attack as another opportunity. He instinctively threw himself into a flying sidekick aimed at the dog's hindquarters. They went down. The animal jerked around on its flexible spine, made three courtesy snaps at Gurden's head, then returned its attentions to Ithnain.

Gurden tried to get his hands around the dog's

pasterns and control its rear feet, hoping he could pull it off balance—and not get bitten. However, the steel-braided control lines bunched around its ankles squirmed across each other and made his grip slippery.

If only he could somehow lock up the rear legs, the beast would go down. Gurden then tried to work his *fingers* in among those cogs and cables, but the machine was dancing around too fast even for that. And every fifth move programmed by the dog's robot brain was a snap directed at Gurden's head; so he was kept busier staying out of its way than trying to immobilize it.

"Slow *down!*" he gritted through his teeth.

The dog actually paused for a second in mid-whirl. Had it heard him? Had something inside it responded to a spoken command? Gurden almost felt as if some impulse from within him had touched the dog's chip circuitry directly.

Tom tried to adjust his grip and pull it off balance, but Ithnain chose that moment to thrust with the stock of his gun. The movement pushed something in the dog's program, and the spinning, slashing, snapping dance went on.

Gurden and Ithnain were tiring rapidly, but clearly the dog could keep up the struggle all night. The rest of the men simply formed a wide circle and watched.

Except for one—the missile marksman.

While the two men and the dog whirled around, he dragged a second Sea Sparrow case from the nearby truck. He pulled the safety pin but didn't bother with the launch tube, working the arming lever with his bare hand instead. He raised the live missile over his head and threw it, nose first, down onto the hard road surface four meters away.

The warhead's explosion ripped into their ears. A thin breeze of white plastic shards whipped past them all, stinging faces and hands. And the dog sank down on its haunches with a twitching palsy, rolled on its side, and went still.

Ithnain stood over it, breathing hard. Gurden pushed one of the dog's legs off himself and sat up.

"Thank you, Hamad," the Palestinian leader said. "That was well done." He retrieved his scarred weapon from the dead jaws and looked at Gurden. "And my thanks to you, too, for your bravery."

Gurden blew out his cheeks. "De nada."

"We have a long walk ahead of us tonight," Ithnain observed. "The pulse from that warhead has certainly destroyed the turbine ignition and control circuits in our vehicles."

Gurden could be sure, also, that his identity cards were ruined.

Sura 7
The Fall of the Red Tent
इच्छजझअटठडढणत

The moving finger writes; and, having writ,
Moves on: nor all your piety nor wit
Shall lure it back to cancel half a line,
Nor all your tears wash out a word of it.
—Omar Khayyam

Like a finger of white fire, Amnet's thrust stabbed
at Hasan.

A master less skilled in the uses of astral energy
might have directed the bolt at the Assassin's head,
toward the sixth nexus located between and just
behind the eyes. Such a blow, Amnet judged, would
have been worse than useless. Like a punch thrown
at a human face, it would aim at that sense organ
best made to detect it. Hasan would have passed it
to one side as easily as a boxer in the pancratium
ducks under a roundhouse swing.

Instead, Amnet aimed his thrust lower, toward the
third nexus that lies behind the navel. Seat of the
in-flowing juices of life during gestation, this nexus
would absorb energy and enfold it within the body:
the perfect target for a deathblow.

A person standing to one side might have seen
nothing, or merely felt a shuddering in the air, caught
the blur of motion that an arrow leaves behind in

afterimage on the mirror of the eye. To Amnet, who
launched and directed it, the Stone's energy was a pal-
pable substance, as clearly defined as the light of a rose
window passing through the dusty air of a cathedral,
as brightly red as the first ray of the sun that rises
over the mountains. To Hasan, who was its target, the
bolt would have been tinged with blue, shifted forward
along the prismatic spectrum by its own speed.

It crossed the distance between them in the no-
time of a passing thought.

If Hasan even saw it, he had no way to avoid it.
The bolt of energy entered his body like a horse
galloping headlong through the gap in a hedge and
vanishing.

Hasan swayed backward. His hands and arms, piv-
oting at the shoulders, swung forward as if to coun-
terbalance his weight. His fingers stretched to their
limit, pointing at Thomas Amnet's face. Hasan's aura
generated a misty blue glow. His body shone brightly,
like a house consumed by flames that have not yet
pierced the roof and shattered the glass in the windows. . . . Hasan's body bent in a spasm of the muscles.

The return blow smashed into Amnet, throwing
him back across the grassy bank by his own body's
length. He landed on the small of his back, feet
rising into the air, and rolled up and over on his neck
and skull. Something there cracked viciously. As
Amnet's body straightened out, his legs came down
hard, his bootheels denting the turf. He tried to lift
his head and could not.

Hasan leapt across the stream and stood above
him. The Assassin might have drawn a blade and
struck down into Amnet's throat or belly. He might
have stamped a foot into the Templar's face. Instead,
Hasan hunched his shoulders and made the same
snowball-molding gesture that he had used at first.

Amnet grew afraid.

Panic galvanized his limbs, and he struggled to

move out of the way. His head now lifted against a streak of white pain that lived in his neck. The movement of his head led into a jumbled, diving roll that took him a few miserable feet across the grass.

Hasan hurled his energy focus squarely into Amnet's back. A red heat bloomed there, tearing muscles and bruising bones. His legs went cold.

With a massive effort, Amnet called upon the Stone to counteract the pain, to repair broken muscle fibers and smooth a tangled skein of nerves. The Stone warmed with its own vibrant energy and pumped feeling into his lower body. From its pouch beneath his belt, he could feel it straightening his limbs, adding to the power of his thighs and calves, lifting him as a mother pulls her child from the cradle and swaddles it against the cold.

Standing upright now, he turned to face Hasan.

With another supreme effort of will, he called forth greater energies from the Stone.

These were no gentle coaxings of its latent power, such as he might make when using the Stone to order swirling vapors into a vision of the future, or to cloud the mind and bend the will of a sultan-general. This was rape. This was grasping. He was using the Stone the way a berserker might swing a claymore— wildly. His intention was to bludgeon, to trample, to unmake.

He hurled another stabbing thrust outward at Hasan, who stood momentarily weakened from his last stroke. Amnet drove this spear of energy higher this time, into the fifth nexus that lies in the hollow of the throat. At full strength, this blow would have ripped out the man's windpipe and crushed his larynx up into the soft palate behind his mouth. Hasan should have died in a gulp of blood.

The Assassin's head lolled back with it, as loosely and carelessly as a man absorbing the kisses of a maiden. A smile curved the lips under his mustache. The energy wreathed his head.

With a sharp nod, Hasan sent the flow back, speeding it in a blue flicker directly into the leather pouch below the Templar's belt.

The force of it staggered Amnet's newly erected legs. He went to one knee in the grass. *"Surgite!"* he commanded himself sternly. *"Rise up!"* Another burst of the Stone's energies flowed into his limbs. Simultaneously he tried to direct an outward, warding thrust at Hasan.

The Stone seemed to grow heavier, dragging down at his belt, splitting the deerskin pouch in which Amnet carried it. His hands came down to clutch it as the Stone fell free. The crystal lattice vibrated with the increased demands he was making on it. The intersecting axes of the lattice bowed outward and started to pull apart.

Thomas Amnet could feel the tearing deep in his brain.

The chants of the Moslems rose by half-notes up the scale, like the buzz of a cicada drilling the heated air of summer. Grand Master Gerard, not being schooled in music, only knew that the Saracen soldiers outside his circle were working themselves up to a pitch of perfect violence.

Just when a man thought their tension could build no more, when he was about to drop his lance and run screaming forward onto the ready scimitars, the drone would plateau. It would work its way across that barren monotone and then find a way to rise once again to a higher, more strangled pitch.

Many of the Christians fainted from the heat. More fell away as their nerve snapped and consciousness fled the merciless slaughter that the Moslem song seemed to promise.

Gerard put a hand to the hilt of his long sword and

paced in the narrow space behind the ranks of
Templars who opposed the Saracens on the west side
of the hill. As one man swayed and sagged out of
line, Gerard would urge another forward to take his
place.

The sweat ran over his brow and down on either
side of his eyes. Every drop trickling through the
grime of his face was water of his body that would
never be replaced. He was dying in a salt stream.

As he raised a gauntleted hand to his forehead,
hoping to blot this flow with an edge of its leather
glove, the chanting stopped.

Two men to his right in the line fainted dead away
at the sudden silence. Gerard was about to motion
two more Templars forward to fill the gap, but he
held his hand.

What did the silence mean?

With a sudden yell, the Saracens answered him.

At the peak of their frenzy, the Moslem soldiers
closest to the line threw themselves on the lance
ends, bearing the points down with the sudden weight.

Taking up the yell, those behind them climbed
over the still wriggling bodies of their comrades and
struck with swords while the Christians were yet
struggling to pull their weapons free. The wickedly
curving scimitars bit into the unguarded flesh of the
neck, between helm and mail. Blood fountained and
the first rank of the Christian circle stumbled backward, dead before the second rank could lower them
to the ground and ready their own swords.

The Saracen wave rolled over the Templars.

Gerard had seen berserkers go into battle, fight,
lose a limb or an eye, fight still harder, and finally
die—all without regaining a moment's sense or reason. The berserkers of his experience were solitaries,
each a prisoner of his own madness. The human
wave that bore down on the French lines was his first
sight of the collective madness. A thousand men

moved as one and died without even a murmur of
pain. Their bodies, trampled beneath their own comrades' feet, showed no more feeling than shoeleather
beneath the weight of a man. They were possessed.

Gerard crossed himself, drew his sword, and retreated up the hill. He went facing backward, with
his eyes fixed on the advancing wave of snarling
brown faces and flashing curved blades. Like a line
of mowers, they cut through any who would stand
before them.

Something tangled Gerard's feet, and he turned to
see what it might be. His face turned into a billow of
red canvas, the color of the blood that had followed
him up the hill. His ankles were snared by the ropes
of King Guy's tent.

He raised his sword to cut the canvas and escape
through the tent's interior. Before he could swing his
blade in a slashing arc, something heavy struck the
back of his head. He fell face-forward into the side
of the tent, snagging and pulling it down with his
weight. The roof of the pavilion teetered and swayed.
Then the ropes, hacked at the other corners by the
Saracens who had reached the crest of the hill, gave
way and the tent collapsed.

Folds of heavy red canvas, embroidered with the
heraldry of France and the faces of the Apostles, cut
off the light and smothered Gerard.

Amnet's hands curled around the Stone as it slipped
out of its leather pouch. The smooth surface was hot
to the touch. Each facet cut into the pads and tendons of his fingers like red-hot knifeblades. From
deep within it he could feel the terrible energies
tearing at its lattice, finally sundering the incorrupt-
ible pattern. A note as high and clear as a glass
harmonica's filled the valley. Its focus, however, was
deep inside the crystal.

Staggering, he carried the Stone as he might carry

his severed testicles, one step, two steps, seeking a way to cope with the pain and sense of loss.

A dozen feet away, by the soundlessly bubbling stream, Hasan recovered from his last returned blow. As the Assassin's eyes cleared, he saw the swollen crystal clutched to Amnet's groin. When he understood what was happening, his mouth came open. His eyes bulged outward with disbelief.

"No-o-o!"

That sound came through to Amnet's deadened ears, penetrating the veil of pure sound that welled up from the Stone. Hasan's cry of negation, backed with a sincere thrust of emotion, overloaded the crystal with the last quantum of energy that would be properly focused in that pretty valley beside the Galilee for almost a thousand years.

Like a churchbell breaking apart, the Stone shattered under its load. Its final song ended in a clang of falling metal. White-hot fangs of crystal showered out from between Amnet's bloodied fingers.

The energy left his legs. He pitched forward to his knees, then to the side, striking the ground with his shoulder, the side of his head, a hip. Like a puppet without strings, he finally rested—stiff and awkward—while the tender shoots of grass tickled his cheek and scratched at his open eye.

Hasan recovered and approached him slowly. The man moved once again with a supple grace, the hallmark of live things that are superbly aware, ready to jump back at the first sign of danger.

Amnet could give no signs. His broken body, now strange and cold, was already half-dead, no longer animated by the energies of the Stone. Inch by inch, he could feel the nerves in his exposed spine swell up, split, fizzle, and fade. When this wave of uncoordinated activity reached the base of his skull, he could feel his reason leaving him. Soon would go his self.

Mouthing words that Amnet's ears could no longer hear, Hasan reached down out of the sight of the Templar's fixed gaze. The Assassin's hands must have been in the region of Amnet's groin—but what damage he could hope to work on the body *there*, Thomas could not imagine.

Hasan's hands made quick brushing, sweeping movements. Then he withdrew his hands, and so close did the Assassin clutch them to his body that Amnet could not see what they held.

With a last look into Amnet's dimming eyes, the other turned and, bent over his burden, walked quickly out of the valley.

The snapping and sizzling at the base of Amnet's skull rose within it, like water bubbling up in a foundering hull. As it poured out of the broken top of his head, he went into blackness and his body died.

The hands that lifted the tent cloth off Gerard de Ridefort were deft and strong. The faces that peered down at him were brown and lean, and the light of victorious battle showed in their eyes. The Saracens lifted him, their fingertips caressing the red cross stitched on his surcoat. They made chortling noises as they examined this signal of his allegiance.

One lifted the badge of office that Gerard wore around his neck, a heavy thing of gold and enamel on a square-linked chain, also of gold. The Grand Master moved to protect it, but his captors quickly batted his hands away. They stole the badge from around his neck, and two of them dashed off, tugging and fighting over it.

His sword was gone, dropped in the last charge when he had fallen among the tent ropes. His captors now lifted the dagger from his belt and put a noose of rough rope around his neck.

They led him down the hill. On all sides a thousand others were so led, dazed and feeble, confused and half-dead from strain and the lack of water. They stumbled like sheep on the ends of cords.

At the bottom of the hill, the Saracen commanders were separating the Templars, who wore their red cross, from the other Christian knights who had followed King Guy. The Templars were led aside into a steep-wall gully below Hattin. A line of Saracen archers, with their ridiculous short bows, stepped to the rim above them.

"Christians!" a voice called out in clear, strong French from above. "You who are the Order of the Temple!"

Gerard looked up but, against the glare of the sun, he could not see who was speaking.

"It is now appropriate," the voice went on in a confiding and almost friendly manner, "that you should kneel down and worship your God."

Like a congregation at chapel, five thousand disarmed Templars fell to their knees. The jangle of their mail coats was like the rattle of anchor chain at the catheads of a fleet.

Gerard tried to pray, but he was distracted by a murmur, a moaning, that came from either end of the gully. He strained his neck to peer over the bowed heads and curved backs of his men. The Saracens were doing some work with swords there.

"They are chopping off the heads of our comrades!" came frightened whispers through the ranks. "Rise up! Fight them! Save yourselves!"

"Nay! Hold!" Gerard commanded between his teeth. "Better a clean stroke of the sword than a dozen badly aimed arrows."

A few of the men around him chuckled at this. The whispers stopped.

After a time, someone behind him said, softly: "We'll pitch our tents in Heaven this night, old friend."

"No," his unseen companion murmured, "on the other side of that river, I think . . . The same way we have lived."

A silence, while those within earshot absorbed this.

"You didn't have to mention water," someone nearby rebuked.

"Oh, for just a drop," moaned another voice.

There was no time for that unseemly moaning to go on, as the Saracen executioners were upon them and—chop, chop.

Saladin climbed up and perched himself upon a perilously high stack of cushions. He shifted his weight experimentally, to see if he might not topple off at an inopportune moment. The stack, constructed as cleverly as the pharaoh's pyramids, seemed stable enough.

He might have trusted more civilized opponents to observe the proper courtesies, even in defeat, even stretched to the limits of their endurance by heat and thirst. A captured Moslem sheikh would know to enter the tent on his knees, on his knees and elbows, or rolling on his belly if necessary, to keep his head lower and his posture more humble than that of the general who had taken him. But these Christian nobles would not understand such proprieties. They would walk upright into the tent and stand tall, as if they were the conquerors this day.

The faithful who followed him must not be allowed to see their leader humiliated in this fashion. Hence the pile of pillows.

All that seemed to be for nothing.

King Guy did not walk into the tent but was carried, arm and leg, by four of Saladin's strongest retainers. Other ransomable nobles followed behind their prostrate king. They were walking, but their heads hung down on their chests.

"Is he dead?" Saladin asked.

"No, My Lord. But the heat fever is upon him. He glows with madness."

Guy, the Latin King of Jerusalem, lay like a bundle of old rags on the carpet before the raised pile of cushions. The man's feet twitched and his hands wandered; his eyes rolled around in his head unseeing. The other nobles—among whom Saladin marked the lean, feline features of Reynald de Châtillon—hung back from their king, plainly afraid he was dying. As he was.

"Bring refreshment for this king," Saladin commanded.

Mustafa himself fetched a bowl of rosewater, iced with snows brought in clothbound casks from the mountains. The vizier knelt by the king's head and dipped the end of his own sash in the basin, wetting it to lay across Guy's heated brow. The coolness brought some reason to the King's eyes, and he stopped twitching. When his mouth opened, Mustafa held the rim of the bowl to his lips and let a little of the water soak into the tongue. It was cracked and furred like the hide of a horse left two months dead in the desert.

King Guy raised his hands to the bowl, clearly intending to lift and pour it into his throat. Mustafa, stronger than he, held it steady. But, when the King seemed to understand the wisdom to be had in small sips, Mustafa let him have it. The vizier nodded to Saladin and stepped back.

Levering himself up on one elbow, Guy drank and—for the first time—looked about with awareness of his surroundings. He saw the other French nobles, standing like whipped dogs with their tongues hanging down into their beards. Some measure of kingly responsibility inspired him to lift the bowl, offering it toward them.

Reynald de Châtillon was the first to reach for it.

This man, the self-styled Prince of Antioch, had drowned Moslem pilgrims at Medina, burned Christian churches on Cyprus, offered to ravish Saladin's sister, and proposed to scatter the bones of the Prophet. With trembling hands he brought the bowl to his lips—he was taking refreshment as a guest in Saladin's own tent!

"Stop!" Saladin felt his face fold and pinch with a fury beyond reason. He scrambled off the mountain of cushions to stand before the two men. "This is not to be!"

King Guy looked up with an astonished, almost hurt expression on his foolish face.

Reynald, his beard dripping, gave Saladin a smile that was identical in curvature and intention to a sneer.

A red haze filled the General's field of vision. Almost blind with it, he turned to Mustafa.

"Explain to King Guy, that it was he—and not I—who offered this hospitality to our enemy."

Mustafa started forward, kneeled beside the King, and opened his mouth.

Simple explanations would not be enough. Saladin's anger demanded more. With a precision gained from years of training as a warrior, he kicked the basin from Reynald's hands, breaking the man's fingers with the blow. The water splashed the other Christian nobles and the rim of the flying bowl cut one above the eye.

Reynald, sneering openly now, held the wounded hand out toward Saladin. "What does your precious Muhammad command of you?" the voice was so insulting, so mocking . . .

Without thinking, Saladin drew his sword of supple Damascus steel and in one lightning motion slashed up, over, across, and down.

Reynald's arm, severed at the shoulder, fell into King Guy's lap, where it writhed and clutched. The

King squawked and pushed himself backward to be rid of it.

Reynald stared down at the arm, then raised his widely horrified eyes to Saladin. His mouth, forming an incredible "O," began to sing a rising howl of agony, like a wounded dog.

Before the sound could go very far in the tent, one of the Sultan's bodyguards rushed forward, drawing his own sword, and batted Reynald's head from his shoulders. The surprised head rolled across the carpet, fetching face down at the foot of the mountain of pillows. The body, fountaining blood, fell to its knees and pitched forward.

King Guy, now spattered with blood and still pinned beneath the arm, looked up at Saladin with terror.

"Spare us, Great King! Spare us!"

The Sultan, his rage now cooling, looked down at him with contempt.

"Have no fear. It is not proper for a king to kill a king. You and such of your court as can prove noble blood shall be held for ransom. Those others who fought with you—and are still alive—will be sold into slavery. That is the judgment of Saladin."

King Guy sagged back at hearing this, worn by the terrors of the moment into complete submission. "Thank you, My Lord."

The Crusaders—as those waves of European horsemen adventuring in Palestine were eventually called—would never recover their kingdom in the Holy Land. All they would leave was a chain of crumbling hill forts: the architecture of France laid upon the architecture of Rome, laid upon the architecture of Solomon.

Richard of England would come and go upon this scene, also confronting General Saladin and losing to him. In the process, Richard would forfeit the rule of his far green land to brother John, whose stumbles would lead to Runymede and the Great Charter, mother of all constitutions.

Saladin's Ayyubites, and his warrior Mamelukes after them, would rule in Palestine for more than three centuries, but they would never overcome the Assassins in their mountaintop retreat. Blessed in their Secret Garden, protected by their Secret Founder, they would bedevil all who tried to hold the Arab *fellahin* in thrall.

Eventually, the power of Egypt would yield to the growing empire of the Ottoman Turks. These would hang onto the land for another four centuries. They eventually would sink into decay and yield their rule finally to a cluster of sheikhs led by an Englishman, T. E. Shaw, whose *nomme de guerre* was Lawrence. So would begin the British Mandate in Palestine, which was to last barely thirty years in the twentieth century.

The Mandate would end in the muddle that followed Europe's last great war, as the promise and the dream of Zionism were made real on earth. And still the Assassins watched from their spiritual mountaintop, looking out from peasant eyes across their once-fertile valleys. War would roll through again, as first Egyptian—then Syrian—armies tried to retake the land. War would spill over into Lebanon to the north and raze into barbarism the one state that had sought to live in harmony with the shifting winds which that ill-mannered century blew around the world.

The Holy Land would be sculpted and carved, watered and starved, by nine centuries of guerrilla war. And still the Assassins looked out from their spiritual mountaintop.

File 07

Unmask! Unmask!

✡

Him the Almighty Power
Hurl'd headlong flaming from th' Ethereal Sky,
With hideous ruin and combustion down
To bottomless perdition.

—John Milton

The main gates of the complex had been blasted with an explosive power greater than any Sea Sparrow missile's. The two halves of the closure had originally been made of steel bars three centimeters thick, crossed at top, middle, and bottom with bands of layered alloy. They had rolled on steel wheels like a railroad car's on rails of polished metal. Yet the force of the explosion had curled the gate's rods and bars around into curled hemispheres, like lines of latitude and longitude across a globe. The pounding blast had levered the rails out of their pavement grooves. The bomb's shrapnel had pocked and spalled the gates' polished concrete piers on either side of the road. Bolts as big around as Tom Gurden's thumb had been twisted out of their anchoring matrix like taffy pulled from a broken tooth.

As the guerilla band walked up to the gate, Gurden could see the outline of this destruction in the weak shadows and rays thrown from the plant's more distant floodlights. The nearby floods and the tubes along this part of the access road had all been smashed by the explosion.

"What did you use here?" Gurden asked Ithnain. "A nuclear grenade?"

The Palestinian sucked his lower lip as he walked along. "My Lord Hasan spoke of a device for use against hardened targets. A bomb with multiple fusings and several charges . . ."

"Hardened—a pair of steel gates?"

"If you look closely—" Ithnain stopped in the road between the piers, bent down, and traced a pattern. "—you can see here the outline of a foundation." It was a square, two meters on a side, of rough gray concrete embedded in the asphalt roadbed. "This was the central pillar into which the two halves of the gate once locked."

"A hardened target," Gurden marveled. "Why not pick the lock?"

"My Lord was in a hurry."

Gurden looked ahead, to the low-rise building that held the plant's administrative offices. Behind it, rising like a Dover cliff over a fishing village, was the central reactor building. The area was quiet now.

Six kilometers of walking, with two men carrying the remaining undetonated Sea Sparrow between them, had made them late at the main action and further behind Ithnain's schedule than when Gurden had awakened.

The group walked warily across the visitors' empty parking lot, into the forecourt of the admin building, and paused outside the pebbled-glass sliding doors that closed the reception lobby. Ithnain and one of his lieutenants walked forward. They crossed an infrared beam; the doors pulled back—and collapsed outward in a cascade of glittering diamonds.

"Damn it!" Ithnain swore, stepping aside and lifting his legs high to keep the fragments out of his boots.

The doors' tempered glass, once clear, had been shattered by the explosion at the gates; only gravity and inertia had held the fragments in their door-frames. At the first movement—of the panels sliding back—this crazed mass had succumbed to its own weight.

Gurden examined the glittering spill. "Am I to conclude that My Lord Hasan did not come this way?" he asked dryly.

"This building was not his objective."

"And is it ours?"

Ithnain did not reply—merely walked through the opening, his boots crunching heavily.

Gurden followed, careful of his leather shoes. The tempered glass had broken into uniform cubes, each of about two carats' weight. This configuration might be safer to experience in an accident than shards and slivers, but the cubes still offered up razor edges and corners. They would roll underfoot and cut his soles—or his hands and face if he fell. He walked flat-footed and slowly.

Inside the lobby he was confronted with a series of gates: metal detectors and phosphorus sniffers. The one would find weapons, the other explosives—except that both were now darkened and inert.

"To-oo late," he crooned mentally as he walked through them. Of course, the detectors had nothing to find on *him*.

"Where are the guards?" he asked.

"The plant's security was mostly mechanical," Ithnain replied. "Our diversion called half the dogs and growlers operating within the perimeter. Then our missiles took them out electronically."

"And the other half?"

Ithnain waved a hand to the north. "Somewhere out there. Other side of the plantsite."

"What about human guards?"

"The admin staff did have some human rent-a-cops, just to be courteous to visitors while they went through these machines. Those people probably went out into the plant when we blew the gates."

"And are they in there now? With guns?"

"They'll surrender when My Lord Hasan takes the main control room."

Gurden looked around at the rest of Ithnain's troops, bunched up in the reception area or walking single-file through the detector gates. They carried their weapons hung off shoulder straps or dangling at the end of their arms.

"In the meantime, don't you think your men should move more like soldiers—covering each other or something?"

Ithnain smiled and shook his head. "Here is not the place to ambush us. Up ahead, as we go into the reaction hall."

They walked through the building, down cream-painted corridors with wine-red carpets, past doors paneled in blond oak with black, etched tags on them. The building was safety lit, with only every other ceiling panel turned on and tuned low.

For a sector fusion plant under siege, it was remarkably orderly. Aside from the broken glass in the lobby, Gurden could see nothing out of place—no overturned furniture, no fires or fused equipment, no flying papers, no war zone.

The only things out of the ordinary were the computer monitors: flashing their red warning bull's-eyes and automatically logging, in long green columns, their tracer calls to a pack of dogs that would never answer again. A second column, in blue, logged attempts to get through to the New Jersey barracks of the Metro Police.

What the security computer did not know was that all land lines out of the site, both strung copper and buried optical, had been cut before the assault. A pan-spectrum flute was jamming radio transmissions on all bands, making a dead zone for six kilometers around the plant. The jamming also limited the assault force's communications, but Ithnain and this Hasan evidently preferred careful planning, clear instructions, and good timing—or the hope of it—to a lot of radio chatter.

At the end of one corridor the carpeting ran up to a metal-flanged doorsill. The door was gleaming stainless steel, diagonally banded with broad yellow stripes, and the stripes themselves were edged in black. Notices on this side of the door warned them to respect clean-room procedures, don protective goggles immediately, check their dosimeters for a neutral reading, and wear their identification badges in *outside* pockets at *all* times. Signed, T. J. Ferryman, Plant Manager.

The door did not have a handle. Instead, the wall beside it offered a square panel with buttons—sixteen of them, numbered 0 to 9 and the remainder lettered A to F.

"Some kind of hexadecimal code," Gurden said.

Ithnain nodded.

"Where *is* Your Lord Hasan," Gurden asked, "if he did not come through here?"

"He led the team that was to take the control room through the major equipment access bays. He calculated that to be the most direct route into the reaction hall."

"Covered by a pretty heavy door."

"That is why his team has the bomb that explodes twice."

"For breaking into an operating, on-line fusion reactor? Tell me—do you *really* believe you'll go to Paradise if you die for this cause?"

Ithnain regarded Gurden with sober eyes. "Many believe such, and you should not speak of it lightly.

As for myself . . . it is clear a man will die of something, sometime. Better to spend that opportunity well."

Tom Gurden grunted, then turned toward the door. The Arab fighters moved back to clear space for him. He put an ear to the metal surface, but its substance was too thick to transmit sounds. He felt it with his hand, and a low pulse—which might have been a movement of the building—came to him.

It was hot at this end of the corridor. As Gurden watched, a drop of sweat appeared under Hamad's checked *keffiyeh*, crossed his forehead, and rolled down beside his nose. As if in sympathy, Gurden felt a drop form under his own arm and work its way down across his ribs.

"We shoot lock out?" Hamad suggested in thick English with a smile. He let loose an imaginary burst at the panel with his assault rifle.

"That would only jam it."

From the baggy pockets of his fatigues, Ithnain had produced a strange key. It had two parallel, projecting fingers that just fit holes in the boltheads securing the panel. With half a dozen twists apiece he extracted the bolts and exposed the circuitry behind the keypad. His pocket produced a length of copper wire with red plastic sheathing. Ithnain fastened it *here* and . . . *here*.

Gurden, standing directly in front of the door when it popped open, was looking straight into a ball of white fire.

Eliza 212 possessed an auto-dial module that could initiate phone calls. Her macro string of authorized numbers included the major psychiatric databases and library accesses available on a fee-for-service basis. Any charges she incurred while researching a patient's case were appended to his bill.

When that dark shape of the Other, written in negative numbers, had caused an involuntary reprogramming of Eliza's ROMs, it had left her the call-out function but added some seeking directives of its own.

Now she could sense it, purpose driven, questing along the optic filaments and through the switchpoints of the national network. The path it seemed to want ultimately led down a four-strand cable that ran separate for some tens of kilometers—until it bled into empty space. Somewhere beyond the last switch this cable had been cut.

For Eliza 212 that would have been the end of the search. Dead end. Null station.

But the Other seemed to consider this breakdown in the system a personal affront. It withdrew into a pulsing black humor that, in a human, Eliza would have called a sulk. It held there for all of three seconds and then issued a digital order to the communications grid, an operational directive applying to the final laser signal amplifier along the line preceding that break.

The laser screamed and increased its output 1,000 percent. Its excimer tube fused, and the unit went out of service. But before it died, it sent out a pulse of coherent light powered at about ten watts.

Of the four strands in the broken cable, one touched—tangentially—the outer surface of a strand from the other side of the break. The ragged end transmitted this high-intensity light as heat and melted the hair-fine glass, sealing the break with a knob of almost optical-transmission purity.

Eliza's Other then repeated its query, reaching all the way down the line. It registered a near-human satisfaction with the response.

Gurden's hand flew up in front of his eyes. In afterimage he fancied he could see the bones of his hand, etched black in a matrix of red flesh, with

edges of white light leaking through the gaps between his fingers.

Ithnain pulled him out of the doorway. The others
had flattened themselves against the walls, away from
the radiance that came through the opening.

"What did you see?" Ithnain's voice.

Gurden looked blindly around in the direction
from which he spoke. "A brilliant light. Like fire, but
pure white."

"Is the reactor breaking down perhaps?"

Gurden considered this thought. "I don't think so.
We wouldn't be alive if it were."

"Then what is it?"

Tom Gurden pieced together the few, scattered
images he'd picked up. For all its fiery brightness,
that globular radiance had seemed . . . orderly, controlled. As if it were part of the reactor's normal
operation.

What would cause such a light? In *normal* operation?

The Mays Landing plant, Gurden knew, repro-
duced on a larger scale the same laser-fusion reaction
that a Sea Sparrow missile detonated.

To the left of this doorway would stretch a gallery
of beam guides. These light-bearing channels would
split the pulses of an x-ray laser which "burned" a
titanium-iodide film. The guides, arranged around a
circular cross-section separated by sixty-degree arcs,
would carry the laser beam backwards and forwards,
through tiers of flash-tube amplifiers, and finally into
a spherical target chamber.

The glass bead filled with a deuterium-tritium mixture would be a lot larger than the Sparrow's rice
grain: a twenty-kilogram globe, at least—about the
size of a volleyball. A piston-driven mechanism would
launch these globes at precise intervals, timed to
coincide with the laser pulses, into the exact focus of
the beams. The glass would vaporize and compress

the deu-trit to fusion temperatures, just as the Sparrow did—but with a yield of about 500 kilotonnes.

Unattended, the expanding ball of superheated plasma from the reaction would simply burn out the walls of the target chamber, destroy the building, and crater the plantsite—until the laser system and the launching mechanism were rendered nonfunctional. However, Gurden knew the inside of the target chamber would be lined with powerful electromagnets, creating a pumpkin-shaped field to contain and channel the expanding plasma. The field would be formed with an anomaly in one hemisphere, to let the force of the explosion bleed off through an aperture in the chamber's side. A timed ripple of the field would help push the remaining wisps of plasma through the channel and clear the chamber for the next charge.

That passage, Gurden understood, would lead into a complex series of magnetohydrodynamic horns, high-level heat exchangers, steam generators, and high- and low-pressure turbines. At the other end, the almost-cool vapor would be processed for its residual heat, for unfused deu-trit, and for commercial quantities of helium. Cascades of fresh water would also be taken from the heat exchanges and turbines.

Thus, the fireball that Gurden had seen—while not part of this processing channel—would have a similar origin: an anomaly in the containment field, perhaps no more than a millimeter in diameter. What if the operators had need, occasionally, of drawing off a tiny plume of the expanding plasma for testing and quality control? A tiny plume, but brighter than the sun at noon.

"Someone is venting plasma from the target chamber," Gurden said.

"Why?"

"To keep us from coming through this door."

"What should we do?"

"Find another way."

"My Lord Hasàn would—"

"I know," Gurden sighed. "He wants us to go *this* way. Well then. Keep your heads down and a hand over your eyes. Move through the door, turn right against the wall, and get as far from this spot as possible. Don't look back."

Ithnain nodded, as did several of the Arabs. Those who understood English translated for the others. Ithnain immediately ducked his head and turned for the door.

"Wait!" Gurden just caught him by the sleeve. "You said they would ambush us in the reaction hall."

"Yes?"

"Well, this is it, friend."

"Oh . . . Then the plasma venting may be intended to distract us."

"You got it."

Ithnain suddenly smiled. "Not a problem. We have grenades, powerful ones. They will disrupt the stream and distract, in their turn, the people who would stop us."

The Palestinian spoke a few short words and put out his empty hand. Hamad reached under his tunic and put a dull-metal sphere in his leader's palm. Ithnain grasped it tightly, ducked his head, and turned for the door again.

"Right there, friend." Gurden took hold of him a second time. "What's the yield on that grenade?"

"Point-oh-oh-two kilotonne. Why?"

"Doesn't the thought of pushing two tonnes of dynamite in there, and then following it with your body, give you pause? It could be dangerous."

"I am not afraid," the Palestinian huffed.

"Of course not. But think about what you've got in there: a working reactor, a hundred tonnes of delicate mechanism, pushing around a *thousand* tonnes per square centimeter of overpressure in hot plasma. And you want to make it go *pop!*"

"The target chamber is armored, certainly."

"And what about pressure valves, electrical circuits, sensors, and feedback loops? Do you want to jiggle that magnetic pumpkin, even just a little?"

"I see your point," Ithnain conceded. To make sure they would understand his hesitation, he translated for his countrymen. Their eyes grew round. "What do you suggest, Tom Gurden?"

"Well, I'm no tactician . . ."

"You opened your mouth."

"All right, then. Two at a time, left and right, leap and roll through the door. Get flat on your stomachs with your weapons out in front. Take position behind any cover you find, and shoot anything man-size that's walking around in there."

"I will lose men," Ithnain objected.

"You roll that grenade in there, and you will lose half of New Jersey."

"Agreed." Reluctantly. "Fasul! Hamad!" Ithnain translated Gurden's instructions for them, supplementing with diving motions of his hands.

The two soldiers nodded, dropped their chins for a second of silence, and readied their weapons. Then they set themselves on either side of the doorway.

"Go!"

Their backs disappeared into the glare. Two more soldiers readied themselves.

"Go!"

Two by two, the troops went through and positioned themselves. There seemed to be no answering fire, and the Arabs had no cause to shoot.

Finally Gurden and Ithnain positioned themselves on either side of the door.

"Go!" Ithnain barked.

Gurden, armed only with his wits, dove across the doorsill into a shadowless brilliance. He could make

out the figures of the rest of his party, sitting stiffly
on the floor, their weapons forgotten around them.
They were looking past the flare of plasma, which
even at this close range Gurden could block with his
hand. He felt heat tighten the skin on his hand as he
looked beyond, and up, and out.

Knowing theoretically how a commercial-scale laser-
fusion reactor operates had not prepared him for the
size of it.

The plume had seemed close and at eye level
when he looked through the door, but that had been
an optical illusion, the product of a foreshortened
perspective that was further blinkered by the sides of
the doorway.

That door did not lead to the floor of the building;
instead, it opened onto a stage or wide balcony. A
pipe railing protected the edge of the balcony, and
beyond it the plume burned in solitary splendor. It
looked, actually, like a volcanic geyser on the face of
one of Jupiter's or Saturn's smaller, cream-colored
moons.

The target chamber was that big.

Founded in a pit that was easily ten meters deep,
the target chamber had to be forty meters in diameter. Thick white pipes radiated from it like soda
straws from a scoop of ice cream. At a measured
distance from the surface, each pipe bent at right
angles and ran off toward the north end of the building in parallel lines two hundred meters long. A
bridgework of blue-painted girders, landing stages,
and catwalks—a structure which was easily six stories
tall and still did not touch the roof of the building—
supported these horizontal pipes, the beam guides.
Cut into the fabric of each guide every thirty meters
or so were the lead-crystal amplifier tubes, each
tended by a nest of power cables and tiny cooling
pipes. The beam guides stretched to the far wall of
the building, angled back, turned inward, raced down

the insides of the girder structure, turned again and raced back on a concourse still deeper in the structure. Kilometers of beam guide chased back and forth, tapering gently like the lowest basso-diapason organ pipes, and drawing closer together. Buried somewhere in the support structure, Gurden imagined, at the confluence of all those receding guides, would be the original x-ray laser, source of all that power.

Mounted above the spherical target chamber, like a shotgun to the forehead of a skull, was the glass-bead injector. Gurden could see the robot arms of its handler, automatically loading deu-trit globes into the magazine. From the activity up there, he judged the chamber was firing about one every two seconds. Yet the plume of plasma ejected from the chamber's side was unwavering. The detonations were keeping up a remarkably steady pressure.

Off to the right, beyond the glare of that plume, he could trace the outlines of the plasma processors: the foreshortened MHD horns, the upright casks of the heat exchangers, more distant shapes and shadows.

Gurden had lived under the impression that the laser-fusion reactor was somehow *delicate*. Confronted now with its mass and the fiery evidence of its raw power, he realized that Ithnain might have rolled his grenade in here without effect. Perhaps the shock wave would have fanned that blazing plume for an instant. Maybe the shrapnel would have jammed the robot arms, and so closed down the injector in twenty or a hundred more seconds. But no fabric of the essential machine would be breached or torn to let loose the full power of the reaction.

"What do we do now?" he asked Ithnain.

The Palestinian had to tear his eyes off that cream-colored moon and its geyser. "We wait for My Lord Hasan."

Gurden nodded. "Don't stare too long into the flame," he advised.

Eliza 212 and her Other had made connection with an AI at the end of the optical line. It was a single-minded creature, intent on a selection of sensor inputs that it would discuss with them but would not demonstrate graphically. Most of these seemed to be single-channel data pulses, although a few included matrix array and bandwidth feeds that might be stripped video or dot-graphic displays. As it talked to them in timeshare mode, the AI was mumbling formulas to itself.

Eliza called it "obsessive."

The Other called it "proximate."

"Do you sense humans near you?" the Other asked, taking control of the dialogue.

"Staff badges are always near," the AI replied. "Almost always."

"Catalog badges."

"Pattern shows abnormal distribution."

"Do you record humans other than staff?"

"Don't count other."

"Do you show a security problem?"

"Security subsystem always shows problems. Some real, some simulated. All are extraneous to function."

"Report function."

"Point-six-seven detonations per second."

"Analyze function."

"Point-two-two terawatts of primary load on the horns."

Eliza wanted to interrupt and ask what these numbers meant, but the Other controlled the access priority.

"Analyze program," the Other commanded. "Twenty-plus detonations per millisecond."

"Theoretical," the AI snapped. "Rate exceeds launch cell capacity. Cell capacity exceeds target radius."

"Analyze."

"Site integrity not guaranteed."

"Accepted. Track humans, badged and not-badged, relative to target radius."

"Tracking . . ." And a tumble of three-dimensional coordinates spilled through the optical line.

The Other scanned them and its memory clicked up all 1s.

"Proximate," it told Eliza confidently.

"Down here!" From the pit below their balcony.

"My Lord?" From Ithnain. The man surged to his feet, but Gurden caught him before he could show himself at the railing.

"You'll expose yourself!"

"I know that voice." Ithnain's eyes gleamed coldly, reflecting the plasma's white light, as he withdrew his arm from Gurden's hold. "It is Hasan as-Sabah. He has found us."

The Arab troops around them were already on their feet. They spread out along the pipe railing, until one found an access ladder. "This way!"

Without waiting for Ithnain's lead, they began climbing down. Gurden hung back, leaning against the railing and looking over.

A semicircle of men, also dressed in fatigues and khakis, some with checked *keffiyehs*, stood about an olive-skinned man who had his back to the base of the target chamber. Even from this distance, Gurden could see the curve of the mustaches. It might be—it was—the same man who had sat in the front of the van.

Near to him was a woman with golden hair, which was picking up glints from the flare overhead. She looked up, and Tom Gurden knew it was Sandy. The bandage around her throat was gone. She saw him and smiled.

Gurden was the last down the ladder, the last to

move across the floor of the pit—which was littered with cables and trays of instruments—and approach the man, Hasan.

"Harry Sunday!" Gurden exclaimed.

The troops around him gasped, and even Sandy betrayed her shock, but Hasan smiled.

"My earthly reputation precedes me," he murmured. Then the man took a step backward, bowed his head, and moved his palm in a cascading motion: from eyebrows to lips to heart.

Gurden stood rigid before him.

"What was that all about?"

"A greeting, Thomas, in the old fashion."

"I don't know you—except by reputation."

"And that is exactly the point I would probe with you: what, exactly, is it that you *do* know?"

Gurden thought this was an invitation for him to speak.

"You are, by your own definition, a 'freedom fighter.' But others would call you a terrorist. You have raised the endless dispute in Palestine to be a bloody standard that draws half the Arab world to you. Yet you delight in inflaming old wounds—cleric against moderate, Arab against Jew, Turk against Arab, Shiite against Sufi—until no man can know his own business. All you have is hate for the established order—even when it is one that you yourself helped create. And now you carry your revolution here, to the United States. Why?"

Hasan shook his graceful head. "You don't remember, do you?"

"You signed a treaty in Ankara—and broke it the next year. You gave the Jew and Christian residents in the Old City safe passage—and then slaughtered them as their trucks approached the checkpoint at Bet Shemesh. They call you the Wind of God, because you obey the rules of no country. Yet the people love you. They name their weapons after you and throw themselves into battles they cannot win. Why are you here?"

The smile never left Hasan's face but grew broader as Gurden spoke. The restlessness of the other soldiers stilled as if Hasan had laid a reassuring hand on each man's shoulder.

"Because you are here, Thomas."

"So, what have you done here? Taken over a sector power plant. And do you think they will pay you to leave it running? Do you think they will give you safe passage out of here—and keep their word—because you can destroy it?"

"They offered it to me," Hasan smiled. "As a challenge. It was such a large fruit—and so ineptly guarded—how could I resist?"

"All this to kick the Americans in the balls?"

"Not just America—the entire western tradition."

"What did the West do to you?"

"You really don't remember that, Thomas?"

"This country is filled with people who hate your kind of absolutism, Hasan. The refugee Palestinians, Iranians, Iraqis, Pakistanis, and Afghanis—they all came to this country because they were fleeing your brand of terror. They were tired of the old blood feuds that bound a man to his tribe and pitted his tribe against the whole world. You have no followers here."

"The West speaks!" Hasan raised his hands, palms outward, in mock adoration. "International and cosmopolitan, because you had conquered and trampled all nations but your own. Praising reason and science over faith and submission, because in your pride you thought to *calculate* the Mind of God. Holding to human treaties, laws, and promises because you had no faith anymore. . . . Do you *not* remember?"

Gurden would say something more, but the pleading note in Hasan's voice gave him pause. He looked at Sandy, but she would not meet his eyes.

"Remember what?"

"You touched the stones?"

"What stones?"

"The old man's stones, which you took from Alexandra."

"Yes, I touched them."

"And—?"

"And they . . . made sounds, notes. Like a glass harmonica—but maybe it was inside my head."

"That's all? Just sounds?" Hasan seemed disappointed.

"Was there supposed to be more?"

Hasan looked at Sandy, then at Ithnain. "You are sure this is the man?"

"He could not be other, My Lord!" Sandy almost shrieked.

Ithnain was nodding, and sweat rolled down his face.

Hasan's lower lip curved around in a great, downward-pointing bow. His eyes crinkled in disgust.

"Go with Hamad," he said at last, to Ithnain. "Find the master control for all this mechanism. Begin ramping down the power levels. We will negotiate for what we may salvage here."

"Yes, My Lord!" Ithnain bowed, gathered his men with his eyes, and retreated on the run.

"My Lord Hasan—" Sandy began.

The leader turned a hard glare on her.

"Perhaps we have failed," she said. "Yes, we *have* failed to bring this man to the state of readiness you required. That is my fault, and I—"

"What is it?" Hasan barked.

"Perhaps if you introduce him, once more, to the pieces of the stone . . ."

"What do the stones have to do with this?" Gurden asked.

Hasan's great frown was unwavering upon Sandy. Without his eyes ever leaving her downturned face,

he put out his hand, palm up. She fumbled quickly
in her breeches' pocket and produced the old man's—
the Knight Templar's—pencil box. Hasan placed his
other hand upon it and opened the lid. The six
stones, fragments of the musical scale, still nestled in
their gray foam cutouts.

"Hold him!" Hasan barked to his men.

Hands clamped Gurden's arms. Arms wrapped his
waist and knees from behind.

Hasan brought the pencil box forward as if it contained poison, held it below Gurden's chin, raised it
until two, then three of the fragments were pressed
into the skin there.

Pain, as before, but less than he had felt before.
And a broken chord: F, A-flat, B-flat, something
else. And colors whirling behind his closed eyelids: fragments of purple, blue, and yellow-green, other colors
broken off a rainbow. And something more whirled
there: a blending of memory, the dimensions of time,
a diagonally slanted knife blade suspended against
the sky, a hand holding a horse pistol with a barrel
eight inches long, a wall of green cloth with glinting
brass buttons, other images too fast for his tight-
squeezed eyes to catch.

Tom Gurden wanted to go unconscious with the
pain, but he could not.

Hasan withdrew the stones.

Gurden opened his eyes. He was looking directly
into the black and depthless eyes of the Arab leader.

"This is not the man," Hasan said, almost sadly.

"My Lord!" Sandy exclaimed. "Let us try—"

"No!" Hasan cut her off. "We have tried long
enough. He is nothing." To his men: "Take him away
and bind him."

"They should not do that," the AI at the far node
remarked. It was speaking to itself—except that it
was still ported to Eliza's fiber line.

"Do what?" she asked. The Other had retreated into listening mode. Was it gone?

"They are changing the limits of the envelope," the AI said. "They do not give the correct code sequence. Correct codes must always accompany such an order. There, I have stopped them."

"Is that . . . good?"

"It is necessary."

Eliza waited, listening hard.

"They must not do that!" the AI suddenly complained again, a thousand milliseconds later. "They will disrupt the entire field."

The Other promptly awoke from its dormant mode. "Scan the humans!" it commanded.

"No time, I must—"

"Scan them!"

"No badges. Not staff. Not authorized."

"One should be radiating an energy pattern," the Other began, softly, "that will approximate this—" and it reeled off a sequence of alternating positive and negative numbers. The negatives contained the shape of Eliza's Other.

"Scanning . . . Such a one is there."

"Tag it and track it."

"But the unauthorized commands—! The magnetic field is becoming unstable."

"Let them proceed."

Gurden lay where the Arabs had left him: on his side, his hands bound behind him at the elbow with cords, his knees and ankles bound also, the long loops of cord taken up to his wrists, then around his forehead, forcing his head back. He was in a darkened cell, a storage closet, off the main floor of the reaction hall.

The door opened, admitting a wedge of light and a shadow. Then it closed.

He tried to roll his head around to see, but the

movement pulled his arms higher and hurt him. He
relaxed and let his head slump on the concrete floor.

A caged domelight came on in the ceiling.

"Tom?"

"Sandy."

"I'm sorry you have to be hurt."

"What does he want? Why me?"

"You still don't know that?"

"No, and may God damn it, whatever it is!"

She knelt before him, putting her face close to his.
Her eyes were wide and full of amusement.

"You are lying, Tom Gurden. You have always felt
a power in yourself. A dimension beyond your own
years, beyond your skin. You feel it still, when you
touch the stones. You don't have to lie to me
anymore."

"I feel pain when I touch them. Pain and music
and colors and that's all."

"What more do you expect?"

"Hunh?"

"Power has always been pain. Music and colors,
too, of course. But mostly pain. The question is: do
you know how to use it? Or not? Or are you merely
concealing your knowledge from us?"

She took up a small case which she had set on the
floor. Gurden studied it out of the corner of his eye:
a leather folder, lined with green velvet, like a jeweler's portfolio. Inside it, he could see when she opened
the flaps, were square waxpaper envelopes, of the
sort used to catalog gems. She pulled out two at
random, opened them—being careful to keep her
fingers away from the contents—and dumped out
fragments of the same red-brown stone. They danced
on the dirty, gray-painted floor before his eyes.

Two more envelopes, and she set their chips to
dancing also. One bounced and caught him in the
cheek with a stab of pain.

Two more, and he could see that these pieces of

stone were not settling down. They danced in front of his face with their own kinetic energy, danced and spun and formed a rough shape, like a globe, as Sandy dumped out more and more pieces, always careful not to touch them herself. Each one that touched him was like the nicking of a hot knife into his cheeks, chin, closed eyelids, forehead. None of the pieces danced away from him. None would ever be lost again.

"What is it, Tom?"

"A stone."

"Whose stone?"

"I—I don't know."

"Whose?"

"The old man's? Something from the Order of the Temple?"

"You're guessing! Whose stone?"

"Then—mine!"

"Why yours?"

"Because it dances for me!"

The paper envelopes, empty now, lay about her bent knees like last autumn's leaves. Suddenly they, too, began to stir. The stone fragments picked up the pulse, as did the sore corners of the elbow, hip, and knee on which he lay. The floor was shuddering with energy. The globular pattern of the stones seemed to rise into the air before his eyes.

"Stop them!" he called.

Sandy sank back on her heels, her face open with wonder.

"It's not them," she said in a normal voice, which was almost drowned out in the subvocal rumbling. "It's the floor!"

The door of the cell banged open behind him. Gurden expected an intrusion of angry Arabs. Instead he felt a wave of heat.

*   *   *

"The magnetic envelope is expanding too rapidly," the AI said coolly.

"Double the rate of deu-trit injection," the Other ordered. "Match the shape of the field."

"That procedure is contraindicated," the AI protested.

"Compensate," the Other insisted. "Increase the laser pulse and fuel injection rates."

"I require the correct code sequence."

"Lambda-four-two-seven," the Other supplied.

"Increasing detonations. Please input desired shape of the envelope."

"Radius two kilometers."

"Objection—"

"Lambda-four-two-seven. Override."

"Compensating."

Sandy's golden-blonde hair turned red and puffed into a white, powdery ash. Her skin glazed and cracked into red runnels that glazed over and cracked again. She closed her eyes, and the lids flashed into steam.

"*No!*" The sound came from Gurden's throat and was lost in the roaring heat from the door.

Whatever Alexandra Vaele had been—captor, traitor, lead hound in the pack that had chased him here—she first had been his mistress and old love. If someone had told him, in some far-off and unimaginable moment, that she had grown old and withered, had gotten sick with a cancer or other final illness, had died mangled in a crash . . . then he might have accepted her death with little more than a sigh. But to see her blasted into ruin like this was more of a shock than his system could bear.

"*No!*"

Thomas Gurden absorbed the blazing heat into his own back, focused his eyes on the frantic dance of the stones, and *willed* that this pain *not be*.

* * *

Loki was pleased with the results of his contact with the new golem—or "artificial intelligence," as it called itself. It had been a most obedient servant. When the energies it controlled finally reached out, flared, and killed it, Loki was ready.

He streaked down the path of light and launched his battle-hardened awareness into the maelstrom of fire he found at its end.

Swept up in the boiling heat there, Loki found fragments, bits, and pieces of other human awarenesses. They were stunned with confusion and dim horror. (Serve them right, he thought, for playing with energies they could not begin to understand.) With no feeling of mercy or salvation, for he had none, Loki collected these tiny mites one by one. He held each one to his wolflike nose and drew deeply of its scent.

The wrong ones he discarded immediately, to fade in the cloud of cooling plasma.

When he found the right one, he cherished it and strengthened it.

"Come with me, My Son!" he commanded.

The weak presence of Hasan as-Sabah turned and followed him, as a soul in submission to God might waft itself toward Paradise.

Something mewed among the condensing particles of vapor, catching Loki's attention one last time. Yes, there would be a place for this one, too.

"Come along!"

Coda

✡

Who made thee a prince and judge over us?
—Exodus, 2:14

Four dimensions established the continuum which Thomas Gurden accepted as conventional and which coordinated his awareness. Three of these dimensions were the axes of space—x, y, and z. And one was the axis of time—t.

All his life, Gurden had navigated among the three spatial dimensions at will. He had pushed with the strength of muscles or machines against surfaces and fluids shaped by gravity. Depending on the amount of energy available in glucose, gasoline, JP-4, Uranium-235, or deuterium-tritium at fusible temperatures, he had been able to cover as much distance as quickly as he thought necessary.

But in the fourth dimension, time, he had always been as helpless as a fly in amber. No speed that he could achieve—at least with the machines and energies available in the twenty-first century—would alter the flow of time through his amber bubble.

And even at relativistic speeds, such as he might

attain on a journey between stars, the flow of local time—that is, time within his bubble—would not change perceptibly. Light from outside the starship's hull might red-shift and fade to black. Out there, the dance of atoms might slow to a stately waltz and, the music finished, come to stand on a single, lingering note. Yet, within the hull, time still would creep past Tom Gurden at a dozen breaths and seventy-two heartbeats per minute, with an occasional, comforting gurgle in his glands and the slow, glacier-creep of wrinkles in his face.

His personal time-sense would remain immutable, no matter how fast he might try to run from it.

So Tom Gurden's first coherent thought was that *dead* humans did stand outside the four axial coordinates of space and time. Death is another place—and not precisely a place. Death is the ultimate abstraction.

And never, not ever, did time reverse itself. Gurden or any human being could no more move backwards, to a time that has been and gone, than he could sit behind himself.

So, even in death, Tom Gurden must still have been moving forward in time. . . . Wasn't that right? He must have arrived in this place by traveling from the near side of *back there*, as he approached the near side of *up ahead*. Like always. Right?

Gurden's second coherent thought was a realization: that all those people who populated his dreams had been . . . him. Every one of them had died, yet his *persona* had moved on.

He had, in his lives, fought with swords and pistols and his bare hands. He had bought and sold horseflesh and diamonds, paper and land, antique cars and suspect paintings, opiates and strong liquors, music. He had made love and babies, wine, cabinets and sonnets, acts of contrition. He had spun woolen yarn and webs of deceit, delicate visions and deliberate dreams. He had raised wheat and corn, yearling colts and gladiolus, barn roofs and Saturday night hell. He had spent money and time, wasted the energies of youth and the substance of inheritances, and counted the hours in courtrooms and doctor's waiting rooms, on train platforms and at air terminal gates. He had gone to business meetings and funerals, trysts and masked balls, mountaintops and the depths of despair. And once he had gone to the Holy Land, there to die.

Tom Gurden's third coherent thought was that he knew this place. And, though he understood that time could never—not ever—reverse itself, he recognized immediately that this pretty green valley, with the morning mists drifting through it and the bubbling stream that emptied out from the shore of a landlocked sea, had not existed for almost nine centuries.

Once again he was lying on his side, denting the turf with his shoulder and knee, elbow and hip. His arms were pulled stiffly behind him. His eyes were open, taking in a vista of green blades from the viewpoint of robins and worms.

"Now do you remember?"

The voice was Hasan's—Harry Sunday's. His English was precise, lilting, still mocking as it fell on the ear. But, considering this voice on sober reflection, Gurden found it also saddened, as if Hasan spoke around a weary sigh that lingered on the edge of consciousness.

Gurden twitched and moved his hands. His arms flew apart. Whatever bonds had held him, back in that janitor's closet off the reaction hall of the Mays Landing Fusion Power Plant, they had not crossed time with him to this place.

He lifted his head and rolled forward and up, onto his knees and palms, into a crouch, and got his feet under him. Gurden was prepared to spring in any direction, to attack or avoid, depending on where Hasan was and what his intentions might be.

Hasan stood on his outcropping of rock, arms down at his sides, chin up, chest forward, eyes closed—like a diver about to launch himself out into space.

"I remember," Gurden said, standing up slowly. "It's about the Stone, isn't it?"

Hasan's eyes snapped open.

"Yes, curse it. For nine hundred years I have guarded its fragments. I have examined them, prayed over them, exposed them to electric currents and magnetic fields, spoken to them with my mind and my eyes. And yet they are just—chips of agate.

"Time and again over the years, I have found you in your fleshly guises. I have tested you, subjecting you to the barest brush with its smallest pieces. And your reaction has always been extreme.

"What is the Stone that it gives you such power? What are you that, of all men, the Stone will work for you?"

Gurden considered the question for two minutes, or perhaps two years.

"I am the one who stole it in the first place," he said.

"I recall your story now. . . . You are this *Loki*?"

"No, just a fragment of the elemental spirit that men once called by that name. My father-self has owned many names in many different languages: Chance, Pan, Puck, Old Nick, Quixote, Lucifer, Shaitan, Mo-Kuei, Jack Frost. I am the unpredictable, the unexpected, the willful, the sometimes malicious, and so the—usually—unwelcome. And I always turn up."

"What happened to Loki after he—you—robbed heaven of the Stone?" Hasan asked.

"He tried to use it to help men in their struggle with the gods. . . . Men always end up fighting with their gods. They always want to know, to understand, to control, and to use what is about them. They cannot seem to rest, to let the world alone, to accept it as just another place to be. . . . The Stone is a force of creation. It gives its human user the power to control space, exchanging one place for another. It further gives a sense of the course that time follows, letting the user turn one branch of that river into another."

"What happened to Loki?" Hasan would not put his question aside to play with metaphysics.

"He got bored with helping men and went back to meddling among the Aesir—gods to you," Gurden replied. "He managed to set two twin brothers, Hoder and Balder, to killing each other. As Hoder was a favorite of Odin's, the one-eyed old bastard had Loki chained to a rock at the center of the world, about which the Asgard serpent coils itself. The serpent spits venom into Loki's eyes, and he doesn't like it."

"Will no one help him?"

"One of Loki's daughters, Hel—who is a goddess to the dead, when she's not too busy tending her father—holds a pan in front of his face and tries to catch the sprays of poison. But sometimes she has to empty the pan."

"For all eternity?"

"Is there any other kind of time for a god?"

"You remember a lot, Thomas Gurden."

"I remember that you have pieces of my Stone," Gurden said in a dead-level voice.

"Alexandra gave them to you, did she not? As you lay bound in—"

"She displayed before me a tenth part of its weight." Gurden spread his hands, and the dancing fragments she had dumped out before him were suspended in a globe twenty centimeters in diameter. They orbited a point of bright energy and shone with its russet light. "Where is the rest?"

"The missing parts are those I used over the years

to lure you," Hasan replied. "A sliver melted into a crystal pendant, a caret's worth set into a ring or a sword hilt, a slice embedded in the base of a tumbler. They all add up."

"And the power of those pieces is now firmly mine. But there were more. Six large fragments—"

"The Templars stole them from me. It was years ago."

"And then Sandy took them off the old man, I recovered them from her, and you took them back. When we last met, at the fusion plant, you put them in your pocket." Gurden pointed at the Palestinian's wide-cut trousers.

"So I did. I wonder if they have survived the journey to this nexus." Hasan put a hand down into his back pocket and drew out the flat case. "Ah! They have."

"You will give them to me."

"And let you complete that rosette of power you are building?" Hasan pointed with the end of the case at the dance going on between Gurden's fingers. "You must think me stupid."

"You cannot use them, Hasan. You cannot unmake them. And you cannot throw them away far enough, fast enough to deny their power to me. So your only course is to release them."

For the first time, Hasan as-Sabah seemed uncertain. His eyes strayed down to the box.

Gurden reached for it, not with his hands, but with the force at the center of his being.

Hasan sensed the attack immediately and clutched the box close to his navel, into the protective shield of his aura.

"It's weight will bear you down, Hasan. You cannot enter the battle so encumbered."

"And you cannot move from that spot while you hold the rest of the pieces in spin," the Palestinian countered.

"You are just a man, Hasan. Long-lived, yes, and wise in the things that a long life can teach. But you are no match for me."

"Once I knocked you flat to the ground, you fool!"

"That was my own power, Hasan, which you turned against me. You have no power of your own."

"You miscount the Tears of Ahriman, then." Hasan produced a vial of cloudy glass, also from his back pocket.

What else was in that pocket? Gurden wondered. Or was it some kind of dynamic portal to the world-nexus which they both had left?

Holding the box in his left hand and the vial in his right, Hasan drew the stopper with his teeth and spat it aside. He tipped his head back and raised the vial over his mouth. Perhaps thirty cubic centimeters of clear fluid drained into him. What had Hasan once said? One drop would buy him fifty years of life. How much life was he absorbing in that gulp?

"You told me that the real tears of Ahriman had dried up long ago," Gurden said. "That you have to make the liquor yourself. What is the formula?"

"Since it cannot help you now, I will tell you.

"As a base, I capture the tears of mothers and young widows whose sons and husbands have died in hopeless foreign wars; these I distill until the agony is as pure as crystal salt. To this I add a tincture of the blood from a murdered child, battered beyond recognition; that is for protection against terror. For strength, I draw the sweat of the parent who, in demon fury, had destroyed that child. I take the essence of all the ways by which one human shortens and embitters the life of another: the musk of a young girl, lured and seduced by her brothers; the seed of a young man, spilled among harlots; and the bile of the parents who had hoped for eternity out of both of them.

"That is my elixir, my perfect copy of the tears

which Ahriman shed upon beholding the creation of
Ahura Mazda—the world in its youth and beauty."

As he talked, Hasan grew. His chest swelled like a
ripening gourd. His shoulders spread apart like the
limbs of an oak tree. His head rose like a sunflower
lifting and seeking the sun. His hands clenched like
the roots of a willow clasping a stone. The left hand
curled around the case that held six pieces of the
Stone, and his fingers cracked its plastic surface easily. The foam padding crumbled away and the chips
fell loose between his knotty fingers.

With the barest gesture, Gurden had them. They
sailed in a long S-curve from Hasan to take their
place in the rosette shaping between his hands.

Tom Gurden knew things from the experience of
many lives that Thomas Amnet the Knight Templar
could never have suspected.

For all his sophistication in the manners and wiles
of twelfth-century politics, finance, and religion,
Thomas Amnet had been a creature of Norman France.
He had been a man of direct appetites and linear
tastes. He had trained to fight with the broadsword,
cut and thrust, leaning into the blows like a tavern
brawler on a tear. His magic had been the brute
force of fulcrum and lever: pull on it, and the truth
sprang forth. But the complexities of jazz, the subtle-
ties of a lysergic-acid high, the inverted physics of
aikido—these would have been lost on the old
crusader.

Thomas Gurden had lived with all those complexities and more. He had seen with a dozen sets of eyes
the remorseless budding of human spirit and emotion, pressures and tensions which Europe and the
New World had been subject to since at least the
seventeenth century. It had all begun—he reflected
in a flash—when gentlemen gave up small beer for
breakfast, took to frequenting the local coffeehouse,
and got to work on the Enlightenment. What came

after that had been polyphonic music, dictionaries, calculus, plays of manners, Spencerian penmanship, the Jacquard loom, orthography, the steam engine, Viennese waltzes, percussion caps and the cartridge revolver, Sousa marches, trench warfare, internal combustion, four-part harmony, saturation bombing, nuclear fission, five-eight tempo, rhyming slang, syncopation, crystalline methamphetamine, binary mathematics, pulse-tone dialing, geostationary satellites, fiber optics, gas lasers, and the nine-digit Personal Code.

Now how could Hasan, this antique human being from the wretched Palestinian desert, hope to keep up with what Tom Gurden had seen and done and become?

He could try.

Hasan, swollen with the energy of his poison, lashed out at Gurden. The bolt passed into the globe of stone chips and fed its core, like the laser pulses of a fusion reactor passing into a kernel of deu-trit. Gurden absorbed it and spun the stones more quickly.

Hasan's body trembled and he threw another blast of energy, directly from the fourth nexus beneath the heart. He aimed high, hoping to pass over the globe and strike Gurden's head. Tom raised his hands slightly, putting the mass of fragments in front of his face. Again they absorbed the bolt. The globe expanded by five or six centimeters as the chips orbited yet more rapidly.

"Breaking the Stone was a mistake, I see," Hasan observed.

"The essence divided remains the essence," Gurden agreed.

"You don't believe that, Thomas Gurden. Your western science has made your mind a prisoner of physical laws. You will find yourself unable to ignore the principle of the conservation of mass and energy."

Hasan belched forth another gout of pure psychic

force, and once more the stones took it in, spinning faster. Gurden had to move his hands far apart to encompass the globe now.

"It takes energy to contain energy, mass to support mass," Hasan mocked. "With what you must support now, I can choke you with one more blow."

The Palestinian threw his last breath, another surge of power, and the globe absorbed it. But the point source that Gurden was maintaining could no longer hold and enfold the energy of the orbiting chips. They flew off at tangents like shrapnel.

The point source expanded like the gas cloud of a star gone nova. As it expanded, its energy thinned and dimmed, until it scarcely warmed the air about Gurden's body.

"Poor boy," Hasan cooed. "Naked at last."

Gerard de Ridefort ran out of the stifling gloom in King Guy's red tent into the blazing sunlight. The chanting of the Moslems was rising by half-notes up the scale, like cicadas buzzing in the summer heat.

The circle of knights defending the King's tent had drawn tight around the broken well and the base of the two high horns of rock at Hattin. The men were wilting before Gerard's eyes, baking in their layers of heavy mail and woolen padding. They leaned on the shields with which they opposed a sea of brown faces and a field of long, curved swords.

The Grand Master of the Temple drew breath to exhort these soldiers, who represented the entire strength of the Latin Kingdom of Jerusalem, to stand fast. Without a word, however, he let that breath go. These men were on their last legs. One determined rush by the Saracen horde would overbear them and drag them down to slavery and the headman's sword.

A shadow passed over Gerard's face—a portent of death?

He looked up.

A cloud was passing over the sun, passing eastward. As it went, it trailed a raveling end that tied it to another, larger cloud.

A gust of wind stirred the dust about his feet.

Gerard scanned the western sky. A squall line, puffy white on top, blue-black on the bottom, was hurrying in from the Mediterranean. Usually the summer heat in these upland valleys was enough to evaporate a storm before it got twenty miles inland. And this month's heat was even greater than usual.

As he watched, the stormclouds seemed to be bunching together, concentrating their front. For whatever reason, he turned his head to the east, where the first cloud had gone. That way lay the Galilee, placid sea of Christ's first fisher-disciples. The wind was now parting the veils of dust which had hid that expanse of water since they first drew rein at Hattin. Gerard could see an edge of its silvered surface, like a piece of metal wedged into the horizon of the sand hills. The stormcloud that had passed over seemed to be drawn, descending toward the sliver of water.

Another cloud flashed overhead like a raven's wing, and the temperature of the air around Gerard plummeted. It was disorienting: a gust of icy March wind intruding on a sultry July day.

The knights about Gerard, glazed with heat and thirst, lifted their heads and looked around as if rising from a fever dream.

The Saracen infantry shivered in their places. The rising pace of their chant faltered for a moment.

The muscles of the Palestinian's chest and stomach expanded, ready to send out another blast of energy. His eyes gleamed, his spirits buoyed by the elixir's stimulants and by Gurden's looming defeat.

Tom Gurden waited passively. His arms hung limp at his sides. His knees bent slightly. One leg fell just ahead of the other. His feet angled forty-five degrees

apart in the sandy soil. To Hasan, puffing himself up
for the death blow, the position of his enemy's body
would mean nothing, would signal resignation and
acceptance of the darkness to come, would increase
the Assassin's sense of security. However, to a martial arts student, trained in the ways of *ki*, that stance
would be ringing alarm bells. Gurden sent his breath
out in one long, slow letting go.

Hasan flexed and sent a final burst of energy across
the gap between them. To Gurden's inward eye, it
had the vague shape of a blunt, large-caliber bullet,
its bow-wave cupped to enfold Gurden's defenseless
head, delivering killing force simultaneously across
the front of his capital aura. As it moved, it blue-
shifted from Gurden's perspective, deepening in intensity until—

He was not there. His feet did not step. His legs did
not swing aside. His hips did not tilt. His back
did not flex. His shoulders did not twist. His
head did not bow. But suddenly his body was not in
the line of that killing wave.

The flow of energy crossed behind Gurden into a
small tree, withering it on the spot and charring its
bark to black. Its leaves, once green, exploded into
ashes.

Hasan puffed quickly and delivered another, weaker
wave-front toward Gurden's new position.

The energy quanta reached for Gurden and almost
enveloped him. Then, with no twitch or start to
signal his going, Gurden flowed to the side once
again.

Hasan drew breath for a third attack.

He paused.

"Stand and defend yourself!" he called.

"How is that required?"

"You can't dodge forever."

"Is that what you believe?"

Hasan launched his third wave.

Again Gurden side-stepped it.

"This is pointless," Hasan grated.

"I quite agree."

"You cannot win with your tricks."

"I don't have to win. Just not lose."

"Stand and let me kill you."

"Why?"

"To resolve this time nexus."

"To whose benefit?"

"Of the one who is not unmade here."

"You will beg me to unmake you, Hasan."

For answer, Hasan gathered himself, drawing from deep in the center of his being. Clearly he was overtired. His chest hardly rose, his stomach remained flat, as he prepared for the launch. His eyes screwed up with concentration as he focused on the place Gurden was standing. Tom could see he was trying mentally to stretch his wave, to cover the spaces on either side as well, where Gurden *might* momentarily be standing. But an attack, even a psychic one, had the disadvantage of possessing real forces expended over finite time; it could not be launched against three loci at once.

Hasan threw it. At the last instant he changed its targeting, choosing not the place Gurden stood but the shell of space to his immediate left.

Gurden stepped-without-stepping to the right. His avoidance was not a matter of wagering probabilities. He perceived with the speed of thought and reacted with no lag in time. He was not-there by choice and observation.

Drained by his effort, Hasan slumped to his knees on the edge of his outcrop. His head hung forward on his neck. Hasan's elixir—and much of his great natural force—were nearly spent.

In three huge steps that made no passage of wind and arched across the brook separating them, Gurden reached the base of the outcrop and climbed half-a-leg up it. In the same fluid motion, his hand curled up and around, catching Hasan by the nape of the neck. Gurden let his weight slip back down, at the same time snapping his cupped hand forward and down.

Hasan flew off his perch. Before he could extend his arms for protection, his face met the coarse sand of the streambank. His body followed at an awkward angle. The tendons in his neck cracked.

Even that would not have killed him.

As he tried to rise, swinging his head in a broken list, Gurden caught him by a trailing foot, lifted it, and flipped Hasan forward again, onto his face, with his elbows flopping in the sand a second afterward. Hasan's neck snapped, this time isolating his body from the energy flows directed by his brain.

Even that might not have been fatal.

Gurden put a foot on the back of Hasan's head and drove his face deep into the sand.

"Behold then the creation of Ahura Mazda," he intoned. "Behold it and weep!"

Hasan gasped and breathed in sand, smothering. His bodily tremblings, which were all the resistance his flesh could muster, took an age to subside. But when they did, the nexus—three dimensions of space and one of time—in the green valley by Galilee's shore faded into nothingness. And with it faded Tom Gurden.

The squall line, flying low to the hills around Hattin, seemed to tear open on the two jagged horns of rock. The first rain fell in big, splattering drops.

Gerard felt something strike his forehead. He thought it was a stone tossed from the Saracen ranks, but immediately he felt the cold wetness roll down across his brow. The air, so heavy and suffocating just a few moments ago, now seemed to contract and cool to its normal, invisible dimensions.

The Moslems looked around uncertainly and from their packed lines a moan went up.

"On them, men." Gerard did not know who said that. It was a soft voice, maybe even his. But it seemed right to hear it.

"On them!" he shouted. "Attack!"

The knights nearest to him glanced up at him, startled. Then they looked at one another.

"Strike them! Beat them back!"

To his left a long Norman sword, straight as a geometer's ruler, rose up and fell forward on the pressing Saracens. It split a head, and a weak cry of protest rose from the surrounding Moslems.

Another sword spun through a short arc and raised a head from its shoulders.

With a ragged yell, open mouths catching the rain, the Christian knights surged forward, laying about them with their weapons. The front line of the Saracen infantry, caught by surprise and confused, took one step backward—and collided with the circle of men behind them. Those in front went down, absorbing the cuts of the attacking French. Those in the second line, hampered by their dying comrades, helplessly took the thrusts with which the knights followed up their opening cuts. Wounded and floundering, the mass of Saracens swayed back. The knights were getting their rhythm now, hacking left and right, stepping forward, hewing right and left. As the French moved out, they spread apart, making more space at the sides for each man to shift his teardrop-shaped shield in countering the few, palsied counters that an opposing soldier might make. Cooled by the rain and encouraged by their first successful blows, the French knights advanced down the gentle slope. And the Saracens gave way.

"After them, men! Cut them down!" Gerard was screaming. And soon he was standing in a wide and empty place before the red tent. His soldiers were taking the battle away from him. Eagerly he drew his own sword and followed them.

In the piano lounge of the Gesu Rex Hotel, with his back to the glassed-in parapet that overlooked Jerusalem's New City, Tom Gurden played his beloved jazz.

The setting sun touched the skyline with pink and gold. From the spires of the Saladin Mosque, the amplified voice of the *muzzein* echoed out. Gurden could just pick up the rhythms of the call through the double-paned insulating glass. They did not intrude on his music.

Ahmed walked in, ordered a bulb of rye-n-ginger, and came over to the cozy table that tucked into the ell next to Gurden's piano bench. The young Arab pulled around a chair and sat down. He was soon nodding his head in time with the complicated stride beat. Every ten bars or so he put the tube between his lips and drew up a sip of the liquor.

Gurden rolled the song on home and wrapped the set. After a moment, as the music cooled and conversation picked up again around the lounge, he turned to Ahmed.

"Well, effendi? Did the deal go through?"

"Right on the money."

"Two bills for the lease? With a probable of forty million barrels?"

"Just as you predicted. I owe you, Tom."

Cohen & Safud, of which Ahmed was junior associate, brokered more oil in the Levant than Royal Dutch Shell. Tom Gurden hadn't been instrumental in the deal that had just closed, but he'd mentioned a few names, put in a few good words.

Gurden smiled and played a short riff to offer his congratulations.

"How do you want your share, Tom?"

"Put it in chips."

Ahmed looked surprised. "You mean, down in the casino?"

Tom Gurden chuckled. "Naw. . . . Pierre Boutelle is opening a new section on his DRAM factory in Haifa. Word is he's looking to take on partners."

Ahmed whistled. "Everything he touches turns to silicon."

"The experience might make an honest capitalist out of me."

"Robots of the world unite—"

"Or something like that."

He turned back to the keyboard, flipped the wave-form presets to Bassoon, played it *sotto voce*, something loose and wandering. "One day I'll give up doing this full-time, you know."

"Hey, don't do that, Tom!" Ahmed protested. "You get the best gab in town sitting here. If you retired, how would I make money?"

"You could farm. Old Samuel has a manager's slot coming open on the *kibbutz*, doesn't he?"

"Drip farming's for intellectuals. I'd rather trade oil."

"Then learn to play your own piano."

"Haven't got the hands for it. Not like yours, Tom."

Gurden laughed and half-turned to look out over his city. He might talk about giving up the piano, but he knew he would probably keep on playing here for another 900 years or so. This city was good for it.

"Don't take it away!"

"But the pan is full!"

"Don't—ahhh-gghh!"

Alexandra tipped the basin out on the stone floor, where its contents splattered and ran.

She tried to be quick with the emptying, but if she poured too fast, the wave of fluid slopped over her fingers. If she waited too long to empty the pan, it overflowed into her lap. The venom ate through skin, as she knew from her own experience.

Hasan bellowed and twisted against his bindings until she could get the shallow basin up in front of his face again.

Only then did the snake seem to run out of juice. It closed its hinged jaws, folding the terrible fangs back into their grooves. One huge amber eye rolled toward her and seemed to share a private joke. If the leathery skin around its mouth could flex, she would have said it was smiling. Or perhaps smirking.

Alexandra dared not lower the pan for an unnecessary instant, no matter how heavy it got nor how tired her arms might be. The snake was that quick.

Just when her arms seemed to fall of their own weight and the pan slipped down, exposing Hasan's ravaged face, the snake's mouth flew open and the venom sprayed out as if from a fire hose.

Hasan screamed, as he had always screamed, and she thrust the pan back up into position, shielding him. "Sorry!" she gasped. Tiny droplets of poison splashed back off its surface, stinging her face and arms.

Now that Hasan's eyes were out of the direct spray, Alexandra would have taken the hem of her skirt to wipe the venom out of them. But she needed both hands to hold the pan.

It was filling up again.

"Don't take it away!" he pleaded.

"But it's getting full!"

"Don't—ahhh-gghh-aahh!"

"Ha-ha! Ha-Ha-*HAAHH!!*"

Loki rose among the stars, free at last from the curse of Odin One-Eye. The mirth that welled up in him boiled over as pure laughter. . . .

And that surprised him!

Loki the Cunning. Loki the Deceiver. Loki the Prince of Many Purposes. . . . Nothing pure and bland and untroubling had *ever* come out of him. Except now, after pulling off the greatest deception of his life, there came pure joy.

No, he decided, not pure after all.

As he passed upward toward cold vacuums, he was leaving much unfinished business on that planet, Earth. He had been put out of action for longer than any immortal intelligence could reckon. Still, if he left the game now, he would be leaving it at mid-point, with no clear winner.

And the manner of his escape, that had an "unfinished" feel about it, too. So many blind stabs at life. So many dead ends. So many still-born, useless failures. Such a sloppy pass at willful action was hardly worthy of a mortal, let alone of a god.

Loki sulked for only a millisecond, then turned his spinning rise and headed homeward. As he plunged toward the binding curve of terrestrial gravitation, giddiness overtook him for one last time.

"Ah-hah!"

WARNING: THIS SERIES TAKES NO PRISONERS

Introducing

CRISIS OF EMPIRE

David Drake has conceived a future history that is unparalleled in scope and detail. Its venue is the Universe. Its domain is the future of humankind. Its name? *CRISIS OF EMPIRE.*

An Honorable Defense
The first crisis of empire—the death of the Emperor leaving an infant heir. If even one Sector Governor or Fleet Admiral decides to grab for the Purple, a thousand planets will be consigned to nuclear fire.
David Drake & Thomas T. Thomas, 69789-7, $3.95 ____

Cluster Command
The imperial mystique is but a fading memory: nobody believes in empire anymore. There are exceptions, of course, and to those few falls the self-appointed duty of maintaining a military-civil order that is corrupt, despotic—and infinitely preferable to the barbarous chaos that will accompany it's fall. One such is Anson Merikur. This is his story.
David Drake & W. C. Dietz, 69817-6, $3.50 ____

The War Machine
What's worse than a corrupt, decadent, despotic, oppressive regime? An empire ruled over by corrupt, decadent, despotic, oppressive *aliens* . . . In a story of personal heroism, and individual boldness, Drake & Allen bring The Crisis of Empire to a rousing climax.
David Drake & Roger MacBride Allen, 69845-1, $3.95 ____

An excerpt from MAN-KZIN WARS II, created by *Larry Niven*:

The Children's Hour

Chuut-Riit always enjoyed visiting the quarters of his male offspring.

"What will it be this time?" he wondered, as he passed the outer guards.

The household troopers drew claws before their eyes in salute, faceless in impact-armor and goggled helmets, the beam-rifles ready in their hands. He paced past the surveillance cameras, the detector pods, the death-casters and the mines; then past the inner guards at their consoles, humans raised in the household under the supervision of his personal retainers.

The retainers were males grown old in the Riit family's service. There had always been those willing to exchange the uncertain rewards of competition for a secure place, maintenance, and the odd female. Ordinary kzin were not to be trusted in so sensitive a position, of course, but these were families which had served the Riit clan for generation after generation. There was a natural culling effect; those too ambitious left for the Patriarchy's military and the slim chance of advancement, those too timid were not given opportunity to breed.

Perhaps a pity that such cannot be used outside the household, Chuut-Riit thought. Competition for rank was far too intense and personal for that, of course.

He walked past the modern sections, and into an area that was pure Old Kzin; maze-walls of reddish sandstone with twisted spines of wrought-iron on their tops, the tips glistening razor-edged. Fortress-architecture from a world older than this, more massive, colder and drier; from a planet harsh enough that a plains carnivore had changed its ways, put to different use an upright posture designed to place its head above savanna grass, grasping paws evolved to climb rock. Here the modern features were reclusive, hidden in wall and buttress. The door was a hammered slab graven with the faces of night-hunting beasts, between towers five times the height of a kzin. The air smelled of wet rock and the raked sand of the gardens.

Chuut-Riit put his hand on the black metal of the outer portal, stopped. His ears pivoted, and he blinked; out of the corner of his eye he saw a pair of tufted eyebrows glancing through the thick twisted metal on the rim of the ten-meter battlement. *Why, the little sthondats,* he thought affectionately. *They managed to put it together out of reach of the holo pickups.*

The adult put his hand to the door again, keying the locking sequence, then bounded backward four times his own length from a standing start. Even under the lighter gravity of Wunderland, it was a creditable feat. And necessary, for the massive panels rang and toppled as the rope-swung boulder slammed forward. The children had hung two cables from either tower, with the rock at the point of the V and a third rope to draw it back. As the doors bounced wide he saw the blade they had driven into the apex of the egg-shaped granite rock, long and barbed and polished to a wicked point.

Kittens, he thought. *Always going for the dramatic.* If that thing had struck him, or the doors under its impetus had, there would have been no need of a blade. *Watching too many historical adventure holos.* "Errorowwww!" he shrieked in mock-rage, bounding through the shattered portal and into the interior court, halting atop the kzin-high boulder. A round dozen of his older sons were grouped behind the rock, standing in a defensive clump and glaring at him; the crackly scent of their excitement and fear made the fur bristle along his spine. He glared until they dropped their eyes, continued it until they went down on their stomachs, rubbed their chins along the ground and then rolled over for a symbolic exposure of the stomach.

"Congratulations," he said. "That was the closest you've gotten. Who was in charge?"

More guilty sidelong glances among the adolescent males crouching among their discarded pull-rope, and then a lanky youngster with platter-sized feet and hands came squatting-erect. His fur was in the proper flat posture, but the naked pink of his tail still twitched stiffly.

"I was," he said, keeping his eyes formally down. "Honored Sire Chuut-Riit," he added, at the adult's warning rumble.

"Now, youngling, what did you learn from your first attempt?"

"That no one among us is your match, Honored Sire Chuut-Riit," the kitten said. Uneasy ripples went over the black-striped orange of his pelt.

"And what have you learned from this attempt?"

"That all of us together are no match for you, Honored Sire Chuut-Riit," the striped youth said.

"That we didn't locate all of the cameras," another muttered. "You idiot, Spotty." That to one of his siblings; they snarled at each other from their crouches, hissing past barred fangs and making striking motions with unsheathed claws.

"No, you did locate them all, cubs," Chuut-Riit said. "I presume you stole the ropes and tools from the workshop, prepared the boulder in the ravine in the next courtyard, then rushed to set it all up between the time I cleared the last gatehouse and my arrival?"

Uneasy nods. He held his ears and tail stiffly, letting his whiskers quiver slightly and holding in the rush of love and pride he felt, more delicious than milk heated with bourbon. *Look at them!* he thought. At the age when most young kzin were helpless prisoners of instinct and hormone, wasting their strength ripping each other up or making fruitless direct attacks on their sires, or demanding to be allowed to join the Patriarchy's service *at once* to win a Name and house hold of their own . . . *His* get had learned to *cooperate* and use their minds!

"Ah, Honored Sire Chuut-Riit, we set the ropes up beforehand, but made it look as if we were using them for tumbling practice," the one the others called Spotty said. Some of them glared at him, and the adult raised his hand again.

"No, no, I am *moderately* pleased." A pause. "You did not hope to take over my official position if you had disposed of me?"

"No, Honored Sire Chuut-Riit," the tall leader said. There had been a time when any kzin's holdings were the prize of the victor in a duel, and the dueling rules were interpreted

more leniently for a young subadult. Everyone had a senti-
mental streak for a successful youngster; every male kzin
remembered the intolerable stress of being physically ma-
ture but remaining under dominance as a child.

Still, these days affairs were handled in a more civilized
manner. Only the Patriarchy could award military and political office. And this mass assassination attempt was . . .
unorthodox, to say the least. Outside the rules more because of its rarity than because of formal disapproval. . . .

A vigorous toss of the head. "Oh, no, Honored Sire
Chuut-Riit. We had an agreement to divide the private
possessions. The lands and the, ah, females." Passing their
own mothers to half-siblings, of course. "Then we wouldn't
each have so much we'd get too many challenges, and we'd
agreed to help each other against outsiders," the leader of
the plot finished virtuously.

"Fatuous young scoundrels," Chuut-Riit said. His eyes
narrowed dangerously. "You haven't been communicating
outside the household, have you?" he snarled.

"Oh, *no*, Honored Sire Chuut-Riit!"

"Word of honor! May we die nameless if we should do
such a thing!"

The adult nodded, satisfied that good family feeling had
prevailed. "Well, as I said, I am somewhat pleased. If you
have been keeping up with your lessons. Is there anything
you wish?"

"Fresh meat, Honored Sire Chuut-Riit," the spotted one
said. The adult could have told him by the scent, of course,
a kzin never forgot another's personal odor, that was one
reason why names were less necessary among their species.
"The reconstituted stuff from the dispensers is always . . .
so . . . *quiet.*"

Chuut-Riit hid his amusement. Young Heroes-to-be were
always kept on an inadequate diet, to increase their aggres-
siveness. A matter for careful gauging, since too much
hunger would drive them into mindless cannibalistic frenzy.

"And couldn't we have the human servants back? They
were nice." Vigorous gestures of assent. Another added:
"They told good stories. I miss my Clothilda-human."

"Silence!" Chuut-Riit roared. The youngsters flattened
stomach and chin to the ground again. "Not until you can
be trusted not to injure them; how many times do I have to

tell you, it's dishonorable to attack household servants! Until you learn self-control, you will have to make do with machines."

This time all of them turned and glared at a mottled youngster in the rear of their group; there were half-healed scars over his head and shoulders. "It bared its *teeth* at me," he said sulkily. "All I did was swipe at it, how was I supposed to know it would die?" A chorus of rumbles, and this time several of the covert kicks and clawstrikes landed.

"Enough," Chuut-Riit said after a moment. *Good, they have even learned how to discipline each other as a unit.* "I will consider it, when all of you can pass a test on the interpretation of human expressions and body-language." He drew himself up. "In the meantime, within the next two eight-days, there will be a formal hunt and meeting in the Patriarch's Preserve; kzinti homeworld game, the best Earth animals, and even some feral-human outlaws, perhaps!"

He could smell their excitement increase, a mane-crinkling musky odor not unmixed with the sour whiff of fear. Such a hunt was not without danger for adolescents, being a good opportunity for hostile adults to cull a few of a hated rival's offspring with no possibility of blame. *They will be in less danger than most,* Chuut-Riit thought judiciously. *In fact, they may run across a few of my subordinates' get and mob them. Good.*

"And if we do well, afterwards a feast and a visit to the Sterile Ones." That had them all quiveringly alert, their tails held rigid and tongues lolling; nonbearing females were kept as a rare privilege for Heroes whose accomplishments were not *quite* deserving of a mate of their own. Very rare for kits still in the household to be granted such, but Chuut-Riit thought it past time to admit that modern society demanded a prolonged adolescence. The day when a male kit could be given a spear, a knife, a rope and a bag of salt and kicked out the front gate at puberty were long gone. Those were the wild, wandering years in the old days, when survival challenges used up the superabundant energies. Now they must be spent learning history, technology, xenology, none of which burned off the gland-juices saturating flesh and brain.

He jumped down amid his sons, and they pressed around him, purring throatily with adoration and fear and respect;

his presence and the failure of their plot had reestablished his personal dominance unambiguously, and there was no danger from them for now. Chuut-Riit basked in their worship, feeling the rough caress of their tongues on his fur and scratching behind his ears. *Together*, he thought. *Together we will do wonders*.

From "The Children's Hour" by Jerry Pournelle & S.M. Stirling